THE FACE I

Alexandra Connor was born in Oldham and still has strong connections with Lancashire. Apart from being a writer she is also a presenter on radio and television. She is a Fellow of the Royal Society of Arts.

By the same author

The Moon is my Witness
Midnight's Smiling
Green Baize Road
An Angel Passing Over
Hunter's Moon
The Sixpenny Winner

ALEXANDRA CONNOR

The Face in the Locket

HarperCollins*Publishers*

This novel is entirely a work of fiction.
The names, characters and incidents portrayed in it are
the work of the author's imagination. Any resemblance to
actual persons, living or dead, events or localities is
entirely coincidental.

HarperCollins*Publishers*
77–85 Fulham Palace Road,
Hammersmith, London W6 8JB

www.fireandwater.com

A Paperback Original 2003
1 3 5 7 9 8 6 4 2

A catalogue record for this book
is available from the British Library

ISBN 0 00 712162 8

Typeset in Sabon by Palimpsest Book Production Limited,
Polmont, Stirlingshire

Printed and bound in Great Britain by
Clays Ltd, St Ives plc

I would like to thank the following, in my own personal roll call of honour:

Susan Opie (editor) for skill
Yvonne Howard (copy-editor) for empathy
Martin Palmer (Sales Director) for support
All the reps on the road for hard graft
and Ella Crossley (my mother) for endurance!

Thanks also to Wigan Tourist Office and Wigan Library.

Dedicated to Robert Wynford –
a man who has learned
how to 'wheel the oils' of life!

PROLOGUE

When I was very young I was delivered into the care of my aunts. They had a book about some place in Sicily. They tried to keep it hidden, but I found it anyway, and couldn't stop looking at it. The book was all about a crypt in which there were thousands of embalmed corpses. A creepy place it looked in the photographs – at least to a child.

Anyway, I hated the book, yet was drawn to it constantly because of one photograph. It was of a child, a little girl of about seven. Her name was Rosalia and she was the best-preserved corpse in the crypt. She looked as though she was just stirring, about to wake up. Her eyelashes were long, eyes half opened, her mouth not quite sure whether it was about to yawn, or not.

Apparently tourists flocked to look at Rosalia. As I did, in that old book. She became famous, nicknamed *Sleeping Beauty*. And she never changed, never got old, never got hurt, or hurt anyone. She died before she disappointed her family or herself. Before she fell in love, or got ill, or even got tall. She stayed locked into that photographic plate, pressed like a pristine violet in a book.

And I envied her.

PART ONE

I am my own soul's ghost.

(Anon)

ONE

Deerheart House, Wigan, Lancashire
The first sight Mildred had of Harris Simons, in the summer of 1931, was a small oval face staring out of the back of a large black car. Unsmiling, the little girl watched the plump woman approach the vehicle and talk in a low voice to Dr Redmond. A shower had made the street greasy, the cobbles shiny and slippery underfoot.

'I think she's still in shock,' Dr Redmond said, wiping his forehead with a handkerchief, the summer evening broiling him. 'I'm sorry about your brother's death.'

'Don't be too sorry,' Mildred replied evenly, but not unkindly. 'We weren't close. A misunderstanding a long while back put paid to any closeness.'

Dr Redmond studied Mildred Simons carefully. She was full-fleshed, still pretty in a print dress, her spectacular ash-blonde hair shimmering in the heat. He had no worries about leaving the little girl with Mildred – but as for her brother and sister . . . Well, that was a different story.

'It's good of you to take Harris on.'

Mildred nodded. Her eyes fixed on the little girl as she slumped in the back seat of the car. 'She's small for eight.'

'Maybe she takes after her mother.'

'I never knew her mother,' Mildred replied. 'You look like you're melting. Come in for some lemonade.'

Without waiting for a reply Mildred turned. Dr Redmond opened the car door and called for Harris. Sullen, the child followed up the drive as he walked towards the curved archway of the house. Around the stone lintel honeysuckle was blooming, overblown roses pumping out a heady scent.

In the hall the doctor breathed the cooled air gratefully, as Mildred waved both her visitors on into the lounge, then went to get the lemonade. Walking in, he looked around. The Simons sisters had money – and it showed. Curiously he noted the walnut furniture, the French ormolu clock, and the gilded mirror over the fireplace. French doors led out into a ridiculously luxuriant garden, crammed with bushes and flowers. The child had landed on her feet, he thought, fanning himself with his Panama hat. Oh yes, little Harris Simons had dropped lucky.

'Can I help you?'

The voice was so sharp that Dr Redmond dropped his hat, wheezing as he bent down to retrieve it. Straightening up, he saw first a pair of thin legs, then a dark skirt, then a long aquiline nose fronting a remarkable face. Irma Simons, he thought wonderingly, a woman with the face of a hanging judge. And the temperament to match.

'Hello there. I'm Dr Redmond –'

'You've got fat,' Irma said simply, walking past him and looking at the little girl standing in the doorway. 'So you're Harris, are you?'

The child nodded.

'Not much of you, is there? Not like Dr Redmond,' Irma went on. 'We knew each other when we were children. He was a runty little thing then –'

'Irma, help me with the tray, will you?' Mildred asked, seeing the doctor's face garnet with embarrassment. 'I've got something to cool everyone down.'

Ice clinked in the glasses as she poured the home-made lemonade, slices of lemon floating on the surface, the scent acidly sweet.

'There you are, sweetheart.'

Unmoving, Harris looked at her.

'Go on, take it,' Mildred prompted the child. 'It's lemonade.'

'I don't like lemonade.'

'You'll like what you're given,' Irma began, her tone colder than the ice cubes.

'Irma, she's only a child.'

'She'll have to get used to our ways if she's going to settle in,' Irma went on, turning away to perch on the edge of the piano stool. For a moment she fixed her eyes on Harris and then looked away.

The little girl glanced up at Mildred appealingly. 'I don't like lemonade.'

'What about milk?'

'I don't like milk.'

There was a snort from the direction of the piano, and Dr Redmond was grateful that *his* time with Irma Simons was going to be limited.

'What do you like to drink?'

'Tea.'

'Tea!' Irma exploded. 'You're a child. No child drinks tea.'

'I do,' Harris said, her tone cowed and belligerent at the same time. 'Mummy always gave me tea.'

'Mummy isn't here –'

'Irma, will you get me some sugar, please?' Mildred asked, and watched as her sister left the room.

When she turned back to Harris, the child was close to tears. Gently she took Harris's hand. The child resisted. 'Sssh, we're going to be friends. And friends hold hands.' Glancing over her shoulder she nodded to Dr Redmond. 'We'll be fine. I'll call by and have a word tomorrow.'

Taking the hint, he drained his glass and made for the door before Irma re-emerged. The heat outside was hard to handle, but anything was better than facing Irma.

Holding on to Harris's hand, Mildred led her down into the garden. The rain shower had made the leaves glossy, heavy droplets falling off the trees, a bird shaking a branch and making a little shower over them as they passed.

'Don't be frightened of my sister,' Mildred began. 'She has a good heart, but she has trouble showing it. It takes a while to know Irma.'

In reply, Harris clung on to her hand.

'I guess it must be pretty strange coming here to live with two old codgers?'

Surprised, Harris looked up at her aunt, her head on one side. 'You're not old, are you?'

'Well, your father was the baby of the family – came after Irma and me – so we're older than him.' She smiled at the child, teasing her. 'Anyway, I thought that anyone over twenty looked ancient to someone your age.'

Mildred sat down on a bench under a tree after wiping it dry with the tea towel she was still carrying. Sliding her hand free, Harris moved a little way away from her aunt, her expression guarded. Mildred noticed the action, but ignored it.

'We've got your room ready.'

Harris took in this piece of information and then looked down. It took Mildred a moment to realise that she was crying. Embarrassed and out of her depth, Mildred stared at her niece. She could see nothing of her dead brother in the child; all she could see for certain was a very small person who was bitterly unhappy.

Acting instinctively, Mildred took hold of the child. Harris struggled for a moment and then relaxed, her face pressed against her aunt's chest, her muted crying hardly equalling the volume of the birdsong from the rain-splashed trees.

*   *   *

Saville had seen them from an upstairs window and then gone off and washed his hands. Several times. Then he had combed his hair, fastened up his jacket and walked downstairs. He was just about to exit the French doors when a shadow fell over him.

'Saville, where are you going?'

He tensed, turning and yet not daring to meet Irma's eyes. 'I was going into the garden –'

She cut across him immediately. 'Have you taken your medication?'

He nodded, looking back to the window. 'I wanted to go out –'

'What for?'

'We have a visitor,' he said, his tone giving away too much excitement. 'Someone new. I want to talk to her.'

'What would *you* know to say to a little girl?' Irma asked, walking over to the window herself and looking out. Good God, Mildred was nursing the child!

'She's only little,' Saville ventured, moving alongside his elder sister. 'Very little.'

Irma said nothing, just kept looking at the tableau in front of her. A long-ignored memory tweaked at her: a young man, Harry Delaney – hardly more than a boy really – playing tennis in the same garden. With her. She had been quite a lot older than he, but he hadn't cared. Said that he loved her and age didn't matter. It had been another day of extremes – heat then rain, followed by a storm in the night. Which didn't wake Irma because she hadn't been asleep. Instead she had been lying, dry-eyed, staring into the darkness and remembering what her father had said earlier.

He had been standing by the desk in the study. A thickset man with glasses. A man who had come from poverty and now despised the Irish immigrant poor he had so eagerly left. As for her mother – Irma knew that there would be no interference from that quarter.

'No daughter of mine marries a man whose family come from Scholes,' her father had said bitingly. 'Are you mad, Irma? The lad's not qualified for any decent work. He's a slum boy who'll turn into a slum man. And take you with him. Oh, and you think you'll not mind, but you will. You're not a kid, you know. You're used to soft beds and good food; you'd not survive on hardship.'

Her heart pinched at the words: the man she loved being prised away from her.

'Father, *please* –'

He had cut her off at once. A bully in a good suit.

'You're too fond of the easy life, Irma. I know you better than you know yourself. You're just grabbing at what you think might be your last chance of love. Hah! What's love when it's at home? Something that sounds fine in books, but it doesn't last. When you're living next to muck, with rats running down the ginnel behind your back door, *then* tell me what love's worth.'

Irma had never been lucky in love and now she was getting to the desperate age – when any man looked better than ending up a spinster. But although Irma might be despairing, *he* wasn't having his daughter marrying a yob.

He had walked over to her. 'You know where I came from – Scholes. Just like Harry Delaney. I know what it's like living with coal stacked up outside the door, no toilet, no electricity. Don't look away! You don't know what you'd be letting yourself in for, Irma. The doctors don't go there, neither do the police –'

'But you got out of Scholes!'

He'd been astounded that she was standing up to him. '*I* did. But Harry Delaney's not like me.'

'You don't know that!' Irma had replied frantically. 'How can you know that?'

'Because I know the type. I look at him and see a lad who thinks he's found an easy way out of the slums.' Her father had paused, letting the rancid words curdle in her brain. 'Don't be fooled by him, Irma. You need a respectable lad from a good family, not someone who'd pull you down with him. You want a nice house, nice furniture, somewhere to be proud of. And a man you don't have to watch constantly to make sure he's not showing you up.'

Irma had found herself wavering. The image her father was painting of life in Scholes was making her queasy. He was right, she didn't want to go *down* in the world, only up. After all, wasn't that what she had been taught all her life? How to be a snob?

Though Irma had continued to plead with her father, her voice had lost its urgency. 'But I love him –'

'When you're broken down with five kids, no money and bad teeth, tell me you still love Harry Delaney. When no one will serve you in a shop or give you credit, when people look at you with disgust and laugh behind your back, *then* come and face me, Irma. And then you can tell me what love meant in the end. *Sod all.*'

She had tried to remonstrate further, but her heart wasn't in it. Something her father had said was true: she wanted an easy life, and she now realised that Harry couldn't offer her that. Oh, his promises might be true. He *might* make something of himself – but then again, he might not. And she couldn't bear that.

Her father had added a final blow, not realising that he had already won.

'I've nothing else to say, Irma. Except this: marry Harry Delaney and you're out on your own. No money from me, no help. You choose the bed you want to lie in. And who you want to lie *with.*'

Blinking, Irma came back to the present. The image of Harry had gone from the garden. Just as *he* had when she told him it wouldn't work out. He had looked at her with loathing, Irma recalled uncomfortably, as though he could read her mind. She never heard from him again. The bed she had

11

chosen was comfortable, but Irma never found anyone to share it with.

Love never came to Irma Simons again. Her first real love affair had been her last.

Taking advantage of his sister's preoccupation, Saville had sneaked out and was now standing in front of Mildred, his eyes fixed on Harris. His brain told him that this was a child, and that she was crying. Why, he didn't know, but he immediately identified with her and started crying too.

At once, Harris stopped and looked up at him. She saw a finely built man with thick wavy hair and a walrus moustache, his eyes watery, his fingers locking and unlocking with agitation.

'Who are you?' Harris asked, fascinated.

Noting that she had stopped crying, Saville stopped too.

'I'm, I'm your . . .' he paused and glanced at Mildred, who mouthed the word 'uncle', '. . . your uncle.'

'How many are there of you?' Harris asked, bewildered.

Mildred smiled to soothe her. 'You've got two aunts, me and Irma, and one uncle, Saville.'

'No one else?'

'D'you want there to be anyone else?' Mildred asked, squashed on the bench as her brother sat next to her.

'Do you like swimming?'

Baffled, Harris looked at her uncle. 'I've never been swimming.'

'I can swim. I can swim!'

Kindly, Mildred changed the subject. 'Saville, this is Gideon's child. You remember Gideon, don't you? Our brother?'

It took several seconds for Saville to absorb the information and then he shook his head. 'No, I don't remember him.'

'He had thick black hair, like yours and brown eyes, like Harris's.'

'Who's Harris?' asked a baffled Saville.

'*This* is Harris!' Mildred replied, pointing to their niece.

'Harris is a stupid name.'

'I know!' Harris replied, agreeing with him and suddenly relaxing. 'I hate it too. Mummy says –'

She stopped short, Saville leaning towards her. 'What is it?'

'She's dead. Both of them are dead.' The child's lips pressed closed as though to stop herself crying.

It didn't stop Saville, though. On hearing the sad news he immediately burst into tears. Harris moved over to him and put her arm around his shoulder. In amazement, Mildred watched the strange couple.

'It's all right,' Harris said softly, 'honestly, it's all right.'

But Saville was beyond consoling. He hated death, feared it with real terror. The family had never even owned another cat after their first one died. It had taken Saville two years to get over the loss.

Mildred caught sight of her sister at the window and waved, but Irma moved away without responding. Oh God, Mildred thought, she would be even more impossible now. But there was no choice, they *had* to take in the child; to refuse would have been inhuman. Mildred sighed. How long had they all lived together? Three unmarried people in one house. Three unmarried people sliding gradually towards middle age.

Saville was laughing again, all misery forgotten. Mildred envied him his handicap in a way. Envied how Saville never grew up, locked into the mind of a seven-year-old. A seven-year-old who was fine if kept on his medication, his irrationality controlled. A seven-year-old with a walrus moustache . . .

Folding her arms, Mildred studied Harris for any sign of her father, Gideon. And then she remembered her brother, the baby of the family, her adored sibling. It was always Gideon this, Gideon that, everyone making allowances for the unexpected baby who had come in their mother's middle years. Gideon was going to take on the world, their father said. After all, Saville couldn't, could he? Mildred hated her father for that; Saville might not understand, but then again, he might. He certainly knew enough to realise that he came a very poor second to his brother. Besides, Saville might be retarded, but he *felt* more than other people. And he could get hurt more.

Not that their father ever gave him credit for anything. Saville was just the idiot son to him, the one he railed about when he thought no one could hear him. The one he saw as a constant rebuke. Why could he have two strapping daughters and a fool for a son? A man like him – a man who had built up his fortune from coal, cotton and property – should have had a son of which to be proud. Not some blathering fool he had to hide away from the world.

So when Gideon came along, Gordon thought his prayers had been answered.

'About bloody time,' he had said to his wife, Rosemary, 'and I know he'll grow up to be a boy to be proud of.'

Mildred sighed again, closing her eyes for a moment, profoundly tired. The memories pulled a blanket over her, lulling her into their iron grip. She could see her mother clearly: pale eyes, pale hair, her smile distant, her eyes vacant at times as though she was in a world of her own. Maybe she was, Mildred thought. Hadn't her father once accused Rosemary of having come from a family of idiots?

Mildred was never sure about that. Rosemary's past was as shadowy as her expression. All Mildred knew for certain was that her mother had been raised by a guardian. At times she seemed ready to rebel against the tyranny of her husband, but mostly Rosemary kept the house, and her temper. And because the staff hated Gordon, they felt protective towards his wife. No one pilfered money, or stole anything from the Simons household. Gordon liked to think that it was due to

14

fear, but it wasn't. It was down to loyalty – to his wife. Loyalty – it was something he had always found hard to understand, and impossible to inspire.

We will have to change now, Mildred thought, opening her eyes and glancing at Saville. He was chatting to Harris excitedly. Well, why not? He had finally got someone of his own age to talk to. If only she herself had. All she had was Irma, and she was little consolation. If it hadn't been for the business she would have gone mad.

Mildred glowed at the thought of the business – a hairdressing salon in the middle of Wigan, close to Market Street. If Irma had had her way only the richest women in the area would come, but Mildred wasn't stupid, or a snob. She knew that women liked to look good, and that a woman who had saved hard for a perm enjoyed it more than someone who had her hair done twice a week. So when she was there Mildred booked in anyone who wanted to come. And when Irma was there, she booked in the rich. And listened to them – especially the spinsters and the widows, bitterness as thick on the ground as clipped hair.

It had been a surprise to Mildred that her sister had even *wanted* to work. But when their parents died – their father very shortly after their mother – suddenly there was little to do for either of them. Years passed, Mildred enjoying a social life without the constraints of her father's rules, but Irma floundering. She had never made friends easily and was naturally suspicious of people.

'There's no one in this world you can trust,' their father had said repeatedly as they were growing up. 'Doubt everyone. Your only loyalty is to me. You understand? *To me.*'

Oh, and how he had made his point.

Irma had been a reserved child, one who could always keep a secret. So she was the natural confidante of the housemaid who had fallen in love with the greengrocer's lad – 'Don't tell anyone, Miss Irma, will you? It would be more than my job's worth for your father to find out.' Tied, and flattered by the confidence, Irma had said nothing.

A few days passed, and then one morning Irma was called into the breakfast room. Her father was standing by the fireplace, a semi-hysterical housemaid sobbing in front of him.

'How dare you?' he had begun to Irma.

She had shrunk back, her voice nervous. '*What*, Father?'

'You know what I mean! You betrayed me –'

'I never –'

'*You did!*' he roared, as his daughter cowered in terror. 'You sided with the staff against me. Against your own father! This common girl here – this t'penny h'penny scrubber – had your confidence. Whilst your father – who clothes, feeds and looks after you – was deceived.'

'Father, I was asked to keep a promise –'

'You aren't allowed promises! Or confidences. It is my duty to know *everything* that goes on in this house.'

'But –'

Realising he had terrified her, he delivered the *coup de grâce*. 'Oh, get out, Irma – I can't bear to look at you! You're a snake in the bloody grass, that's what you are. You stay out of my sight, you hear? Stay away from me until you know which side your bread's buttered on.'

Tears burned behind Irma's eyes. She had been asked to keep a promise and she *had* done. What was wrong about that? How was that a betrayal of her father?

'Please, listen –'

'Keep quiet!' her father had snapped back. 'You answer to *me*, girl! I rule you, and I set the rules. If there's anything going on in this house *I want to know it*! You don't keep secrets with the bloody staff. There *are* no secrets from me – and it's time you learned that.'

Irma had kept her distance from people after that. Better not to get too close than risk paternal exile. But when their father

16

died Irma found time hanging heavily on her hands. Friends might be all right for Mildred, but they were out of the question for her. So Irma decided she would do good works.

But she wasn't a natural do-gooder, and after a couple of years the British Legion and the Women's Institute – usually delighted to attract members – had had a bellyful of Irma Simons. So gradually Irma had found herself spending more and more time at home. She began to read voraciously, did crossword puzzles and ran the house immaculately. 'I'd make a first-class recluse,' she said once wryly. But there was a bitter note of truth in the words.

Then, as the next few years passed, Mildred began to tire of her social life. Freedom from restrictions was all well and good, but it seemed an idle existence. She liked people, but small talk wearied her and after another indifferent year had passed, Mildred was ready for change.

The change was quite something.

'Why don't we open a hairdressing salon?' Irma had said when Mildred suggested they go into business. 'It would be better than a shop.'

'I was thinking more of a dress shop –'

'Too common,' Irma had responded, glowering out of the window.

'But we aren't qualified hairdressers, Irma.'

'No, but I dare say we could learn. I mean, cutting hair, curling it, it's easy. Neither of us is stupid,' Irma had replied evenly. 'Besides, we would *own* the salon, not just work there. And we could employ people. *Staff*.'

Ah, Mildred thought, so that's it. Not only are you bored after years of doing little, you want an empire. Suits me.

So the two sisters went to look at several premises and argued about all of them, until one day Irma came in late. It was December, a bitter night before Christmas, when she slammed the front door and pounded into the drawing room. Decorating the tree, Mildred paused with some holly in her hands.

17

'I've done it,' Irma enthused. 'We now own a hairdressing salon.'

The holly immediately fell from Mildred's hand. 'But I never –'

'It's all organised.'

'The hell it is!' Mildred snapped. 'We're in this together. You should have talked to me first.'

'Talking to you is like trying to plait sand. We had to get on with it. So I've sorted it out for both of us.'

Angrily Mildred approached her sister. 'Don't try making yourself into the boss, Irma. You might be older than me, but I have a say in all of this. It's *our* money, not *yours*.'

But Irma was already brittle with power. 'I'm the business head –'

'You're the big head, you mean,' Mildred retorted sharply, pushing past her sister. 'I'm not working somewhere I haven't picked myself.'

'It's in Library Street, hardly somewhere you *wouldn't* like.'

Mildred wasn't about to be placated. Irma had always tried to keep the upper hand, but no longer.

'Now look, you and I have to get on, although frankly if we weren't sisters, I doubt if we would even pass the time of day with each other.'

Stung, Irma had slammed down her umbrella then put her hands on her hips. 'I've walked my feet off finding the right place –'

'You should have taken me with you!'

'What for?'

'Because we're joint partners in this venture, that's what for.'

Irma's eyes hardened. 'Well, I wanted to talk to you about that.'

In a millisecond Mildred had known what her sister was up to. This was to be no partnership: Irma's boredom with life was to be redeemed by success in business. And that meant her being top dog. Oh, Mildred had thought to herself, there's more than a little of our father in you.

'Forget it.'

'What!' Irma had shrieked.

'I'm not coming into business with you.'

'But we agreed –'

'We agreed to a *partnership*.'

Thwarted, Irma's eyes fixed on her sister. 'You fat bitch.'

And that was it. Years of patience evaporated at the words. It was almost funny now, Mildred thought, looking back. But at the time . . . She had pushed Irma over as those words left her lips. Irma had lost her footing, falling clumsily backwards into the Christmas tree. Unfortunately the tree didn't break her fall, and she took it with her, the whole mess of branches, arms, holly, legs, lurching against the drawing-room wall. It was the first, and last, time Mildred ever needed to take her sister on physically.

Still smiling to herself, Mildred looked at Saville. Her brother was walking with Harris by the bird table, waving his hands about because he was excited. He has more sense than any of us, Mildred thought suddenly: he sees the child's coming as an adventure, not a trauma. She would do the same. So what if she knew nothing about children? She had known nothing about hairdressing once. But she'd learned. Just as she would learn about bringing up a child.

And besides, Harris wasn't likely to bond with her sister, was she . . . ? Getting to her feet, Mildred walked back towards the house. Unexpectedly she had been offered the role of mother – Fate giving her a chance she thought would never come her way.

She would make the most of it; be the girl's mentor, her confidante. She would teach Harris about life, give her standards, ambitions. Oh yes, Mildred thought, giddy with hope, this would be a whole new part of her life.

How difficult could it be?

TWO

Looking back now, I can see it more clearly. Seems strange, that, but as a child of eight I was too shocked to take in much. And now, time having passed, I can look back to those first days at the Simonses' house and remember.

I can see myself walking up the path that first evening, following Dr Redmond. The rain has stopped, but he brushes some droplets off an azalea bush as he passes and the water makes a stain on his jacket sleeve.

The house seems enormous. I was used only to cramped flats, my father moving us on constantly, my mother pliable, sweet. 'I love your daddy very much,' she told me often, 'and we have to do everything to make his life easy . . .' And he loved her too: told me that every day, picking me up and swinging me in the air, promising good times. Which never came.

I was toted about with them like a mascot. I know now that there was nowhere else to put me, and no one to leave me with, but I think that even if there had been they would have kept me with them. They were wonderful parents, a complete success. But only in that; in everything else they were failures. My father could never hold down a job and my mother was sickly, her health not improved by the conditions in which we lived. By the time I was old enough to understand I hated *the conversations about money, and the lack of it – how my father's family had thrown him out, penniless. My mother would cry then and he would comfort her, telling her over and over again that he would have it no other way. That she was worth it, that money didn't matter. I don't think either of them believed that.*

Then when I was about three my father took me all the way to Wigan. It took over two hours from Yorkshire. When we got there he walked me to his old house and pointed at it, through the azalea hedge. 'I was born there,' he said. 'We should be living there now.' His face tightened with bitterness. 'My father was wicked, Harris. They all are. Never trust any of them: they're bad to the bone. Except one . . .'

And I remembered his words as I followed Dr Redmond up the path, the same azaleas now glossy with rain, a honeysuckle making music with its scent. Whilst we waited for the door to be answered I glanced up, and there – half hidden under creeper – was the name Deerheart House. Moss had grown over much of it, the stone mottled with age, a drowsy bee throwing its tiny shadow over the letters.

I wanted to run away, but there was nowhere to go. My parents were dead and now I was to be left in amongst the enemy, the very people I had been told never to trust; the people who had broken my father's heart.

It was up to me not to love them.

THREE

As Dr Redmond said to his wife, Harris Simons was a handful, and no mistake. Far too much for two spinster sisters to take on. Despite numerous warnings about climbing, Harris had, within six months, broken her collarbone and knocked out two teeth.

'It's her mother's fault.'

Dr Redmond frowned. 'But her mother's dead, love.'

'I know that! I meant that giving a girl a boy's name is asking for trouble. Poor mite's confused.' Irene Redmond warmed to her theme. 'You can't take a child away from its parents –'

'They died.'

'– and put her with a family like that one and then expect miracles. I mean, that Irma can't get on with anyone.' She touched her hair thoughtfully. 'She can cut hair, though, I'll give her that. Knows how to charge too. I asked for a trim the other day and she took all of an inch off. *And* charged me for it.'

Dr Redmond tried to stop the flow. 'About Harris –'

'They should have changed her name,' Irene went on. 'Given her a good honest name instead. *A girl's name.*'

'I like her name –'

'You're a man, what do you know about it?'

22

Defeated, Dr Redmond disappeared into his surgery off the main house. He had known the Simons sisters since childhood. Although they were now registered with him, neither of them had ailed a day. Amazing that, he thought. Maybe having the salon was keeping them too busy to get ill. Then again, nothing would *dare* to make Irma sick. As for Mildred . . . he smiled at the thought of her. Now there was a fine lady. Surprising that she had never married. He knew himself of a couple of young men who had once had ideas in that direction, but nothing came of them. Somehow other people got in the way. Like Irma. And Saville, of course.

An unpleasant memory knocked into Dr Redmond at that moment. It had been so long ago, Mildred had been barely more than seventeen and he had called round to see her with a Christmas present. For once, no one had answered the door at Deerheart House, so he had walked round the back, carrying the present under his arm. Snow had crunched underfoot as he'd walked over to the drawing-room window and lifted his hand to knock.

But instead he had frozen, chilled not by the snow but the scene inside. Gordon Simons was towering over his wife, terrorising her. Mildred was putting her arms around her mother protectively. He couldn't hear what Gordon Simons was saying, only muffled shouting. Horrified, he had seen him pull Mildred off her mother and raise his fist, striking Rosemary on her shoulder. In an instant, Mildred had pushed her father away, desperate to protect her mother. And then Lionel Redmond – later to be Dr Redmond, well-respected professional man – witnessed something he had tried for years to forget.

Enraged, Gordon Simons had picked up the poker in the hearth and brought it down on his daughter's back. Mildred collapsed like a tent cut loose from its guy ropes. A moment passed. And then, as though nothing had happened, Gordon Simons had taken his wife's hand and led her out of the room.

Without a protest, she had gone with her tyrant of a husband. *Rosemary Simons had chosen him, over her child.*

For many minutes Lionel Redmond had stood watching, too terrified to do anything, and yet afraid that Mildred was dead and he had witnessed a murder. Cold to the bone he stared in at the window and then finally he had seen Mildred stir. Slowly she had sat up, wincing and rubbing her back. Then she had got to her feet and walked, unsteadily, to the door.

Whether she went to cry in her room, or joined the family for dinner, he never knew. What he *did* know was that Mildred had tried to protect her mother and had been punished for it. She had cared and yet no one had cared for her. The path of her life had been set.

Sighing, Lionel Redmond returned now to his previous thoughts. Mildred Simons should have married. Should have had children of her own. Mind you, he thought again, she hardly needed a child of her own with Saville around. A couple of times in the past Dr Redmond had suggested that Saville might benefit from a stay in a home. His suggestion had been rebutted immediately. And firmly. Saville was no trouble, Mildred told him. Who would talk of putting a child of seven in a home?

But he *wasn't* a child of seven, Dr Redmond thought. Saville was now a lanky man of fifty with a walrus moustache. Most people didn't have seven-year-olds over six foot and weighing in around twelve stone. But then again, Saville was harmless. Oh, they had to keep an eye on him, Dr Redmond knew that full well, because Saville wandered. But he wouldn't hurt a living thing. If he kept up his medication he was fine. Silly, but kind.

And into this strange mêlée of people had come a small girl. God knows what Harris had thought of it, but she had seemed to settle in quite well. Mildred probably had a lot to do with that . . . Dr Redmond eased himself into his chair and glanced at his list of patients. At the bottom was written 'Harris Simons'.

Another broken limb, he thought. Why in God's name didn't they stop her climbing? But then how *could* you stop a child if she had the energy and skill of a monkey? He thought of Harris, of her dark-featured, elfin face. Like her mother, he had been told, but when he pressed for details no one knew much else about Kate Simons. What Dr Redmond – and all of Wigan – *did* know was that the beloved Gideon had blotted his copybook by marrying outside his social circle.

It had been a right scandal. Old man Simons had thought that his blessed son would take over the family business, and in that way make up for the retarded Saville. But Gideon had other ideas. It was wrong to spoil a child, Dr Redmond thought, and the charming Gideon had been idolised. Nothing was too good for him, nothing too much trouble. Old man Simons had plotted out Gideon's future like a military campaign. And then, when Gideon met Kate Ward, the whole strategy crumbled. You could hear the arguments from a hundred yards off, someone told him, the old man shouting at his son day after day. But in a way it was all expected. Gideon had been denied nothing before and thought that in this, as in all things, his father would give way.

Only this time old man Simons *didn't* give way. Kate Ward was a nobody – how could his son marry a woman of no importance? In reply Gideon had thrown down the gauntlet: 'I marry Kate or I leave.' Old man Simons had been in no mood to allow Gideon to rebel. Besides, he thought his son would back down. But he couldn't cow Gideon. They were too similar, and Gideon had been indulged for too long.

So Gideon left and married Kate Ward and they moved away to live in Yorkshire. The old man never referred to his son again, but all his fury descended on his remaining children. Girls couldn't run his business, he decided, and as for the idiot Saville, what good was he to anyone? Within a year old man Simons had driven his wife to death. He could hardly say a civil word to Irma and berated Saville every time he saw him. But how he treated Mildred, no one knew. No gossip had escaped about her, no broken romances, no fights, no rebellions.

Dr Redmond sighed to himself. He had seen a little of her past, and it had been shattering. But the rest of Mildred's story remained firmly locked within the walls of the Simons house. Not for public consumption.

Once again, his gaze fell on the name 'Harris Simons'. It would be interesting to see if the girl was assimilated into the family – or if she would change it. Or if, like her father before her, she would cause havoc.

'I said the other day – oi, watch my ear, that's flesh you're cutting!' Mrs Leonards settled back down into her seat and stared into the mirror as Mildred continued to trim her hair. 'I saw that little one of yours the other day.' She peered into the mirror again. 'Not too short, I don't want to look like a boy.' Mildred tried to imagine a boy with the chest of a pouter pigeon. 'She's a strange-looking little thing.'

In the mirror's reflection Mildred could see her sister at the reception desk behind her. Where did your good looks go? she wondered. You were a stunner once. Her gaze moved from Irma and drifted around Simons Coiffeuse. It was a lovely salon, Mildred thought with pride, all pink and grey. *Pink and grey,* people had said when they first opened, *in Wigan?* But that was the point, Mildred thought; they weren't going to be like anyone else.

Besides, she had seen this picture in a magazine of some film star's bedroom – Mary Pickford, was it? – and that had inspired her. Irma had only wanted the business to be busy, but Mildred had wanted it to be a roaring success. In that way she could cock a snook at everyone. Especially her dead father.

26

'. . . yes, I hear your Harris is quite a little terror,' Mrs Leonards babbled on. 'Fallen off the bakery roof, I gather.'

'It wasn't the bakery roof,' Mildred said evenly.

'You're not cutting it too short at the back, are you? My husband doesn't like it too short. He doesn't like women to be mannish.'

Mildred thought of Mrs Leonards' husband and had a sudden impulse to shave the back of her client's head.

'. . . You have to keep children in check. I mean, I know you haven't got children of your own, Mildred, but I have and I can give you good advice –'

'On your collar?'

Mrs Leonards frowned, baffled. 'What?'

'D'you want your hair to rest on your collar, or not?'

'Depends on the collar.'

Mildred was standing with her scissors poised. '*This* collar.'

Mrs Leonards frowned. 'Wouldn't it be too short?'

'All right then, the collar of your blouse.'

'Too long.'

Why doesn't she just wear a bloody hood and solve all our problems? Mildred thought acidly.

'I think I'll take a bit more off.'

Mrs Leonards relaxed. 'Do what you think best, Mildred. Like I was saying, I've had children, I know how difficult it can be.'

'Harris has been with us for six months. She's fine.'

'Oh, you imagine so, but you don't know what she's thinking. You never what's going through another person's mind.'

You're right there, or you'd be out of this seat in a jiffy, Mildred mused to herself.

'. . . All I mean is this – you and Irma are businesswomen, not family types.'

Businesswomen – oh, that sounded so good to Mildred's ears. What would her father have thought now if he could see this salon, see their takings? Bigger every year. Not so stupid now, are we? Mildred thought. We did better than you expected, better than Gideon ever did. You tried to break our spirits, Father, but you failed. *You failed*.

'What did they die of?'

Mildred frowned. 'Who?'

'Harris's parents. I heard rumours, but you know how it is, people gossip.'

'They drowned.'

'Good Lord, in water?'

No, in bloody soup, Mildred wanted to reply.

'They were on that ferry going to Ireland, you remember the one –'

'That one!' Mrs Leonards was all excitement, moving round in her seat, her wet hair dripping down her back. 'There were no survivors, were there?'

Mildred shook her head. 'No, none.'

'But Harris wasn't with them?'

She really is a master of the obvious, Mildred thought, turning Gladys Leonards back to the mirror. 'Harris was at school. She didn't go with them that day because she had a cold.'

This was real news, Mrs Leonards thought, something to pass on to her friends when they met for tea that afternoon. Everyone had wanted to know the full story, but *she* had come up trumps. It was worth giving Mildred a good tip just for that.

'Does she miss them very much?'

'No,' Mildred said quietly, 'she said they were very cruel to her.'

Mrs Leonards' eyes bulged under her wet fringe. 'Cruel?'

'Yes, they killed people and then ate them. In Yorkshire.'

Stunned, Mrs Leonards gawked at Mildred in the mirror. 'They were cannibals?'

Mildred nodded. 'I know you won't tell another soul, Gladys,

28

but there's a lot of it in Yorkshire. Inbreeding – all those generations of farmers living away from the towns. I heard there are goings-on no decent person could imagine.' Trying hard not to laugh, she turned back to cutting Gladys's hair, then delivered the *coup de grâce*. 'They're into devil worship too.'

This was too much for Gladys. She fidgeted as Mildred finished her haircut, wriggled as the rollers went in, and fretted under the cumbersome, noisy steel hair dryer. Glancing over to her on several occasions Mildred could see she was about to self-combust with frustration. And she knew that within minutes of Gladys leaving the salon, the ludicrous story would be retold.

Most, knowing Mildred, would see the joke.

It was all right if you liked pink, Harris thought, but she had always liked yellow. Sitting on the side of her bed she ran her tongue along her gum where she had knocked out two teeth. Her mother would have kept them and put them under her pillow for the tooth fairy . . . Harris sighed and walked over to the window. It was a lovely garden. Her father had always talked about how they would get a garden someday. But it had never come about. Instead they had lived in a grimy, gloomy terrace, her father always losing his jobs for fighting, her mother very sweet, very quiet.

And very kind . . . Her parents had been looking forward to the new baby, telling her all about it. And she had pretended to be very pleased, but she wasn't. At night she had prayed to God to get rid of the baby because she wanted things to stay as they were. Just the three of them. She had prayed and prayed and God had heard her. Only he took the baby *and* her parents away.

She could never tell anyone. About the baby, or what she had done. She had to be very tough, like her father taught her: 'I know you're only a little girl, Harris, but life's hard and you have to learn how to keep people from hurting you.'

She had rested her head against his shoulder, not really understanding what he said. He'd been in a fight again. Someone had said something he didn't like, or he'd been asked to do something he thought *was beneath him*. Harris didn't understand what the phrase meant, only that it was important to her father. So it mattered to her. Hugging her, he had laid his head against her, his lip cut and swollen. She had caught a faint smell of iodine; a familiar smell after every fight.

'You have to struggle in this world, Harris, never forget that. And don't tell people anything. Only tell us, your mother and me. No one else. This is your world, Harris, the three of us. We have to stick together, don't we, darling? The three of us, for ever.'

That three had been about to swell to four. But now – because of what she had done – there was only one left . . .

Harris stared into the garden. It was so different from how it had looked the summer evening she'd arrived. Then it had been drowsy with scent and fallen rain. Now it was chilled, emptied of flowers. But she hadn't broken down again. Oh, she cried at night, but not when there was anyone around, because they would ask her why she was crying. They would think it was because of the death of her parents and if they pressed her she would have to tell them that she had killed them.

You went to hell for that, didn't you?

'I think we should give her more food,' Saville said, ladling his eggs on to Harris's plate as Mildred looked on. 'Lots of food.'

'She's had enough. No one likes a greedy child. Take your tablets, Saville. Go on, take them now,' Irma said, wiping her mouth with her napkin.

It was a cold day, chilly and unwelcoming. Soon she would leave for the salon, walking as she always did. It was good to walk, Irma thought, kept you fit and meant that you knew what was going on in the town. And there was always something going on.

Usually Mildred and she would set off together, but not today. Today Harris had to go to the dentist and Mildred was going with her. Good thing too, Irma thought. She and the child seldom had any conversation.

'I'll take Harris on to school afterwards,' Mildred told her sister. 'Saville, leave your food alone.'

He looked up, pained. 'I just thought that she might like some more.'

'If Harris wants some more, she'll ask.'

'She might not like to. Might think it's rude.'

It was a fair point. Smiling, Mildred turned to her niece. 'You can ask for anything, sweetheart. Don't be afraid.'

'Can I not go to the dentist then?'

Saville burst out laughing, clasping Harris to him with delight.

'You should learn not to cheek your elders and betters,' Irma said coldly. 'You should count yourself lucky that you have people who are prepared to pay for you to visit a dentist.'

Saville's good humour sank like a dropped soufflé.

As she looked over to her sister, Mildred took Harris's hand. 'No one wants to go to the dentist, Irma. When was the last time you went?'

She bridled. 'I have perfect teeth.'

'I'll remind you of that when you have to put them in a glass at night,' Mildred retorted smartly, leading Harris out of the room.

Together they walked down Wigan Lane, then continued a little way further, finally catching a bus for the last part of the short journey. Mildred looked out of the bus window at the cars passing by. Big, unwieldy machines, she

31

thought, and yet she longed for one. People wouldn't expect that of her, she thought, not of Mildred Simons. In fact she had even begun to dream of her own car. If she got one they could all go out on trips together. Maybe Blackpool – no, Irma would say that it was too common. St Annes, then – yes, that would be nice. They could get their housekeeper, Mrs Turner, to make them up a lunch and all go off some Saturday. After all, how hard could it be to learn to drive?

'I don't want to go.'

Mildred turned to Harris sympathetically. 'Oh, the dentist's not so bad.'

'But Mummy never took me to the dentist.'

Mildred digested this piece of information carefully. 'Maybe your mummy didn't think you needed to go.'

'No . . . we didn't have the money.'

Surprised, Mildred studied her small charge. 'Were you poor?'

'I suppose so.'

Curiosity got the better of her. Mildred had promised herself not to pry, to let Harris open up when she wanted to, but the waiting was getting hard. Mildred had loved her brother, felt bitter for his loss. Gideon had been pushed out of their family so suddenly, without a goodbye. There one day, gone the next. And she had missed him, because Gideon was glamorous, charming and entertaining.

She had never resented him. Even though he had been the chosen one. Even though their father had poured all his energy and affection into him. Even though, by loving Gideon, he had neglected his other children. Somehow, to Mildred, Gideon was worth it. Irma had grown to hate him, Saville had tried hopelessly to compete, but Mildred had accepted that Gideon was not only the brightest, but the *only* star in her father's firmament.

'You must miss your parents very much.'

32

Harris looked down at her feet. Smart shoes, not the ones she used to have. 'I miss home.'

No wonder, Mildred thought. They were hardly a substitute. 'We love you, Harris. I know we're a bit odd, Irma, Saville and me, but we do love you.'

The little girl kept her head down.

'Are you very unhappy?'

Mildred had tried over the preceding months to get close to Harris, but she wasn't a child who opened up readily. Buying her clothes and taking her shopping was a pleasure, but to whom? Harris, or her? Besides, she wasn't a typical little girl – always getting grubby in the garden, scuffing her new shoes and asking repeatedly if she could have her hair cut. Irma refused, adamant on that – *a girl should look like a girl*. Mildred felt that to cut such thick dark hair would be criminal. But how much did such things matter to a child?

'Harris, tell me, *are* you unhappy?'

But the conductor cut into their conversation at that point, calling out their stop.

There was to be no answer that day.

The Simonses didn't have close neighbours, only the Barracloughs down the road, with whom they had no communication, except indirectly – as the Barracloughs' gardener, Mr Lacy, was very much in love with Mrs Turner. Mrs Turner, having been widowed earlier than she could have expected, was not in love with Mr Lacy, but liked to flirt. And keep her options open. After all, as she said to a friend, 'When I'm old enough to retire Mr Lacy might look a lot more attractive.' And so might his pension, her friend thought meanly.

The besotted Mr Lacy – ginger-haired and built like an outside privy – waited for Mrs Turner most evenings when she had finished at the Simonses. She would make dinner, serve it, and then head for home. And usually on the way she would have a drink at the Bishop's Finger with her paramour. It was a routine that was comfortable. But Mr Lacy's conversations were more heated than his affections and Mrs Turner had long since become bored. There was only so much any man could say about a dahlia, and over the years Mrs Turner felt as though she personally had ploughed, manured and planted every inch of the Barraclough garden. Unfortunately she had had little of interest to say either. Until Harris had arrived.

It was a revelation for Mrs Turner. Now she really had something to tell Mr Lacy – and everyone else at the Bishop's Finger. *Oooh*, they said when she told them about Harris's parents' death. *Ahhhh*, they said when she confided about the child's falls. And, *Well I never*, the night Mrs Turner talked about the visit to the dentist.

Hugging her port and lemon tightly, Mrs Turner saw the small circle of faces watching her avidly. It was a cold night but inside the pub it was cosy, a coal fire blazing, the light flashing off the optics and the lines of bottles behind the bar. Smoke curled over her head as Mrs Turner – resplendent in a checked coat and blue wool hat – began her tale.

'I was just finishing the dusting when I heard a terrible commotion.' She stopped. Mr Lacy nodded as though Plato couldn't have said anything wiser. 'Miss Irma was home unexpectedly . . .' a sigh around the assembled customers; Miss Irma wasn't to be tangled with, '. . . when Miss Mildred and the little girl came in.'

A clock sounded the hour ominously behind the listeners.

'Go on, luv,' Mr Lacy urged, although he had heard the story twice already.

'Well, like I say, in walks Miss Mildred and the child. She was cross, you could see that –'

'Who were?' a voice queried.

Mrs Turner peered into the smoky gloom. 'Miss Mildred, who else? Her face was as red as a smacked arse.' Mr Lacy nodded as though he had seen it for himself and knew it to be true. 'She came in and told Harris –'

'Who's Harris?'

'The little girl!' Mrs Turner replied hotly. 'I've talked enough about her before and it's not a name anyone with half a brain is likely to forget.' She settled back down again. 'She told Harris – "Don't you ever behave like that again! How could you show me up like that?"' Mrs Turner looked round the watching faces. 'Miss Mildred's not one to shout, but she was spitting feathers. "What kind of child acts like an animal?" she says. Well, all of a sudden in comes Miss Irma.' There was a communal intake of breath. '"What's been going on?" she asks. Miss Mildred jumps – not expecting her sister there and knowing she's no soft touch. "It's nothing, Harris was just naughty at the dentist . . ." Well, you should have seen Miss Irma's face. "Naughty!" she repeats. "How naughty?"'

Mrs Turner paused for effect and sipped at her port and lemon. Everyone watched and waited. Finally she spoke again. '"She was naughty, that's all," Miss Mildred goes on, but then the child looks at Miss Irma – dead defiant – and says, "I bit the dentist!"'

Everyone gasped.

'Never!'

'I don't believe it!'

'Which dentist?' came the voice from the back.

'Mr British,' Mrs Turner replied.

'Serve him right. That bugger nearly broke my jaw once.'

There was a rush of laughter, Mr Lacy chiming in, 'Go on, Mrs Turner, finish the story.'

'Well, she drew blood, did Miss Harris. She bit the dentist that hard, she drew blood.'

'How d'you know?' came the voice from the back again.

'I heard about it,' Mrs Turner said, miffed. 'I'm the Simonses' housekeeper, as you well know. There's nothing that's happened in that house that I miss. She's like a little animal, that child. And mischievous. Oh, she'll be trouble. You mark my words, she'll be trouble.'

FOUR

This is the last straw! Irma thought, grabbing Harris by the arm and marching her out of the garden and into the kitchen. A surprised Mrs Turner watched them pass, but said nothing, hearing the footsteps come to an abrupt end as they entered the morning room.

'How dare you?' Irma raged, her normal control evaporating by the second. 'How dare you go through my things?'

Keeping her head down, Harris trembled. It was true, she *had* gone through Irma's clothes, but she had had to. Hadn't everyone at school said her aunt was a witch? *Well, hadn't they?* And witches, Harris knew, had weird things that gave them away, like frogs, cats, broomsticks . . .

'I will NOT have you nosy-parkering around!' Irma hollered.

Mildred hurried into the room anxiously. She took in the scene with a glance, immediately putting her arm round Harris protectively. 'Lower your voice, Irma, you're frightening the child.'

'I will not lower my voice!' Irma snapped back. 'Harris needs controlling. She's been going through my things – be stealing next, no doubt.' Her voice was metallic with rage. 'And when I first asked her about it, she didn't tell me the truth. So she's a liar too!'

Mildred faced up to her sister. 'She is only a child –'

'A bad child!' Irma replied, leaning towards Harris, who immediately stepped back. 'She can't see how lucky she is. She should be grateful to us for taking her in. After all, we didn't have to. She could have gone to some home somewhere with all the other orphans –'

Shaken, Mildred shouted at her sister. 'Irma, stop it! That's enough!'

'Nothing near enough!' Enraged, Irma pointed at Harris. 'Look at her! Just look at her! She's our brother all over again. And she'll turn out bad, just like him. As wilful and stupid as he was –'

At that, Harris lunged forwards, her fists pounding Irma's corseted stomach, her face contorted with fury. Caught off guard, Irma nearly lost her footing.

The child was beside herself. 'Don't talk about my father like that! I hate you! I hate you! I never wanted to come here. I want to go home! I want to go home!'

Mildred tried to pull Harris off, but she kept on pummelling her aunt's body, Irma fielding the blows as best she could.

'Now look what you've done!' Mildred reprimanded her sister, as she pulled the child away.

'What *I've* done –'

'I hate you!' Harris repeated, her dark eyes flecked with fury as she stared at Irma. 'Daddy hated you too; he hated all of you. Said you were cruel to him. And you *are*! You're all cruel!'

And with that she ran off, leaving Mildred standing with her mouth hanging open, Irma red in the face with fury, and Mrs Turner listening gleefully behind the morning-room door.

Sitting on the side of his bed Saville shuddered. He hated arguments. They frightened him and reminded him of his

38

father. But he was dead, Saville told himself, and dead men don't come back to life.

Breathing in, he gradually relaxed, as the house fell silent. Slowly he got to his feet and peered round the door, looking out on to the landing. There was no one about. Confusion muffled his thoughts. His father wasn't here. It hadn't been his father shouting. He's dead, Saville told himself again, Father is dead. There's nothing to be frightened about any more.

And yet the shouting had traumatised him and although Saville tried hard to leave his room, old memories – clammy and treacherous – locked the door on him.

Her temper still simmering, Irma hurried into Simons Coiffeuse and slammed the door behind her. It was early in the morning, half an hour before they were due to open. Hurriedly she made herself a cup of tea in the room at the back and then walked out into the salon. A neat little row of chairs and mirrors faced her, the fierce contraption of the perming machine standing to attention in the corner.

Irma stared at it. They had invested in it when the Marcel wave had become popular, forcing the hair of the Wigan women into the steel rods attached by wires to the main machine. For weeks no one had had the nerve to use it and all Irma's protestations that she had visited the manufacturers and knew *exactly* how it worked won no volunteers. Finally Mildred had stepped forward. 'H. G. Wells would have been proud of us,' she had said at the time. It had taken Irma half a day to perm her sister's hair, reassuring her repeatedly – even when the perm lotion was searing into Mildred's head like a flame-thrower. Minutes had passed, Irma watching in rigid anticipation. More minutes had passed, Mildred's head haloed with wires, her face by then the colour of a ripe strawberry. Both sisters had watched the clock, and when the allotted minutes were finally up, Mildred had leaped from her chair with impressive speed for a plump woman.

In the end, the result was spectacular: Mildred's ash-blonde hair had been transformed into a froth of bubbles. For weeks people came to stare at Wigan's answer to Shirley Temple and then, mercifully, the perm began to sag and from a nest of wiry ringlets luxuriant waves appeared. From then on, Irma hadn't looked back.

She had always been a quick learner, and besides, who was likely to complain to Irma? So she permed and curling-tonged unruly heads of hair into submission, and mostly the hair obeyed. The occasional disaster still happened, of course. The thought of Gloria Osborne's hair still caused pain to Irma. She had come in for a tint and had left as a blonde bombshell. When she looked in the mirror later her head was a froth of platinum, extending three inches from the scalp. Crying, she had phoned Irma. Irma had stood her ground: 'You wanted blonde hair, you got blonde hair . . .' 'But I wanted a soft blonde,' Gloria had wailed. Luckily her husband had liked it and from then on Irma coloured Gloria's hair every six weeks, Gloria walking around Wigan looking like Jean Harlow.

Sipping her tea, Irma continued her scrutiny of the salon. They had done well, made a little fortune from the place. After all, there was nowhere else like Simons Coiffeuse. Not that it had been easy at first. When they had opened people had wondered what the well-off Simons sisters knew about hairdressing – and also how a notorious snob like Irma would take to serving customers.

But Irma didn't *serve* her customers, she *terrorised* them. Her skill with scissors and her natural eye for copying fashions meant that she didn't have to take any lip from anyone. Women came in with a picture from a magazine and Irma copied it. Others came in with an idea and she did something else – but no one ever dared to complain. They were scared of Irma and, anyway, she made them look good.

It was funny, that. Irma wasn't interested in her own appearance; looking clean and tidy was all that mattered to her. But she was incredibly generous in getting the best out of other women. So they endured her moods, her silences and her snobbery to get the smartest hairstyles in Wigan. Woe betide anyone who offered a suggestion when Irma was cutting their hair. Or worse, gossiped. Irma had no time for gossip. Besides, her customers weren't so much flesh and blood, as objects for her to practise on. If she could have made each one of them comatose she would have done.

Taking another sip of her tea, Irma felt her rage bubbling. That damn child was impossible, she thought. Here she was, driven out of her own home by some uncontrollable brat. Oh, Mildred might like to play at being mother, but Irma could see Harris for what she was – a temperamental, difficult, wilful child who needed controlling. Fast.

As for Saville, he was besotted by the child . . . Irma stared fiercely at a passer-by and then walked over to the row of customer chairs. One by one she corrected their angles so that they were directly facing the mirrors. Then she checked the mirrors for dust, then inspected the floor. It was all well and good for Mildred to pick pink and grey, but they showed the dirt quickly. And Irma hated dirt.

A sudden rattling at the front door made her jump. Mildred hurried in, her face pink from the cold morning.

'What the hell were you playing at, shouting at Harris like a madwoman?'

Irma waved aside the rebuke, her tone bitter. 'We have to do something about that child. You heard what she said – she hates us and she hates living with us.'

Mildred folded her arms. 'So what do you suggest we do about her?'

'Something quick. She's out of control.'

'She's a child who's just lost her parents.'

'That was six months ago!'

'Dear God!' Mildred snapped impatiently. 'Give her a chance.'

Irritated, Irma turned away and began to count the towels. She would have to have a word with Rose, the junior. They weren't clean enough for her liking.

'She bit the dentist –'

'He hurt her.'

'– and she attacked me.'

'You frightened her!'

Irritated, Irma threw down the towels she was holding and spun round. 'So that makes it all right? I can't discipline her, and as for the dentist, *he hurt her*, so it's fine for her to hurt him back! We've known Mr British for years – how d'you think it makes us look, the child behaving that way? Anyway, he's a JP.'

Mildred's eyebrows rose. 'I don't suppose Harris realised that when she bit him.'

'Oh, go on, make a joke of it! That's what you usually do,' Irma snorted. 'But we have a position in this town. One that I personally don't want to see threatened by some demented child.'

'Harris is our niece.'

'So we have to excuse her *everything*?' Irma snapped, her face righteous. 'Personally I don't think she should have come to us. We don't know anything about children.'

'And where else could she have gone? She's Gideon's daughter, for God's sake.'

'And naturally we all have to put Gideon first – even when he's dead.'

Shocked, Mildred took in a breath. Irma was seething, moving quickly round the basins, hoping to find something else to rebuke poor Rose with.

'I didn't know that you were still so bitter about Gideon.'

Irma stopped, her hands on her hips. 'Gideon let down the family. And now *we* have to clear up his mess.'

'His mess is a child –'

'I don't want his child around!' Irma shouted, frustrated beyond measure. 'Life was orderly before. We had a good business, money and status in this town. We knew where we were.'

Mildred's stared incredulously at her sister. 'We were two dried-up spinsters.'

'Speak for yourself, Mildred! I was very content. I had my bridge evenings and this salon. The Simons name means something in this town. I don't want Gideon's offspring ruining everything.'

Frowning, Mildred studied her sister. 'This isn't just about Harris, is it?'

'Then who *is* it about?'

'I don't know! You tell me.'

'We have customers. I have to get ready,' Irma replied hotly, turning away.

Annoyed, Mildred followed her. 'It's bound to be difficult for all of us –'

'Difficult!' Irma snapped. 'That's an understatement. I liked things the way they were.'

'Well, I didn't. I was bored,' Mildred retorted, her tone even. 'I like having a child around.'

'So far that child has bitten the dentist, fallen off the roof, and tried to injure me. She's always telling stories and now she's decided that she hates us and doesn't want to be with us,' Irma said coldly. 'It's obvious that our brother never taught her any manners. That would be typical of Gideon, letting his child run wild.'

'You always hated him, didn't you?' Mildred asked, her tone confrontational. 'Always resented Gideon.'

'And you didn't?'

'No,' Mildred snapped. 'I loved him.'

'Well, fat lot of good that did you!' Irma replied sourly. 'He obviously didn't feel the same, or he would have been in touch with you. Or any of us. But no, Gideon got what Gideon wanted and that was all he cared about. We never entered his head after he left. Never a thought for us, being left at home with our parents.' She shuddered, old memories just below the surface. 'Gideon had what Gideon wanted and *we* could boil in hell. And to cap it all, he was even poisoning his daughter's mind against us from a distance. So you tell me, Mildred, why *should* we look after his child? What exactly do we owe our brother?'

'I *want* to look after Harris.'

Slamming down a pair of steel scissors, Irma rounded on her sister. 'Well, I don't! We've had enough problems with Saville over the years, we didn't need more responsibility. You've seen for yourself how Harris's presence has affected our brother. He's wandering off all the time. Mr Lacy had to bring him back from the Barracloughs' only the other day.'

'Saville has always had a tendency to wander,' Mildred countered.

'But he'd settled down a lot – until that child came along. Now he's got worse, and I know why, even if you're too stupid to see it. He looks at Harris as competition for our attention.'

Grudgingly Mildred had to admit that her sister was right. Saville was alternately delighted with, then jealous of, his niece. But why did Irma have to make the situation even more difficult? Why couldn't she help out instead of simply criticising? Harris wasn't going anywhere; they all had to find a way to cope with the upheaval she had caused.

'Irma, just think of Harris as a confused little girl –'

'Who is causing havoc.'

'– she's away from home, without the parents she loved, and thrown into some strange house with even stranger people.'

Irma stiffened. 'Speak for yourself, Mildred! There's nothing strange about me.'

'Oh, look at it with the eyes of a child! We're two oddities to her, and Saville is like some huge child. We live in a house which has been cleaned and organised like a pharaoh's tomb – nothing out of place, nothing disturbed. So in she comes and is probably frightened to even move – and when she does you're on her like a ton of bricks. Living with us is hardly what she's used to, is it?'

'We don't know what she's used to,' Irma countered. 'All we know is that they were poor.'

'And we're well off. We could buy Harris whatever she wants. But all she wants at the moment is to feel safe.'

'Climbing roofs, falling out of trees and attacking her own aunt are hardly likely to add to her feelings of security, are they?' Irma answered. 'I thought she might settle down when she started her new school, but she's worse.'

'You have to give her time.'

Irma's voice was hard. 'I don't have to give her anything! She's been invited into a comfortable home, shares good food and sleeps in a good bed. Harris ought to count her blessings. She has to be made to toe the line.'

Mildred flinched. 'Dear God, listen to yourself. You sound like our father.'

Irma stopped in her tracks. Mildred thought for a moment that the words would shake her enough to make her realise what she was becoming. But they didn't. It was as though Irma had decided that after a childhood of being terrorised she was going to offer no quarter to anyone else. She would no longer be bullied; she would *be* the bully. She wasn't going to reject their father's traits, but embrace them.

'You can mollycoddle that child all you like, Mildred, but Harris has to understand that she comes a long way down the pecking order. Life will be a lot sweeter when she learns to control herself and fit in with us.' Irma's expression was stony. 'And if *you* don't tell her that, *I will*.'

FIVE

Despite what Irma said, there was peace for a while. In fact, Mildred was enjoying the run-up to Christmas. After all, it was the first she had spent shopping with – and for – a child. She took Harris round Lowes department store, showing her the kids' toys, the clothes and all the foods in aromatic piles on the stalls.

They were just passing a display of boxed biscuits when a passer-by stopped Mildred, looking curiously at Harris.

'So this is your little nephew –'

'Niece,' Mildred corrected the woman.

'Oh, sorry, it's just that . . . well, Harris is rather an odd name for a girl, isn't it?'

The child looked at the woman with an impassive face. 'It's my father's middle name,' she said simply.

Mrs Ramsbottom smiled uncomfortably, as though she hadn't actually expected the child to talk. Looking back to Mildred, she asked: 'Will you be having her for Christmas?'

'Roasted or boiled?' Mildred retorted, squeezing Harris's hand. 'Of course we've having Harris for Christmas. She lives with us now.'

Nodding her head, Mrs Ramsbottom digested the news, then looked back to Harris. 'I must say, you're a pretty little girl.'

On cue, Harris smiled – the huge double gap between her front teeth rendering Mrs Ramsbottom speechless.

Of course Mildred had known that Harris had done it deliberately. She already had a wicked sense of humour. Still clutching her niece's hand, Mildred walked on, until they came to a large, mock-Georgian doll's house.

'What do you think of that?'

Solemnly Harris stared at it. A memory came back so painfully that she took in her breath. There had been another doll's house in a shop window once. Her mother had shown it to her, long ago. Or was it? Maybe it just *seemed* a long time ago.

Her mother had looked at the doll's house, and so had Harris, their eyes huge. 'One day I'll buy you that, sweetheart. When Daddy gets his new job, then I'll buy it for you.'

'Harris?'

She blinked at her name, jolted back into the present. The doll's house her mother had showed her had been cheap, gaudy, not like this one. But that night, holding her mother's hand and staring in at the window, it had seemed like a mansion.

Concerned, Mildred bent down to the child. 'Harris, are you all right, dear?'

She nodded, a lump in her throat.

'Would you like the doll's house?'

'No!' Harris wanted to scream. 'I want the one my mother showed me. I don't want *your* doll's house because you're just buying it to make me be good, to make me be quiet.'

'Harris, do you want it?'

And then, without warning, Harris started to run. Customers watching could see her move away from Mildred's side and run down the aisle towards the stairs, her hat falling off as she did so. Shouting and waving her arms about, Mildred called for help. At once a shop assistant ran over to her.

'Can I help you, madam?'

'My niece has just run off. She's going down the stairs. RUN AFTER HER!'

The man did as he was told, Mildred trying to keep up, a couple of other men joining in the chase. But Harris had long since outrun them and was on the pavement before they managed to make it out of the building.

The cold air shook its fist at the child as she looked from right to left, searching for something, anything. Where was she going to go? And to whom? Again Harris looked round, tears in her eyes. It was useless, there was nowhere to go. Nowhere to run . . . She would have to go back into the shop and say she was sorry. Mildred was kind; she might not even scold her.

But just then one of her pursuers ran up behind Harris and caught hold of her arm. Panicked, she ducked out of his grip – running straight into the Christmas traffic.

They said afterwards that you could hear the screeching brakes across Wigan. In the last moments before impact Harris saw the car and tried to jump out of its way. That action saved her life, Dr Redmond said later. Unfortunately the car still hit Harris's left side.

When they took her to the hospital they discovered that her pelvis was broken in three places.

That night Saville was inconsolable. He would not believe that his playmate was still alive. Harris was dead, he wailed constantly, she wasn't coming home. In the end it was Irma who came up trumps. Taking her brother's hand firmly she marched up to the infirmary and faced the night nurse.

'I need to see my niece.'

'I'm sorry,' the young woman replied, not yet daunted by the hanging judge in the navy coat, 'she's asleep and this is well past visiting hours.'

48

Irma's reply was to walk past the night nurse, dragging Saville along with her. Guided by the soft night lights she scrutinised every patient, the nurse running behind, her protestations ignored. Finally Irma spotted a bed separated behind curtains.

With one firm movement she pulled back the curtains.

'There!' she said, pointing to the sleeping Harris. 'Look, Saville, she's not dead at all.'

Relieved, he laid his head on his sister's shoulder.

Irma stared at her niece. Dear God, she thought, she's so tiny and so bruised. Harris's face was marked, her lip cut, the dark eyes swollen. Guilt swelled up in Irma all at once. She had been cruel to this child, to her own flesh and blood. How could she? Wasn't Harris a Simons? One of their own?

'I have to ask you to leave,' the night nurse repeated, her face flushed.

'I know the principal of this hospital and the Simonses have donated enough money to build your X-ray department,' Irma replied coldly. 'That gives me some rights, surely?'

'You can have five minutes,' the young nurse said, backing down in the face of such power. 'But no longer.'

'She looks dead . . .'

Irma dug Saville in the ribs. 'Nonsense! She isn't dead. She's sleeping.'

'Is she hurting?'

'Not at the moment, but I dare say she won't be climbing any trees for a while.'

Irma's voice betrayed little of what she was really feeling. How could she have been angry about Harris climbing trees, roofs, losing her temper – any damn thing? She was broken now, a little doll, limp as a glove.

It was a silent Irma who left the hospital that night, Saville jabbering beside her. When she got home to Deerheart House, Mildred was waiting by the door.

'Well?'

'No . . .' Irma said quietly, 'she's not well at all.'

Harris came home a week before Christmas. She was carried into her room by the ambulance men, Mildred fussing round her as Harris was put to bed. Silent, she lay against the pile of pillows and then, minutes later, fell into a deep sleep.

It was only when she woke Harris remembered where she was and winced as she tried to turn over. Homesickness, painful and consuming, washed over her. It seemed in that instant that there was no one else in the world. And yet Harris could hear footsteps moving in the house below. She longed for someone to come. Saville or Mildred. But they thought she was asleep and wouldn't disturb her . . . Lonely, she stared out of the window, as she would for a long time to come.

And so the days followed. Soon snow was banked up against the glass, icicles hanging from the trees outside. It hurt Harris to move. It hurt her to sleep. It hurt her to think, it seemed. Over and over again she could see the car coming towards her and then feel the impact. Many times she wondered why she had run away to begin with. After all, she was just about to go back to Mildred, wasn't she? So why *had* she run away?

And then she would remember the doll's house.

Puffy-faced from exertion, Dr Redmond came into the Simonses' hall. He had been walking instead of driving and was patently exhausted, his florid face shining, steam rising from his shirt collar, his goatee beard absurdly small on his massive jowls.

'I have to ask you something,' Mildred said, leading Lionel Redmond into the drawing room and sitting him down. She seemed embarrassed, then hurried on quickly: 'Will Harris be able to have children?'

He blinked. 'Well . . .'

'If she needs to see a specialist, that's fine. Money's no object. We want Harris to have the best.'

At that moment Irma walked in and Dr Redmond flinched as though he was about to be struck. Stern-faced, she sat down by the fireside and fixed Lionel Redmond with her black stare.

'So?'

'So what?' he squeaked.

'So what about Harris?' Irma replied, with a look that intimated that she was talking to a moron. 'Can she be a mother?'

'No one can be sure about anything at the moment. But Harris is very young. She might recover completely –'

'Or she might not?'

He looked balefully at Irma. 'Or she might not.'

'So she could be an invalid for life?' Irma asked. 'Bedridden?'

Shocked, Mildred looked at her sister. She must be wrong, she thought. It wasn't *hope* she was reading in her face, was it?

'No one said Harris would be bedridden for life, Irma.'

Slowly Irma turned to Mildred, her head on one side. 'No one said she wouldn't be, did they?' She glanced back to Lionel Redmond. 'I think we should give Harris the best care available. My sister and I will look after her, and we'll get in a nurse to help.'

'We will?' Mildred asked, bemused.

'Harris has to have round-the-clock care if she's to be properly looked after. No half-measures,' Irma said firmly. 'Poor little mite will need all the help she can get.'

Glassy-eyed, Dr Redmond studied Irma Simons. He was wondering if he had heard right, or if someone had exchanged the old Irma with a new, kindly version without his noticing.

'Harris is a child,' he said finally. 'Children do recover from –'

'We don't want to hurry anything!' Irma said with a tone

that invited no contradiction. 'If Harris is to be an invalid, so be it.'

Mrs Turner was sipping her port and lemon and nodding sagely into her glass.

'The little lass is broken like a doll, all plastered up in bed. Miss Mildred and Mr Saville are fussing over her all the time. As for Miss Irma, well, she can't do enough for her now. I pity the poor nurse, bossed from pillar to post.' She paused, checking that the inebriated Mr Lacy was listening. 'You know something? I think Miss Irma likes the child now she's in bed, all sickly. She can manage her now.'

'How long will it take?' Mr Lacy asked, leaning back in his seat, his face shiny.

'For what?'

'For the little one to heal?'

'Oh, I don't know. To hear Miss Irma tell it, you'd think Harris would be bedridden for life.'

'Nah!'

Mrs Turner nodded. 'She said to me this morning – and that was a first; she hardly exchanges a word with me usually – that we all had to be "very careful with Harris. She's a poorly little thing," she said, "never going to be strong."'

Mr Lacy digested the words, along with a swig of beer. 'No more climbing then?'

'No more climbing.'

'The Barracloughs will be glad.'

Mrs Turner slapped the back of his hand. 'How can you be so heartless, Mr Lacy?' she snapped. 'Speaking for myself, I'd give anything to see Harris knocking down their bloody apples again.'

*   *   *

After a while the bed had been pushed over to the window where Harris could look out on to a winter garden. Much of her room had changed: its pink and white prettiness punctuated with towels, medicine, hot-water bottles and books. Dozens of books.

She was finding her forced confinement frustrating. Living with the Simonses had been bearable when she could get out, but now she was locked in, almost tied to her bed, in pain – and there was no mother to comfort her. Upset, Harris turned her face into the pillow. She had tried to be brave, tried ever so hard, but this was too difficult. Mildred was kind to her, and sometimes, in pain, she had wanted to cling to her aunt and be petted. But she couldn't, could she? Her father had told her the Simonses were wicked, so how could she look to any of them for comfort? All of them were bad, he had said, except one. *But he had never told her which one.*

For a moment Harris doubted her father's words. How could *Saville* be wicked? He was simple, silly even. How could he be wicked? And if her father had been wrong about Saville, could he also have been wrong about Mildred? She sighed, breathing out into the soft pillow, her crying muffled. Irma was certainly wicked, Harris knew that much. Even though she pretended to be nice now, she was bad. Irma was glad she was ill, smiling when she came in as though she was thinking – I've got you where I want you now. You have to do as I say.

But Mildred couldn't be bad. Hadn't her aunt tried over and over again to get close to her? Little presents had materialised, treats, meals made that Harris constantly picked at. And in the evenings, hadn't Mildred read to her hour after hour, weaving stories, making the pain lift? Would a wicked person do that?

But who knew for sure? Harris wondered. After all, they didn't know that she was wicked too. They thought she was just a child; pitied her, even. Would Mildred like her so much if she knew what her niece had done? If she ever found out that Harris had prayed for the baby to die? If she discovered that God had heard and taken all of them?

She would hate her then, Harris thought, flinching. No more being read to, no more shopping trips. Mildred might even lock her away in the cellar, and no one would ever know what happened to her. And Irma would make potions out of her bones ... Terrified, Harris hid under the blankets. She *had* to stay quiet. Had to resist throwing herself into her aunt's arms.

She was only a little girl, but Harris knew enough to realise that she was being punished. And if you couldn't trust God, who could you trust?

It was Saville's surprise, a tree so large that it took Mildred, Irma and Mrs Turner to help him carry it into the drawing room. When they finally managed to erect it, Saville stood back beaming, while Irma wiped her hands on a tea towel. 'For Harris,' he said simply.

'Do you want her to look at it, or live in it?' Mildred asked drily, nudging her brother.

They spent the rest of the evening decorating the Christmas tree, tying ribbons on it and candles, the whole topped with an angel all of them remembered from their childhood. Standing back to admire their work, Mildred remembered her mother buying the angel one Christmas a long time ago. Their father had come home and said that it looked like something off the bloody market.

A sudden noise brought Mildred's thoughts back to the present. Saville walked in carrying Harris in his arms. Her plaster had been removed and now she was merely bandaged from knee to waist.

'Look, Harris,' Saville said, the child looking tiny in his bear-like arms. 'It's a Christmas tree.'

Excited, Harris stared, her gaze slowly moving upwards to the angel on top of the tree. 'It's an angel!' she said, her tone unguarded for once. 'An angel!'

'Just like you,' Mildred replied, brushing her cheek with her hand.

None of them knew quite why Harris started crying. Irma put it down to excitement, but Mildred wasn't convinced. Something other than her parents' death was bothering Harris, something deeper. Something no child should have to carry alone.

The salon was incredibly busy, everyone wanted perms and tints for the Christmas season. And there was plenty of competition. No one wanted to look unkempt at the Mayor's Ball, and certainly no woman worth her salt was going to miss out on a Marcel wave before 25 December. As the run-up to Christmas hotted up, so did Irma. Her usual monosyllabic conversation was now at an end. She had work to do and no time to talk. The rush meant money in the till, more in the bank. Irma might not like Christmas, but she liked the profit it brought.

'. . . and then he said – This towel's wet!' Mrs Brewer said suddenly, interrupting her own story.

Rolling her eyes, Mildred signalled to the harassed Rose. 'Fresh dry towel here, please.'

'. . . as I said,' Mrs Brewer went on, letting Rose tuck the dry towel around her scrawny neck, 'both of them were hardly more than twenty-one. Twenty-two at the most. With three children. A disgrace, I call it. And there they were, expecting others to give them a hand-out. Well, you make your own bed and you lie in it.' She considered what she had said, then added slyly, 'Mind you, if there had been a little less lying in bed they wouldn't be in the state they are now.'

Mildred watched her customer in the mirror. Mrs Alma Brewer was involved in every charity in Wigan. She loved to give, providing everyone knew how much, and how often, she gave. It wasn't even her money, Mildred thought, but her husband's. And how he had made his fortune no one was really sure. And no one was about to find out.

'It's the Mayor's Ball Saturday. Well, you know that, Mildred. You'll be going, won't you?'

Mildred shook her head. The excuse of Harris was welcome. She had always hated the Mayor's Ball, always loathed sitting on the sidelines with the old maids and the widows. But Irma would be going as usual. Nothing would stop a snob like her sister. In fact, she would have crawled naked over broken glass to get there.

'Not this year. I've got Harris to think about.'

'How is she?' Mrs Brewer asked, applying some powder on the end of her shiny nose. 'I heard she was likely to be crippled for life.'

Mildred winced. 'No, Alma, she's just going to take a while to get back on her feet. The plaster's off already. You'll see, in a few years she'll be dancing at the Mayor's Ball.'

Staring at her reflection, Alma was thoughtful. 'I remember your brother Gideon at the ball.' She caught Mildred's face in the glass. 'Oh, come on, you can't not talk about him now you've got his child! Like I was saying, I remember Gideon well. Oh, he was a good-looking man. All the girls were after him. But he danced with me . . .'

Must have been desperate, Mildred thought meanly.

'. . . I think he had a bit of a thing for me,' Alma droned on, 'until that woman came along.' She sniffed, smarting at the old memory. 'If ever a man was ruined by a woman, your brother was.'

At that, Mildred deliberately caught the back of Alma's ear with the comb.

'Oi!' Alma snapped. 'Mind what you're doing.'

'Oh, sorry, Alma,' Mildred said, craftily changing the subject. 'Would you like a cup of tea?'

By the time they closed the salon that night both sisters were exhausted. Saville was at home, sitting with Harris, the nurse now off duty. And Mrs Turner was staying on, as usual, to make dinner. Her feet throbbing, Mildred sat down in the room at the back of the salon, Irma counting the takings next to her.

Outside the snow was falling heavily. Ice was clinging to the window-ledges, and the skies were leaden.

'We could retire.'

Irma looked up, money in her hands. 'What?'

'I said, we could retire,' Mildred repeated. 'We don't need to work. We have oodles of money, and we have Harris to look after now.'

Irma turned back to the money. 'Don't be ridiculous!'

'Why it is ridiculous?' Mildred asked, looking down at her sister's feet. 'You look like you've got two doughnuts round your ankles.'

Annoyed, Irma pulled her skirt lower and kept counting. 'I like working.'

'So do I. But this Christmas rush has damn near killed me.'

'It'll be quiet in January, it always is,' Irma went on, snapping: 'Stop talking to me, I'm trying to count!'

Falling into silence, Mildred fiddled with the locket around her neck. The one she always wore, the one that wouldn't open. It pained her to admit it, but Irma was right. They *would* miss the salon if they retired.

'But –'

'Shut up!' Irma barked, her head bowed over the money on her lap.

You should have married Harry Delaney, Mildred thought suddenly. So what if it had gone wrong? You might have had children. *I* might have married and had children. Bugger it!

Christmas did that to you: made you think of kids. Not that the Simons children had had good Christmases – not with their father around. A man who didn't believe in giving, but woe betide anyone in the family who didn't buy *him* a gift. Their Christmases were in reverse to the rest of the world's:

the Simons children looking on in awe as their father opened his presents.

With a sigh, Irma finally leaned back in her seat. 'We've made more money this Christmas than ever before.'

'We could go on holiday.'

'What?'

'All of us. We could take Harris. It would do her good.'

'She's too sick,' Irma said flatly.

'She's making progress,' Mildred contradicted her. 'Dr Redmond said so.'

'And what does he know, the fat fool?'

'You can't keep her walled up in that bedroom for life, Irma –'

Irma turned, face flushed. 'I beg your pardon! I'm just trying to do the best for her.'

'Then let her breathe –'

'There's no pleasing you, is there?' Irma countered. 'I don't know why I bother. Maybe I should pack up and go and leave you to it. You'd like that, wouldn't you? Having Harris all to yourself. I suppose even a child is better company than me.'

Mildred sighed. Irma had a knack of making herself into a martyr. Better to change the subject. Christmas was upon them and Irma in a mood could ruin the holiday for everyone.

'What are you wearing for the Mayor's Ball?'

At once, Irma relented. 'I got a new dress from Lowes, lovely navy-blue silk. Very expensive, but you have to put your best foot forward, don't you? After all, the Mayoress thinks she's everyone, but people know where she came from.' Getting to her feet, Irma stretched. 'Not that I really want to go to some silly ball, but still, someone has to represent the family, don't they?'

A sudden image of Gideon slid into Mildred's head: Gideon dressed in black tie, laughing as he walked to the door. Full of hope, knowing all the women would want to dance with him at the ball. You had your pick of the town, she thought. What made you choose Kate Ward?

For an instant Mildred wanted to know all about her. What she looked like, sounded like, how she acted. What was it about Kate Ward that had made a man give up his family and his fortune? And would Harris display some of that fascination? Mildred sighed to herself. Her niece might be only a child but there was already a haunting air about her, a quality as unusual and unforgettable as her name.

Something compelling, amusing and infinitely sad.

SIX

That night – Christmas Eve – Irma went to the Mayor's Ball. Saville had gone up to bed, and downstairs Mildred checked the food for the next day and then crept upstairs to look in on Harris. The child was asleep. Silently Mildred crossed the room and drew the curtains, moonlight and snow making the room white as a wedding cake.

Walking over to the bed she looked down at her niece and then tucked the coverlet around her. If she had been awake, Harris would have resisted, but in sleep Mildred could cosset her . . . In the distance the sound of carols came on the still air. The Salvation Army are out in force, Mildred thought, humming 'We Three Kings' along with them.

I want so much to love you, she thought, staring at Harris. I want to know you and watch you grow up. I want you to like me. Drawing up a chair to the bedside, Mildred sat down, her hand resting an inch away from the child's. And then she began to talk, very softly.

'When your daddy was little we used to play in the garden. He fell off walls, just like you do. He would be so pleased with you, sweetheart. So proud of your bravery.' She paused. Harris was still soundly sleeping. 'He never knew it, but when he left I was heartbroken. He was my favourite, you see. We always

60

had a good laugh together. I thought we would both marry and have our own families and enjoy visiting each other. But it didn't happen, he went – and I was left here.'

Astonishingly, Mildred found herself moved to tears. If she was honest she felt a failure. Gideon's child didn't love her, didn't even like her much. Obviously she didn't have what it took to be a mother. She was just some silly old maid, playing at life. But somehow she couldn't stop talking.

'I do love you, Harris. I do. I know I'm not what you want, or who you want, but I love you. I want to reach you and I can't. I want to make it all better and I can't. I don't know the words. I'm just someone who wants to make you happy.'

At that moment Harris reached for her aunt's hand, her fingers tightening around Mildred's. *She was awake and had been listening*. Without hesitation, Mildred took the little girl in her arms and hugged her, Harris sobbing and clinging on to her aunt as though it would kill her to be parted.

'I'm bad –'

'No, no, sweetheart . . .' Mildred soothed her.

'I am, I am. They're all dead because of me,' Harris blurted out, her head buried in her aunt's neck. 'I killed them.'

'It was an accident, love, it wasn't your fault.'

'It was!' Harris shouted, her little figure rigid with unhappiness. 'I killed them.'

Holding her niece at arm's length, Mildred looked into her face. 'How did you kill them?'

'I can't tell you. You'd hate me.'

'I wouldn't hate you, whatever you did, Harris. I'll never hate you.'

In the cold white light Harris stared at her aunt. Could she trust this woman? One of the Simonses, the people her father had warned her against? And yet he wasn't here, he was dead, and she was alone with no one. Unless she trusted her aunt. Unless she risked it.

'They were going to have another baby . . .' she began, watching Mildred's face eagerly. 'I didn't want it, so I prayed . . . I prayed to God to kill the baby. He heard me. He killed the baby and he killed them too! I killed them all!' She stopped talking, almost breathless with sobs, her face wet against her aunt's neck. 'You hate me now, don't you? You hate me.'

Mildred's voice was very quiet when she answered. 'You know, when I was little I was jealous of your father when he was born. I prayed to God that he would die too.'

Stunned, Harris looked into her aunt's face. 'No!'

'It's true,' Mildred assured her. 'I did. And I imagine a lot of children do the same. It wasn't God that killed the baby, Harris, or your parents. And it certainly wasn't you. It was an accident. That was all, Harris. An accident.'

'But –'

'But nothing,' Mildred said, smiling and touching Harris's forehead. 'What a lot you've had to carry in that little brain. Listen, love, *I promise you* that the accident was nothing to do with you. And no one will ever know what you told me tonight. It will be our secret. I know your secret, and you know mine.'

'It wasn't my fault?'

'No.'

'Are you sure?'

Mildred looked over to the window and pointed to the moon. 'Is that the sun?'

Harris laughed, 'No! It's the moon.'

'Are you sure?'

'Yes, of course I am!'

'And that's how sure I am that none of this was your fault.' She pulled Harris to her. 'A wonderful life is waiting for you, Harris. And whatever happens, I'll be here for you. Remember that. Whatever you do, wherever you go, I'll be with you.'

SEVEN

'And if you turn the ground over there, it'll be ready to sow in spring –'

Mr Lacy stopped short, staring over his young companion's shoulder. Just coming into view was Mrs Turner, with a young boy and girl in tow. Passing the Barraclough house she nodded to Mr Lacy briskly and then walked on.

'Well, I never,' Mr Lacy said to the undergardener. 'I wonder what she's doing with those two.'

'Aren't they her children?' the lad asked.

'Nah, Mrs Turner hasn't got –' Mr Lacy stopped talking at once, turning on the boy with indignation. 'What business is it of yours? I'll not stand for anyone talking about Mrs Turner.'

'But, I wasn't –'

'No buts!' Mr Lacy replied, flinging a spade in the lad's direction. 'Now, less talk and more digging.'

This was a turn-up, and no mistake. Aggrieved, Mrs Turner opened the small side gate and walked up to Deerheart House. When she reached the back door she turned, studied the two children, and then sighed.

'Now you both stay here. And don't touch anything. I'll be back in a minute.'

That was the trouble with injuries, Mrs Turner thought, you never knew when they were coming so you could never plan for them. Her poor sister, laid up with pneumonia, and no husband to help out at home. Never been a husband around for years, not since the boy had been born. Just upped and left, and no one had heard a thing about the toerag until someone spotted him in Bury with a bottle blonde. Mind you, Madge wasn't the kind of woman who would be easy to live with. And after her man left she got worse. Drinking too much and swearing fit to bust . . .

Taking a deep breath, Mrs Turner knocked on the morning-room door.

'Come in,' Irma commanded, looking up as the housekeeper entered. ''Morning, Mrs Turner.'

Mildred also looked up from reading the Saturday morning paper, but had the perception to see at once that something was wrong.

'Are you all right, Mrs Turner?'

'I have a problem.' She glanced over to Irma, whose eyes were glassy with disinterest. 'My sister's poorly –'

'Oh, I *am* sorry. Is it serious?' Mildred said, tossing aside the paper and leaning forward in her seat.

'She's got pneumonia –'

'Good God!'

'Trouble is,' Mrs Turner hurried on, knowing she had Mildred's full sympathy, 'she has two children, and now she's in hospital there's no one to look after them.'

'What has this got to do with us?' Irma asked coldly.

With an impatient gesture of her hand, Mildred waved aside the question, prompting Mrs Turner to continue. 'What about the children?'

'She can't look after them.'

'What about their father?' Irma asked, from the other side of the room.

'There is no father.'

'There must have been once,' Irma retorted, turning back to her toast and biting into a piece noisily.

'Their father ran away when the children were little,' Mrs Turner continued gamely, 'so now there's no one to look after them. I mean, they go to school for most of the day, and I can tend them at night – they can stay at my house with me – but from three in the afternoon until I leave here –'

'No.'

Mildred looked over to her sister, her eyebrows raised. 'No *what*?'

'Can't you see what's coming?'

'No, *what's coming*?' Mildred replied, baffled.

'Unless we are very careful, we're going to have two other children in this house – or at least that's what Mrs Turner is hoping.'

Cornered, the housekeeper hurried on. 'It would only be for a few hours in the day! And they'd be useful. The girl can help me to clean and the lad's strong; he'll be good in the garden.'

Irma wasn't impressed. 'And I suppose you'd expect wages for them?'

Mrs Turner shook her head vehemently. 'No. I just want them to be where I can keep an eye on them, that's all.' Her eyes held Irma's steadily. 'Otherwise I can't work here – until their mother's better again.'

The threat tingled on the air between the two women, Mildred breaking the spell as she stood up and looked to the door.

'So where are they?'

Intimidated by Irma's unwavering gaze, Mrs Turner dropped her eyes and turned back to Mildred. 'Outside. They're waiting in the back porch.'

'Well, bring them in!' Mildred cried. 'It's far too cold out there.'

Relieved, Mrs Turner looked at her with gratitude. 'So you don't mind that they come here for a while?'

'Of course not!' Mildred retorted. 'What other choice is there?'

Irma watched Mrs Turner hurry off and then turned immediately to her sister. Her expression was disbelieving.

'Are you crazy?'

'They have nowhere to go –'

'We are not running a charity home here.'

'They're only children, Irma –'

'Oh, you exasperate me! You've never been the same since Harris came here. You think you're some kind of mother figure, don't you? All warm bosoms and cocoa?'

'Hey, that's enough –'

Irma cut her off. 'Harris is our flesh and blood. She is a Simons. But we have no idea what these children are like.'

'Whatever they're like, they'll be company for Harris. It'll be good for her to have someone of her own age around.'

'A servant's children!' Irma replied, genuinely astonished. 'Our niece is not going to mix with the likes of some slum cast offs.'

'You don't know what they're like –'

'I can imagine!' Irma hurled back. 'Harris is a very special child, Mildred. And she's not well enough to be fooling around with a couple of rowdy children –'

The door opening cut her off in mid-sentence. Ushering in two children Mrs Turner then stood back, letting the Simons sisters study the newcomers. To Irma's eyes they looked like two strapping farm animals, ungainly, unkempt and too big for the room. To Mildred, they looked like two healthy, normal children who could prevent Harris from getting lonely and spoiled.

'This is Richard,' Mrs Turner said, 'and this is Bonny.'

Hardly appropriate, Irma thought. The girl was about as bonny as a cow shed.

'Hello, children,' Mildred began, warming to them immediately. 'You'll be spending some time here, at least until your mother gets well.'

'She's not gonna get well,' Bonny replied, wiping her nose on her sleeve. 'She's gonna stay there in that place and die. She said so.'

Biting hard into a fresh slice of toast, Irma gave her sister a triumphant glance. It said, as clearly as words could have done: *See, slum kids. What did I tell you?*

'Now then,' Mrs Turner said hurriedly, 'that's nonsense –'

'Mam said the hospital food stank,' Richard added, suddenly coming to life. Mrs Turner's expression was pained. 'She said it were like eating –'

'How you children do chatter!' their aunt said frantically, pushing them out of the morning-room door and then turning back to her employers. 'I'll keep them out of your way.'

In reply, Irma bit savagely into the dry toast. Cowed, Mrs Turner flushed and backed out.

Harris's first glimpse of the Baker children would remain with her for life. Propped up in bed she was restless and had leaned on the windowsill to look out. And that was when she saw them. To her they looked familiar: similar to the kids she had known in Yorkshire. Poor kids, raw-boned and clumsy, running about in the snow with chapped knees, whooping like banshees.

Then suddenly there was silence. Someone was calling them in and a second later the garden was emptied of children. Excited, Harris rang the bell by her bed and waited. Then she rang again. Finally Mildred walked in.

'Who are the children?'

Mildred smiled and sat down on the side of the bed. Oh, Harris was so different now. No longer so sickly-looking. The confinement had filled out her bones, her elfin face now smooth, her eyes less wary.

'They're Mrs Turner's nephew and niece. Richard and Bonny –'

'Are they staying here?'

'In the afternoons,' Mildred answered, briefly touching Harris's cheek. 'When you're better you can meet them.'

'I'm better now!' Harris exclaimed. 'Dr Redmond said I could get up more. He said I *should*.'

Mildred hesitated. 'You're not really strong –'

'I am! I am!' Harris insisted, getting overexcited.

'Sssh,' Mildred soothed her. 'Calm down, you'll meet them in time. All in good time.'

But Harris wasn't about to wait. The following evening, she moved to the window and looked out. The winter evening was coming down, the snow looking purple in the shadows.

Struggling to open the window, she called out to the children below: 'Hello, down there! Look up! Look up!'

The boy did, smiling at the tiny figure at the upstairs window. 'Hello, there.'

She beamed down at him: 'I'm Harris! Are you Richard?'

He nodded, face raw with cold. 'And this is Bonny,' he added, his sister coming out and looking up too.

At once Harris took to them. 'Can you come up?'

They shook their heads.

'Your aunt would kill us!' Bonny called up to the window.

'Not Mildred –'

'Nah, the other one. The scary one.'

Harris leaned further out. 'That's Irma. She's at the salon working. They have a hairdressing place in town.'

'I know. Our aunt told us all about it.'

Bonny nudged her brother quickly in the ribs. 'We could climb up.'

He looked at his sister, grinned, then nodded, grabbing hold of the thick bare branches of the honeysuckle and climbing upwards. Laughing, Harris watched his progress as he stepped onto the top of the bay window and faced her.

'Hello,' he said simply, looking her straight in the eyes.

'Hello,' Harris replied, excited.

'Hey! What about me?' a voice came from below. Quickly Richard helped his sister onto the roof of the bay.

'I'm Bonny,' she said, spitting on her hand, then rubbing it on her skirt before offering it to Harris. 'Bonny Baker.'

And then the roof gave way.

EIGHT

As Dr Redmond told anyone who would listen, it was a miracle that the Baker children escaped unharmed. Irma saw it another way. The bay window, she explained with brittle fury, had been their father's pride and joy. It had cost a fortune, and now who was going to repair it? Mrs Turner – red-eyed, her bulbous nose scarlet – stood to attention in the drawing room, the scene of devastation behind her.

'They didn't mean it . . .'

'The roof will have to be rebuilt,' Irma hurried on. 'And the glass replaced. What were they doing up there, anyway?'

'I saw a nest,' Bonny said hurriedly, covering up their visit to Harris. 'I thought it might have eggs in it.'

'If it *did* have eggs in it,' Irma went on pitilessly, 'they should have stayed there. Or were you thinking of having a late breakfast?'

'Miss Simons –'

'Windows like these cost money!' Irma continued, still staring at the children. 'Money, I might add, that you don't have.'

Mrs Turner was wretched with misery, as were the two Baker children standing on either side of her.

'You would have to work here for years to pay off the debts,' Irma continued. 'Luckily we have insurance – but that's not

70

going to let anyone off the hook.' She turned to Richard, splay-footed, cap in hand. 'You'll have to labour hard to make up for this. And you,' she looked, basilisk-like, at Bonny, 'can help your aunt.'

Mrs Turner tried to interject: 'They were going to anyway –'

'I don't mean playing at it!' Irma exploded. 'I mean *real* work. Children these days don't understand the value of things.'

'It were an accident,' Richard ventured, Bonny silencing him with a look.

'Accidents like this cost money,' Irma replied, storming over his protestations. '*Real* money.'

'Well, all I can say is, thank God no one was hurt,' Mildred said from her seat by the fire. 'A window can be mended, but just think how terrible it would have been if you'd injured yourselves. Your poor mother would have been out of her mind with worry.'

Irma stared at her sister, incredulous. 'Honestly, did Mildred *always* have to see the other person's point of view? What about the blasted window?'

'Look!' she commanded the children, pointing to the ruin behind them. 'That's what silliness did. Reckless behaviour like yours should be punished –'

'Oh, I've punished them,' Mrs Turner chipped in hurriedly. 'No treats, and no playing out for a while.'

'Hardly Draconian, is it?'

'Huh?' Mrs Turner didn't know who or what Draconian was, but she knew it was bad.

Impatiently, Irma waved them away. 'Oh, go on, get out of here! And if I ever – *ever* – see either of you climbing again, there'll be real trouble.'

Falling asleep by Harris's bedside, Saville started snoring. He was dreaming about apples, big as coaches, pulled by giant ants. Snapping awake, he looked over to his niece. She was sleeping deeply, her mouth slightly open. It was lovely to have her here, Saville thought, especially now she was stuck in her room. He had enjoyed the past couple of months, liked visiting her and reading to her. But now he was unsettled. Change was in the air.

Saville knew he was slow, but he didn't miss much. And he knew that Harris was getting better fast. Before long she would be up and about again – no longer his captive little friend.

Saville coughed by the bedside, desperate for Harris to wake up.

Stirring, she rubbed her eyes and sat up, looking at him blearily. ''Lo there, Saville.'

He beamed. 'Were you dreaming?'

She nodded, yawning, then frowning. 'I was dreaming about caves, all dark and gloomy. You know that Irma's a witch?'

'No!'

She nodded emphatically. 'I've read all about witches in one of my books. It said that they look just like Irma.'

'Witches do?'

'Yes,' Harris said, warming to her theme. 'And it went on about things witches have. Weird things.'

His eyes were enormous. Mildred might remind her brother constantly about Harris's overactive imagination, but he had forgotten the warning and was hooked.

'What kind of weird things?'

Harris thought for a moment. 'They have cats.'

'Irma doesn't have a cat.'

This was a snag. But Harris wasn't about to be put off. 'They have *invisible* cats.'

'No!'

She nodded. 'Irma has one. I've seen it.'

'But –'

'Only at special times of the day, of course. When the cat's *not* invisible,' Harris added, anxious to cover any loopholes in her story. 'And she flies.'

'The cat flies!'

'No!' Harris replied impatiently. 'Irma flies.'

Now this was a huge lie, one that even a devoted admirer like Saville found hard to swallow.

'I don't think –'

'But I saw it!' Harris said firmly. 'I saw her fly past that window,' she said, pointing to the bay and dropping her voice. 'It was very late, the moon was full, and she came past on a broomstick. Flying.'

'I . . . I don't believe it.'

Immediately Harris folded her arms, looking wounded. 'Fine! Don't believe me then.'

Saville was quite at a loss. 'But I've never seen Irma fly.'

'That's because you're a boy!' she said, as though it was perfectly logical. 'Only girls can see witches flying.'

He stared at her and laughed. When his niece got better, where would he be? Who would he have? He would be relegated to the shadows again, the idiot brother of the Simons sisters. Of no use to anyone. Harris would grow up, but he would stay locked into his child's brain. And stand by, helplessly, watching her go.

The thought was anguish to him.

In March the newspapers were full of the news of the Lindbergh baby kidnap, Mildred reading out the headlines to Irma. All over Wigan people had been talking, customers at the salon asking how a baby could be kidnapped like that, and how likely was it that the child was still alive?

'I remember when our Gracie wandered off – oh, that must be ten or so years ago. She was by my side one minute and gone the next. I was frantic with worry . . .'

Mildred paused with her scissors raised, studying the back

of Gladys Leonards' head. Her eyesight wasn't what it was; she had to get some glasses, and fast.

'. . . And then I found her. In the manager's office. They had seen her wander off and . . .'

Mildred was glad to leave the salon that night, her feet aching badly. Back at Deerheart House she plunged them into a bath of Epsom Salts and let her mind wander. Harris was making good steady progress, Dr Redmond insisting that she take more exercise. So Mildred would walk Harris up and down the hallway several times, morning and evening, before returning her to bed. And always Harris complained, begging to come downstairs. And always Mildred said 'later'.

So just who had put the frog in Mrs Turner's teacup, and who had eaten half of the cooked chicken in the fridge?

'It was all there earlier,' Mrs Turner said to Mildred, looking at the mangled bird. 'When I asked, Miss Irma said she wasn't in the habit of eating things off the bone like an animal,' she sniffed. 'And Saville hates chicken. You haven't had it and Richard and Bonny know that it's more than their lives are worth to take anything.' She paused. 'So who ate the chicken?'

They exchanged glances.

'Harris is not allowed out of bed. Unless she's supervised.'

Mrs Turner raised her eyebrows. 'For someone poorly your niece gets a lot of exercise. I saw her only yesterday at the end of the corridor, letting down a basket to Bonny in the garden.'

'Letting down a basket?' Mildred was baffled. 'Whatever for?'

'Harris said that it's like the fairy tale. The heroine lets down the basket and her admirers put jewels in it for her.'

Mildred rolled her eyes. 'How many "jewels" did she get?'

'A rotten apple and half a ball of twine,' Mrs Turner replied. 'Honestly, I've never known anyone with such an imagination – and she's always the heroine. Fanciful, that's what she is.

Your Harris must be living in a world of her own, because it's nothing like this one.'

A moment later Mildred was up in Harris's room. Her niece was pretending to read a school book, even though Mildred could see the lump of the hidden comic under the bedspread.

'Harris, did you eat half of the chicken?'

Her niece laid down the book, all innocence. 'Which chicken?'

'The one in the fridge.'

'Downstairs?'

'We only have one fridge, Harris. Yes, the one downstairs.'

'I can't go downstairs.'

'Maybe it walked up by itself,' Mildred said drily. 'You've been downstairs on your own, haven't you?'

'No!' Harris said, shocked. 'You told me not to.'

Patiently Mildred sat on the edge of the bed. 'You mustn't lie, Harris. It's naughty. Poor Saville nearly frightened Irma to death earlier, screaming something about her invisible cat. And as for that frog . . . You can't go around making up wild stories.'

'But –'

'And telling Richard that your mother had been a famous actress – that wasn't true, was it?'

Biting her lip, Harris looked down. 'She *could* have been –'

'Harris!' Mildred said firmly, then dropped her voice. 'Did you eat the chicken?'

'Well . . . in a way . . .'

Folding her arms, Mildred was staring at her niece when the sound of something hitting the bedroom window made both of them jump. Harris – obviously guilty – avoided Mildred's eyes.

'Harris!' a loud whisper sounded. 'Harris, are you there? Come to the window.'

Mildred's voice was even. 'How often does Richard visit?'

Harris was all bluster: 'He comes with his sister –'

75

'How often?'

'Three, four times a week,' Harris admitted at last. 'We're not doing any harm! We just talk.'

Mildred sighed. 'You shouldn't encourage them, Harris. When you're better you'll be playing with children of your own type –'

'THEY ARE MY TYPE!' Harris shouted, getting out of bed and walking stiffly to the window. 'I like them. They're my friends.'

'Harris, listen to me,' Mildred replied, catching hold of the child's arm. 'Richard and Bonny are nice, but they're ordinary kids, not like you. You live here now, you have the Simons name, you have a bright future ahead of you.'

Angrily, Harris shook off her aunt's hand. 'I thought you were different! I didn't think you were like Irma. I never thought you were a snob!'

'I just want the best for you.'

Another stone hit the window. Harris hesitated, looking from her aunt to the window.

'Go back to bed, sweetheart,' Mildred said kindly. 'I'll have a word with Mrs Turner tomorrow – and Irma need never know.'

Still Harris hesitated.

Then another pebble hit the glass. A moment yawned between Mildred and her niece – and then suddenly Harris hurried towards the window, flung it open and climbed out into the cold night air.

NINE

I remember it perfectly – the heady sense of defiance, combined with the cold making my head giddy. And I remember how much I hurt. Oh, how my bones hurt. The bay window had been repaired and I stood on it, Richard and Bonny's heads peering up at me. There was no moon that night, the only light coming from the bedroom.

The stone of the roof was cold on my feet and I shivered, wanting momentarily to jump off – into God knew what. I was torn between two worlds that night. The world of kindly Mildred looking down at me from my bedroom window, and the world of the Baker kids, looking up from the garden below.

I remember thinking that if I jumped into their world, I might never be allowed back into Deerheart House. But then again, if I stayed, would I ever escape the liniment, lectures, and the crushing sweetness of cosseting?

It was a chill night, snow still on the ground, me too small and weak from being so long bedridden to jump off. Or climb back up. The moment seemed to be locked like a moth in amber. Which way I would have gone, I cannot tell you, because as I shivered on that roof a pair of hefty arms came down from my window and lifted me up.

They lifted me quickly, from cold to warmth, from freedom to confinement. And although I would have hated anyone else for it the decision lay with the one person I could never hate – Saville.

And so, from then onwards, I lived as a Simons.

PART TWO

For I cannot be
Mine own, nor anything to any, if
I be not thine.

Shakespeare – *The Winter's Tale*

TEN

Scholes, Wigan

'I've told yer, watch where yer going!' Madge Baker snapped at her daughter. 'Yer always in the bloody way.'

Bonny paused, her hands on her hips, her chin jutting out. At fourteen, she was tall for her age, rangy, her limbs poking out of her clothes like a bird scarer. Their mother had finally recovered and was back at work at the pie factory, Bonny just starting at R. & J. Gorner's, the bakers. Unfortunately Madge had been a reluctant mother and had let Richard and Bonny run wild.

Further excuse for her neglect had come in the shape of Bert Shaw. To hear her tell it, Bert was the answer to a woman's prayers. Didn't he have lovely thick hair, Madge said repeatedly, and such a way with him? *And with other people's money*, the neighbours said, watching Madge make a fool of herself. *Look at her, dyeing her hair – she looks like a bloody carrot. And surely someone should tell the silly bitch that there's not many beds round here that haven't had Bert Shaw's shoes under them.*

Madge wouldn't listen. She had a man and, by God, she was going to keep him. Whatever her children said.

'I hate him,' Bonny declared defiantly, staring at her mother's violently hennaed hair.

81

'Yer no reason to say such things!' Madge replied, pushing past her daughter and applying her lipstick in front of the mirror. 'I'm going out.'

'Yer always going out now –'

'Yer watch your tongue! Yer not too big to get a bloody hiding.'

Sulking, Bonny looked round. It had never been much of a home, down in Mill Yard, Scholes, the slum side of town. The side that everyone avoided visiting; the side its inhabitants longed to escape.

The fact that the Simons sisters had once indirectly helped with the care of her children cut no ice with Madge. After all, for all their airs and graces, hadn't their father come from some rat hole round the corner on Vauxhall Road? She had heard people talk about old man Simons. His father had been Irish, dog rough. Many had seen him fall asleep in his own vomit, dead drunk. Gordon Simons might think that money wiped people's memories, but he was wrong. Everyone remembered where he came from. Wasn't his sister on the game, sores around her mouth and swearing like a miner, and with two kids who didn't know who their fathers were? He might pretend he had no family, but Dora Simons could tell a pretty tale about her brother when she'd had a skinful. 'He were a right little shit,' she'd say. 'Started out running errands for the market traders, and taking home fish heads for our mother to make into soup . . .'

And yet money changed everything, Madge thought bitterly. Old man Simons had been a fly kid, quick on the uptake and even quicker on the make. He had worked down the pit and then made some money on the side selling off the slack. He would load it into bags and then put some good pieces of coal on the top so that people would think they'd got a bargain.

Before long, Gordon Simons had expanded – left the pit and moved into debt collecting. He had been ideally suited to the work. There was many a tenant down Crawford Terrace, Mill

Yard and Collard Street who had had reason to remember Gordon Simons. The few who had tried to object had been roughed up by one of Simons's henchmen. By the age of nineteen, Simons was feared – not least by his own parents. Then, after a violent row, he had left home and set up house with a tup'nny tart who worked the Tramway.

His climb was unstoppable and by the time Gordon Simons was thirty he had a fortune everyone envied – and a reputation everyone feared. Having bought a pit outside Ince, he moved into buying his own miners' properties, and then he purchased his first mill. He also purchased a wife; the oddly remote Rosemary with whom he shared nothing.

Madge was still thinking about old man Simons when Bonny interrupted her.

'I'm going out.'

'Where to?'

'Why?'

'I'm yer mother!' Madge said, clipping Bonny round the ear. 'Don't cheek me.'

Bonny rubbed her ear. 'Yer seeing Bert Shaw tonight?'

'What business is it of yers who I see?' her mother replied, moving to the door. 'I'm off now. If yer go out, lock the door behind yer. Meg Riley had her bloody armchair nicked last week.'

Disconsolate, Bonny threw herself into the old chair by the fire. Richard was off somewhere with his friends. He thought at the advanced age of eighteen – and working at the pit – he was too grown up to be seen with his sister. Idly, Bonny kicked the fender. If her mother married Bert Shaw she would run away, with Richard, whether he liked it or not.

The cheap clock on the undusted mantel read 6.15. It was a cold night, but then it was a cold house without a fire lit or much to eat in the larder. She could tidy up, but what was the bloody point, she thought miserably. She wasn't ever going to get a good job. Wasn't going to get out of bloody Scholes either unless she looked sharp about it.

Closing her eyes, Bonny leaned back her head and played her favourite game – Being the Count of Monte Cristo. Harris had lent her the book and although it had taken her a while, and Bonny had forgotten almost as much as she had read, the salient point remained – the count was so rich he could do anything.

It was a delicious thought, a thought Bonny plunged into like a warm lake. Walking down Market Place she would imagine herself riding in a car, dressed in furs, and driving miles away from Wigan. At school she would daydream herself onto a warm beach. There *were* such places – she had seen them at the flicks – and besides, if she was the Count of Monte Cristo, she could *buy* the bloody beach. No more sneaking into the flicks whilst her brother caused a diversion, no more stuffing brown paper into her shoes to stop her feet getting wet in the winter. Oh no, the Count of Monte Cristo would have the money to wear his shoes once and then throw them out.

'What you doing?'

Startled, Bonny opened her eyes, then grinned. 'Wow, Richard! That's a real shiner.'

He covered his face with his hand automatically and turned away.

'Aw, come on, let me see!' Bonny pleaded, ducking and diving around her brother to get another look. 'How d'you do it?'

'I fell.'

'Yeah, right,' she said dismissively. 'You wait till Mam sees that. She won't half give you a seeing-to.'

Richard shrugged, belligerent. 'She doesn't give a damn about me or you. She's all caught up with that pig Bert Shaw.'

Forgetting his black eye, Richard hacked off a lump of bread and passed his sister some. 'You know what I heard?'

'Nah, what?'

'He'd been in gaol.'

'So's half the people round here.'

'But not for murder.'

Bonny's eyes widened. *'He killed someone?'*

'So Kenny said.'

'Aw, Kenny's a liar!' Bonny replied, suddenly deflated. 'Yer can't trust a word he says. He told yer last week he were emigrating.'

Richard chewed his bread thoughtfully as he leaned back against the grubby oven. 'Well, he seemed to think it were true about Bert Shaw. It were all over Bury a while back, Kenny said, about how Bert Shaw's girlfriend disappeared.'

Bonny slumped back into her chair, her eyes narrowing. 'Yer should tell Mam.'

'Why? She wouldn't believe me.'

'But we *should* tell her.'

Richard grimaced. 'She thinks the sun shines out of his arse.'

'She might think differently if she thought he was going to *kill* her. I mean, surely that might put her off?' Bonny chewed her lip. 'She's gone to meet him tonight.'

'Where?'

'I dunno . . .' Bonny considered her mother's situation seriously. 'Did Bert Shaw *really* kill his girlfriend?'

Brushing the breadcrumbs off his hands, Richard studied his sister. She was worried, he could tell that. And he hated to see Bonny worried. Besides, she was right, Kenny *was* a bloody liar. There was probably nothing to worry about after all.

'I were thinking,' he began, rubbing his face with the back of his sleeve to smarten himself up, 'that I might go over and see Harris. You wanna come?'

*   *   *

85

It would be a good idea to decorate the window of the salon, Mildred thought. I mean, how often did the King and Queen visit Wigan? It was going to be such an honour, everyone already talking about the visit in the coming May, Irma delighted that it meant brisk business. After all, she said quite seriously, who'd want to be caught in curling rags at the procession?

Mildred sighed to herself. She would buy Harris a special dress, something unlike any other girl's. They might even go over to Manchester for it. After all, Lowes was a good shop, but it wasn't Kendal Milne. Putting down her glasses, she thought about Harris. To everyone's surprise she had turned out to be rather stupid at school. No one expected that, but the sisters made excuses, saying, what could you expect when she had been ill for so long?

They didn't like to mention that during her extended illness Harris had been taught at home, by no less a tutor than Irma. French, mathematics and English literature had been crammed down her throat along with the medicine, her brain as medicated and massaged as her limbs. By the time Harris had been allowed back on her feet she was an impressive example of Irma's tutelage. Miles ahead of her class at school, Harris should have progressed in leaps and bounds.

But she didn't. She flopped. Lazy, she was forever daydreaming or telling wild tales to the other children. A born leader, Harris was followed by them, her background making her all the more glamorous. She had no mother and father, she lived with her aunts at Deerheart House. They were rich – the rich Simonses . . . And so the other children idolised Harris and, spoiled at home and at school, she was indulged for years.

It was mostly Mildred's fault. 'We have money,' she told Harris consolingly. 'Don't worry if you're not academically bright; you'll never have to work.'

After a while even Irma came to terms with Harris's lack of progress. She would marry well, Irma decided, and who cared whether a wife had an education or not? If she had money, she would sail through life.

As for the Baker children, they had – over the previous six years – become frequent visitors to Deerheart House. Irma might disapprove, but Mildred had only to remind her of Harris's earlier rebellion to make her relent. Besides, Irma was making new plans for her niece. Harris was going to marry into money, hoisting the Simonses even further up the social ladder by a marital coup.

Even Mildred began to get caught up in the dream. 'Look,' Irma told her, 'Harris could grow up to be a beauty. A beauty with money has the world in her hands.' And they, she didn't have to add, would bathe in her reflected glory. Irma could imagine the Mayor's Ball when Harris was of age, the parties they would throw at Deerheart House, the young men she could vet for her niece. No mistakes for Harris; no doomed love affairs; no curtailed romances with unsuitable people. Love might have missed Irma, but by God, the same wasn't going to happen to Harris.

Besides, Harris had charm – everyone recognised that. Charm and money, Irma thought – empires had been built on less.

'Saville will be so excited,' Mildred said suddenly, cutting into her thoughts. 'He loves a procession, and as for seeing the Queen –'

'We must get a good spot,' Irma interrupted her. 'I shall have a word with the Mayoress about it. And I was thinking that we should have a little garden party. Invite a few important people . . .' Usually Irma didn't like to socialise, but this was business. 'As for this place, we should get in the decorators and spruce it up a bit . . .'

'But, Irma –'

'. . . and jab that lazy gardener of ours into life,' Irma mused. 'I'm wondering if the Barracloughs need Mr Lacy full time.'

'Ask Mrs Turner.'

'Why?' Irma replied, eyebrows raised.

'Because Mrs Turner and Mr Lacy have an understanding.'

Which was more than Irma had. 'About what?'

'They walk out together.'

'They're *courting*? At their age?' Irma snorted, although Mrs Turner was younger than she was. 'How ridiculous.'

Mildred winced at her sister's words. Irma could be so casually cruel. What was wrong with falling in love at forty, fifty or even sixty?

'I think she wants to marry him.'

'Marry a gardener!' Irma replied, amused. 'Ah well, I suppose he'd do for a housekeeper.'

'I seem to recall that you were once in love with a very common boy,' Mildred said, unusually vicious.

Irma flushed. 'At least I *was* in love once. Which is more than you managed.'

'What makes you so sure of that?' Mildred blustered.

'No one had any secrets in this house,' Irma replied with absolute certainty. 'If you'd ever been in love the family would have known about it.'

Mildred picked up the evening paper and appeared to read. In fact, she was hiding her face from her sister. How little Irma really knew about her, Mildred thought. How little *anyone* knew about the open, happy-go-lucky sister. The last person anyone would have suspected to have a hidden life.

Hearing the door close as Irma left the room, Mildred lowered her newspaper. I will allow myself to remember, she thought, just for a little while.

Richard soon tired of Bonny and Harris talking about clothes and make-up, and went home. Left alone, Harris leaned towards Bonny and nudged her.

'Have you ever been kissed?'

'Yer what?'

'It's *you*, not *yer*,' Harris said simply. Then, warming to her theme: 'Well, have you?'

'Sure I have,' Bonny replied, flushing.

Harris was impressed. 'What was it like?'

'All right.'

'Did he close his eyes?'

'Yer what?'

'It's *you*! *You!*' Harris corrected her. 'I said, did he close his eyes?'

'I dunno,' Bonny blustered. 'I had my eyes closed.'

Harris considered this vital piece of information. It was important that she knew everything about kissing, otherwise how would she make a man fall in love with her? Oh, it was all right watching the films, but that wasn't real life.

'How did it feel?'

Bonny wanted to change the subject, fast. 'Listen, you want to see that new flick at the Roxy –' She stopped, mesmerised, as Harris pursed her lips and planted a smacking kiss on the back of her own hand. 'What the hell are you doing?'

'It said in one of the magazines that you should practise kissing on the back of your hand.'

'What bloody magazine?' Bonny asked, stunned.

Harris ignored the question, rolling onto her back on the bed and staring upwards. 'You can get pregnant kissing. You know that, don't you?'

Bonny's grasp of sex was shaky, but she wasn't about to let Harris see that. 'Nah, you can't. You can only get a bun in the oven if you sleep with someone.'

This was news. 'Why would you want to *sleep* with them?'

'People do,' Bonny said uncertainly.

'But I thought sex was something else. You know, rolling about together,' Harris went on, biting her lip. 'Not sleeping. I mean, what's exciting about *sleep*?'

Sensing that she had the upper hand, Bonny warmed to her

theme. 'Did you know that you can get pregnant if you share a toothbrush?'

Goggle-eyed, Harris stared at her. 'Are you sure?'

Bonny nodded.

'But what if you didn't know? I mean, what if someone had broken in and used your toothbrush – and then you used it?'

'How many people,' Bonny said wryly, 'break into houses to clean their teeth?'

'But what if they did? I mean, that would be awful,' Harris replied, her imagination scaling new heights. 'What if it was a horrible old tramp? Then you'd have a tramp baby.'

'Babies aren't born tramps,' Bonny said with conviction.

'Or a monster? What if it was a monster who broke in? Then you'd have a baby with two heads and a hump.'

'On the other hand,' Bonny said cheerily, 'it could be a handsome prince.'

Harris stopped frowning. A handsome prince could use her toothbrush any day.

Mrs Turner was getting more than a little bored with Mr Lacy. I mean, she said to her friends, it was nice to have a man around, but what good were they unless they married you? Thoughtfully she walked to the back door, arching her spine. God, it had hurt, lifting that coal. Wasn't a job for a woman, and no mistake. And she wasn't getting any younger. But for all Mr Lacy's obvious adoration, it had never come down to a proposal. Not once, in eleven years.

'How do, Mrs Turner?' Mr Lacy called out to her.

Smiling, she moved over to him and leaned on the back stone wall that separated the Simonses' estate from the Barracloughs'.

'I got you some early spuds.'

She took them, smiling dully. *Spuds*. Not a ring, or even a bunch of flowers. Just spuds.

'Thanks, Mr Lacy. I'll put them in water.'

He missed the sarcasm completely as Mrs Turner turned and spotted the two Baker children coming up the driveway.

''Lo, there, you two.'

''Lo there, Auntie,' Richard replied. 'We came to see Harris. Miss Irma in?'

'It's her bridge night – as if you didn't know,' Mrs Turner replied, watching as they moved across the lawn to the backdoor. 'Kids . . .' she said dreamily.

'Would you like a family of your own?' Mr Lacy said, staring at his object of unfulfilled desire.

'Oh, Mr Lacy, what kind of a question is that to ask a lady!' she replied, apparently flustered.

'I never meant –'

'I don't like familiarity, Mr Lacy, you know that.'

He was mortified. 'I just thought –'

'I'm a respectable woman – you ask anyone. Now I know my sister's a bit on the rough-and-ready side, but not me. I'm a respectable woman with a respectable home and a respectable job. You might do well to remember that.'

His contrition was total. 'Mrs Turner, I never meant to insult you. It were just the way you looked at them kids, I just thought –'

'Aye, and you know what thought did, Mr Lacy,' she replied, walking off.

Back in the kitchen, Mrs Turner began laughing, throwing her apron over her face to stifle her snorts. Now, if that didn't force that slow bugger to propose, nothing would! Still laughing, she leaned against the stove. *I'm a respectable woman with a respectable house . . .* My God, Mrs Turner thought when she finally controlled herself, it was incredible what you had to do these days to get a husband.

It had been summer. They had met over by the Bloody Mountains, not far from the disused quarry, Mildred leaving

Deerheart House after an argument with her father. They had been fighting about Saville, Mildred taking her brother's side.

'He's no bloody good to anyone!' her father had roared. 'Get him out of my bloody sight!'

What had been going on in her brother's mind, Mildred could only guess at, but the expression in Saville's eyes had been one of complete hopelessness. He knew he was despised by the father he adored – by the father who in turns bullied or ignored him, but always terrified him. The few grains of kindness Gordon Simons had ever given Saville were treasured like another person treasured love letters. He could – and would – at the slightest encouragement repeat his father's tiny ration of charity as if to say, *look, he loves me really*.

Her father's cruelty had hurt Mildred to the bone, and on that day she'd walked out of the house and kept walking. Before she knew it she was out in the open countryside, on the Bloody Mountains, the site of a battle, fought long ago, over something no one could remember. It had been a warm day, sun hazy, flies drowsy with warmth. Taking off her jacket she'd lain down in the grass and felt the sun on her face.

It hadn't been her turn to go to Derbyshire that summer. Every June either she or Irma would visit their old, gently potty cousin, who never knew, or cared much, about what was going on. For a couple of months one of them would be free to do as she liked, with no interference. It was a brief glimpse of how normal people lived – but that year Mildred was to be stuck at Deerheart House, whilst Irma flew the coop.

Sighing, Mildred was just rising to return home when a man had approached her. He had been walking with his back to the light, seeming neither very tall nor very short, neither very fat nor very thin. Only confident, easy in his movements. And then, when he reached her, he'd stopped, turning his face to the sun and smiling into the light.

'Lovely day . . .'

Transfixed, Mildred had stared at him, at the hooked nose,

the heavy-lidded eyes, the slightly overlong fair hair. His face was burned into her memory for ever: a profile cameo sunk into the yellow heat of the sun.

'It's hot, though,' he had gone on, turning and putting out his hand. 'I'm William Kershaw, I live quite near you, at the other end of Wigan. I wasn't too keen to come at first, but it's not bad here. Not bad at all.'

Mildred had stared at him in astonishment. He had talked so easily, so freely. Not like she did, nor anyone else in Deerheart House.

'I have to go home –'

'So soon?' he'd said, obviously disappointed. 'I was hoping you'd talk for a while. I don't know anyone round here and I miss my old friends . . .'

Now jump a year, Mildred told herself. That's right, go on a year. She had been so much in love, and so aware that this might be her last chance to find love . . .

It was raining, Liverpool bleak, the sign reading 'Doughty Street'. She had travelled by tram and bus to get there, her body shaking with cold and terror. No one had suspected anything at home. Mildred had simply been going to a concert at the Town Hall, something she did frequently. No one had noticed anything unusual when she left.

Or when she got back. And in between Mildred Simons went for her abortion. The price was five pounds. Which wasn't a lot to Mildred, because money had never been a problem. She could remember the woman in Doughty Street – tall, with a hoarse voice and rough, big-knuckled hands . . .

Opening her eyes, Mildred stared ahead, shaken to the bone. She should never have allowed herself to think back. Because that's where the dead lay.

ELEVEN

It was the talk of the town, that May of 1938, the King and Queen's visit to Wigan. People had dressed the shops for days and then lined the streets to watch King George VI and Queen Elizabeth's procession from Skew Bridge, along Wallgate, Market Street then finally Market Square. All the schoolchildren had been given a day's holiday and the Mayor had asked local businessmen to do the same for their employees. Naturally parades were organised, the Manchester Regiment, British Legion and St John Ambulance Brigade all taking part. Bunting and flags were everywhere, even tastefully adorning Simons Coiffeuse, and the church bells rang out across the town from morning to night.

Irma had managed to secure a wonderful vantage point on Market Square for herself and the whole Simons clan. Harris was decked out in a white frilled dress and straw hat. 'Jesus,' some said, 'they look more bloody royal than the royals themselves.' Of course Irma was still smarting from the fact that she had not been chosen to be one of the twenty local citizens to be presented to Their Majesties, but took comfort from the envious glances thrown their way as the Simonses stood next to the Mayor's party. 'Makes you wonder how they dare to look so smug,' someone said tartly.

'If only the King knew about old man Simons and how he got his money.'

Jealousy had been building for some time around the Simons household. Irma had always got up people's noses because of her snobbery, but Mildred's patent adoration of her niece, and Harris's inherited grandeur were fanning the flames of the townspeople's envy. 'I mean,' one local said, 'their money was built on other people's misery.' 'That's not the sisters' fault,' another replied. 'They suffered enough from the old man's bullying.' 'Yeah, but they didn't say no to his money, did they?' came back the sour reply.

As Their Majesties made their way around Market Square there were many as interested in the Simons family as the visiting aristocracy. It had not escaped anyone's attention that Harris was rapidly turning into a spoiled snob. Only poor, stupid Saville stayed the same, waving his flag and laughing like a jackass.

If Mildred realised what people were thinking, she never let on. She was happy, secretly delighted at their prominence and overjoyed by Harris's behaviour. The girl was glowing, posing like an actress in her white dress, the local paper taking a photograph of her. It was clear to Mildred that her niece was revelling in the attention. Smiling, she turned to have a word with Irma.

This was the day Irma had lived for. To be in amongst her peers, to be standing next to the Mayor, the King and Queen passing only feet from her, and all of Wigan watching . . . Mildred could almost feel her sister's heart beating with pride and knew that when the photograph of Harris came out Irma would have it framed for everyone to see. *Look, this is my niece, this is Harris Simons.*

The triumph had made Irma ecstatic, and under the brief afternoon sun her face lost its bitter edge. The navy veiled hat she had so carefully chosen threw a shadow over her eyes and for an instant she was young again. All the bitter remarks, the carping, the snide innuendos about people were forgotten. All the regrets, the loss, the dreaded slide into old age were somehow bleached out by her social victory.

At last Irma Simons was having her day in the sun.

'I won't be going there again. Never again!' Mrs Ramsbottom said hastily as she waddled down the street with her friend. 'Did you hear about Saville Simons?'

Mrs Brewer nodded eagerly, her scrawny face animated. 'I heard! All of Wigan heard. And after all that posing the Simonses were doing the other day. Goes to show, pride comes before a fall.'

Silenced by the sight of Mildred coming down the street, they hurried off. Having seen them, Mildred unlocked the door of the salon as fast as she could and once inside, leaned against the door heavily. Dear God, who would have thought it of Saville? He was a child, for God's sake – hadn't the doctors always said that? He was harmless, just a big kid with the mental age of seven.

She shuddered. Saville Simons – caught in the local park, flashing. It was unbelievable! And coming so soon after their triumph at the royal visit, it was devastating. It hadn't reached the papers yet, but an old friend of Mildred's had tipped her off that it would be all over the front page that evening. God, she thought again, what a showing-up.

Her friend also said that he had heard that the police would be kind, and that Saville wouldn't be prosecuted because of the fact that he was handicapped and didn't know what he was doing. The woman who had been the object of his unexpected affections had been talked out of taking him to court when she understood the situation.

No one had ever suspected that Saville – dopey, dreamy Saville – had even had a sexual thought in his life, let alone acted on one. That's what comes of cutting down his medication, Mildred thought, flushing to her hair roots. That her brother could think sexually and then expose himself in Mesnes Park . . . Oh God, Mildred thought, slumping into one of the salon's chairs, what were they going to do now?

For the first time in her life she was glad that Irma had been laid low with a migraine. Up in her darkened room, her sister had not heard the news. *Yet*. Mildred winced: she would have to tell Harris. Prepare her.

It was lucky that someone had tipped her off, Mildred thought. At least it gave her time to prepare everyone else. But how could she prepare her sister? How could she take away the thing Irma held most dear – her position? God, if she'd only had an inkling, Mildred thought, she would have kept a better eye on Saville. But then again, he had stopped wandering off lately, seeming to be happy at home with Harris.

Harris . . . How would her niece take the news? Would she understand? And how would she face up to her peers at school? Mildred's head sank down further onto her folded arms. A flasher in the family – it would have been funny if it had been someone else's family. But not theirs. She thought then of Mrs Turner and the Baker children, anticipating their whispers and sniggers. It was too much, Mildred thought angrily, way too much.

Although Mildred didn't know it, Irma had heard the news already. Dr Redmond told her, when he was passing on another visit. Or rather he had come to tell Mildred, but could hardly walk off, his mission aborted, when Irma faced him.

Her response to the news was one sharp word. 'What!'

He stammered the information out again. 'Saville was caught in the park, er, flashing.'

'Don't be ridiculous! He hasn't even got a camera,' Irma replied icily.

'Er, flashing *himself*.'

'What?'

'Your brother was exposing himself.'

'Get out!' Irma had exploded. 'I won't have filthy talk in this house.'

Hardly knowing how it happened, Dr Redmond found himself on the doorstep of Deerheart House a moment later, Irma's strident tones ringing like the Trump of Doom from behind the closed front door.

He would just sit in his room and it would all stop, Saville thought as he rocked himself on the side of the bed. It was safe up here, no one bothered him. Usually. His thoughts moved back to the previous night. He didn't know *why* he'd done it. He had just had an urge. It wasn't something he'd done before – and now he could hear his sister shouting for him.

Only it wasn't Mildred, it was Irma. His mind slid back years, to his father shouting for him . . . 'Come down!' Gordon had barked. 'Come down here and answer for yourself!' Saville started to shake, and kept shaking. He wouldn't answer his sister and after a while she would stop shouting.

In time, if he kept very quiet, she would stop.

Her head bowed, Harris was walking alone to school. I can go on my own, she had told Mildred that morning. I'm not a baby, I can cope . . .

Yet only yards away from Deerheart House, an unfamiliar voice called out to her, ''Ere, is it true about yer Saville? Yer balmy uncle's been flashing in the park? Showing 'is thingy to any and sundry?'

Her face flushing, Harris walked on, the boy following her. Within a minute he had been joined by several others, all mocking the stuck-up Simons girl.

'Yer uncle's a flasher. Yer uncle's a flasher,' they chorused. 'He shows his privates in the park. Ever so quick, comes out his dick!'

Shocked, Harris began to walk faster. She wasn't used to anything like this. After all, the boys weren't from round her way; they were slum kids, up from Scholes, deliberately come to mock her family. They must have been waiting outside the gates, Harris thought helplessly. Waiting for her, or for her aunts, anyone they could laugh at. Because it was an opportunity too good to miss for them – one of their rich betters getting caught with his trousers down. Literally.

'Hey, Harris Simons! Yer uncle's a flasher!'

Sobbing now, Harris began running, the boys running after her. Several passers-by saw them, but no one intervened, thinking it was just kids having a lark. Tripping, she dropped her school books, her hair untying itself from its tidy plait. And still they kept running after her, their voices more angry now, more vicious, Harris's mouth chalk dry with fright.

If only she could get into the school gates, Harris thought. But the school seemed a long way away and suddenly she was as frightened as the time they told her that her parents had died. She was alone, and under threat. Again.

'Oi! Stop running away! Yer a coward, like yer uncle!' the ringleader shouted behind her.

Then suddenly the shouting stopped.

Hearing a scuffle, Harris turned to see Richard hitting the biggest boy square on the nose. Running up beside her brother was Bonny, ungainly in her mother's shoes as she reached Harris's side.

'You all right?'

Harris nodded. 'They were saying all kinds of things. About Saville.'

Bonny pulled a sympathetic face. 'I know all about it. Everyone does. Mam can't stop talking about it. Made her day, it did.' Her head on one side, Bonny watched as the boys ran off and Richard turned back to them. 'Yer a regular hero, yer are.'

Pulling a face at his sister, Richard turned to Harris. 'Are you OK?'

She was trembling, her face white. 'Fine, just a bit shaken.'

'I know a couple of those lads,' Richard said calmly. 'They won't bother you again.'

'See, he's yer White Knight,' Bonny replied, sniggering. 'Yer should have a bloody horse, Richard, and do it right.'

'I'll give you one if you don't stop it.'

Bonny put up her hands to feign fighting. 'Yeah, yer and whose army?'

The three of them dropped into step, Harris in the centre. Having proved himself the hero, Richard was now rigid with embarrassment, Bonny left to do the talking.

'We had a bloke down our way who were a flasher. He was done for three year in Manchester – not that your uncle will be. I mean, everyone knows Saville's soft in the head.' Her brother gave her a warning look. 'It's the truth! Saville's not all there, so they'll let him off. Anyway, he's not done it before, has he? Not and been caught, anyway.'

'Bloody hell, Bonny!' Richard said, exasperated. 'Don't you *ever* know what to say?'

It was Harris's turn to intervene. 'She didn't mean anything by it, Richard. Anyway, Bonny's right, perhaps Saville won't go to gaol.' She stopped, the thought punching her square in the gut.

'Now look what you've done!' Richard snapped at his sister.

'What *I've* done! It weren't me flashing in the bloody park.'

'It were a lousy picture of your uncle,' Richard said, turning to Harris again. 'Perhaps no one will recognise him from the paper.'

'It had his name underneath, stupid!' Bonny replied, swinging round a lamp-post as they continued their walk. 'I suppose everyone at yer school will be talking about it. Just let it run off yer back, Harris.'

Over Harris's head Richard motioned for his sister to be quiet. 'Perhaps you shouldn't go to school today.'

'Then I'd have to go tomorrow,' Harris replied truculently. 'They'd still be talking about it then.'

'Not if our mother gets murdered in between,' Bonny offered helpfully.

Harris stopped walking. 'Murdered?'

'It's just something someone said,' Richard explained, his voice strained. 'Some ass said Mam's boyfriend had knocked off his old lady –'

'Girlfriend,' Bonny corrected him. 'It were his girlfriend –'

'He murdered her?' Harris asked, momentarily forgetting her own problems. 'How?'

'We don't know. And the lad that told me is a born liar.'

'But it might be true. Aren't you worried about your mother?' Harris asked, stopping on the pavement and looking from brother to sister.

'Mam can look after herself.'

'But if he's a killer –'

Richard moved in quickly. 'It were Kenny who told me, and no one takes anything he says seriously. He came to school once and said he were going to have his leg taken off because he had some rare disease. He only did it so the teacher would give him extras at dinner –'

'It worked,' Bonny said, thinking back grudgingly. 'He got three portions of slab cake.'

'But why would he come out with a story about this man being a murderer? I mean,' Harris said smartly, 'I doubt if there's any slab cake in that.'

Bonny stopped swinging round the lamp-post and looked over to her brother. 'Harris has got something there – why *would* Kenny lie about Bert Shaw?'

'He lies about everyone. He said that the woman in Hunter's had had a freak baby. She wasn't even pregnant –'

Harris's thoughts were whirling on. The anguish of her situation at home had lifted temporarily as she was captivated by the idea of some maniac in the Wigan streets – a maniac who knew her friends' mother. It was a relief to think about something else, Harris realised, something other than Saville.

'We should follow him.'

'Who?'

'Your mother's boyfriend,' Harris answered with certainty. 'We should follow them when they go out and see what happens.'

'I don't have to follow them to tell you that,' Bonny said drily.

Richard grimaced. 'And if Mam caught us she'd hit the bloody roof.'

Harris waved aside their objections: 'She wouldn't. Not if we were just looking out for her. Trying to save her life.'

Harris was warming to her theme. She had had enough of her beloved Saville for a while; enough of Mildred's sombre mood and Irma's hysterical disappointment. For the last forty-eight hours Deerheart House had been a hellhole, and besides, her aunts didn't seem to notice her now that their attention was focused on Saville. And Harris hated to be ignored.

'We could do it,' Harris urged the Baker kids. 'When's your mother seeing Bill –'

'*Bert*. Bert Shaw,' Richard corrected her.

'When is she seeing him again?'

'Tonight.'

'What time?'

Bonny shrugged. 'After seven sometime.'

'OK,' Harris said, the matter decided. 'I'll see you round your place at seven.'

'And just how will you get away?' Bonny asked.

'I'll say I've gone up to bed. They won't check on me. They don't now; they're too busy watching Saville.' Harris moved away from them, then turned, her face animated with excitement. 'See you at seven.'

TWELVE

Dr Redmond called by that evening to see Mildred, Irma thankfully keeping to her room. Showing the doctor into the drawing room, Mildred offered him a sherry, her hand shaking as she passed it to him. Poor woman, Dr Redmond thought, what a shameful thing to happen to such a wonderful person . . . Carefully he sipped his sherry, stealing glances at her. She had lost some weight and it suited her, made her look younger.

Easing himself forward in his upright chair, Lionel Redmond began, 'I've had a word with the chief constable. You know, a nod and a wink here and there keeps the wheels turning.'

Mildred stared at him. She should be grateful but she hated to feel beholden, to have to kowtow to people again. It was too acute a reminder of her past to sit easily with her. Lionel continued to talk, his tone sympathetic and all Mildred wanted to do was to slap his red face and watch his jowls wobble like a turkey's wattle.

'Don't you worry about a thing, Mildred. No one's talking about a trial, or prison. Everyone knows that Saville's not quite . . . normal.'

'If they didn't know it before, they know it now.'

'I understand how difficult it is for a lady such as yourself to talk about these matters. I understand that you've led a sheltered, decent life, Mildred.'

Her thoughts took her momentarily back to Doughty Street and she sighed emptily.

Misreading the action, Lionel blurted out, 'Sorry if I've offended you! I didn't mean to –'

'It's all right, just go on with what you were saying, please.'

'Saville will not have to go to trial, I'm assured of that. The case will never come to court.'

Mildred had known as much the previous day from another friend, but let the good doctor have his moment of glory.

'Thank you.'

'It was nothing,' Lionel bleated on, his face flushed further with pleasure. 'You know how I admire you.'

Well, I don't admire you, Mildred thought to herself. I should be flattered, but you're nothing but a fat, posing buffoon. And you're breaking one of my best chairs.

'All this will blow over in time,' he went on, leaning further forwards, the seat protesting. 'Tell me, have you thought about having Saville put in a home?'

'For flashers?' Mildred replied evenly.

Dr Redmond was momentarily taken aback. 'No . . . I mean for people like Saville. People with problems.'

'No, I haven't thought of putting my brother in a home. And when you mentioned it before I said I never would – and that hasn't changed.'

'But your brother's exposed himself in public!'

'Well, there's plenty round these parts that do that in private where they shouldn't,' Mildred replied, watching the doctor's shock with some satisfaction. 'I'm grateful to you, believe me, but what my brother's done won't ruin my life. I was never that worried about people's opinions myself. I worry about my sister and my niece, though. It's no laughing matter for Irma. And as for Harris . . .'

'Do you want me to talk to her?'

'No, she isn't one to confide in outsiders,' Mildred replied quickly. 'But she's had enough trauma in her life already, I'd rather not have added to it. Besides, it's not exactly the kind of thing you can explain to a young girl.'

Lionel nodded wisely. 'And how's your sister coping?'

'Having hysterics every hour, on the hour.' Mildred paused. 'I'm sorry if I sound heartless, but there's not a lot I can do for my sister. All Irma cared about, all she protected and prized, Saville wrecked in an instant. I don't know how I can restore that for her. My sister saw herself as Lady Wigan. She's a snob through and through – and making Harris into one too. I should be grateful to my brother in a way.'

Lionel Redmond raised his eyebrows. 'Grateful?'

'Yes, I've been thinking about Harris, about how we've worshipped her, spoiled her – and I know I'm as much to blame as Irma. But now I wonder how she'll cope with this scandal – if she'll come up trumps, or let us all down. I suppose I want to know one thing, and one thing only: did we make a goddess out of her or a monster?'

At the very moment Mildred was talking to Lionel Redmond, Harris was making her way down towards the outskirts of Scholes. It was not yet dark, the streets still busy, a couple of regulars staring as she passed. Having read one too many of Mildred's detective books, Harris was wearing her school mackintosh with the collar up, her woollen hat pulled down over her forehead.

Leaning against a wall Bonny was the first to spot her.

'What the hell . . . ?'

Richard followed his sister's gaze, took in Harris's outfit and tried hard not to laugh. 'You got out all right, then?'

'Climbed out of the bedroom window,' Harris told him proudly. 'So, has your mother left yet?'

Bonny shook her head, turning to stare down the street. At

first she had been ashamed of Harris knowing where they lived, but her friend had reassured her. This was nothing, Harris had said magnanimously. Where she had lived with her parents in Yorkshire had been much, much worse. Touched by the kindness, Bonny had still doubted it. You couldn't get much worse than the Scholes slums – the mean terraces dark, streets piled with rubbish and dog muck, the Golden Fleece throwing out its drunks after closing time. And always that smell, the odour of unwashed clothes and sour food.

Her reminiscences were curtailed by the sight of Madge coming out of their front door. She was wearing a red coat, too tightly belted, her dyed hair in a pageboy, her make-up garish. God, Bonny thought to herself, she looks a right sight.

'There she is!' Richard whispered, pushing the girls back against the wall and into the shadows.

They watched Madge walk on a way and then began to follow her. She moved quickly, her heels clacking on the pavement. At the end of Vauxhall Road she stopped at the Tramway and looked round.

'Maybe she's seeing a friend –'

'Ssh!' Harris said, silencing Bonny and pointing to a thickset man waving at Madge from across the track. 'Is that him?'

'Ugly pig,' Bonny replied, by way of verification. 'Look at that skin, pock-marked. I reckon he's got VD.'

Richard gave his sister a withering look, then glanced over to Harris. 'Now what?'

'We follow them.'

'But –'

She silenced him with a glance. 'We're doing it for your mother's own good. After all, we'll be heroes if we save her life.'

And we'll be dead if she catches us, Bonny thought, falling reluctantly into step.

*   *   *

'He's asleep,' Mildred said, checking in on Saville and then turning to her sister, hovering in the corridor behind her. 'What's the matter?'

Irma's face was blotchy with crying. She had always been tough, but this was too much for her to bear. Shame, exposure – and what difference did it make that they were going to hush the whole thing up? Everyone knew what Saville had done. You couldn't hush that up.

'Lock his door.'

Mildred stared at her. 'What?'

'Lock his door,' Irma repeated. 'I won't sleep a wink unless I know he can't get out.'

Taking her sister's arm, Mildred led her downstairs and into the drawing room. Mrs Turner had finished for the day, making their dinner as usual, but avoiding their eyes.

Ruefully Mildred sat down and faced her sister. 'Saville's not a prisoner.'

'Then he should be.'

'I've been talking to Dr Redmond –'

'Hah!'

'He said there might be some other – stronger – medication they can put Saville on. Something which stops him having . . . *feelings*.' She stared at Irma, expecting a response. There was none. 'I must say I never thought of Saville as having sexual ideas –'

Groaning, Irma slumped further into her seat.

'But it's only natural. He's a man, after all.'

'He's supposed to have the mental age of a seven-year-old! When was the last time you read about a seven-year-old flashing in the park?'

Trying not to laugh, Mildred kept calm. 'Children have sexual feelings.' God, this was difficult, she thought. They had never talked about sex before. But now they had to – and Irma wasn't about to make it easy. 'I've been reading –'

'About flashers?' Irma snapped shortly.

'About why these things happen. You know, about why men do this kind of thing.'

'Well, all I can say is that you can't have got a book like that from our library. I'm on the judgement panel there and we won't buy anything sordid.' She paused, her eyes wary. 'Oh God, do you suppose they'll ask me to resign?'

'Why? It wasn't you exposing yourself.'

'Oh, go on, make a joke of it! You make a joke about everything,' Irma wailed. 'But this isn't so simple. No one's going to shrug this one off in a hurry.' Her eyes darkened. 'I suppose there'll be no more invitations to the Mayor's Ball – or to renew my membership of the bridge club.'

'Irma, calm down.'

'*Calm down!* How can I calm down? You've never been much interested in society, but I was accepted around here. One of the top rank. Because of me, the Simons name meant something.' Frantic, she stood up, walked around a bit, then sat down again. 'I'm not going to the salon any more.'

It was Mildred's turn to be surprised. 'You can't do that!'

'I can, and I will,' Irma replied. 'I'm not going to be the butt of jokes, seeing our customers whispering behind our backs, talking about us.'

'But *I'm* supposed to face everyone?'

'It's different for you,' Irma said imperiously. 'You don't mind the same. People like you, Mildred; you're friendly. People will be sympathetic with you. But not me. Oh no, no one cares much for me. Anyway, I'm more sensitive.'

To her astonishment, Mildred burst out laughing. 'You, sensitive! Now that *is* funny. You're about the most insensitive person I've ever known.' Warming to her theme, Mildred went on. 'You don't give a damn about anyone but yourself, you and your ridiculous snobbery. If Saville had murdered someone it wouldn't have been half so bad for you, would it? I mean, he could be put away then, forgotten. But the fact that he's a flasher – that's too much!'

109

'And you *don't* mind?' Irma countered bitterly.

'Not as much. I mind more about the effect all this will have on Harris than I do about myself.'

'Always so noble,' Irma replied, her tone thick with sarcasm. 'I recall, however, that Harris is no stranger to upheaval. She had a very rum upbringing before she came here. I mean, Gideon was hardly the perfect father, was he?'

'This isn't about Gideon!' Mildred replied, her tone needle sharp. 'And Harris's difficult start should make you more, not less, concerned for her.'

'Harris will be all right!' Irma snapped, impatiently. 'She's upstairs sleeping like a baby. Hardly upset, I'd say.'

Sighing, Mildred turned the subject round. 'We have to make the best of this. We have to keep our dignity and carry on as –'

'I'm not going near that salon!'

'Well, I can't cope alone!'

'You've got Rose.'

'She's a half-wit! A kind girl, but a half-wit.' Mildred's tone softened. 'I need you, Irma.'

'Well, that's a pity, because I'm not leaving this house again.'

'Great!' Mildred exploded. 'So you're going to wall yourself in, are you?'

'I'm going to keep away from people.'

'For ever? I mean, do let me know. I have to tell your bridge club –'

'There you go! Making jokes again! And at my expense, as usual,' Irma shouted, getting to her feet. 'I give you notice now, Mildred. I'm too ashamed to face the town, or the gossip. From here onwards, if anyone wants me they have to come here. Because I'm not going out.'

*   *   *

Harris's eyes were huge as she watched Bert Shaw slide his arm round Madge and then squeeze her bottom. Did people do things like that, she wondered, and was it what they did before they killed you? Fascinated, Harris stared at Madge's face. She didn't look frightened.

'How she can let that ugly pig touch her bum –'

'Bonny!' Richard hissed. 'That's enough.'

'It doesn't look like enough for Mam.'

'I don't think this was a good idea after all,' Richard said shortly. 'We should leave.'

'Not likely!' Bonny replied. 'I wouldn't miss this for the world.'

'He wouldn't kill her out in the street,' Harris said knowledgeably. 'I mean, no one kills people out in the street.'

Richard sighed. 'I don't think Bert Shaw's a killer. I think Kenny's lying.'

'He'd have to take her somewhere,' Harris went on, 'somewhere quiet. Look! They're off again!'

Laughing, Bert Shaw and Madge walked down the Tramway and then turned back into Wellington Street, hanging on to each other as they walked. The place was shabby, like the other Scholes slums, many of the windows boarded up. Suddenly Bert stopped outside a grimy house with a chalked 17 on the door.

The watchers stopped too, hiding behind a ruined wall, Bonny's knees scraping against the rubble. They couldn't hear what Bert Shaw said from that distance, just watched as he fumbled for a key and inserted it into the lock. At that moment Madge put her arms around his neck and kissed him.

'Wow!'

Bonny pulled a face. 'I'd rather kiss a scabby dog.'

'Give it time,' Richard replied from behind them.

And then suddenly Bert caught hold of Madge, putting his hands round her face and kissing her roughly.

'He's killing her!' Harris said, startled.

'He's kissing her.'

'He's horrible,' Bonny added.

Eager not to miss anything, they leaned forwards, a couple of bricks working loose from the wall and falling onto the street. Hearing the rumpus, Bert Shaw turned. Madge turned. At once, the three of them ran. Bonny, struggling to her feet, followed the other two, but she was slower and at the end of Wellington Street she was stopped by Madge grabbing her ear violently.

'By heck, Mam, yer can't half run fast in them heels!' Bonny said desperately.

'What the hell –' smack – 'are yer –' smack – 'doing here?'

'We were watching out for yer, Mam,' Bonny replied, trying to wriggle out of her mother's grip.

'Yer were spying! That's what yer were doing!' Madge hollered.

'He's a murderer!' Bonny cried, playing her trump card. 'Bert Shaw's a murderer.'

'If I catch yer spying on me again, he won't be the only bloody one.'

THIRTEEN

Creeping up the driveway to Deerheart House, Harris stopped and listened. There were no lights on. Good, that meant that everyone was in bed. Carefully she caught hold of the ivy that ran from the ground to her bedroom window and began to climb. It took her several attempts before she managed to swing her leg over the sill of the window and then, noiselessly, push open the glass pane.

A light went on immediately, Mildred watching as Harris fell into the room. 'Where have you been?'

Getting to her feet, Harris stammered, 'I was . . . walking.'

'At this time of night?'

'I was just –'

'Don't lie to me!' Mildred snapped, for once truly angry. 'I've been waiting for you for over an hour. I came in here to see if you were all right and what did I find? A pillow put in your bed, to look as though you were there. Very clever, Harris. It nearly fooled me. I was worried about you, wondering if you were upset about Saville, but you'd sneaked out.' She stopped talking and turned away.

Wrong-footed, Harris blustered, 'I didn't think you'd find out –'

'So that makes it all right, does it?' Mildred snapped, facing

Harris again. Suddenly she was more like Irma than her gentle self. 'Have you no consideration? After all this family is going through, did you have to *add* to our problems?'

'I didn't think –'

'You never do!' Mildred exploded, frustrated by her earlier conversation with Irma and taking it out on Harris. 'You're a wilful, ungrateful girl. We didn't have to take you in; you could have gone to a home. You wouldn't have been sneaking about then, Harris. Oh no, they lock the doors at night to stop that kind of thing. What were you thinking of? Don't you care about yourself? Your reputation? What kind of girl sneaks out? And to do *what*?'

Shaken, Harris tried to remonstrate. 'I'm sorry –'

'Sorry isn't enough! I've had a bellyful of sorry from Saville. All of you seem to think that I can cope with anything. *Good old Mildred, she'll sort it all out.* Well, I won't! You hear me, I won't!'

Trembling, Harris stood by her bed. This wasn't like her aunt; she had never been cruel before, always understanding. Seeing Mildred angry was a shock, but realising that she was close to tears made Harris burn with shame.

'I'm sorry, really I am,' she blundered.

'Where were you?'

'With Richard and Bonny. We were following their mother. Her boyfriend's a murderer.'

'Oh, Harris!' Mildred snapped, sitting down on the side of the bed and bursting into tears. 'Not more stories. Dear God, don't lie now.'

Hurriedly Harris sat down next to her. 'I'm *not* lying! Bert Shaw was supposed to be a murderer. We went to see if Mrs Baker was all right.'

'What about me?'

'What?' Harris said softly.

'What about me?' Mildred repeated. 'Did you *have* to go off tonight, Harris? Did you have to run off on some silly

114

adventure? Everyone knows Bert Shaw's no killer – he's a wide boy, nothing more.' She looked at Harris despairingly. 'But you *wanted* to believe it, didn't you? Wanted to be a heroine of the hour, as usual.'

The criticism was too close for comfort. Harris tentatively put her arm round Mildred. 'I'm sorry.'

Mildred shook her head, her plump hands lying limply on her lap. 'All I ever wanted was to come first with someone. All I ever wanted was that. It never happened with a man, but when you came along and we got on so well, I thought I meant something to you. I thought I mattered to you.'

'You do!' Harris said helplessly.

'No, I don't. Not enough.' Mildred got to her feet and walked to the door, then turned. 'I love you, Harris. Maybe too much . . . but if you promise me one thing we'll say no more on the matter. Promise you'll think about what you did, will you? Think about how easy it is to hurt someone. The world's full of people who are casually cruel. Don't be like them.'

FOURTEEN

I don't think she ever realised how much those words affected me because I knew Mildred wasn't just talking about some kid's prank, she was talking about her life. The stinging rebuke actually encompassed all her disappointments, regrets and frustrations. I was her whipping boy that night. But deservedly so.

Often we grow to understand only when it is too late. Looking back now, I can see the whole picture. But then all I really knew was that the woman I had grown to love I had let down. After that, if she smiled at me a thousand times, I would never forget that look of disappointment. And I would wonder often, over the years to come, if I could ever make up for the injury I had so callously inflicted on her.

She would have said that it didn't matter, that I had taken her too seriously. But that was the point. No one – including myself – took her seriously enough.

FIFTEEN

True to her word, Irma didn't leave the house again. Within the safety of Deerheart House she found her new role: gaoler. Saville was never to be far from her reach; monitored, watched, considered, controlled. It was to be Irma's new mission in life. She was looking after her brother and protecting the public. It was the honourable thing to do, wasn't it?

So Mildred went back to the salon alone. For months hardly anyone came to have their hair done. They came to stare, to commiserate, but not as customers. To hell with all of them, Mildred thought as she saw them pass the window. Irma might hide away, but that wasn't her style.

Another Mayor's Ball came, and went. But no regulars came to the salon to have their hair done. They walked past instead, their eyes averted, their hair newly permed elsewhere. No more Lady Mayoress, no Gladys Leonards. But stubbornly Mildred kept the salon open.

Then one day a woman came in off the street. She was young, but obviously poor, a world apart from the customers of old.

Looking round, she smiled uncertainly. 'I was . . . I think I'm in the wrong place.'

Mildred hurried to reassure her. 'No, dear, no. What did you want?'

'A haircut,' the young woman replied, looking about her nervously.

Mildred had flung a cape around her shoulders and hustled her into a seat before the young woman knew what had hit her. 'But . . . I was wondering how much it would cost.'

Mildred looked at her squarely. 'You need a haircut, my dear, and I need a customer. You pay me what you can afford. And don't worry, I'm past being insulted.'

The following Friday Harris came into the salon unannounced. She was wearing a spring coat of pale yellow, her dark hair falling over her shoulders. At sixteen she was – as her aunts had hoped – a stunning young woman. But what kind of man would she attract now? Mildred wondered. What kind of rich husband would want to marry into the disgraced Simons household?

'Hello there,' Mildred said simply. 'Want your hair doing?'

'I was wondering . . .' Harris began and tailed off. Slowly she walked around, touching the scissors and combs, then she looked up again. 'I was wondering if I could learn . . . you know, how to do hair.'

'You want to work here?' Mildred said, astounded. 'With me?'

'I know you had to let Rose go,' Harris said tentatively. 'I just thought I might be able to help. I could learn the trade.'

Mildred was thoughtful. She had seen a difference in Harris – and not just the obvious one of her gradual maturing. Her spoiled ways had mellowed: this was no brat come looking to gloat. In fact it had surprised Mildred to see how much their argument had affected the girl. She would have expected Harris to shrug it off, but she didn't. Instead she became thoughtful, quiet.

'Why do you want to learn hairdressing, Harris?'

'I should work.'

'We have enough money. You don't ever have to work.'

118

'I can't sit around all day,' Harris said simply. 'Besides, Bonny's had her job at R. & J. Gorner's for ages.'

'Bonny Baker's not from your background.'

'I know, but she's enjoying it at the café. They're even making her speak properly, something I never managed.' Harris pulled a face, then hurried on. 'And Richard's down the pit.'

Mildred frowned. 'I've always said that was a waste of a good brain. With money and education Richard could have become someone.' She looked back to Harris. 'Why don't you stay on at school?'

'What for? I'm not bright! It would be a waste of time. You know it and so do I. Anyway, why work for someone else when I could work for the family business?'

This was a new Harris, Mildred thought, impressed. A very different girl from the one who had sneaked out with the Baker kids just months before.

'You're only sixteen –'

Harris was adamant. 'I don't want to stay at school! Besides, I don't have anything in common with anyone there. Not now.'

So that was it, Mildred thought. Harris had never admitted it – however many times she had been questioned – but Saville's fall from grace had obviously made her life difficult at school. Mildred could imagine how her peers had sneered – *Look at her, stuck-up bitch, not so clever now, is she?*

'Do you get bullied?'

Harris shook her head emphatically. 'I did at first . . .'

'You should have told me!'

'It's OK now.' Her eyes moved to the window and then returned to her aunt. 'I feel like an outsider there. I seem to feel like that a lot nowadays.'

The words tickled the air between them. Mildred was the first to speak.

'We don't talk like we used to, do we?'

'No.'

'I miss those talks we used to have.'

'Me too.'

'I thought you were ashamed of the family. That you regretted coming to us,' Mildred admitted, her voice quiet. 'I mean, your father was right all along, wasn't he? We are no good.'

'You *are*!' Harris said, flaring up suddenly. 'You've been wonderful to me and all I've thought about for so long was myself. And then the other day I walked past and saw you in here on your own, with all those stuck-up cows snubbing you –'

'Harris!'

'I don't care!' she blurted back. 'They *are* cows, all of them. Going off to that crummy salon on Market Square, when everyone knows it's not a patch on this place.'

Touched, Mildred put her arm round Harris's shoulder. 'It's life . . .'

'It's not fair!'

'Like I said – it's life,' Mildred replied calmly. 'But in time people will forget all about Saville's little adventure. When something bigger or more scandalous happens.'

'I feel so sorry for him,' Harris replied. 'He didn't mean to do any harm, I'm sure of that. But the way Irma's treating him is horrible.'

'Look,' Mildred said patiently, leading Harris to a chair and taking one herself, 'you have to understand something about your uncle. What Saville did is against the law. If he had been normal, he would probably have gone to prison. The fact that he's backward saved him from that. But people don't understand about him being slow. And harmless. They just fear people like Saville.'

'No one could be frightened of Saville!' Harris replied hotly.

'They're frightened of *what he did*,' Mildred said, her voice very calm. 'So now we *have* to keep a close eye on him, Harris, for his own good. You think Irma's hard, but she's actually helping him.'

'He's frightened of her.'

'Saville is frightened of punishment,' Mildred explained. 'Even now, so long after the event, he thinks he'll be punished for it. Our father used to prolong punishment, you see, so we were never sure when it was coming. Sometimes we thought he'd forgotten, and then, weeks or months later, he would make us pay for it.'

Harris frowned. 'That's wicked. My father hated him –'

'And yet he loved Gideon. So just think what it was like for Saville.'

'And you?' Harris asked, head on one side. 'What about you?'

'I could cope with it. Irma found it difficult, but she learned to cope in her own way.' Mildred paused – why was she talking about the past now? 'Saville has to be protected by us, Harris. Or he might have to go away somewhere –'

Harris jumped as though she had been slapped. 'You can't send him away!'

'I didn't say we were going to.'

'You sent my father away and now you're going to send Saville away!'

'Harris, for God's sake!' Mildred protested. 'Do calm down. I never knew anyone who could get so worked up so fast. Saville is not going anywhere. But that's why we have to watch him and make sure he doesn't do anything "odd" again.'

Harris considered her words for a moment. 'But why does it have to be Irma who's always with him? I could stay with Saville sometimes.'

Mildred coloured and looked away. Harris saw the reaction and asked hoarsely, 'You think Saville would do something to me?'

'Harris –'

'How could you? He wouldn't ever hurt me, or do anything

121

bad. I hate this life!' she snapped, suddenly beside herself. 'People are so cruel. You have to do this, live this way, say this, or everything goes wrong. If anyone's different, people hate them. Well, I hate everyone that hates Saville! And who are these people, anyway? I bet not one of them is as kind as my uncle. Not one of them!'

'Dear God, Harris,' Mildred replied, laughing, 'you get more like your father everyday! He was always so certain of everything. Always so passionate, like you.' She stopped laughing and reached out for Harris's arm. 'But Gideon was *too* wilful, *too* sure of himself. Be careful of that, love. Stand up for yourself by all means, but keep your feet on the ground – and always know when to compromise.'

It was very strange – maybe it was something to do with the light – but that morning Harris seemed different. Richard studied her, careful not to let her see his scrutiny. She was certainly growing up. And suddenly. It seemed as though he knew what she would look like as a mature woman – then there would be a rapid change, and she would seem totally different. A chameleon in Wigan. Typical, he thought, Harris never did anything like anyone else.

But this Sunday morning she was *definitely* different. They were sitting on the lowest part of the wall that separated the Simonses' property from the Barracloughs', Bonny reading a copy of *Picture Post*, Richard narrowing his eyes against the sun as Harris whistled to herself.

' "A whistling woman and a crowing hen, drive the devil out of his den." '

She stopped whistling and looked over to Richard. 'Huh?'

'That's a saying.'

'Rubbish,' Bonny said, putting down the magazine. 'You just made it up.'

She had grown fast, her raw-boned limbs, as ever, too long

for her slim body. Even her face had an elongated look. And yet, despite the odds, Bonny had a chemistry about her, a humour that made her crackle with life.

'Mam used to say it.'

'She never! Oh, you do go on, Richard.'

He sighed to himself and turned his head up to the sun, Harris watching him. She had burned to ask the question for years and now, suddenly, it was the right time.

'Is she an alcoholic?'

Richard flinched. Bonny leaned across her brother towards Harris.

'You mean Mam?'

'Yes.'

'Of course she is! Some of the best people are lushes,' Bonny replied, waving the magazine in front of Harris's nose. 'Errol Flynn and Carole Lombard are drunks –'

'Never!'

'It's in *Confidential Magazine*,' she said, as though citing the oracle, 'and I believe it.'

'It's a mental problem,' Richard said suddenly.

'It's a throat problem,' Bonny countered. 'Mam just keeps swallowing.'

'Is it difficult to live with?' Harris asked, unable to let the matter drop.

'Yeah, she's –' Bonny stopped suddenly, catching Richard's warning look. 'Oh, why *shouldn't* she know? It's Harris, for God's sake! She knows everything else about us.'

'It's not something to be proud of.'

'Who said it was?' Bonny asked, amazed. 'Honestly, what's got into you? The three of us have never had any secrets before.' She turned from her brother to look at Harris. 'Your mam and dad never got drunk then?'

'I don't remember –'

'She was a child, for God's sake!' Richard interrupted, obviously irritated. 'How would she remember?'

'You're turning into a right bore, Richard!' Bonny snapped, sliding off the wall and walking off.

A minute passed as he watched Bonny depart. Desperately Richard hoped that Harris would stay and not follow his sister. Why the hell did Bonny have to talk about their mother? . . . The sun was high, making the grass luminous, a dragonfly casting its aeroplane shadow on the ground. He stared for a long moment at the back of Harris's head. Such thick dark hair, he thought, waving onto her shoulders. Had it always been so brown? Harris sighed, her shoulders rising for an instant in her cotton dress. He could sense her heartbeat: knowing he could not hear it, but imagining the steady thump of life inside her.

God, Richard thought suddenly, what *is* the matter with me?

'What's it like?' Harris asked suddenly, turning to meet his gaze.

He was pale with embarrassment at being caught out. 'What?'

'The pit.'

He let out a long sigh of relief before answering. 'Grim.'

'You've got a good brain, Richard, you should have stayed on at school. You could have had a decent job, even a profession.'

Was she talking to him? he wondered. Was this dark-eyed, dark-haired idol telling him that he was clever, that he could do something worthwhile? And if so, what did Harris really mean? Was it a subtle message – *you could be good enough for me, if you tried?*

'Are you all right, Richard?'

He was dizzy with confusion, one part of him longing to hope, the other chiding himself for being a bloody idiot.

'I have to bring in a wage, like Bonny does.' He winced; why the hell did he have to bring his *sister* into this?

'It's not the same. Your mother should have realised you

124

were clever. She should have let you go into further education.'
Harris stared at the dragonfly for a long simmering instant
before it made upwards for the summer clouds. 'I'm stupid,
I know that –'

'You're not.'

'I am!' she insisted, laughing. 'Oh, I'm clever enough to get
by, I've got common sense, but my brain's nothing special. I
take after my father. He wasn't very clever either.' Her tone
was wistful. 'But he had charm.'

'You have loads of charm.'

She smiled, looked over her shoulder at him. 'You think so?'

Was she flirting with him? Oh God, Richard thought, was
she *flirting*?

'Yeah, you've got loads of charm.'

Jumping off the wall, Harris lay down on the grass at
Richard's feet, looking up at the sky. He wanted to copy
her, but hesitated. What should he do? Was it an invitation?
Had she, like him, this smouldering summer's day, suddenly
felt some attraction between them? They had been friends for
years, neither of them noticing each other sexually – until now.
That was what he was thinking. But was it what Harris was
thinking?

Taking his chance, Richard slid off the wall and lay down
beside Harris, staring upwards. He could feel the pulse in his
neck thumping, his heart beating like a piston. He would die
there, staring up at the sky for ever. Die next to Harris Simons
– and he didn't mind a bit. Because he felt like a man, he felt
powerful and clever. He would get a decent job, he would
make money, he would work for his princess and then claim
her. He would – Richard trembled at the thought – *he would
marry Harris Simons*.

'Well, thanks for coming after me!' Bonny said suddenly,
her shadow throwing them both into gloom before she flopped
down on the other side of Harris. Copying them both, she
stared up into the sky. 'So what are you looking at?'

A lost opportunity, Richard thought grimly, a lost bloody opportunity.

Mrs Turner wasn't about to compromise. Not a bit. Flicking her duster out, she moved towards the back wall and then sidled along to where she knew there was a gap in the stonework. Checking that she was unobserved, she then peered into the Barraclough garden.

It was true! she thought, shattered. Mr Lacy was being unfaithful to her. And with some trollop called Nelly Fisher. Some cheap, racy piece whom the Barracloughs had hired temporarily after their usual maid had caught TB. Mrs Turner burned with fury as she gawked through the spy hole. Far off, by the rhubarb clumps, Mr Lacy was talking to the willowy Miss Fisher. The *young* willowy Miss Fisher.

Craning forwards further Mrs Turner jumped as her name sounded.

'Mrs Turner.'

Spinning round, she lost her footing and fell heavily into a patch of heathers.

'What *are* you doing?' Irma demanded.

'I was just . . . just checking on the garden.'

'We have a gardener for the garden, and you for the house,' Irma replied deadly, her gaze going up and down the dishevelled Mrs Turner. 'You look flushed. I do hope you're not going to get TB like the Barracloughs' woman. It would be so difficult to cope without help.'

For the first time in her life Mrs Turner wished consumption on herself, if only to make Irma's life unbearable. Summoning all the dignity she could, Mrs Turner then climbed out of the heathers and moved back towards the house.

Idly, Irma watched her and then, just as she drew level, said: 'That pie last night. What was in it?'

'Rabbit.'

126

'I don't like rabbit,' Irma replied. 'I used to keep rabbits as a child. They were sweet little things . . . Don't serve rabbit again, Mrs Turner, it brings back memories. You should never make friends with your dinner.'

You should never make friends with your dinner! Stupid bitch, Mrs Turner thought as she moved on into the kitchen. Irma Simons was bloody lucky that she had stayed on after Saville's spot of bother. Not that Mrs Turner minded Saville, for all the gossip. Like she had said to Mr Lacy, 'He's a poor soul, but I reckon Mr Saville's harmless. After all, he's never looked funny at me. Not once . . .'

She stopped short, tea towel in hand, suddenly reminded of her faithless paramour next door. So Mr Lacy was playing fast and lose with her, was he? Flirting with some cheap piece who everyone knew was only out for what she could get. That Nelly Fisher should never have tried it on. Didn't the whole town know that Mrs Turner and Mr Lacy had had an understanding for years? Hadn't he promised himself to her?

Well, no, Mrs Turner thought sadly. He hadn't promised himself at all. He had stayed firmly unpromised. Unshackled. Unwed.

The bastard.

SIXTEEN

Mildred had been right when she said that people forgot. They did, when something bigger happened to wipe their memories. And war, now that was big. Sighing, Mildred walked up the front drive to Deerheart House. The neglected stone plate caught her eye suddenly and she reached out, tugging away the ivy to reveal the letters.

Her mother had christened the place Deerheart House. 'Should be *Dearheart*,' Gordon Simons had said disparagingly. 'You can't even bloody spell!' But she could, and she meant *Deer*heart, not *Dear*heart, because sarcasm had never been a weapon she used.

Another memory came back to Mildred unexpectedly and hazily. She had been very small – God, she had *never* remembered this before – and her mother had been sitting beside her in the garden.

'I love deers,' she had said, forthcoming for once. 'When I was a little girl, like you, I could see them from my bedroom window. I promised myself that when I had my own house I would call it Deerheart House – after them.'

Now why had that old remembrance come into her mind, Mildred wondered, walking into the house, the newspaper in her hand. The silence that greeted her was complete. The

128

stopped clock stared out sullenly from its walnut case, the Delft vase was still on the polished table in the centre of the hall, and the painting of *The Judgement of Solomon* facing her, the baby as fat and unprepossessing as it always was. Nothing had changed that day, or any day for decades. Why *was* that? Why hadn't they changed the house? After all, it wasn't as though they had wanted to preserve good memories.

'WAR!'

The sudden shout made Mildred jump, Saville running down the stairs towards her, his thin face flushed behind his walrus moustache. 'WAR –'

'Ssssh, love,' Mildred said kindly, taking her brother's arm. 'I know all about it. But we'll be fine here. Safe.'

'It's very noisy, war.'

'Yes,' Mildred agreed, remembering how upset Saville had been during the Great War. 'But it's quiet here.'

'GUNS!' he said suddenly, his eyes wide. 'I could fight. No.' He changed his mind and hid behind her. 'I can't fight, I can't fight at all.'

Hearing all the noise, Harris ran down the stairs and took in the scene at once. 'Hey, Saville, Mrs Turner's made parkin.'

'Parkin?' he repeated, his terror lifting. 'I love parkin.'

Breathing in deeply, Mildred watched as Harris led her uncle to the kitchen. The panic had been contained, but how many more panics would there be in the months to come? And how long would this war last? Flinging down her handbag on the table, Mildred looked about her and promised herself one thing.

If she got through the war she was going to decorate.

Enlistment took the unemployed men off the streets, some even eager for war if it meant employment and a wage. Women who had fought to bring up children on meagre funds soon found themselves drafted into war work at the industrial sites around

Wigan and further afield in Manchester. They had their own money and were needed.

Oddly enough the women still needed glamour too. And so Simons Coiffeuse stayed open. The wealthy old guard had drifted away, but the cheerful working women came in for a bleach or a perm, passing over their money willingly for the morale boost. Then Mildred's greatest rival, Doris Collins, closed up in Market Square.

Her husband had deserted her, the rumour went, and she had gone back to her mother's in Cornwall. Either way, it was good news for Mildred.

'You watch, Harris,' she said cheerfully. 'They'll have to come back now.'

'Who will?'

'The Mrs Leonards, Brewers, Ramsbottoms and all the smug others.' She smiled to herself. 'They've nowhere else decent they can go – *except* come back to us.'

Surprised, Harris studied her aunt. Who gave a damn about hairdressing when there was a war on? Wasn't her aunt frightened? Here she was blabbing on about perm lotion and hairnets, and Hitler was all over the papers . . . Harris stared at the scissors in her hands. Was it true what she had overheard a customer say? That the Germans raped every woman they could find? Even little girls? And that they killed Jews and idiots . . . ? She thought of Saville. Maybe they should hide him away, so no one would find him and kill him.

Behind her, Mildred rattled on, 'Oh yes, you just wait and see, Harris. Those flaming women will be crawling back here. "Please, Mildred, there's no one can cut hair like you. It's not been the same since I've been away . . ." As for the Mayor's wife, well, I won't be making it comfortable for her. And as for her hair, have you seen it lately? If that's a perm, I'm Mussolini –'

'What about Hitler?'

'Does he want a perm?'

'It's not funny,' Harris said soberly. 'What if the Germans invade?'

'They tried it before and failed. They'll fail again.'

Harris was unconvinced. 'They say Hitler's –'

'Hitler's an ass. Anyone with a moustache like that must have a slate loose,' Mildred retorted, bustling round the salon.

She was as worried as Harris, but was not about to let her niece know that. They would face what was to come, when it came, and not a minute before. Besides, they had the air-raid shelter in the garden, tinned food put aside and enough vegetables growing to keep them through the autumn if there was a shortage. They would be comfortable, they would survive – unless a bomb hit them.

Down in Scholes and parts of Ince they weren't so lucky. Mildred thought of the Baker children, grown up now. How would they manage through the war with a mother like Madge? Bert Shaw had dumped her and she was drinking heavily. But then again, Madge Baker was probably the one person who would know all about the black market. More than enough silk stockings and powdered eggs would be coming her way . . .

'You're doing well, you know,' Mildred said, to distract Harris from the war. 'That haircut you did yesterday was good. Very good.'

'What if Hitler takes over England?'

'We have Churchill, love, so there's nothing to fear.'

'But –'

'Harris,' Mildred said kindly but firmly, 'I've already lived through one war and I know a bit about it. We have to live one day at a time. You, me, Irma and Saville. One day at a time, because no one knows how long or hard this is going to be.' She slapped a comb into the palm of her niece's hand. 'Now, comb out that lady under the dryer, will you? And look quick about it.'

SEVENTEEN

'You're mad!' Bonny snapped. 'Didn't Mam teach you never to volunteer for anything?'

Pushing his sister aside, Richard moved across the cramped space of his bedroom. Having worked down the pit since he was eighteen he had had a bellyful. Whatever was out there, away from Wigan, had to be better than labouring in some freezing dank hole underground.

He looked round. The money he had brought into the house had made no impression. His mother bought food for them all, she said, but in reality The Fox saw most of Madge's cash. As for the housekeeping – Madge was as sloppy as ever. Nothing was clean, nothing tidy, stacks of old newspapers and cheap magazines piled up in the lobby, the yard outside overflowing with broken bottles, old cans and cast-off pieces of wood.

Richard had tried to tidy up the place, but it was no good. And as for Bonny, she had given up long ago. It seemed that if her children tried to make any improvement on the squalor, Madge resented it. The only places they could make reasonably comfortable were their own rooms.

Richard studied the four walls that surrounded him. He hated the faded wallpaper, mildewed in the corner, and the bed, which had come from some old fella when he died. As for the wardrobe, whatever he did with it, the door fell open constantly, lolling like a drunk into the depressing room.

'It's war, for God's sake,' Bonny went on, watching her brother. 'Who volunteers to get their head shot off?'

'I might be lucky.'

'Yeah, our family were always lucky,' Bonny said drily, then got to her feet and flung her arms around her brother's neck. 'I don't want you to go. It's bloody silly.'

'I want to do something worthwhile –'

'Then paint the hallway,' Bonny replied, dropping down on the side of the bed. 'If you volunteer, I will.'

'Girls don't go off and fight.'

'I'll join the WAAF.'

'You like your job. Why change?'

'Why change yours?'

'I hate the pit. It's a job that leads nowhere.'

'Oh, and being a waitress at R. & J. Gorner's or working at Burneys bloody handbag factory will land me in the arms of Howard Hughes, will it?'

Sighing, Richard sat down beside his sister. 'I want to feel useful.'

'You *are* useful. You keep me from killing Mam.'

'I mean *really* useful. I could turn out to be brave, win a medal, or something.'

'You could turn out dead,' Bonny replied, folding her arms truculently. 'They could send you anywhere. Abroad even.'

'That wouldn't be so bad.'

'You hate the heat.'

'It's October, Bonny.'

'They could send you to Egypt.'

'Look, the war will probably be over soon,' Richard said gently. 'I could be home for Christmas.'

'Dead or alive?' she snapped. 'Don't bother coming back if you'll be put in the cemetery on McCormack Street. I won't

133

come and see you there, Richard, not there. You've left me alone with Mam, so don't go making matters any worse, you hear me? You bloody come home, or else.'

The two of them lapsed into silence, each thinking his or her own thoughts. Richard squeezed his sister's hand tightly. She was wondering how she would exist without her brother. They had been inseparable since childhood; one always looking out for the other, the resourceful offspring of a neglectful mother. Where Richard went, Bonny went. And now he was going to leave her. There would be no brother around any more. No one to tease, no one to go to the flicks with, talk daft to, even share dreams with.

Richard was wondering if he was crazy. Was war so much more appealing than the pit? But it was true, he *could* do something useful in the army, even become someone, perhaps. People wouldn't know him as the raggedy kid who ran around in his mother's cardigan, his soiled nappy hanging below the uneven hem. Wherever they sent him, wouldn't it be better than Scholes? But if he died . . . The thought puzzled Richard. It should frighten him, but it didn't. It only made him fearful for Bonny.

'I know you. You'll desert.'

He laughed; looked at his sister. 'I could make general.'

'You could make a bloody mess of your life, you mean. They don't make generals out of our sort.'

'You won't be all alone, Bonny. You've got your friends at work, and Harris –'

Bonny winced. 'Have you told her?'

'No . . .'

'Don't you think you should, Richard?'

'You tell her for me. I hate saying goodbye.'

'She's a friend,' Bonny continued. 'Aw, come on, you can't just walk off and leave her flat.'

'She's not my girlfriend.'

'I bet if she were you wouldn't be running off to bloody

war!' Bonny replied smartly. 'Sorry, I didn't mean to tread on your corns.'

'Why stop now? You've been treading on my corns all my life,' Richard replied, nudging her. 'We both know nothing will come of me and Harris. I used to hope, but she's destined for better things than me. She'll marry some rich man if the Simons sisters have their way.'

'Why don't you talk to her?'

'No,' Richard said after a moment. 'If she'd felt anything for me – other than as a pal – she'd have let on.'

Bonny shook her head. 'Like you did, you mean?'

Mr Lacy had not anticipated the back of the trowel striking him on the head. And he had to admit, even though the pain was making his eyes smart, that Mrs Turner was a damn good shot.

'You sod!'

'Now then, Mrs Turner,' Mr Lacy pleaded, feeling blood under his fingertips as he touched his scalp. 'I were only showing Miss Fisher how to stake a sapling.'

'I bet she's staked enough saplings in her time!' Mrs Turner threw back, advancing on him with a bamboo cane. 'I heard you were snuggling up to her in the Rose and Crown again. Well, this has been going on long enough.'

'She had something in her eye –'

'Something in her eye! There soon will be – my bloody fist.'

'Mrs Turner! I never knew you swore.'

'There's a lot about me you don't know, Mr Lacy,' she replied, chucking the bamboo cane at him. He ducked just in time. 'You've made me into the laughing stock of this town. I thought it was just a little flirtation you were having with that trollop. I even thought it would blow over in time. But no! Well, now you have to choose – it's Nelly Fisher, or me.'

Mr Lacy floundered. 'Mrs Turner, I'm very fond of you –'

'Argh!'

'But the truth is, I'm engaged to Nelly.'

Mrs Turner stopped short, her mouth hanging open. *Engaged to Nelly Fisher*. Her man was engaged to another woman. Rejection hit her hard, her steely gaze finally moving back to Mr Lacy and fixing him to the spot.

'You'll rue the day you crossed me, Lacy –'

'Mrs Turner, we can still be friends. There's no need to get all worked up about this. Life's hard enough – there's a war on.'

'Yes there is,' Mrs Turner replied, turning away, 'and your little girlfriend is going to be one of the first flaming casualties.'

Irma hadn't thought about Harry Delaney for a very long time. But now, as the light faded on that October afternoon, she let herself look back. Only a couple of yards away Saville was dozing in his chair, snoring softly as Irma stole to the window and looked out.

Harry Delaney was standing there, waving up at her . . . Irma blinked, then looked back into the garden. He was gone, of course, and in his place was Mildred, her head down as she bustled past. Slowly Irma let her memory slide back again.

'Hey there!' Harry had called out to her. 'Come out here. It's wonderful.' She'd looked behind her quickly. 'It's OK,' Harry had gone on, 'your father's out.'

There I go, Irma thought, watching herself in the past. Was that really me?

She had been attractive then, dark-haired, sensual for a time. Such a little time. When she'd entered the garden the smell of honeysuckle brushed against her, the late summer roses blowsy with scent.

'I love you,' Harry had said, kissing her.

Now, Irma's fingers stole up to her lips, lingering for an instant on the soft flesh.

'I love you too,' she'd replied, touching Harry's cheek. And then he'd kissed her again, pulling her into the azalea bushes, the glossy leaves brushing summer rain onto their clothes, both of them laughing. Laughing . . .

Suddenly the door of the morning room slammed shut, Mildred walking in with a newspaper.

Irma was still standing by the window, her fingers resting against her lips. She seemed locked into some kind of trance, her expression bewildered.

'Are you all right?' Mildred asked.

'He courted me in this garden . . .' Irma said unexpectedly.

Surprised, Mildred frowned. 'Are you talking about Harry Delaney?'

Irma winced, then hurried on to cover her vulnerability, 'I heard that Gregory Barraclough was killed. I suppose his fiancée will get over it soon enough. Things aren't how they used to be. Women these days don't have to obey anyone. They can do as they like. No wasted lives now. War or no war, they live as though life will never end for them. We had to do what we were told.' Her voice was bitter. '*We were special, we were the Simonses*. But we weren't, were we, Mildred? We didn't make the grand matches or carry on the family name, we just did what we were told. And look where it got us . . .' Her gaze moved out into the garden longingly. 'I should have married Harry Delaney. I should have taken my chance. It was the only one I ever had.'

Then she stopped and, without saying another word, left the room.

EIGHTEEN

January 1943

Dr Ben Ramsey entered Dr Redmond's surgery and looked round, frowning. Rheumatic fever had kept Ben out of the war, but he didn't mind – there was more than enough illness to cope with away from the front. Sighing, he moved the blotter around on the old desk and then toyed with the heavy blackout curtain.

Wigan wasn't a bit as he remembered it. But then the last time he had seen the town was when he was a boy. The intervening years had been spent in Yorkshire, near Barnsley. His father had always wanted his son to be a doctor, and Ben hadn't disappointed him. Not that it mattered now: both his parents were dead.

'Everything all right?' Irene Redmond asked, putting her head round the door.

'Fine,' Ben replied evenly. 'How's Dr Redmond?'

'Getting well, but it's slow,' she answered, taking the question as an invitation to enter.

Approvingly she studied the stand-in for her husband. Well now, this was a handsome man, and no mistake. There would be plenty of ailments amongst the ladies from now on.

'Where are you staying?'

'In Standish.'

'Nice.'

'Comfortable,' Ben agreed.

Mrs Redmond waited for him to confide further, but was disappointed.

'It's still busy here, even though there's a war on. Still the same children's ailments, the usual things. We had a lot of flu last winter, and there's a few casualties sent home you have to keep an eye on.' She warmed to her theme. 'Mrs Carter's son, Morris, came back without his legs. Shame, that – he was a lovely dancer.'

'Is there a list?'

She blinked. 'Of what?'

'Calls I have to make. Do you write me out a list daily?'

'I could,' she said, anxious to be helpful. 'My husband usually did it for himself, but I like to be useful. I could write a bit about each patient by the side of their name, you know, just to fill you in.'

'That would be helpful, thank you,' Ben replied, turning back to his papers.

Mrs Redmond admired his thick hair and then jumped at the sound of her husband banging a stick on the floor above.

'I have to go now.'

'Yes.'

'See you later,' she said, turning, and then adding eagerly, 'You can rely on me to give you any help you need.'

It was soon agreed that being attacked by the enemy wouldn't be so bad after all, if Dr Ramsey came to look after you. His dark good looks and brooding air soon inflamed the Wigan women. He must have a past, they said. All that melancholy must hide a lot of pain. Perhaps he was injured and that was why he wasn't called up . . .

'Perhaps he's got flat feet,' Mildred offered, shampooing Mrs Brewer's long grey hair with soft soap. Not that Mrs Brewer would know that – believing that she was getting the last of the shampoo allowance.

'I heard he was related to a famous surgeon in London,' Mrs Brewer confided, drying the inside of her big ears with the edge of the towel. 'It wouldn't surprise me. A man like that looks like he was born to money.'

'So why end up in Wigan?' Mildred countered.

'There's nothing wrong with Wigan!' Mrs Brewer snapped. 'Is he married?'

'How would I know?'

'I thought you'd have heard, with all the gossip in this place.'

'Well, I heard that he was divorced,' the stout Mrs Ramsbottom said, leaning over from her seat, water dripping from her wet hair. 'Ready to be snapped up.'

'Why did he get divorced?' Mrs Brewer asked, fascinated.

'His wife died.'

'So he's a widower?'

'No, he's divorced.'

'But why did he need a divorce if she died?'

Mrs Ramsbottom pulled the towel around her thick neck to catch the drops before she continued. 'She died *after* the divorce.'

'Any children?'

'They came after the divorce too,' Mildred chipped in smartly, Mrs Brewer giving her a bleak look.

'No children that I know of. Although he's not exactly the chatty type. He was with Mrs Short for all of half an hour and she still didn't find out where he lives.'

Good for Dr Ramsey, Mildred thought to herself. Frowning she checked the bottle in her hand – Amami setting lotion, the label said. She shook it. Empty. Sliding behind the curtained partition Mildred then emptied some of the sugar and water she had made up earlier into the empty bottle and walked back into the salon, smiling.

'Lucky for you, Mrs Brewer, I've just got a little setting lotion left.'

Sighing with relief, Mrs Brewer leaned back in her seat. 'Thank God for that. I mean, war or no war, you want to look your best.' Her attention was then drawn to Harris as she entered the salon. 'All grown up now, that niece of yours.'

'She should be. She's twenty now.'

'Go on!'

'Yes, time flies.'

Mrs Brewer watched the girl carefully. Enough time had passed, hadn't it? And there was a war on. Things were different now. No one remembered Saville's sordid little patch any more. After all, you had to let bygones be bygones, didn't you? It was only Christian.

'So is Harris going to the Mayor's Ball?'

'There's going to be another ball?' Mildred asked, agog.

Mrs Brewer wriggled her finger in her large right ear to get the water out. 'There're always two balls a year.'

'Yes, but I thought with the war on –'

'Well, it won't be like it was before,' Mrs Brewer replied, miffed, 'but it does a fine job of keeping up morale.'

Whose? Mildred thought. The town's, or yours?

'It's next Saturday, at the town hall, eight o'clock. Of course I'll bring in an invitation if your niece is interested in coming. We need all the pretty faces we can find. You know, the kind of people I mean. People like us, Mildred, not the common sort.'

Welcome back into the fold, Mildred thought bitterly. And it had only taken years. So Saville's indiscretion had been forgotten, had it? Mildred doubted that, but the war had put things into perspective, and besides, Harris was turning into a remarkable young woman. The kind that people couldn't help but notice and be curious about. The type society ladies liked to take under their wing. Despite her background, Harris had none of her grandfather's coarseness, the Scholes scum making no impression on her.

Mildred studied her customer in the mirror. For a second she wanted to tell the woman just what she could do with her invitation, but paused. *She* wasn't interested, but Harris might be. After all, which eligible men would she meet in a hairdressing salon? It was time Harris got out into the world.

'I'll mention it to her,' Mildred said calmly, as though it hardly mattered. 'Who knows, she might already have something on.'

Dear Bonny,

Well, what can I tell you? It's cold, but then I bet it's cold in Wigan too. Is Mam all right? She never writes. As for you, thanks for the letters, they are a real life-saver. I don't want to talk about how it is here, enough to say that I get on fine and have some good mates. A lad from Wigan here, called Hancliffe, sends his love and says he knew you. You'd served him tea once at R. & J. Gorner's. I think it's a bit of a lie myself. How many lads of our sort go into Gorner's? Maybe he just wanted to make your acquaintance – we'll have to see about that.

I wrote to Harris, and she wrote back. Did I tell her how I felt? No – I was always a coward, wasn't I? Talk of leave at the end of March. Do you think I should have a word with her then? War makes you think different, Bonny. Maybe I should just take the risk and hope it comes to something.

As for you, take care and don't do anything Mam would.

Your loving brother,
    Richard

Idiot brother –

Of course you should talk to Harris! Stop messing about. I am enclosing a pic of me – if any lad in your barracks is interested, let me know!

Bye for now,
    Bonny

Dear Richard,

How good to get your letter and yes, I *am* looking forward to seeing you on your next leave. I'm glad you're keeping well. Stay safe, won't you?

Life is so different now. So odd. Mildred copes, of course, and the salon is busy. Can you believe it? We could all be bombed and women still come and fight over the shampoo ration. Saville is having a hard time of it. The noise of the air raids terrifies him and Irma never leaves him. I wonder sometimes who needs who.

Did I mention that she's not been well? Some trouble with her heart, Dr Redmond said. Not that we've seen him for a couple of weeks, since he ran his car into a wall and broke a couple of ribs! Luckily, there's a new doctor in the practice, so I suppose he'll take over for a while.

In answer to your question – of course I think about you! Honestly, what a thing to ask! I was thinking the other day about the time you and Bonny wrecked the bay window. It was so long ago, when we were children.

See you soon,
    Harris

Dear Harris,

I love you. I love you so much I can't breathe when I think about you, or even speak your name. Look, I'm writing like a poet, and that's down to you. Sweetheart,

I want to marry you after the war. I want children with you and a house somewhere out of Wigan. Maybe one with a bay window that our kids can wreck . . .

Say you love me, say you'll never leave me, say you'll wake up next to me always. For ever. For ever . . . Just say you love me, Harris. Write back now and say you love me. Say you love me, darling, now . . .

Always,
Richard

The last was the only letter he wrote but never sent.

'God, it sounds so close,' Mildred said, pulling the door of the air-raid shelter closed after her.

The raid seemed to be almost overhead, bombers making for Liverpool or the River Irwell, hellbent on destroying Manchester's industrial heartland. Flicking on the paraffin lamp she had brought with her, Mildred looked round. Irma was sitting perfectly still, another lamp giving her a ghostly appearance. Beside her, Saville was rocking hysterically, his nails digging into his drawn-up knees.

'War! WAR!' he said repeatedly, his voice rising.

Irma put her arm round him, her own voice tight: 'Hush now, there's no point being a baby –'

'War . . .' he moaned again, his head lolling onto her shoulder. Another plane droned on overhead, bombs falling a way off. At once Saville jumped, his eyes rolling, a smell suddenly filling the air-raid shelter.

'WAR!' he snapped, beside himself, his trousers soiled. 'WAR . . .'

Patiently Irma held on to her brother, Mildred watching.

You never knew who was going to be brave and who wasn't, she thought. Who would have thought that Irma would have turned out to be so tolerant? Irma, who hated mess and weakness; Irma, who had barely tolerated her brother for years. And now here she was, sitting in the semi-dark, holding on to a man who was so scared he had soiled himself.

'Where's Harris?' Mildred asked.

Irma glanced up. 'With Bonny Baker.'

Her sister wasn't *that* changed, Mildred thought wryly. She still managed to get a whole load of disapproval into the girl's name. 'She should be home.'

'You tell her. You can't tell that girl anything nowadays. She thinks she knows it all.' Irma stopped, carefully unfastening Saville's grip on his knees. His fingers were rigid, white-knuckled, his voice a low murmur of terror. 'I suppose I should get on with my knitting.'

It was incredible, Mildred thought. There they were, huddled together in a foul stench, and her sister was talking about knitting.

'What are you making?'

'A jumper for Harris. She won't wear it, of course. It won't be modern enough.'

Silence fell. Saville's wide-open eyes looked around, then closed again as another raid began. This time it was Mildred who spoke first.

'Richard Baker's in France now.' An explosion sounded overhead, Saville whimpering into Irma's neck. 'Harris had another letter from him this morning.' Another explosion, Mildred jumping, then settling herself down again. 'I think that lad is soft on our girl.'

'The Baker boy?' Irma said, her hand closing on her knitting as though she was trying to throttle it. 'Never! He's a pit lad – from Scholes.'

'Our father came from Scholes –'

'Which is something I don't need reminding about,' Irma snapped, another plane flying low overhead, Saville shaking uncontrollably. 'She's grown up fast, has Harris. I don't suppose anyone has talked to her about . . . ?'

'What?' Mildred said, frowning.

Irma gestured to Saville with a jerk of her head. 'About, you know . . . things.'

'What things?'

'Life.'

'*What* about life?' Mildred repeated, baffled.

'You can be stupid at times!'

'You don't explain yourself, that's your trouble.'

Another plane, then silence. Then, far away, another bomb. Saville's eyes were huge with terror, his body racked with shaking. He looked pathetic, his huge moustache out of place on the childlike face.

'Nearly over, Saville,' Irma said, beginning to knit, her head down as she addressed her sister again. 'The birds and the bees.'

'What about them?'

Irma shot her sister a violent look: 'Are you being deliberately stupid?'

'You don't mean . . . ? Oh. God, Irma,' Mildred said, laughing, 'you don't mean talk to Harris about the facts of life, do you?'

'Well, someone has to tell her.'

'Harris is twenty! I imagine she knows about those things.'

Irma flushed. 'Well, I've not told her.'

'I bet Bonny Baker has.'

'I bet *she* has personal experience to call on,' Irma replied sourly.

'You weren't *really* going to talk to Harris, were you?'

'Why not?' Irma asked, her tone reasonable. 'You wouldn't know where to start.'

Another plane flew over, very close, Mildred watching her sister knit. The lamplight flickered around them, the three misfits cramped together, none of them fully understanding what the others were feeling.

'He's asleep,' Mildred said softly, gesturing to Saville.

'Good,' Irma replied, still concentrated on her knitting.

Mildred watched her, curiosity burning into her guts. Did she dare? After so many years, did she dare to ask? They might never get out of the air-raid shelter; they could be killed – how much did one little question matter in such circumstances?

'Did you ever . . .' Mildred tailed off, then began again. '. . . Did you ever sleep with Harry Delaney?'

She expected Irma to react violently, but she just carried on knitting. Her hands worked rhythmically, the wool spooling on her lap.

'Harris will never wear this.'

'Irma, I asked you a question.'

'I heard you.'

'So, what's the answer?'

Only then did Irma look up. Her eyes fixed on her sister, then her gaze moved upwards to the ceiling of the shelter.

Finally she spoke. 'It's over. Listen, there's the all clear.'

There was to be no answer that night.

NINETEEN

One thing Ben Ramsey was sure about – he would have to marry well. If his career was to progress as he wanted he would need a good consort, someone who could mix socially, a woman who would be at home married to a doctor on Rodney Street, the medical Valhalla in Liverpool. He savoured the thought. He had the looks and the charm; he could manage to get there. But not alone.

Hadn't his father always said that it was imperative to marry the right woman? Beauty is all well and good, he had implied, but breeding is what people respect. Besides, you want a respectable mother for your children. He was right, Ben thought – but then his father had always been right.

Yet time had passed and Ben still hadn't found his ideal match. He had fallen in love a couple of times, but to unsuitable women, his feelings running roughshod over his ideals. *But never again*. He had made up his mind to settle down and this time he would pick well.

It was easy for a handsome man to attract attention. Ben had never been short of admirers, seldom run the risk of rejection, and now – in wartime, with few men around – his chances were even greater. Irene Redmond might prove to be a good help too. She seemed very eager to matchmake the eligible bachelor. Maybe he would drop a few hints, Ben thought, let it be known that he was looking . . .

At the very same time Irene Redmond was also thinking about Ben Ramsey's marital status. As she told her injured husband, if she found him a local wife Ben Ramsey would stay in the practice. But Lionel Redmond wasn't sure if he liked the idea of that. Having been used to running things his way he didn't welcome an interloper who was smarter, better-looking and younger.

'I don't like him, Irene.'

'You'd like him a lot better if he had a walleye,' she replied frankly, redoing the bandaging around her husband's corpulent torso. 'Everyone else likes him.'

'All the women, you mean,' Lionel replied, wincing as she pulled the bandages tight. 'Hey, watch out! I can't breathe.'

'For someone who can't breathe, you can talk loud enough,' Irene retorted, sitting down beside his bed and looking at him through her thick glasses. 'Dr Ramsey will be quite a catch for some lucky girl.'

'He's got a big head.'

'So had you, at his age.'

'I never did!' Lionel replied vehemently. 'And I didn't eye up all the women.'

'You didn't have his looks,' his wife said wickedly. 'Besides, you were smitten with me.'

I was smitten with your father's surgery and the thought of an easy practice, more like, Lionel thought to himself. If it had been a question of choice, he would have fallen in love with Mildred Simons. But her father wasn't a doctor . . .

'Go on,' Irene teased him. 'Say what you do when we're alone.'

He flushed. 'Not now!'

'But there's no one about,' Irene insisted, snuggling up to

her husband on the bed. 'The cleaning woman's off, and Dr Ramsey's out. Go on, Lionel, say it.'

He was crimson with embarrassment. 'I love you.'

'I love you, what?'

'I love you, *kiss kiss lips*.'

She squirmed with delight. It was funny, Lionel thought, but you could say something affectionate to a woman *once* and she never forgot it. He supposed that at first it had been cute, but as age had caught up with them the words were now excruciating.

Not that Irene thought so.

'You're my little rabbit baby,' she crooned, tweaking his ear, 'Mummy loves her little rabbit baby.'

He was going to be sick, Lionel thought miserably. One more day of 'kiss kiss lips' and 'little rabbit baby' and he would be taken from the house gibbering. Perhaps he *should* encourage his wife with her matchmaking – anything to stop her constant, cloying attention.

'You know, you *could* be right, Irene –'

'Call me your little kiss kiss lips.'

He swallowed and then struggled manfully on. 'Darling little kiss kiss lips, you might be right – perhaps you *should* find a nice wife for Ben Ramsey. It would be wise, like you said, to keep him here.'

'You think so?' she asked, her eyes blinking behind her heavy lenses. 'But if I looked all over Wigan I could never find another like my little rabbit baby.'

And then she tickled under his arms, Lionel smiling like a man in pain.

That summer was hot under a sky of white clouds, the quiet punctuated by air raids. In the shops the rations were biting hard, though Madge Baker somehow still managed to find enough booze. Bonny was now working at one of the factories given over to munitions work. As for Richard, he wrote from the front, and shared his dreams with his sister.

Bonny had her own dreams, mostly centred around an American she had met on a train going to Manchester. 'How romantic is that?' she asked Harris. 'I could marry him and go and live in New York.' The difference was that Bonny knew her dreams were just that – dreams. Richard was too far gone in love to see reality.

And yet he could not put his feelings down on paper, or even tell Harris when he was home on leave. Instead, the three of them – sometimes four if Bonny had her Yank in tow – would go out dancing, or to the cinema. Together they watched *Gone With the Wind*, Richard teasing Harris about her likeness to Vivien Leigh. But he never crossed the line from friend to lover. He knew from the looks other men gave Harris that he had to move fast, but his lack of confidence stopped him. What if she rejected him? Laughed at him?

But why would she? Richard asked himself. Harris had never been cruel – that wasn't her way. Yet all the reasoning in the world never forced the words from his lips and that June he returned to fight a frustrated man.

Bonny had offered to tell Harris herself, but Richard had forbidden it.

'I'll tell her when the time's right.'

'She'll be dead by then!' Bonny had replied. 'Get in there quick, before someone else does.'

He'd winced. '*Is* there someone else?'

'Not yet, but that's only because she works in a bloody hairdressing salon, surrounded by women! If she was amongst men you wouldn't stand a chance.' She'd paused, considering how nice he was – nice but slow. 'Aw, Richard, get a move on . . .'

'What if she won't have me?'

'She'd be mad.'

'But I'm not her sort. She's got money –'

'And a potty uncle,' Bonny had replied phlegmatically. 'The Simonses are rich, but they're odd. Those two old biddies might think they can pull off a great marriage for Harris, but I wouldn't be too sure. One more flash from Saville, and it's over.'

'Bonny!'

She had pulled a face and then linked arms with her brother. 'Hey, this is me you're talking to, remember? Don't hang back, Richard. If you want Harris – go get her.'

It was a burning summer's day when Ben Ramsey drove out to the Bloody Mountains and parked his old Austin car. Breathing in deeply, he stood on the high ground and looked out. He was depressed by the morning's visit to one of the lads who'd returned home from the war. The man had been young and bedridden, lying paralysed in a makeshift pram, his expression a mixture of bewilderment and despair.

Coming down the Scholes street Ben had noticed the women hanging out their washing, a few children playing hoops on the cobbles. The area was bitingly poor, a vast Bovril sign fading on a street corner. Women with exhausted faces had stood in the doorways, an old man selling tat from his rag-and-bone cart.

'Rag and bone!' he had shouted as he urged his nag on. 'Rag and bone!'

There had been few takers, Ben's appearance attracting more interest. A couple of younger women, on a factory break, had smiled as he passed, another sitting on her stone front step. Slowly she had swung her leg at him, inviting interest, her laughter echoing behind him as he passed . . .

His thoughts came back to the present with a jolt. After the war he would move on, Ben decided, looking out over the town. No more slums, no more desperate people who couldn't even pay the sixpenny visiting fee. No more Wigan. After all, what was there to keep him here?

'Hey, you!' a voice said suddenly.

He turned to see a good-looking young woman staring at him.

'Me?'

Harris walked up to him. 'Have you seen a dog?'

'Have you lost one?'

She nodded, pushing her thick dark hair off her forehead. 'It's a stray that latches itself on to my aunt, visits for a few weeks and then goes off again. I walk it sometimes.'

Again, she looked around and whistled. The noise bored into his brain like a train whistle. *Hurry,* it seemed to say to him, *hurry, catch the moment, time's short.*

'What kind of dog is it?'

She shrugged. 'I dunno. A terrier of some sort. Are you sure you haven't seen it? I'd hate to have to go home without him.'

Ben watched her greedily, propelled into speech. 'Do you live round here?'

She nodded. 'Wigan Lane. Deerheart House. And you?'

'I'm working at Dr Redmond's practice.'

Alerted, Harris stared at him. 'You're Dr Ramsey?' He was inordinately pleased that she knew of him. 'We've heard all about you. How's Dr Redmond doing?'

'Getting better slowly.'

She whistled again, driving the notes into his skull. 'I suppose you'll be looking after my aunt then? Irma Simons.'

He had heard the name *and* the reputation. At once Ben was on his guard. The Simonses were notorious, Irene Redmond had said as much. The father had been a lout and the brother was mentally retarded. And there was more . . .

'Oh well,' Harris said, shrugging as she looked round one last time. 'I'll go and call for him on the other side.'

With that she moved away. Ben watched her. And then, like

a fool, he hurried after her. Already running, Harris was calling loudly for the dog, the heather crushed under her feet, her hair bouncing up and down on her shoulders. It was not just her beauty that had fascinated him, but the fact that she had not been impressed by him. Nor had she wanted to be admired by him.

And yet, mesmerising as she was, she was unsuitable, Ben thought, utterly wrong for him.

So stop running, logic told him. *Stop now. She's not a woman to get close to, not someone who would be a credit to you.* Yet something compelled him to follow her.

Her voice echoed behind her, her whistle calling the dog. And him. Then suddenly the animal broke cover and ran to her. It was giddy, turning round and round, pleased to have fooled her and delighted to have found her. And she laughed, running on, the dog now at her heels.

And the doctor close behind.

PART THREE

Do not go forth today. Call it my fear
That keeps you in the house, and not your own.

Shakespeare – *Julius Caesar*

TWENTY

The thing about money was that people listened to you. They might not *like* you, but they listened. And the more money you had, the more they heard you. Sydney Clough knew about such matters – after all, he was the richest man in Wigan, probably amongst the wealthiest ten in the North-West. The Depression hadn't touched him; he was in beer. And however poor a man got, he usually found enough for a half-pint. Now, Sydney was rich in his own right, but when he had the good fortune to marry into one of the richest brewing families in Ireland, he was made.

His wife, Birdie, was devoted to him. Or so Sydney liked to think. He also liked to think that she was rather stupid, an opinion she did nothing to contradict. Dizzy, silly Birdie, never grew up. Stayed just as Sydney wanted her: the obedient wife who never interfered in business. What was the point? If he asked Birdie anything she would simply say, in her soft Southern Irish tones, 'What do I know, darling?' But then again, Sydney had to admit that Birdie had been a wonderful mother. It was just a shame that they had only had the one child, Eve. Still, better to have one perfect daughter, than a brood of morons.

'Daddy?'

His thoughts were shattered by the very person he had been

considering. 'Hello, sweetheart,' he greeted her warmly. 'What have you been up to?'

Eve Clough sidled into the room, tall and elegant. She had a cool way of speaking – not her mother's lilting brogue; that soft, slow speech that made everyone hang on every word – Eve was quick, direct.

'I was thinking about the party,' Eve replied, perching herself on the side of her father's armchair. 'Can we go?'

'I don't like parties. Besides, there's a war on. People shouldn't be having parties in a war.'

'It's to raise money for the war effort. We *have* to go to this one. It's at the Thorsons'.'

'Oh, Eve, can't we give it a miss?'

'Why should we?' Eve replied abruptly. 'God knows, there's little enough to look forward to.'

Sydney wriggled in his seat. He hated arguments – not at work; that was meat and drink to him – but at home he couldn't stand even a black look.

'Well, you and your mother could go –'

'And have the whole town thinking she was a widow?'

Sydney's eyebrows rose.

'You want to go out with Mummy more. She has admirers, you know.'

Sydney didn't know how he was supposed to respond to this. Birdie had admirers? Dozy Birdie? Ah, but dozy, *pretty* Birdie. He shouldn't forget that.

'Only the other day Mr Tobar was flattering her –'

'Where?'

'In the town. We went out to do some shopping, and he came over to have a word with us.' Eve paused, enjoying stoking her father's jealousy. 'I bet that Mr Tobar would be more than grateful to escort Mummy and me to the Thorsons' party.'

'Lenny Tobar's a Jew!'

'I dare say,' Eve replied calmly, 'but a very rich one.'

Putting on his best vexed tone, Sydney stared up at his

daughter. But it didn't work, because Eve was still perched on the edge of his seat and he had to jerk his head back to look at her.

'I don't want you mixing with the likes of Lenny Tobar –'

'Oh, Daddy, you do worry! Anyway, if it upsets you so much you should come with us. Then Mr Tobar wouldn't be able to pay court to Mummy, would he?'

She had him, and he knew it. Funny, Sydney thought, how even women could sometimes trick you.

Around town there had been a buzz of interest amongst the younger women that had slowly become a hum of concentrated rivalry. Whatever they had first thought, Dr Ben Ramsey wasn't married, or divorced, or even engaged. *He was a free man.* The thought made every unattached woman perk up. The men had been away too long, and it was hard coping with the news of casualties or, worse, deaths. To have a good-looking young man on your doorstep, a professional man, no less, was just too tempting to resist.

The race was on. And suddenly women who had been friends for years became deadly rivals. To marry a doctor would be a coup; to marry a young, good-looking doctor would secure their place in the town's pecking order for life. It was one thing fighting over an indifferent man, it was quite another vying for the attention of a Ben Ramsey.

In the dirty, war-weary, devastated streets, under skies blasted by air raids, in shelters, in terraces, lonely, hopeful women looked to Ben Ramsey and dreamed. They dreamed of him when all the other men were fighting or missing. Those who had lost their men looked at him with envy, those who had no man looked at him with longing. Every woman wanted him, saw him as the only bright spot in a world of trouble. And he was within reach.

Or so they thought.

*   *   *

Nelly Fisher was only sure of one thing – she was going to bag Mr Lacy. If only to spite that bitch Mrs Turner next door. Savagely she cut up the carrots for dinner, although why she bothered she didn't know. Since their son's death. Mrs Barraclough only ever played with her food, and Mr Barraclough ate in his study. It did Nelly good to realise that money brought no happiness. In fact she had seen more fun in the poorest house. Like her mother's, the run-down bed-and-breakfast establishment, which had done quite well before the war.

But not now. There were no commercial travellers any more, only the odd wide boy who stayed and offered her stockings cheap. Give us a kiss and we'll call it quits, they'd say. I'll give you a back hander, Nelly would reply. But she'd take the stockings anyway. Well, a girl had to live by her wits, hadn't she?

Sighing, Nelly looked out over the back garden. Mr Lacy saw her and waved. Oh, he was hooked all right. There was nothing so easy as getting an old man eating out of your hand. The other girls might fancy their chances with Ben Ramsey, but Nelly was no fool. Mr Lacy would do nicely and, besides, once they were married she could always find her amusement elsewhere.

Far away she could just see the top of Mrs Turner's head as she moved out into the Simonses' back garden. So she really thought she could win, did she? Hah! Fat chance. She must be fifty if she was a day. Nelly turned back to the carrots. Mr Lacy had confided that he had a pension, a little nest egg put away.

'Nothing too fancy,' he had told her, 'but enough to keep you comfy.'

Her eyes had widened. 'Oh, that would be so lovely. I want to feel safe.'

His arm had gone round her reassuringly. 'You're safe with me, luv, and you always will be.'

She had pretended that she didn't get on with her mother. Told some wild tale about being thrown out. It had been her mother's idea. 'Tell a man a sob story and you're halfway there,' Mrs Fisher had said. And her daughter had duly obliged. Mr Lacy had fallen for it. In his eyes Mrs Fisher was a cruel harpy, a woman who had used his beloved as a skivvy. It was his duty to get Nelly away from the dismal bed and breakfast. *His duty.* It appealed to his sense of chivalry. Mrs Turner was a fine woman, but she could look after herself. As for his Nelly, who would look after her? No one. Except him.

A bell started ringing behind Nelly's head. Sighing, she looked up. Mrs Barraclough wanted something. Damn it! she thought, wiping her hands. Before long she wouldn't have to keep running after a miserable old woman. She would have a home of her own and that nice little pension to tide her over.

It was a shame that Mr Lacy came with it. But then, nothing was perfect.

The pain started quickly and soon had Irma breathing hard as she leaned against the hall table for support. It was that blasted ginger! she thought. She could never eat ginger. And yet there was something more than indigestion to this. Another pain shook her, made her cry out, Mildred hurrying from the breakfast room.

'God,' she said, running over to her sister and helping her to a seat. 'What is it?'

'Pain,' Irma replied, clutching her chest.

'Where?'

Irma gave her a slow look. 'In my foot! Where d'you think?'

In one quick movement Mildred was on the phone, calling Mrs Redmond at the surgery.

'So your husband's not seeing patients today? . . . What about the other doctor?' There was a murmur down the line. 'Yes, I *do* want him to come out here. As soon as you can. It's my sister's heart.'

Putting down the phone she returned to Irma. Her sister's face was waxy, sweat on her forehead. It's not good, Mildred thought, this is not good at all.

'The doctor's coming.'

'Not that idiot Redmond!' Irma gasped.

'No, love, Dr Ramsey.'

'I don't want to go into hospital.'

'You won't have to.'

'I want to stay here.'

'Yes, Irma, I hear you. You can stay at home,' Mildred assured her, sliding her arm around Irma's shoulder. She expected to be pushed away, but instead her sister leaned against her heavily.

No one said anything else until Ben Ramsey arrived ten minutes later. Walking in, he put his bag on the table and looked at Irma carefully.

'Where's the pain?'

'In my chest.'

'How long have you had it?'

'About twenty minutes.'

'Ever had anything like this before?'

'A couple of times.'

Mildred looked at her, surprised. Irma had never mentioned it.

'Miss Simons,' Dr Ramsey went on, 'I have to examine you now.'

Mildred closed her eyes to the protestations that were sure to follow, but she was wrong. Irma was in too much pain to protest. And besides, she was afraid. Helping her undress, Dr Ramsey examined Irma thoroughly, took her pulse and temperature and then turned back to Mildred.

162

'Your sister's had an angina attack –'

'If it's *my* angina attack, you can tell *me*,' Irma croaked from the settee.

He turned back to her, his voice patient. 'You've had an angina attack. I can give you something for it, to take away the pain, but I would suggest that you take things easy for a while.'

'Hah!' Irma said in response.

Her colour was coming back, Mildred noted – and so was her temper.

Beside her, Ben packed his case, then straightened up and glanced round the room. The Simons money was obvious in the furniture, the rugs, the silverware. No shortages here, Ben thought. But then hadn't he heard as much about the Simons fortune as he had about the Simons scandal? His gaze moved to a side table where there was a photograph of Irma shaking hands with the Mayor. The snob in her heyday.

'Thank you for coming,' Mildred said, smiling as she showed him to the door. 'Will my sister be all right?'

'Your sister's healthy otherwise, so she should make a full recovery. She has to rest though, no strain, no lifting, no emotional distress.'

His attention was suddenly taken by a figure moving out on to the landing at the top of the stairs. A tall, thin man was looking down at them. Then he backed away, startled.

'That's Saville,' Mildred said simply, 'our brother.'

Ben Ramsey knew all about Saville. 'He's an idiot,' Irene Redmond had said simply, then dropped her voice. 'Disgraced the family, did Saville. The Simonses have never been the same since he exposed himself in the local park.' It sounded funny, the way she put it, but seeing Saville it was no longer amusing. He looked hunted, his thin face dressed with its music-hall moustache, giving him the appearance of a child who had raided a costume box. Only Saville wasn't a child.

'He's not been in any trouble for a while. He's on medication,' Mildred went on, knowing that Mrs Redmond would have been sure to pass on the old scandal. 'But the war's not helping him. You know, the bombing and all the noise, it sets him off. Scares him badly.'

Ben studied the practical woman in front of him. 'Do you want some kind of sedation for him?'

Mildred blinked. 'You could give him something?'

In answer, Ben put his bag on the hall table and quickly wrote a prescription, which he then handed to Mildred.

'Give your brother this when he gets agitated. It should help, but it will make him slightly drowsy for an hour or so.'

Mildred took the prescription gratefully. 'Thank you for that. I don't like to see him suffer. He's suffered enough.'

There was a momentary pause, before Ben asked kindly, 'And how are *you*, Miss Simons?'

'Oh, I'm all right. It's all these other folk,' she said briskly. 'We have it easier than most here. God knows how people cope in Scholes. Besides, it doesn't do to complain.'

Their conversation was interrupted by a loud crash from the kitchen, followed by a low curse and the sound of Mrs Turner banging a steel pan on the hob.

A moment later the kitchen door swung open and a dishevelled Harris walked out.

'Really, she's in such a temper!' she said hurriedly to her aunt, then stopped, seeing Ben Ramsey.

A slow smile spread over her face, her eyes warming with pleasure. Mildred caught the look and turned to the doctor with open curiosity. For his part Ben was caught somewhere between joy and guilt. Should he have mentioned to Mildred that he already knew her niece?

But before he could say anything, Harris stepped in. 'How d'you do, Doctor. I'm Harris Simons.'

He took her hand and felt the warmth of her skin against

his palm. Tingling. She was mocking him, pretending that she didn't know him.

'Pleased to meet you,' he replied, but less surely. 'So you're Miss Simons's niece?'

Harris nodded. 'Her one and only.'

She slid her arm round Mildred, her dark eyes fixed on Ben. God, he was good-looking, she thought. All the women were after him. Hadn't she heard them talk in the salon? Hadn't she caught the whispers? He was like something out of a film . . .

'Are you settling in well, Dr Ramsey?'

He flushed, angered by his gaucheness. 'Things are better since I moved from Standish. The Redmonds have made me very comfortable.'

Harris nodded. 'Did you come to see Irma?'

Back on sure ground, Mildred chimed in, 'She had an angina attack.'

'Angina?' Harris echoed.

'She has to take things easy from now on. No lifting, no getting upset.'

'She *thrives* on getting upset,' Harris said simply. 'That's her nature.'

Mildred sighed. 'Then she has to change her nature.'

'Well, you tell her that. I wouldn't dare.'

Ben was watching Harris with fascination. She seemed to be glowing. Was that because she was enjoying her little deception, or because she was just pleased to see him? He hadn't been able to stop thinking of her in the weeks since they had met.

After their first accidental meeting Ben had passed the salon – just as it was closing – waylaid Harris, and asked her to go out with him.

But, to his surprise, she had been evasive, agreeing only to a brief conversation on the phone. She made it seem furtive, exciting, as though they were doing something that was forbidden. And maybe it was, Ben thought. Certainly she wasn't wife material for him. Yet he was sure Harris wasn't the kind of girl to fool around with. Besides, hadn't Irene Redmond said that she was only twenty? And he was thirty-one.

'Never had a boyfriend, that girl,' Irene Redmond had gone on. 'Mind you, what kind of respectable lad would want to get involved with that family?'

Ben had flinched at the words, but had already learned how much such things mattered in a small town. He would have to be careful of the company he kept. If he picked a wife from Wigan, she would have to be someone who could fit in with his grandiose future. Not someone anyone could point the finger at later. Not someone with an uncle like Saville.

But then again, who said anything about marriage? Ben studied Harris out of the corner of his eye. She was a stunner, that wasn't in doubt.

'Perhaps you would like to come for dinner one evening?' Mildred said pleasantly, having noted the attraction between the doctor and her niece. 'Nothing too special, shortages being what they are. But we do all right.'

Smiling, Harris lifted her eyebrows, challenging Ben. Her look seemed to say – *well, do you want to get involved or not?*

'I'd love to come to dinner,' Ben said at last, looking at Mildred. 'It would be an honour.'

Much, much later in her room Mildred remembered the look between Ben Ramsey and Harris. They already knew each other, she realised. Well, everyone had secrets, didn't they? And who was she to judge? Slowly she brushed her hair and then stared into her bedroom mirror. In middle age a bit of flesh was kind to a woman; Irma's leanness was doing her no favours now.

Sighing, Mildred's eyes fixed on the locket around her neck. Thoughtfully she fingered it, the silver cool to her skin. It was the only tangible thing left of William Kershaw; the one present he had given her. And she had never taken it off – even after he had gone. She told everyone that it didn't open, but it had done. Once. Then after William had gone Mildred took it to a jeweller's out of town and had it sealed. Whatever was inside, no one would ever know. Except her.

Still deep in thought, Mildred sat down on the edge of her bed and began, rhythmically, to rub her arms with some home-made lotion. What for, she didn't really know. For a long time she had done it to keep herself young, attractive to a man. But now it was unlikely that any man would come into her life. Funny how the years passed and suddenly what might have been was laughably unlikely.

She would have treasured Harris's confidence. After all, it was obvious that her niece was smitten with the new doctor. But unless Mildred was much mistaken – and she doubted it – Ben Ramsey wasn't the kind of man he pretended to be. There was something about him that unsettled Mildred. He had, she realised with some apprehension, the capacity to be cruel.

Cruelty had figured so much in Mildred's life she had developed a sixth sense about it. She could anticipate it in a person or a situation long before it became apparent. Her father and then her lover had been masters of unkindness, her encounters with them leaving her damaged and bitterly wise. Yet Mildred had learned to accommodate her feelings. Harris however, was another matter.

Her niece was too reckless, too trusting, and too innocent for her own good. And much of that fault must lie at her aunts' doors. An orphan is easily indulged, Mildred thought, a pretty orphan with wit and cheek all the more so. But now Harris had grown up she was more worried than she had ever been. She could guard her niece as a child, but Mildred was all too aware that in an adult love could make a fool out of a genius, and a wasteland out of a kind heart.

TWENTY-ONE

Bonny wasn't having much luck with her hair. It was all right everyone saying that you could roll it up with rags and sugar water overnight and in the morning you would have a head of curls, but they didn't have hair that was as straight as pump water. Hopelessly Bonny looked at her reflection and at the mixture of waves and spiky tufts leaping at right angles from around her face.

'Bloody hell,' Richard said, walking into the mean little kitchen. 'I thought I'd seen some sights, but you take the biscuit.'

'Oh, dry up!' Bonny snapped.

'The last time I saw hair like that it was on a coconut,' he carried on, laughing as he slumped into a kitchen chair. 'It was worth coming home on leave just to see this.'

Flinging a tea towel at her brother, Bonny grabbed a headscarf and tied it firmly over her hair. Then she sat down, glowering at him.

'You going out?'

'I was going to pop up to Simons Coiffeuse.' She always managed to mangle the French word. 'And see if Harris could do something with this.'

'A direct hit with a bomb couldn't do anything with that!' Richard went on laughing.

'One joke goes a long way with you, doesn't it?' Bonny replied, folding her arms and looking round.

In the cold, early December morning the kitchen looked dismal. No sign of Madge, but then she was coming and going at all hours now. A slattern, to hear everyone tell it, and who could disagree? Not her children certainly. But Bonny wasn't going to turn out like her mother – oh no, she'd promised herself a good marriage with a decent man. Which wasn't likely if she didn't get her hair sorted out.

'I wanted to see Harris as well,' Richard said, reaching for his mug of tea.

He had changed too – fitter now, his face more weathered. Never the type to moan, he didn't complain about the conditions he was fighting in, but his dream of rising in the ranks had remained just that. A dream.

'Harris was asking after you last night. Said she was surprised you hadn't called by.'

Richard flushed, then held his sister's gaze. 'I want to talk to her. You know, serious, like.'

'About politics?' she teased him.

'Nah. You know what I mean.'

'Oh,' Bonny teased him, 'you mean love stuff.'

He flushed, looked down. 'It's time I said something. I mean, all that talk before I volunteered, well, it's not come to anything. I'm not a hero, or general material.'

'Just brave.'

He smiled at the compliment. 'Yeah . . . but I can make a good life after the war. It's not going to go on much longer now, everyone says so. Should be over soon and then I'll be back home for good. I hoped I could get my leave over Christmas, but I've got to go back tomorrow. Anyway, it gives me enough time for what I want to do.' He blushed. 'I want to ask Harris to marry me.'

'Wow!'

'You think she'll refuse?'

Bonny widened her eyes. 'Well, it's just, like – well, it's quite a jump from being a good friend to being a husband. I mean, a bit of courting in the middle might ease things along.'

'I mean to court her!' Richard hurried on. 'I just want to ask her to get engaged, and then all that courting stuff can follow.'

'You got a ring?'

'Nah. Should I?'

'Course you should, you daft bugger! What are you going to use when you're down on your knees asking for her hand and there's no ring? You can't draw one on with a laundry pen.'

Frowning, Richard stared at his sister. She was sitting with her arms folded, her headscarf on, looking like a younger version of their mother.

'Take that bloody scarf off!' he snapped. 'I can't talk to you wearing that.'

'Oh, get on with it!' Bonny replied shortly. 'You're always distracted by something, that's your trouble. As for Harris – if you want to propose, get on with it.'

'But I've no ring.'

'Not yet . . .'

Smiling, Bonny got to her feet and beckoned for her brother to follow. Together they walked up to their mother's bedroom and pushed open the door. The curtains were drawn, the bed unmade, a smell of cheap perfume and stale booze coming thick on the air.

'Old bag,' Bonny said as she edged round the bed. Suddenly her foot hit something and made a loud clanking sound.

Richard flinched. 'Is that a bottle?'

'Well, it's not her wooden leg,' Bonny replied smartly, walking over to her mother's dressing table and beginning to search through the drawers.

'Hey, you can't do that!'

Bonny waved aside her brother's protestations. 'Mam

170

doesn't know what she's got. But I do. There's a ring somewhere that some Irishman gave her . . .' Bonny kept on rummaging.

'Wouldn't she have flogged it by now?'

'Nah, she said she was keeping it as a nest egg.'

'We can't take it!'

Bonny spun round. 'What has Mam ever given you? Eh? Good food? Caring? A nice home? Nothing! So don't get sentimental now, Richard. You can't go to Harris empty-handed. She knows you're poor, but you have to look like you've made an effort.' Turning back to the drawer she kept on rummaging. 'I know it's in here somewhere.'

Behind her, Richard sat down heavily on the bed, looking round. 'I remember this room so well. When we were kids . . . You remember the men she had in here?'

Bonny nodded, but didn't stop her search.

'I remember all those comings and goings. How she used to put her belt on the door handle to let us know there was someone in with her . . . They'd all talk about her at school: Madge the Slag, Boozy Baker . . . She's not so much for the men now, though, is she? More for the booze.'

'The men went when her looks did,' Bonny replied, finally pulling out a tiny box, her voice triumphant. 'Got it!'

Together they stared at the small square box.

Bonny nudged her brother. 'Go on, open it.'

'You do.'

'No, you.'

'I can't –'

'Oh, here, let me!'

Taking in a breath, Richard flipped up the lid. The box was empty.

'The bloody old cow!' Bonny said, throwing it across the room. 'She hasn't even got anything left to steal.'

*   *   *

It was pouring that afternoon, an air raid sounding around three. In town women ran with their children to the nearest shelter, Bonny bumping into Harris as they found the shelter in Herald Street.

'Hey, I was coming to see you,' Bonny said, pointing to her hair. 'What a mess, eh?'

Harris pulled a face, letting a fat woman pass with her crying son. After another moment they huddled in the shelter together, pulling their coats around their knees. The siren sounded overhead, the fat woman rocking her son and crooning to him.

'It smells down here,' Bonny said quietly.

'You're right there,' Harris replied, looking at her friend excitedly. 'I've got something to tell you.'

'Scandal?'

'In a way.'

'Great,' Bonny said delightedly, leaning closer to catch everything Harris whispered.

'I'm in love.'

Bonny smiled, almost giddy. Oh, this was going to be easy. Harris loved Richard! Their childhood dreams of romance were finally coming true. OK, so there weren't any White Knights, but Bonny's own American and Harris's Richard would do just fine. Bonny stared at Harris, hardly able to stop grinning. When they all met up tonight Richard would propose, Harris would accept – and if he didn't have a bloody ring, so what?

Smiling, Bonny stared into Harris's face as the siren wailed overhead. 'Took you long enough.'

'Huh?'

'Oh, go on, I won't interrupt again.'

'It was so sudden,' Harris went on, her mouth only inches from Bonny's ear. No one was to overhear what she said. 'I just looked at him and knew . . . Just like that. Can you imagine?'

Bonny frowned. Had Harris seen Richard already on this leave? She must have done. 'Go on.'

'He's so handsome. All the women want him.'

This was news. Richard was OK to look at, but hardly Errol Flynn.

'But I'm going to get him, Bonny. *Me*.'

'I think you already have.'

It was Harris's turn to be surprised. 'What? You know Ben?'

And then Bonny knew that Harris wasn't talking about her brother. This had nothing to do with Richard. Bonny had been right all along. Her brother *had* left it too late. Another man had come in and stolen the prize from under his nose whilst he had hesitated. Bonny had been right and, God, how she wished she hadn't been.

'He's so handsome. You must have heard about him,' Harris went on, drumming the words into her friend's skull, inflicting pain after pain without even knowing it. 'He's Dr Redmond's partner.'

'Ben Ramsey?' Bonny croaked.

'Yes,' Harris replied, her eyes brilliant.

She was so beautiful, Bonny thought – even more beautiful now she was in love.

'Well, actually Ben's not Dr Redmond's partner yet, but he will be. He's ambitious, I know that much.' She paused, dropped her voice even lower, the fat woman shifting her position, another woman knitting, the click-clacking of her needles echoing inside Bonny's head. 'It's early days, but I know one thing for sure. I'm going to marry Ben Ramsey.'

'Marry him?' Bonny repeated, her eyes fixed ahead.

She wanted to shake Harris then. To say, 'how could you? How could you go and fall in love with a stranger, when all along Richard has loved you? Richard, who never judged you, who doesn't give a damn about your background or your potty uncle. Richard, your pal . . .' But how could she say anything like that? After all, her brother had never spoken up. Never let on. Never staked his claim or said, 'I love you, Harris Simons.

I want you.' He had just kept silent. For too long. So how could she blame Harris now for what she was about to do to her brother? It wasn't Harris's fault that she was going to pull a razor across his heart.

Suddenly overhead the siren wailed again, Bonny putting her hands over her ears, Harris following suit. Little did she know that Bonny was trying to block out her words. Not the sound of the German engine overhead, but the sound of lost hopes falling as deadly as bombs.

TWENTY-TWO

Sitting in his room Saville looked at his reflection and wondered what he would say to the stranger. He had been told by Irma to be on his best behaviour. Ben Ramsey was a doctor, his sister had said. You have to be polite. Otherwise . . . She had let the intimation hang, but Saville's imagination had run riot from that moment. Was the doctor coming to have a look at him? Was he going to judge him? *Were they finally going to send him away?*

It had been threatened before. Especially after Saville had disgraced himself in the park. Irma had told him then that if he ever did anything like that again he would be put in a home. In a home, with the crazies, she had said. And she had touched her forehead, wiggling her finger around. With the crazies . . .

He didn't want to go with any crazies, Saville thought, brushing his hair frantically. He was better now; he'd been good for a long time. Didn't even want to go off to the park, not now he had his medication . . . He knew he'd been silly, but that was a long time ago. He was better now . . . Saville paused, staring into his reflection, his eyes bewildered. This was a new doctor, Irma had said. So did a new doctor mean trouble for him? Would a new doctor do what the old doctor hadn't? *Put him with the crazies?*

'I don't want to go!'

Harris walked in, frowning. 'What?'

Panicking, Saville turned and gripped her hand, his eyes filling. 'Don't let them send me away!'

'No one's sending you away, Saville,' she said sweetly, sitting next to him. Slowly she picked up his special comb and tidied his moustache, pulling a face as she did so. 'It's a very fine moustache you have, Mr Simons.'

Saville smiled, pinked up.

'In fact, no one has one as fine as yours.'

He was relaxing, Harris could see that. Whatever had spooked her uncle had passed.

'Now, are you ready? Dr Ramsey's coming to dinner.'

At the mention of his name Saville leaped off the bed and huddled in the corner.

Confused, Harris approached him cautiously. 'What is it?'

'I'm not going with the crazies!'

'Which *crazies*?'

He was huddled against the wall, his eyes petrified. 'The crazies in the home. The home they're going to send me to. Irma said they would. She said they would one day. And now there's a new doctor –'

'Ben Ramsey is a friend of mine, Saville. He's not going to do you any harm. He's not going to harm *any* of us.' Slowly Harris led him away from the wall and then brushed some imaginary fluff off his shoulder. 'You want to know a secret?'

Saville nodded, goggle-eyed.

'I like Dr Ramsey,' Harris admitted, then added quickly, 'Not as much as I like you. But I like him a lot.' She put her index finger over Saville's mouth. 'Promise me, not a word to anyone? Especially not Irma?' He nodded eagerly. 'I'm going to marry Ben Ramsey, you see if I don't. I'm going to have the biggest wedding Wigan's ever seen. Every woman in this town will envy me, hate me for bagging him.' She smiled, then looked hard into her uncle's face. 'And no one's putting you with the crazies, Saville. Not whilst I'm here. No one will hurt you whilst I'm around.'

Silly little fool, Mrs Turner thought bitterly as she served the makeshift dinner. It was all right putting out the best silver and china, but that didn't make anyone forget about Saville. She eyed up Harris carefully, then looked over to Ben Ramsey. You think you can bag him, do you? Fat chance.

'Mrs Turner works wonders with the rations,' Mildred said pleasantly, trying to ignore the way the housekeeper slapped down a bowl of beetroot on the table. 'And Mr Lacy's so kind about vegetables.'

There was a strangled cry as Mrs Turner left the room.

Raising her eyebrows, Mildred continued, 'So, how are you liking Wigan, Dr Ramsey?'

'Please call me Ben,' he replied, Harris staring at his profile as though he might disappear if she looked away. 'I like it a lot. There are some sad cases, though – lads sent back from the war injured. Some crippled; paralysed. Some my age . . . It makes me feel guilty, as though I should be fighting like all the rest.'

Harris's admiration was boundless. What a noble man, she thought, not only to feel such things, but to confess them. A hero, in his own way.

'You're not fit to fight with your medical background,' Mildred replied, not at all impressed by his openness. What was clever about putting in words something that everyone was thinking?

'I'd like to fight!' Saville said suddenly, from down the table.

Smiling patiently, Ben turned to him. He had to admit that he had been surprised to find Saville Simons invited to the dinner table. Although he *was* a member of the Simons family, after all. Yet if they had wanted to impress him, wouldn't it have been better not to have included Saville? After all, his presence was a constant reminder of his sordid past – something which did nothing for, and actually counted *against*, the family.

'I want to fight!' Saville went on, banging the handles of his knife and fork on the table top.

'Careful, Saville, calm down,' Mildred said patiently. 'You don't like guns, Saville. The noise they make frightens you. It makes you jump, doesn't it?'

He looked down, crushed. 'But I *could* fight.'

'You could,' Harris said emphatically. 'I bet that you could rescue me from a dragon any day.'

Saville looked up, luminous with delight. 'I would! I would!'

'You would pierce it through the throat until it bled to death, wouldn't you, Saville?'

'Harris,' Mildred said patiently, looking towards Ben, 'don't forget we have a guest.'

'I didn't forget,' Harris replied, holding Ben's gaze for a scintillating moment. 'Would *you* rescue me from a dragon, Dr Ramsey?'

The flirtation caught Mildred in the short ribs. She paused, holding her last forkful of beetroot halfway to her mouth, her eyes moving from the flushed face of Harris to the young doctor.

It was the housekeeper who finally broke the spell.

'Pudding,' Mrs Turner said suddenly, slamming down another plate onto the table. A huge round lump of steaming suet sat like a bleached frog in front of all of them, Mildred trying hard to keep a straight face.

'It looks lovely,' she lied, staring, unblinking, at the leaden mound. 'Is it your own recipe?'

Mrs Turner wasn't even grazed by the sarcasm. 'My mother made it and passed the secret on to me.'

We can only hope it stops there, Mildred thought to herself, digging a serving spoon into the boiling mass.

'Currant pudding, anyone?'

Harris stared hard at the dessert and then looked at Mrs Turner. '*Currant pudding?* Did you stand at the top of the stairs and throw the fruit in?'

Mrs Turner had had enough. 'I do what I can on the rations! No one else could make a dinner party out of nothing.'

Throwing Harris a bleak glance, Mildred hurried to reassure her. 'You did very well, Mrs Turner.'

'Indeed,' Ben agreed, his expression unreadable as a plateful of pudding was laid in front of him. 'Umm. It smells . . . delicious.'

Mollified, Mrs Turner left the dining room.

Saville leaned forward and sniffing the pudding. 'It smells like everything else she cooks.'

'Ssssh! She'll hear you,' Mildred replied, turning back to Ben. 'You don't have to eat it.'

'Oh, yes you do,' Harris said, teasing him. 'You have to eat every morsel.'

What the hell had got into her? Mildred wondered. She was acting like a giddy teenager. She had never seen Harris behave like this before. Usually she was cool with boys. But then again, this was hardly a boy. This was a handsome man of thirty, with she guessed a goodly amount of experience with women. The kind of man Harris had fantasised about since childhood. Oh God, Mildred thought. Save us from Prince Charming.

'How's your sister?' Ben asked, aware of Mildred's discomfort and trying to ease the tension.

'Much better. Irma sends her apologies. Said she was sorry she couldn't join us for dinner –'

'She never eats downstairs,' Saville said, shovelling the pudding into his mouth. 'She eats with me, upstairs.' His voice speeded up, the food spitting out as he talked. 'She looks after me, you know. Keeps an eye on me all the time. Says she'll put me with –'

'Saville, calm down,' Harris said gently. 'Everything's OK, honestly.'

He paused, then breathed in, then turned back to his pudding. Panic over. For Saville, at least.

The dinner was turning into a small pocket of hell, Mildred realised. But then again, what had she expected? They were hardly a normal family. Ben Ramsey would probably go back to the Redmonds later and tell them all about it; have a good laugh at their expense.

Still, better to keep struggling on. 'So are you going to make Wigan your home?'

Ben nodded. 'For a while.'

'Then what?' Mildred asked, pushing him.

'I have ambition.'

I bet you do, she thought. 'Ambition's good. But then that does depend on what your ambition is. I mean, you have ambition to achieve *what*?'

He shifted in his seat, suddenly aware that this cosy-looking woman was actually sharp. 'I want to have rooms on Rodney Street one day.'

Ah, Mildred thought, the good doctor craves the smart practice, the golf club membership, the big car – and the right wife.

'What's Rodney Street?' Harris asked innocently.

'Liverpool's answer to Harley Street,' Mildred retorted, turning back to Ben. 'That would be a fair assessment, wouldn't it?'

He nodded. 'It's what I'm aiming for.'

'You can do it!' Harris chimed in, hopelessly eager.

Slowly, Ben turned to her, thinly disguised irritation under the attraction. 'You hardly know me, Harris, how can you know that?'

'I just do,' she went on, her face flushed with giddiness. 'I bet you could do anything you set your mind to.'

And that was the moment Mildred knew. That was the moment that Ben Ramsey saw Harris and realised that she was besotted with him. She was smitten. Hooked. In the bag.

Embarrassed by her attention, he was plainly uncomfortable, but instead of directing his conversation to Mildred, he turned to Harris. And smiled. His smile was one of control, of certainty. His smile was inviting and as dangerous as a land mine. Welcome, it said, come on. You might be lucky – or you might get blown to bits.

And then it passed. He was the handsome young doctor again, leaving Mildred wondering if she had imagined it.

'Harris, honestly,' Ben said, his tone light, 'you flatter me too much.'

'Can a person be flattered *too* much?' she replied, her head on one side.

'I imagine you've grown up with flattery,' he answered, playing the good guest. 'A pretty girl usually does.'

It was a kind comment, but Mildred was unsettled. Pushing aside her pudding she looked at the handsome couple in front of her. Harris was no longer aware of her aunt, and when Mildred studied Ben Ramsey she could see that he was mesmerised. He might fight it, but he was falling for Harris.

Which could be good news, Mildred thought. On the other hand, if Ben Ramsey *ever* hurt her niece he was going to wish he had never been born.

TWENTY-THREE

Richard had been standing at the corner of the road for nearly an hour, waiting. In a few hours' time his leave was up and he would have to go back to fight. He dreaded it, and then again, he didn't care. Did it matter what happened to him any more? After all, he had thrown away his reason to fight, his reason to hope, his chance of a good future.

It was his own stupid fault, no one else's. Bonny had warned him often enough – 'Talk to Harris, tell her you love her.' But he hadn't listened. Wasn't that the difference between the winners and the losers? The men who made generals, and the ones who ended up down the bloody pit coughing up their guts at forty? He was a no one, a wet, ineffectual private with no chance of catching a girl like Harris. But he *could* have done, if he had followed up on his luck – the luck that had made them friends for so long. He could have changed that friendship, nourished it, made her love him. After all, he knew everything about Harris and whatever she was, or whatever she did, he would always love her. Didn't she know that? How couldn't she have known that?

Because you never bloody told her . . . And now some doctor, some flash bloody professional man had swept her off her feet. She was in love. Bonny had told him – after he had forced her to. Told him because she didn't want him to make a fool of himself.

'Don't, Richard, please.'

'I have to talk to her,' he had said helplessly. 'I have to ask her to marry me.'

'No, don't!' Bonny had snapped, desperate to save his pride, if nothing else. 'It's no good, it's too late. She's fallen for someone else.'

He hadn't expected the pain. Couldn't imagine how people lived with it. And it was no good Bonny saying that maybe Harris's infatuation would blow over. Ben Ramsey didn't look the type to be serious, she said. In the end Harris might get hurt. Then you'll have another chance.

But he didn't believe her, and although he hated the idea of Harris loving someone else, he didn't want her to be hurt. Didn't want to have to piece together broken remnants of the beautiful original. And besides he knew, *knew,* that he had missed his chance once and for all. The girl he had rescued from the bullies, the girl he had called into the night garden, the girl who had made up a hundred crazy stories, was gone. She had walked away from him.

And now what was left? Only a speech he had prepared too late. Which said too little. And had been held back too long.

The winter snows came down hard and fast, the terraces whitened, people struggling with the lack of food and coal, the air raids almost nightly. Some Christmas it was going to be, Bonny thought to herself. The hardship was felt most down in Scholes. Bonny was working at the tea shop in the day and at the munitions factory at night. She said she did it to help the war effort. In truth, it was to keep out of the way of her mother and to get over the fact that her American boyfriend hadn't written.

And she was late with her period.

'What the hell's the matter with yer?' Madge said, her voice slurred as she bumped into a chair in the kitchen. The sleeve of her blouse was torn, a grubby bra strap showing. 'Yer want to cheer up. Men don't like a sour face.'

'Oh, go to hell!' Bonny exploded, pulling on her coat and walking out into the night.

It was cold and she walked fast. It wasn't important where, only that she kept walking to try to clear her head. Richard's leave was over; he was going back that night. Where he was now Bonny had no idea, but suspected that he was waiting until Madge left the house. Shivering in the cold, Bonny dug her hands deep into her pockets and walked on. Passing a man she knew, she nodded briefly and then hurried by, deep in thought. Why the hell had she slept with the American? Had she no sense? God, she hated this bloody town, this bloody war, this bloody life . . . Skirting some bomb-damaged houses, she made for the centre of Wigan. There would be people there, wouldn't there?

But did she want to see people? Bonny stopped, lighting a cigarette and inhaling deeply. One thing the Yank had been good for – fags. Oh, and sex . . . She thought of him lying on top of her, his hands running over her breasts, between her legs. The way he had held on to her as though she mattered. And that feeling, that warm rush she'd felt as he entered her. It had been good, his teeth biting softly on her bottom lip, her back arching to take him in . . . Bonny stubbed out her cigarette briskly. No good thinking about sex. He'd been a bastard, like all men. Her mother was right. God, she never thought she'd say that, but Madge was right about men.

Slowly Bonny turned for home. Her mother was sozzled already, but not drunk enough. Madge would go out again, beg or do whatever it took to get more drink. And then come back late. Or not at all. Hadn't she passed out on the pavement of Boundary Street only the other night?

Oh, get a grip, Bonny told herself. You're not your mother

and you never will be . . . She walked on quickly. There was time for her to grab a bite to eat, make a sandwich for Richard and then go with him to the station; try and make him feel wanted, see him off. It was the least she could do for him. After all, hadn't she been the one to smash his dream?

Bonny stopped, hanging her head. But what choice had she had? Let her brother make a fool of himself with Harris? Let his hurt be worsened by embarrassment? Not bloody likely! It had been hard to hurt him, but she had done the only thing she could to lessen Richard's humiliation.

The trouble was that humiliation seemed to be the least of Richard's problems. She hadn't known just how infatuated her brother had been with Harris. His shock on knowing that he had lost her was frightening. His colour had gone; he had even faltered and sat down heavily, as though his legs couldn't hold him up any longer. She had tried to soften the blow, to tell him that he might have a chance later, if it didn't work out with Ramsey. But the words hadn't made any impact – she could see that. Her brother had turned off, imploded inside himself. His face was a mask, devoid of expression, his voice flat. And the severity of his reaction had frightened her.

Reaching the end of her street, Bonny stopped. It was impossible to tell if there was light in her house, because the blackout curtains masked any illumination. Slowly she looked round at the bleak terrace, the blacked-out windows, the walls bellied out in places with subsidence. It was a hole. And she had dreamed of going off to New York with her Yank. What a fool she'd been, what a poor bloody fool . . .

Taking a deep breath, Bonny was relieved to find the house empty as she entered. In the kitchen Madge had evidently tipped over her tea, the newspaper that served as a tablecloth soaking up the liquid. Disgusted, Bonny picked up the paper and screwed it up, dumping it into the overflowing bin.

Something was wrong. She could sense it. Bonny's ears pricked. She listened. Silence. Slowly she turned and looked round the room. Nothing was changed. But it *was* different. Something was different. Her skin crawling, Bonny moved out into the cramped lobby and gazed up the dark stairwell. Flicking on the dim bulb, she began to climb.

Her breathing quickened, fear like fire in her veins. Oh God, she thought, oh God . . . When she reached the top of the stairs she paused. The laundry basket was full of clothes, an unemptied chamber pot outside her mother's room. Go on, she told herself, go on. Extending her hand, Bonny turned the handle and walked in. The room was empty.

Sighing, she backed out, but felt no relief. And then she looked across the landing. Slowly, she moved towards the back room – Richard's room. The house was silent, only her breathing sounding loud as she opened the door. Her eyes took a moment to adjust to the darkness, and then she saw, in the dim light from the landing, her brother's body on the bed.

'Jesus! NO!' Bonny screamed, flicking on the light.

There was blood everywhere. It had poured and was still pouring from the slashes on his wrists. It had soaked the bed sheets and blankets and dripped onto the floor where Bonny slipped on it as she ran over to her brother. Frantically, she cradled his head and then began screaming, over and over again, knowing that through the paper-thin walls someone would hear her.

She screamed like an animal, Richard unmoving in her arms. Soon her clothes were sticky with his blood, his body heavy against her as she tried to stanch the flow. His blood was warm, the smell thick in her mouth, but she kept screaming. And then, as an air-raid siren started up, she heard the sound of footsteps running up the stairs.

It was two days before Christmas.

TWENTY-FOUR

No one told me why Richard tried to commit suicide. I learned the reason many years later and then it was too late. Timing in death is as important as timing in life, I suppose.

Oddly enough, what I remember most was not the horror of Richard's attempted suicide, but the way Bonny arrived at our house that night in her old winter coat. Upstairs Saville had his radio on and they were playing Bing Crosby singing 'White Christmas' . . . She stood in the middle of our dining room whilst Mildred poured her a brandy and said nothing.

A moment passed, another, and then Bonny took off her coat – and I saw her dress.

It had been an ordinary grey wool dress, but now it was clotted with Richard's blood, splatters extending down to her wool stockings and one tiny droplet – just one – on the white collar around her neck. Richard's blood. So much of it. I didn't think that anyone could lose so much blood and live. And after she had taken off her coat Bonny just stood there, in that damned dress, and looked at me as though it was all my fault.

And I didn't know why. Then.

TWENTY-FIVE

Mrs Turner was wringing an apron in her hands, her face red raw, her eyes blank with shock as she stood in the kitchen, shaking under the overhead light.

'Richard tried to commit suicide!' She shook her head, looking at Mildred with flat eyes. '*Why?* He slashed his wrists and Bonny found him –'

'I know,' Mildred said calmly, 'we're sorting it all out.'

'She was screaming like a mad thing and the watchman heard her. They got an ambulance, took Richard to the infirmary.' Mrs Turner clutched Mildred's hand, leaning towards her. 'Why would he do it? He's not a coward. People will say that, though, won't they? They'll say he didn't want to go back to the front when his leave was over. They'll say –'

'Nothing,' Mildred replied flatly. 'They'll say what we *want* them to say.'

Leaving Mrs Turner in the kitchen, Mildred moved back into the drawing room. Picking up the phone she hesitated, and then dialled Lionel Redmond's number.

He came round fast. He had put on more weight and was puffing like an ox when he entered the drawing room. Heavily he sat down, another chair giving up the ghost.

'Richard has tried to kill himself –' Mildred began.

'Oh, my Lord!'

'You and I are friends, Lionel, we always have been . . .'

'Indeed, indeed,' he agreed eagerly.

'We have to cover this up. Otherwise you know as well as I do that Richard will be branded a coward. Maybe even a deserter.'

Dr Redmond was torn between wanting to help the woman he admired and being put slap-bang on the spot. If anyone found out that he had pulled strings it might go badly for him.

'Oh, come on, Lionel!' Mildred snapped. 'Stop thinking about your own blasted skin. We can pull this off. It's wartime – no one will bother to check the facts.'

He flushed, ashamed that his cowardliness had been so easy to spot. 'Why did he do it?'

'I don't know. Neither does Mrs Turner. Mind you, there's always been trouble in the Baker family. Madge – well, everyone knows how she is.'

'Quite.'

Mildred held his gaze for a long instant. '*Can* you cover it up? Say Richard had an accident? Well, can you?'

And so together they concocted a story that Richard had been knocked down by a van in the blackout. An unfortunate thing to happen, but not something scandalous. By doing so, Richard dodged what would have been the inevitable psychiatric examination. It would have been bad on his record, they all knew that. What Mildred *didn't* know was why he had tried to commit suicide in the first place. Easy-going, happy-go-lucky Richard – what had changed him so much? *Was* it the war? Or something else entirely?

So whilst Richard was recovering from his 'road accident' Mildred called Bonny in to see her. Harris had been hysterical, desperate to see Richard, but his sister had prevented it. And Mildred wanted to know why.

It was obvious at once that Bonny didn't want to see her. She came into Deerheart House like a stranger, no smiles, no jokes. Baffled, Mildred's mind went back, seeing Bonny as a child, her and her brother crashing through the bay window. Or playing conkers in the garden under Harris's window. Two slum kids making a friend out of the rich kid with the odd family.

To Mildred, Bonny had always been admirable in a way. With a family background that should have made her turn out bad, Bonny had somehow managed to claw her way through, still grudgingly supportive of the odious Madge and clinging to some vestige of respectability. And still Harris's closest friend. But not lately – not since Richard had tried to kill himself. Instead she had actively avoided Harris.

Now, Mildred thought, why was that?

'Come and sit down here,' Mildred said kindly, 'next to me.'

Bonny took the seat as though it might at any moment electrocute her.

'I like you, I always have,' Mildred went on. 'I miss your visits and I know Harris does. It was terrible about Richard, and I can't imagine how much it must have affected you, how difficult it must have been finding him –'

'He's fine now,' Bonny replied brusquely. 'But I wanted to say thanks. Thanks for what you did. I mean, you know, stepping in like that and covering it all up.' She hesitated, awkward on the edge of her seat.

'How's he doing?'

'Not bad. At home now.'

Mildred's eyebrows rose. 'Is that wise?'

'Richard's fine. It wasn't as bad as it looked. He'll be going back to fight soon.'

'But –'

She cut Mildred off. 'He wants to. He can't believe what he did. Ashamed, I think.' She bit her bottom lip hard. 'He wants to fight, make himself into some kind of hero. You know, make up for what he did.'

Mildred paused. 'Why did he do it?'

Bonny shrugged. 'I dunno.'

'Yes, you do.'

She shook her head. 'Nah, not me.'

The clock on the mantelpiece chimed twice. Between them the silence intensified.

It was Mildred who spoke first. 'What about some tea?'

'I should go home.'

'Bonny,' Mildred reached out and tapped the back of her hand, 'you need support –'

'I don't need anything!' the girl snapped. 'I'm fine, just fine. Soon as Richard goes back to fight, it'll all be over. I mean, he might make a bloody general after all! Or he might get killed. Either way, you get on with it. After all, he'd be dead now if I hadn't found him.' She stared at Mildred, her eyes hostile. 'I know what you're thinking – how could I be such a bitch? Well, maybe I need to be. You know, in case he does go and get killed.'

'Oh, Bonny,' Mildred said, her tone soft. 'Isn't life a bugger?'

Bonny smiled, nodded once, then suddenly hung her head.

Mildred put her arm round her. 'People are responsible for their *own* lives, Bonny. And for what they do.'

'I never thought Richard would try and kill himself!' she said, her tone hard. 'It was bloody cowardly.'

'War is frightening –'

'WAR!' she snorted, sitting upright. 'If only it *was* the bloody war. I could understand that. I wouldn't want my sodding head blown off. I wouldn't want to be out there, in all the muck and filth, away from home. Who would? If he'd deserted I would have hidden him.' She looked at Mildred defiantly. 'Yeah, I would! Because I love him, because he's my brother. Because it's not really our bloody war, it's the politicians' war. I would have hidden him and lied to everyone – and done it gladly.'

'So if it wasn't the war, what was it?'

'Love,' Bonny said, spitting out the word. 'He wanted to die for love.'

Surprised, Mildred looked away. 'Had he met someone? Someone who hurt him?'

Bonny laughed suddenly. 'Yeah, he'd met someone and yeah, she hurt him.'

'Does she know that he tried to kill himself? And why?'

'She knows what he did. But not why.'

Mildred frowned and looked back to Bonny. 'Shouldn't someone tell her?'

'You think she's a right to know?'

'Of course!'

'Even if she wasn't in love with Richard? Even if she never knew that he loved her? Even if she was besotted by someone else?'

'But *why* didn't she know that Richard loved her?'

'Because he was a coward and he didn't speak up,' Bonny answered, looking at the clock when it chimed the quarter-hour. 'I should go –'

'No, Bonny,' Mildred said, catching hold of her arm. 'I want to understand and I don't. I want the whole story. Who's the girl?'

'You have to ask?' Bonny countered. 'Do you *really* have to ask?'

Realisation came to Mildred in that instant. 'Harris?'

Bonny nodded. 'Richard's loved her for years. Talked about it for longer than I can remember. I kept saying – tell her, take her out, let her know you want to be more than friends –'

'*Harris?*' Mildred repeated, staring into the fire.

'Sorry it's come as such a shock,' Bonny said bitterly. 'I know you wanted a grand match, not some slut's offspring. Not some snotty-nosed slum fodder –'

'Now cut that out!' Mildred snapped, her eyes flaming. 'You were never made to feel anything other than welcome here.'

'Irma hated us –'

'Irma hates everyone!' Mildred countered. 'You weren't any different to anyone else. But me, I always liked you around. I wanted you around to be with Harris.' She paused. 'There's nothing wrong with Richard –'

'If Harris doesn't marry him.'

'Now look, young lady!' Mildred said, her tone unexpectedly cold. 'You might have a chip on your shoulder, but I didn't put it there. My own father came from Scholes and I've never forgotten it. Don't you dare to judge me! Irma might have made a career out of being a snob, but I didn't. How could I – in all honesty – after what's happened in our family?'

'But you've got money –'

'And Saville. And believe me, if you're embarrassed by your mother, I know the feeling.' Mildred leaned back in her seat and folded her arms. 'What a mess – Richard in love with Harris. No wonder you didn't want to see her.'

'I can't tell her why he did it. Richard made me promise I wouldn't.' Bonny relaxed suddenly, resting her head on the back of the sofa, her legs stretched out in front of her. 'You know, I always thought you looked down on us.'

'Oh, grow up, love,' Mildred replied gently. 'Richard's a good boy, always was. I know how he always looked out for Harris. He might have made a good partner for her.'

'I thought you wanted a great match.'

'Irma wants a great match for Harris.'

'And Harris wants a great match for Harris.'

Slowly Mildred turned her head to look at Bonny. 'Go on.'

'Nothing . . .'

'Get on with it! I've no patience left.'

'Is this in confidence?'

'No, I'm going to sell it to the *Wigan Herald* tomorrow! Yes, it's in confidence, Bonny, now get on with it.'

'Harris is in love with Ben Ramsey.'

'Oh, I know that she *thinks* she is,' Mildred replied dismissively. 'But it's just a crush.'

193

'She wants to marry him.'

Mildred jerked up in her seat. 'Marry him!'

Bonny nodded her head emphatically. 'She told me that she was going to marry him. And she meant it. I could tell.'

'Ben Ramsey won't marry someone like Harris. He wants the right wife, someone with a respectable, rich family behind them. We have the money, but not the right pedigree.' Mildred stared into the fire, stubby blue flames picking at the bank of coal. 'It'll blow over.'

Bonny shook her head, her tone steady. 'Nah, it won't.'

'You're right,' Mildred agreed reluctantly, 'it damn well won't.'

TWENTY-SIX

Dandy Gilburn was standing by the corner, by the Old Lion pub. The night was moonless, the street empty. Only a little while ago there had been an air raid; soon the all clear would sound. He had to work fast. Whistling three times, Dandy waited, his angular body pressed against the wall. After a moment, an answering whistle sounded back, then footsteps.

Without looking back, Dandy made his way up Vauxhall Road and then turned into Mill Yard. He knew full well that someone was following him in a car, its headlights turned off as it crept along the dark street. Finally Dandy stopped and opened the back door of a lockup backing on to a seedy row of houses, many empty.

'You there?' someone whispered. 'Oi, Gilburn, you there?'

Dandy's feral face poked out of the lockup. 'Keep yer bloody voice down!' he hissed. 'Got everything?'

A large heavyset man materialised out of the darkness, Dandy's torch picking out the sharp suit and shined shoes.

'Now you don't want to go using that tone of voice with me, Gilburn, do you? There's some might say you were getting a bit above yourself.'

'Aye, and them's the ones that's doing well enough not to mind a tone of voice,' Dandy replied.

'I've got whisky and some brandy.'

'That last lot could rip the skin of an alligator.'

'What can I say? It's the war.'

'What are they putting in it?'

'Why should you care, Gilburn? You're getting enough out of it.'

'I don't want to kill anyone.'

'No one ever died from my booze. They might have gone blind – but they never died.' The man laughed wheezily. 'I got the cigarettes too. The Yankee camp are being very helpful.'

Dandy let out a snort. 'Those bloody Americans! They could put an honest man out of business.'

'You won't have to worry then, Gilburn, will you?'

The thickset man lumbered off and a moment later returned with a colleague, several crates of booze and a plain brown box full of cigarettes. Hurriedly, Dandy stuffed them into the lockup and then threw a couple of old blankets over the top.

'It stinks in there.'

'It's meant to,' Dandy replied, straightening up and brushing the dirt off his hands. 'Stop people nosing around.' He paused, put his head on one side. 'No stockings?'

'I didn't know you wore them.'

'You know what I mean!'

'You got a girlfriend then, Gilburn?'

He sighed, irritated. 'We agreed that there would be some stockings.'

The big man leaned forwards, towering over Dandy. 'Now you listen to me, you little runt. I tell you what you're getting, not the other way around.'

At once, Dandy put up his hands in submission. 'OK, OK, whatever you say, whatever you say.'

Watching the men walk off, Dandy stood in the shadows and then winced as the all clear sounded. That was close, he thought, enjoying the frisson of excitement. The police had had him in a few times now, but found nothing. And that was how it was going to stay. He smiled to himself. The thing that was important was to pick the right accomplice. And Madge Baker was perfect. Always too drunk to notice much of anything, she asked no questions, just took the booze he gave her and never asked why he wanted the key to the lockup.

All she wanted was what he could give her – black-market goods and a bit of slap and tickle once a week. Where, she wasn't fussy. Poor old Madge, Dandy thought, hardly worth a look. God knew how she got anyone to pay for it. He would call by and visit her at the weekend. Make sure he picked a time when her bloody daughter wasn't around. Now that was a cute one, Dandy thought. Bonny Baker was sharp and no mistake. He had tried at first to win her over, but she had looked at him with such loathing that he'd never tried his luck again. And he'd made damn sure that Madge told her that he wasn't around any more. It might be easy to con the mother, but the daughter was another matter altogether.

'Psst!'

He spun round at the sound, Madge creeping up behind him in the darkness. Her perfume was cheap, hardly covering the smell of gut rot brandy.

'What you doing here?'

'I live 'ere!' she snapped. 'What the bloody hell d'yer think I'm doing 'ere?' Smiling, she wrapped her arms around his skinny neck, dragging his face towards her own.

'Aw, Madge, leave off! I've got business to go to.'

'Monkey business, I'll bet,' she said, laughing tipsily and then stroking the fly of his trousers. 'I bet yer can spare a minute for yer little Madgy, can't yer?'

He wanted to clear off, but knew better than to cross Madge. She was easy to manage – if he gave her what she wanted. So he did.

Slowly he pulled up her skirt and slid his hands over her bottom.

'I love yer big arse . . .'

Her lips closed over his, her tongue probing his mouth. The smell and taste of brandy came powerfully strong. Gamely, Dandy unzipped his flies and sighed as Madge began to stimulate him.

It was bloody amazing, he thought, what a man would do for a lockup.

It was 5 January when Eve Clough developed a rash. It had happened very suddenly, her left arm speckled with little red dots, the size of freckles. Birdie had noticed them at breakfast.

'What happened to your arm, darling?' she asked in her lazy Southern Irish brogue.

'I don't know,' Eve replied, realising that she now had her mother and father's attention. 'It just flared up.'

'I knew a man who had a rash which just flared up. He was dead in a week.'

'Now then, Sydney,' his wife cajoled him. 'You tell such stories.'

'It's true –'

'We'll call the doctor,' Birdie went on, ignoring Sydney's protestations. 'Let him have a look at it. Just to make sure.'

Ben Ramsey arrived at the biggest house in Wigan at eleven thirty-five that morning. A cold wind was blowing, but the sun was trying its best to make an impact as he was shown into the drawing room. Dear God, Ben thought, looking round, there must be thousands of pounds' worth of artefacts. Slowly he looked round at the selection of swords, shields and guns. What did a man want with so many instruments of fighting? In the middle of a bloody war, what did anyone want with an armoury? Ben stopped suddenly in front of a suit of Japanese armour. It was set upon a life-size figure, the head, complete with long moustache and beard, encased in a terrifying helmet.

Behind him the door opened suddenly, Ben jumping as a short, stocky man walked in.

'Oh, hello there, sorry to startle you,' Sydney said easily, eyeing the doctor up and down. 'You like the samurai?'

'Pardon?'

He pointed to the figure. 'Part of my collection of Japanese armour. Very rare.'

Ben frowned. It was quite a mix – a broad Lancashire accent coupled with antique Japanese armoury.

'I like unusual things,' Sydney went on, taking in Ben's height, weight and general deportment. 'Life's too short to be surrounded by dull objects. Birdie!'

He shouted his wife's name so loudly that Ben jumped again, smiling wanly as the pretty Mrs Clough entered the room.

'Has Sydney been boring you with his silly costumes?'

'Suits of armour, darling,' her husband corrected her, lighting up a cigarette and offering one to Ben. 'Smoke?'

He shook his head. 'Not when I'm on duty.'

'I want to go to Japan after the war and set up a business there,' Sydney went on, his short bulky frame pausing beside the warrior. 'I think the future's in the East.'

'What about Eve?' Birdie asked patiently, turning to Ben and taking his arm. Chatting, she guided him to the door. 'We wanted you to have a look at our daughter, Dr Ramsey. She's developed a rash all of a sudden.'

'You mind my words and watch the East, that's where the future is,' Sydney called after them.

'My husband's a regular clairvoyant,' Birdie replied, smiling at Ben. 'The future's no mystery to Sydney.'

Immediately Ben took to her, suspecting that beneath the easy Irish charm and prettiness there was a ferocious brain. Still chatting, Birdie led him upstairs, Ben trying hard not to stare at the marble floor and the heavy gilded blackamoors on the landing. He had thought the Simonses had money, but this was in another league. This was riches.

Birdie was still chatting as she opened the door to Eve's sitting room. For a moment the sunlight flooded the room, blinding him.

'Dr Ramsey, this is my daughter, Eve.'

She rose up from the chair she was sitting in with one fluid movement, her height surprising him. How on earth could the diminutive Sydney and Birdie Clough have a daughter so tall? And so effortlessly elegant. For the first time in his life Ben wondered if class *could* be bought. Maybe money *could* buy grace, refinement, the kind of played-down English looks that normally resulted from generations of careful class interbreeding.

'Dr Ramsey,' Eve said pleasantly, 'I think I might have called you out for nothing.' She shrugged and rolled up the sleeve of her silk shirt. 'Look, it's all gone. Nothing to see.'

Ben disagreed with that and set down his medical bag. 'Maybe I should check you out anyway.'

Eve shrugged. 'If you think it's necessary.'

Smiling, she sat down on a high chair and allowed her pulse, temperature and heartbeat to be measured. When she caught Birdie's gaze she raised her eyebrows as though to say, what a fuss about nothing. But under her polite indifference Eve was sizing up Ben as eagerly as her father had done. So this was what all the fuss was about? she thought. Well, for once rumour hadn't lied. He *was* a good-looking man and no mistake.

'You have a regular heartbeat, Miss Clough, a strong pulse and no skin abnormalities,' Ben said at last. 'There's nothing I can find wrong with you.'

She looked up at him gratefully and he smiled back at her. But Ben didn't feel any attraction for Eve. He could admire her, yes, but not feel that thumping rush of sheer pleasure Harris invoked in him. *Harris* . . . Her name came like a dinner gong into the room, shattering the calm, cool richness.

'Well, I must be going –'

Surprised, Eve rose to her feet. 'Perhaps you would like a cup of tea? Or a drink?'

'I have other patients to see, so I'd better be off,' he replied politely.

Birdie was standing by the door with her arms folded. So that was it, she realised. Her daughter had a fancy for the doctor, did she? Well, whatever Eve wanted . . .

'Dr Ramsey, we know how busy you are and we're sorry that you've had a wasted journey. Let me show you out. How are you liking it here?' Birdie asked, again linking arms with him as she led him out onto the corridor. 'I find Wigan a delightful town, and the people love strangers. Take to them so easily. Reminds me of home.' She glided down the stairs with him, effortlessly charming. 'Mind you, a young man on his own, with a busy medical practice, could find himself too tired to go out and find company. I dare say that could be true of you.'

Ben smiled. 'I get out and about when I can.'

'But not often enough, I imagine. I'll tell you what, Dr Ramsey, I would like to propose something. And I give you plenty of time to arrange your business. Would you care to make up our party to the next Mayor's Ball on the twenty-second of April?'

At once, Ben stopped walking, Birdie looking up at him expectantly.

'There will be many influential people there – people you should meet, people who can help careers. Many a charming, ambitious man has leapfrogged his way up the ladder using useful contacts.' Her head tipped to one side. 'The delightful Dr Redmond won't be able to hold on to you for long – if you have a mind to advance yourself.' She paused, letting the words take time to settle into Ben's brain. 'Should we expect you on the twenty-second of April then?'

He nodded. Just as she knew he would.

A couple of moments after Ben had left Birdie could hear a

slow hand clapping from the landing above. Looking up, she caught sight of Eve, smiling down at her.

'That was masterly.'

'Not at all,' Birdie replied, her tone nonchalant. 'By the way, what did you use to make your arm flare up?'

Eve's face was all shocked surprise. 'Mother!'

'Oh, don't Mother me! I know you, you're my daughter after all. So, what was it?'

'Some of Dad's snuff rubbed in hard.'

'Snuff?' Birdie repeated thoughtfully. 'Very inventive.' Slowly, she climbed the stairs and then stopped halfway, looking up at Eve. 'Dr Ramsey's good-looking and personable. But he's only a doctor, darling.'

'Some doctors make a lot of money.'

'Some starve.'

'Not with the right contacts.'

Birdie laughed melodiously. 'Get to know him, Eve. Don't be in such a rush. We have to watch our pretty doctor, see what he's made of. See what he wants. See if he could fit in with us. Besides, you don't even know if his heart's already set on someone else.'

'How could it be!'

Birdie laughed that tinkling laugh. 'Just look at him. You're interested – and so must every other girl be.'

'I'm a match for anyone.'

Birdie sighed, toying with the pearls around her neck, her eyes steady. '*If* he's interested in you.'

Hurriedly Eve took the stairs two at a time until she was level with her mother. 'You don't think he liked me?'

'He *admired* you. But he wasn't bowled over by you.'

Disappointed, Eve leaned against the banister rail. 'How dare he not want me!'

'Oh, hush now, darling. Hush,' Birdie soothed her. 'There's not a man born who can't fall in love with a fortune.'

*　　　*　　　*

My dearest sister,

What I put you through – how could I? And worse, I couldn't even say sorry when I was home. So I'll say it now – sorry, sorry, sorry, from the bottom of my heart. I was mad, wasn't I? Went off the deep end, something I never thought I'd do. But there you go. You never know how things will hit you.

Miss Simons and Dr Redmond were better than I deserved. I can only thank them by making a good fist of the war. Maybe not a general, but would a sergeant do?

God, Bonny, I'm so sorry. I know what madness is like now and I don't ever want to go there again. It's not Harris's fault, so don't blame her. There's no need. When I get back on my next leave things will be as they were before. I promise you.

And I never asked how you were? Never asked how you were coping with Mam and all the problems at home. I was too selfish, wasn't I? Say you forgive me, I didn't mean to let you down.

From now on, I'll be there for you always.

Your loving brother,
    Richard

Dear Dopey,

You did let me down and frighten me and I hated you for a little while for even *thinking* of leaving me. But I've forgiven you now.

How are things at home? Mam's like she always is. I don't think she even took it in about your 'accident'. Why do all the wrong people have children?

In a hurry to catch the post. Keep your head down and your spirits up. Do not commit suicide when I'm not there to save you.

I suppose I still love you – against my better judgement.

Bonny

Slowly, Bonny laid down her pen and folded the letter in two, slotting it into the envelope. She was pregnant. And yet, funnily enough, she was glad. A baby would make some sense out of life. Give her someone to look after, someone who might be there for her. Because others weren't. Her mother wasn't, and even Richard had let her down. Richard, the one person she would have bet her life on being reliable.

It wasn't his fault really. He had been potty, a moment of sheer bloody-minded bile had made him try to carve his own arteries open. So if her brother – the kindly, supportive, normal Richard – could do it, how frail was everyone else?

A door below slammed shut, Bonny wincing. Madge was home, singing an Andrews Sisters' tune about love in June. It must be nice to be a drunk, Bonny thought suddenly. Her mother probably didn't even know there was a war on.

Probably just walked down the dark streets and wondered who'd fused the bloody lights.

TWENTY-SEVEN

'Mildred! *Mildred!*' Irma shouted over the phone. 'Saville's gone!'

A moment earlier Mildred had been applying perming lotion to Gladys Leonards' hair. The woman was watching her through the mirror avidly, wondering what new scandal might be taking place under her very nose. It couldn't be Saville again, could it? Could she be so lucky to be around when the news broke?

'Calm down, Irma,' Mildred said, turning her back to her customers and dropping her voice.

'I *am* calm,' Irma said icily. 'He's gone off.'

'Where were you?'

'In the lavatory, if you must know.'

Mildred fought the desire to laugh. 'Look round the house.'

'I've done that!'

'The garden?'

'Do you think I'm a total imbecile?'

'I thought we were talking about Saville,' Mildred replied smartly. 'Go and look down the lane.'

'You know I don't go out!'

'Maybe it's time you did.'

'You're so selfish!' Irma snapped. 'I can never look to you for support.'

'You can talk! I get more support from my corset.'

There was a snort of irritation down the line. 'Are you coming home, or not?'

'I'm doing Mrs Leonards' hair –'

'You can leave her. Nothing you could do with that woman would help. I've seen better hair on bacon.'

Hoping her customer hadn't overheard, Mildred turned and smiled at Gladys, who had put her thick glasses back on and was watching her with overt curiosity.

'Irma,' Mildred went on quietly, 'where's Harris?'

'Well now, that's a question we'd all like answering. I thought she was at the salon with you.'

'No, she's due in at one.'

'She said she was going there at eleven!'

Mildred digested the information and decided to cover for her niece. 'Oh yes, now I think about it she's coming in late today.'

Irma snorted. 'So what about Saville? He could be any-where.' A long pause. *'Like the park . . .'*

Mildred dropped her voice even lower, trying to keep any mention of Saville out of the conversation and knowing that Gladys was hanging on her every word.

'I'll call you back.'

'What the hell are you talking about!'

'Yes, I do want some more bread, Irma. Send Mrs Turner out for it, will you?'

At the other end of the line, Irma's temper exploded. 'Bread! Are you crazy? I'm talking about Saville –'

Gladys Leonards' eyes were magnified to twice their size behind the thick lenses of her glasses, and they were fixed on Mildred. Please God, Gladys thought, let it be scandal . . .

'Oh, and ask Mrs Turner to get some more tea –'

'TEA!'

Mildred flinched as the word scorched her ear. 'I have to go, Irma.' Hurriedly she put down the phone and turned back to Gladys.

'Trouble?' the woman asked hopefully.

'The dog's gone missing.'

Gladys frowned. 'I didn't know you had a dog.'

'We haven't really. He just adopted us. But he comes and goes as he pleases, always wandering. We should get him done, but I haven't the heart.' She bent over Gladys's head and then wheeled an iron contraption over to her, leads dangling out of the back. 'I'll just pop you under here for a while, so that the perm will take.'

Gladys hadn't believed the dog story for an instant and immediately ducked away from the hood. 'If I can help in any way –'

'No help needed,' Mildred replied lightly. 'Homer –'

'Homer?'

'The dog . . . He'll come back eventually, he always does.'

Irritated, Gladys put her head under the hood and then immediately popped out again. 'Are you going to the dance?'

'I might. Harris has asked me to go with her.'

'And Irma?'

She gave Gladys a slow look. 'You know my sister doesn't go out.'

'I just wondered . . .'

Mildred flicked a switch and the metal hood clanged into life, Gladys leaning back – then leaning forwards again immediately.

'Everyone's going to the ball, Mildred. All your old friends. They'll be so pleased to see you.'

I can imagine, Mildred thought grimly, pushing Gladys back under the hood.

Returning to the back room Mildred sat down heavily, rubbing her left knee. So where was Harris? It wasn't like her to lie – or was it? She had been different lately, something Mildred put down to Ben Ramsey. Fiercely she rubbed her knee. She wasn't impressed by the good looks and easy charm. And yet she wanted to see more, not less, of the doctor. Wanted time to assess him. To work out if her suspicions were justified or if she was just being overprotective.

Mildred knew Ben Ramsey's type. Trouble was, Harris didn't.

'I adore you,' Ben said, stroking Harris's face and staring at her. God, she was beautiful, ridiculously so. His fingers rested against her skin, feeling the warmth of her cheek. She was so fascinating, in love with him and yet still capable of being unpredictable. Never a walkover. He was certainly in love, Ben thought, but Harris wasn't the right woman for him. *Why did he never learn?*

She snuggled against him. 'I was thinking of you all day. Kept looking at the present you bought me.' She fingered the chain around her neck lovingly. 'It's beautiful.'

'Like you,' he replied softly.

Harris laughed, drowsy with happiness. She had found her White Knight; it hadn't been a fairy tale after all. Even her imagination hadn't been able to match this. 'I don't ever want anything to change. I want it all to stay like this for ever.'

The words jangled in Ben's ears. How *could* it stay the same? He was destined for Rodney Street, for the top branch of his profession. And yet he couldn't imagine life without Harris . . . Damn it, he thought, what the hell am I doing?

'It's wrong what we're doing,' Ben said, leaning back in the driver's seat of his car.

Beside him, Harris smiled. 'What's wrong about it? Don't you want to see me?'

'Not like this,' Ben said sullenly. 'Creeping around behind everyone's backs.'

'We're not creeping around,' Harris cajoled him. 'You just asked me to meet you up here.'

'And you lied to your aunt to get away.'

'Mildred would understand.'

'I doubt it,' Ben replied, looking out of the car window. 'She doesn't like me.'

'How on earth can you say that?' Harris answered, laughing. 'You two were getting on fine when you came to dinner.'

'She was sizing me up,' Ben said, not without a trace of irritation. 'And you didn't help – flirting with me like that.'

Stung, Harris looked down at her hands. 'She knows I like you.'

'I'm thirty-one years old. Years older than you,' he said, his tone unusually curt, 'hardly someone your aunt would approve of her little niece seeing.'

'But –'

He cut Harris off in mid-flow. 'You should be with a boy of your own age.'

'I don't like boys of my own age!'

'How many have you known?' he countered, looking at her. 'God, Harris, you live in such an ivory tower, don't you? All cosy and safe. No wonder you think you like me – the "mysterious stranger" coming into your hick town.'

Uncomfortable, Harris kept looking down at her hands. Why was he being so mean to her? Hadn't he just been holding her, kissing her? And now he was making her feel like a fool. They had been meeting regularly for the last month. Sometimes in town for coffee, but more often in between Ben's patients visits. He would ring Deerheart House and ask Harris to meet him, and she would duly obey.

'Ben, don't . . .'

'Ben, don't,' he parroted. 'Don't what? Don't mock, don't be mean, don't touch?'

He was fully aware of the hurt he was inflicting and yet unable to stop himself. He wanted Harris so much that it unnerved him. He'd been in the same situation before, besotted by women, and it had thrown him off course. Not again, he told himself. I'm not losing my head again.

'I want to go home,' Harris said softly, close to tears.

Ben burned with shame. He knew that he had to keep control of himself, but at the same time he didn't want to alienate Harris and lose her.

Sighing, he leaned over to her and tipped up her chin, looking into her eyes. 'Sorry . . . God, I'm so mean to you. Say you forgive me, Harris.'

She wasn't about to be mollified so easily. 'You're so horrible sometimes.'

His hand traced the line of her chin, her cheek and then her forehead. Her dark eyes watched him, unblinking. God, was she really only twenty-one? He had seen women of thirty-odd without her pungent sexuality.

'Sorry, sweetheart,' he murmured, his lips brushing against hers.

She moved forwards, eager to kiss him, Ben responding, and then after an instant, pulling back.

'I have to get back to work now,' he said, starting the car. 'I'll drop you at home.'

In a minute he'll change, Harris told herself, in another minute he might park the car again and cuddle her and make her laugh. He was under pressure, busy because Dr Redmond wasn't well again. That was all it was. Surely.

And then another thought hit her, the accusation out of Harris's mouth before she could check it.

'Are you seeing someone else?'

At once Ben pulled the car over to the kerb, turning off the engine and staring ahead. 'What?'

'Well, are you?' Her face coloured as he stared at her.

'Listen, I'm not married to you, Harris.'

'I know!'

'So you don't own me.'

She was mortified. He would hate her now; think she was a nag.

'I just thought . . . Oh, I don't know what I thought. I mean, other women must be interested in you. I know they are, they

210

talk about you in the salon all the time.' She stopped. Should she be telling him this, or not? 'I just wondered if I was special to you. Or just one of a few.'

'Of course you're special to me, Harris,' Ben replied honestly. 'It's just that you're so possessive . . .'

He tailed off, thinking of her words. So women were talking about him, were they? The thought tickled his vanity and yet he had to admit – to his own astonishment – that he was only interested in Harris. She was the one who inflamed him, irritated him and yet fascinated him. But she didn't own him, and she had to know that. Harris Simons had to realise that she was never going to be the wife of Ben Ramsey.

'I'm sorry,' Harris said, her tone soft. 'I didn't mean to irritate you.'

Gently he kissed her forehead, avoiding her mouth. Avoiding the feelings she aroused in him. If he had any sense he would skirt clear of Harris Simons, aim for Eve Clough instead . . . Ben studied the curve of Harris's cheek, the full top lip. God, I want you, he thought. But in my own way, and by my own rules.

When he was younger he would have let himself fall in love completely. But now he was harder and no woman was going to lead him away from his ambitions. Ben Ramsey was heading for the road that led all the way to Rodney Street.

And that was a journey Harris Simons would never make.

'Where have you been?' Irma asked, her hands on her hips as a quiet Harris came in.

She was preoccupied, thinking about Ben and wondering if she had pushed him away. They had been so much closer recently. He had brought her presents, left little jokes on scraps of paper in her handbag. Wooed her . . . And now maybe she had ruined it by her stupid accusation. Maybe he wouldn't want to see her again . . . The thought was panic-making.

'Harris, did you hear me?'

'I was just walking around.'

'Where?'

'Does it matter?'

'You can watch your tone with me!' Irma snapped. 'I asked a civil question and I expect a civil answer. I can't tell you what a morning I've had. Your uncle went missing –'

'What!'

'I found him by the pond. He was trying to catch a shark. Sharks in Wigan! I ask you, he gets worse.'

'He can't help it,' Harris said, forever rising to Saville's defence. 'I'll go and talk to him.'

But Irma was in full flow. 'I could have had one of my angina attacks, and then where would we all have been? I could be lying here dead, Saville drowned in the pond. And you off somewhere walking around like a sleepwalker.'

She studied the silent Harris critically. The girl was handsome, but sullen. What kind of a man would marry a sullen wife? Irma found herself irritated with Harris afresh. Her niece should be grateful for everything she had. If Gideon had lived, what kind of future would she have had then? No cushy home, no easy work with Mildred, no freedom. Just some slum hovel with a bitter father and a mother so unremarkable even Harris couldn't remember much about her.

Irma wasn't going to allow her niece to let her down. The Simons name had been dragged through the mud – time to restore some of its polish. And there was only one way to do that: get her niece a grand marriage.

'You want to look your best for the big dance, Harris. It's –'

'That's not for ages.'

'People plan these things a long time in advance. They look forward to such events!' Irma snapped. 'The dance will be well attended – you never know who you might meet.'

'I don't want to meet anyone.'

Irma frowned. Was she *trying* to annoy her?

'Of course you want to meet someone! Every woman wants to get married.'

'So why didn't you?'

This was mutiny! Irma thought. Her eyes glacial, she faced up to Harris.

'I don't have to take your cheek. You might think you're all grown up, but you're not. You've no experience of life at all, and you would do well to listen to someone who has.'

A seething resentment boiled over in Harris at that moment. Her relationship with Irma had always been strained. And as the years had gone on she had spent more time with Mildred to avoid her other aunt. Their conversations had been restricted, with the occasional half-hearted attempt at pleasantries, which were mercifully short-lived. In fact the only time Harris found Irma palatable was when she was ill. *And quiet.*

'I'm not a child!'

Irma raised her eyebrows. 'Really?'

'I'm twenty-one. I'm grown up now.'

'So when did this transformation take place? I don't recall reading anything about it in the paper.'

Harris's temper uncoiled slowly. She was confused by Ben's attitude and wanted someone to take it out on. And Irma was the only person available.

'What do you know about life anyway? You never even leave the house.'

'What I do is my own concern.'

'Hah!' Harris replied, surprised by her own bravery. 'You've hidden away for years, so afraid of what people were saying about Saville flashing in the park –'

'Harris!'

'No one cares any more; no one gives a damn. What my uncle did happened a long time ago, and there are other things more important than the bloody Simons family. Like the war. You *did* know there's a war on?'

Glassy-eyed, Irma studied her niece, then smiled with all the warmth of a iceberg.

'That was quite a speech, Harris. I just wonder what brought it on. Feeling hard done by, are you? Ready to join the real world? Perhaps you'd like to have your friend's life? You and Bonny could work in the munitions factory together, and go out drinking with a couple of Yanks in the evening. I'm sure she could teach you all about life. Or then again, you could talk to Richard. He's led quite an admirable existence –'

'Leave them alone!' Harris retorted heatedly. 'They have nothing to do with this.'

'So what has?' Irma asked coldly. 'What part of your easy life is so hard to take?'

'Oh, shut up!' Harris snapped, turning away.

Irma moved fast, catching hold of her niece's arm and pulling her round to face her. Her expression was hostile, her tone frightening.

'*You* think you're missing out on something? *You're* dissatisfied? You don't know you're born. Look around you, Harris. Look at me, at Mildred, at your crazy uncle –'

'Don't!'

'Saville *is* crazy. And it's small wonder. The only thing that surprises me is that Mildred and I didn't turn out the same way.' Her face moved closer towards Harris's, only inches away. 'I have nothing left. I have nothing to look forward to. You think I'm cruel to Saville – well, maybe I am. But I was taught to be cruel. I was scared into being cruel.' She stared into Harris's eyes. 'You ask Mildred. Ask her about our father, ask her why Saville's the way he is. Oh, our brother was born slow, but in different circumstances he might have improved.'

'Why are you telling me all this now?' Harris's voice wavered.

'Because you have to know,' Irma answered. 'You have to make sure that you don't end up like any of us. That's the one thing I can do for you, Harris. The one thing no one did for me – *I can warn you.*' Footsteps sounded over their heads. Irma's voice dropped lower. 'We were controlled by our father, frightened into doing everything he said. He manipulated every one of us. There wasn't any safety in this house. We were told how to dress, to think, to act. We were told where we could go, and with whom. I had a chance to get away, but I didn't take it. I stayed, because somehow being frightened was easier than being happy. You *never* let anyone control you. You hear me?'

Disquieted, Harris backed away from her aunt and then ran up the stairs to Saville's room. She had been more shaken by Irma's demeanour than her words. It was only later that Harris would come to understand what her aunt had said.

And then it would be too late.

TWENTY-EIGHT

Standing by the barrier at the train station Bonny searched every face that passed her. She had long ago given up on seeing her American lover, he had been posted overseas, away from the army camp. It had all been very sudden. So sudden that she never had the chance to tell him she was pregnant.

Standing on her toes, Bonny struggled to get a better look. A rush of steam was rising from the train and obliterating the figures as they moved, like ghosts, towards her. All around people were hugging their fathers, brothers, lovers, women shouting with excitement as another loved one approached the barrier.

And still Bonny kept looking. The cold April weather chewed into her clothes, the damp making her shiver as she rubbed her arms to keep warm. She was wearing one of her mother's coats, because it was larger than her own. Madge hadn't noticed her daughter's weight increase – in fact no one had, because Bonny had been clever. Nothing was tight-fitting any more and besides, her lanky form with her slim arms and legs took attention from her stomach area.

Suddenly there was a shout, Bonny screaming with delight and then flinging her arms around Richard's neck.

'You're late!'

He hugged her, smelling the nostalgic scent of cheap soap on his sister's skin. 'You look well.'

'I'm fine,' she replied, linking arms with him. 'How are you?'

'Good,' he said, meaning it. 'I've got forty-eight hours' leave.'

'Forty-eight hours! Jesus, the army really knows how to spoil you.'

Together they walked out of the station towards the town. Others walked with them, in front and behind, the lads in army uniforms getting waved at from passers-by. Inordinately proud of her brother, Bonny smiled beside him, nodding a welcome to the fishmonger on Market Place as they passed.

'You hungry? I made an apple pie.'

Richard looked impressed. 'Apple?'

'I have my sources,' Bonny teased him, walking along happily.

She wanted more than anything to tell him about the baby, but she didn't dare. Richard would be shocked and demand to know who the father was. And to what end? She had slept with a Yank and was having a Yank's bastard. That was a truth and she could live with it. The one thing she couldn't live with was disappointing Richard. Would he judge her? Lose affection for her? Think she had turned out like their mother?

Did *she* think that?

'Home,' Richard said as they turned from Vauxhall Road into Mill Yard. He stopped and studied the poor houses, the windows taped up, the streets littered with rubble. 'It looks good.'

'God, you *must* be homesick,' Bonny replied, opening the door and walking into the kitchen. 'Mam's out.'

He was hurt. 'I thought she might be here to welcome me. How is she?'

Bonny shrugged. This wasn't the time to tell Richard just

how far Madge had fallen. Or the fact that their mother spent more and more time away from Mill Yard.

'She should get some help for her drinking,' Bonny said, putting on the kettle and then banking up the fire. 'Mrs Robins –'

'Who?'

'She works at the factory with me,' Bonny explained, going on, 'She was telling me about some place alcoholics could go. On the other side of Manchester. A place they lock them up till they dry out.'

'Mam that bad?'

'She couldn't get worse, and that's a fact,' Bonny replied, taking off her coat. She waited, tensed, for a comment. But Richard hadn't noticed anything different, just smiled as she passed him his tea and a slice of pie.

'We could go to the flicks tonight.'

'Fine. What's on?' he asked, eating hungrily.

Time flipped backwards. Richard was a kid again and they were on the rise, just by the Bloody Mountains, watching foxes. Quietly they had lain on their stomachs and waited for dark. Then they had seen the animals arrive, picking at the bread they had thrown out for them. Another memory followed – Richard in the drawing room of Deerheart House, trying manfully to explain just how they had fallen through the roof of the bay window. And then there was the image of her brother on the bed, blood all over the floor and over that cheap grey dress . . .

Bonny's thoughts came back to the present with a jolt. Richard's head was bowed as he ate. For a moment she longed to reach out and touch his hair, but resisted. Don't think badly of me, Bonny willed him. Please, don't hate me.

Quickly, Richard finished the pie and then wiped his mouth, leaning back in his chair.

'Now, *that* was good.'

'I should think so. I had to sell my fillings for it.'

He laughed, patting the seat next to him. 'Come on, sit down and talk to me. Tell me what's been going on.'

'I thought we were going to the flicks?'

'Later,' he said, studying his sister. And then he saw it. Not what Bonny had feared – he had noticed no change in her weight – but in her expression. 'What is it?'

'Huh?'

'What's the matter?'

'Nothing!' she said lightly.

'Don't lie to me.'

'Oh, Richard, you do go on! Nothing's the matter.'

He sighed. 'Still working at Gorner's?'

'Yeah. And the factory at night. I like it there, the women are a good lot.' Bonny thought of the rows of tables all piled high with machinery, the women lined up behind them, grease and noise everywhere. And above the clatter the sound of a radio playing Glenn Miller tunes. Strange, she thought, how such a dump could be so comforting.

'What else?'

'Nothing much . . . More pie?'

'More information,' Richard said, putting his head on one side. 'Are you seeing someone?'

'No!'

'Sure?'

'I'd tell you.'

Frowning, Richard leaned forwards, his elbows on his knees as he looked as his sister. 'You can't keep a secret from me. We never have secrets, remember?'

'I don't recall you sending me a telegram before you cut your wrists,' Bonny replied smartly.

He ignored the joke. 'What is it?'

'OK. There *was* someone. You remember, that Yank . . . But it's over now,' Bonny said slowly.

I can't tell him, she thought, I can't. He'll think I'm a slut, a slag like so many others in Scholes. Like our mother. Me,

219

with all my big ideas, and look where they got me – up the duff.

'Did he leave you?'

'He was posted overseas.'

'That's hard,' Richard said, genuinely sympathetic. 'Do you keep in contact?'

'It's not like that,' Bonny said, getting to her feet.

Hurriedly, Richard caught her hand. 'Sit down and talk to me. I'm not going anywhere until you tell me what's the matter.'

'I miss him,' she lied.

He saw the lie. 'No, you don't.'

'OK, so I don't.'

'Bonny, what happened? Was he married?'

'No.'

'Did he treat you badly?'

'No!'

'So what was it?'

'I'm pregnant.'

He rocked back in his seat as though he had been punched. Glancing away from his sister, Richard shook his head and then opened his mouth to speak – but no words came out.

Oh, dear God, Bonny thought, he's ashamed of me. He's shocked. I've lost the best ally I have in all the world.

'*Pregnant?*' he repeated at last.

'You know, having a baby,' she said, her tone brittle. 'In the club, a bun in the oven –'

'Stop it!' he snapped. 'It's not funny.'

'I know, I stopped laughing a while back.'

Richard could tell that his sister was distressed but trying hard to cover it. Bonny, pregnant! What did that mean? His little sister was going to have a child. And she was on her own. Because Madge would be no help, and he was away. Oh God, his sister pregnant . . .

'When's the baby due?'

'Huh?'

'The baby – when's it due?'

'End of August,' Bonny said, her tone quiet. 'You don't hate me, do you?'

Richard looked at her in genuine amazement. 'What *are* you talking about?'

'I was worried. I thought you might think I was a slut, you know . . . like Mam. I thought you'd hate me.'

'You're having a baby,' Richard said softly. 'How could I hate my sister and my future nephew?'

She was finding it hard to speak. 'It might be a girl.'

'My niece then.'

'People will talk, Richard. There'll be gossip.'

'I don't think so. Girls are born every day.'

'You know what I mean! There'll be a scandal.'

'We're used to that.'

'But I wanted to be different! Not like all the other people round here. Not like Mam. I wanted to be respectable.' She laughed suddenly, bitterly. 'I'm having some Yankee bastard and *I want to be respectable*.'

'It's a baby,' Richard said sharply, 'not a bastard! I don't ever want to hear you call it that again. It has a mother and an uncle. That's more than enough.' He paused, looked round the shabby kitchen. 'It's going to be hard, Bonny. Can you do this alone?'

'I won't be alone. The war will end soon and you'll be back.'

He nodded. 'But what about friends? Is there anyone you can turn to when I'm away?'

He wanted to say the name Harris, but couldn't quite manage it. She still didn't know why he had tried to kill himself, only that he had been upset about a woman. Well, as Bonny said at the time, it was *almost* the truth. Harris never thought for one moment that the woman was her.

'You mean Harris?' Bonny asked, looking at her brother curiously.

221

'I'm OK, I can talk about her now,' Richard replied, almost meaning it. 'She'll help you.'

Bonny hesitated. She hadn't told Harris and wasn't at all sure how she would take the news. Besides she was so besotted with Ben Ramsey that they hadn't met up for a while. It wasn't just because he had usurped her brother that Bonny didn't like the doctor, it was because of the things Harris had said about him. That, and Mildred's suspicions.

'Is she OK?'

What *was* the answer to that, Bonny wondered. 'Yes, Harris is fine.'

'She'll help you. She's always been a good friend to us.'

'Yeah.'

'I even thought . . . I thought the three of us could go to the flicks together.'

Bonny's head jerked up. 'You ready for that? I mean, you know Harris has met someone else – what if she wants to talk about him? Could you handle that?'

'Without cutting my wrists, you mean?' Richard teased her. 'I think I could. I don't dream about Harris any more, Bonny. It's over. I still love her, but I've accepted that nothing will come of it. And I can live with it now.' He leaned forward and tapped his sister's knee. 'We make quite a pair, don't we?'

'You can say that again.'

'But we've got each other,' Richard said, adding gently, 'and there's a baby coming. A new life, Bonny, a new generation.'

'Another addition to the Baker clan. Gee, maybe I should ring Reuters now. They could put a note on the palace gates.'

Without answering, Richard leaned forward and hugged his sister, Bonny finally breaking down and crying as she held on to him.

It was a hell of a world, he thought, rocking her. A hell of a world. And a baby with no name and no father might well find it cold and unwelcoming.

TWENTY-NINE

Considering that it was wartime, the dance was well attended. Some of the high-ranking officers from the nearby American camp hung around in groups, talking amongst themselves, braver souls approaching women who were more than eager to dance. On the other side of the ballroom – the nobs' end – the Mayor and Mayoress held court.

Mildred arrived late with Harris, who hadn't been able to find her gloves.

'What d'you want with gloves?' Mildred had asked patiently. 'It's a dance, not a fishing trip. Anyway, you're lucky I agreed to go with you. I hate these things.'

But agree she had and now Mildred was sitting in her dark velvet dress feeling totally out of place amongst the proud mothers and wives in the dainty chairs watching the ballroom floor. The only consolation Mildred had was looking at the various hairstyles and seeing – with no little satisfaction – that her clients looked much better than everyone else's.

'See her? She never came to Simons Coiffeuse after that do with Saville,' Mildred whispered, digging Harris in the ribs, 'and now look at her hair. Natural blonde! Oh, it's natural all right – on someone else's head.'

Harris wasn't feeling too comfortable either. She had expected to be fêted, but was finding that the other young women her age were giving her a wide berth. The Simonses' reputation had preceded her.

'I'm sorry I came.'

'*You're* sorry!' Mildred said, resting first one buttock and then the other on the tiny seat. 'You were the one who wanted to come.'

'I didn't really. It was Irma who forced me into it. You know that.'

Mildred turned to her niece and slowly eyed her up and down. 'You look marvellous. No wonder everyone's snubbing you. They're all jealous.'

'I can't believe Irma ever liked coming to these things.'

'Oh, but she did. In the good old days, before Saville, she used to hobnob with everyone who mattered.' Mildred dabbed at her forehead with a lace handkerchief. 'It's as hot as fire in here.'

'It's that dress, it's too heavy.'

'It's cold.'

'Outside, yes, but not in here,' Harris replied. 'You'll be melting in another hour.'

Groaning, Mildred shifted on her seat again. Harris thought that her aunt had come to the dance to please her, but there was more to it. Mildred had come because of Ben Ramsey. She didn't like the effect he was having on Harris, and hoped, probably illogically, that her niece might meet some nice young man at the town hall. Away from Ramsey some other man might get a look-in.

Mildred looked around, suddenly depressed. Nice young men were thin on the ground. Most of them were off fighting, and the ones at the dance were either Americans (God forbid) or servicemen home on leave. Her gaze rested hopefully on a naval officer but in an instant he was swallowed up by a gaggle of giggling females. Drowned, in white tulle – the Wigan women managing what the Führer had not.

224

'What about him?' Mildred said suddenly, gesturing to a quiet young man standing alone at the window.

'What about him?' Harris replied, getting steadily more embarrassed by their obvious ostracism.

'He looks nice.'

'He looks dull.'

'Dull can be nice.'

'Dull is dull,' Harris replied emphatically. 'Did you *ever* enjoy these things?'

'I never went to them.'

'Even when you were young?'

'We weren't allowed to balls,' Mildred answered simply, her eyes following the dancing couples moving in front of her.

She used to dream of such nights, long for a man to hold her and waltz, long for the candles flickering, the silly whispers in her ears. In Deerheart House she had conjured up images of dances from the magazines she kept hidden in her wardrobe. The magazines her father wouldn't allow in the house. Her thoughts drifted, her head swimming pleasantly with the heat and the music . . . Suddenly Mildred was back in her youth, giddy with anticipation. William Kershaw was waiting for her at the end of Wigan Lane, whistling, the tune soft in the summer air, their meeting all the more precious because it was secret. He would take her away from home, look after her for life. They would have children and a home a long way away from Deerheart House. They would be happy. They would be free . . .

A sudden pinch to her arm made Mildred's attention snap back. Harris was staring across the room, at a handsome couple who had just walked in.

'Oh God,' Mildred said simply as she watched Eve Clough enter – *with Ben Ramsey*. She could feel Harris tense beside her, could imagine her pain and humiliation. 'I didn't think he was coming.'

Harris's voice was low. 'Neither did I. He never said . . . *Why* didn't he say? Why didn't he bring me?' Her voice was shaky. 'He came with another girl. *Why?* Why didn't he ask me?'

She was rising to her feet when Mildred caught her arm and pulled her back down into her chair.

'Don't show yourself up, Harris.'

'Don't show myself up!'

'And keep your voice down,' Mildred warned her. 'Now, *smile*.'

'What!'

'You look at him and *smile*.' Mildred's tone was steely.

Transfixed, Harris saw Ben crossing the ballroom floor as though in slow motion. He was with another woman! He had linked arms with her! They looked comfortable, as though they had known each other for a while.

And then, finally, Ben saw Harris. He hesitated and then walked over to her, nodding to Mildred before turning back to Harris, whose face was scarlet.

'Good evening. I didn't know you were coming tonight.'

'Evidently,' Mildred said, her smile warm as stone.

He glanced at Eve. 'This is Miss Mildred Simons and her niece, Harris.'

'Quaint name,' Eve replied, looking round, anxious to move on. 'We should have a word with the Mayor, Ben. After Daddy's spoken to him.'

'Who's Daddy?' Mildred asked guilelessly.

'Sydney Clough. You might have heard of him.'

'No,' Mildred lied, turning to Harris. 'Have you heard of Sydney Clough?'

But she was too shocked to enter the game, just stared at Ben with a look of bafflement.

'We *should* move on,' he said hurriedly. 'It was lovely to see you Miss Simons – and you, Harris.'

It was lovely to see you. How damning kind words could

be, Mildred thought. Beside her, she could feel Harris's body as tight as cat gut, and when she turned to her niece Harris's expression was blank.

'Can we go?'

'No.'

'I have to go!' Harris said quietly, fighting tears.

'And that's why we stay,' Mildred replied. 'You never let your feelings show, Harris. Now you hang on for a little while, love, and then we'll go home.'

'He never said he'd be here. *He never said . . .*'

'I know.'

'He looked comfortable with her, didn't he?' Harris said, her tone distant. 'They looked like a couple. Like they belonged.'

'Harris, we'll talk about this at home,' Mildred replied, watching the quiet young man approach her niece from across the room. 'Now, I want you to accept this man's invitation to dance.'

Harris's head dropped down. 'I can't!'

Mildred gripped her hand tightly. 'Yes, you can. You get up and you dance. And you smile, like you're having the time of your life, you hear me?'

The young man approached and bowed, looking admiringly at Harris. 'Would you like to dance?'

Holding her breath, Mildred dug her fingernails into Harris's palm.

Her niece suddenly found her voice. 'Thank you.'

In slow motion Harris rose, in slow motion she took the young man's hand and allowed herself to be guided out onto the ballroom floor. Above her head the chandelier shone on the gloss of her hair. Other men looked at her, wanted her. And the young man who had been brave enough to ask Harris Simons for a dance thought for a few minutes that he was up amongst the angels. In his arms, Harris was moved and turned like a beautiful marionette. She listened to what he said and remembered nothing; she spoke and thought of nothing; but when they found themselves alongside Ben Ramsey and Eve Clough she finally reacted.

Holding her breath Mildred watched from the sidelines. She saw Ben and Eve approach within a couple of feet and then she turned to look at her niece. Harris was brittlely beautiful, turning towards the man she was in love with, her head tipped upwards as she *laughed*. The sound tinkled across the piano keys, swung amongst the crystal lights, danced on the top of the glasses.

And it echoed inside Ben Ramsey's head like a funeral note.

THIRTY

In the kitchen of Deerheart House Mrs Turner was counting up the coupons.

'Oh, hello there, luv,' she said pleasantly as Bonny walked in. 'I haven't seen you for a while.'

'I've been busy,' Bonny replied. 'Is Harris in?'

Putting down a tin of corned beef, Mrs Turner jerked her head upwards.

'Yes, and in a mood. Been in a bad way since Saturday. If you ask me that girl's making a fool of herself over Ben Ramsey. He'll never have her,' she said with secret delight. 'Never marry her.'

Bonny moved to the door. So Mr Lacy hadn't been run to ground yet, hey? Still, her aunt would get some mileage out of *her* news. Her unwed niece pregnant. Now that was a disgrace . . .

'How's your mother?'

'Search me,' Bonny replied evenly. 'I haven't seen her for days.'

Mrs Turner sniffed. How could she get Mr Lacy to marry her when she had a sister like Madge?

'I'll tell you something, though,' Bonny said, leaning over the scrubbed wooden table, 'I saw that Nelly Fisher the other day. Snogging some airman.'

The words danced in Mrs Turner's head. Joy unbounded lifted her from her seat, her coupons, and her corned beef.

'You never!'

Bonny nodded. 'I did. At the Co-op dance. She was tarted up – all new stockings and lipstick.'

'*Lipstick!*' Such luxury, Mrs Turner thought, such decadence. No decent woman got lipstick unless she paid over the odds for it. And she didn't mean with money.

'She was dancing cheek to cheek with this airman, and then I saw them outside later. The last time I saw a woman enjoy herself so much she was acting next to Cary Grant,' Bonny went on gleefully.

It did her good to see her aunt's hopes rekindled. Besides, she had never liked Nelly Fisher since she had called Madge a scrubber. It was true, Madge *was* a scrubber, but she was Bonny's scrubber.

'An *airman* – and you know what they say about airmen?'

Mrs Turner frowned. 'What *do* they say about airmen?'

Bonny shook her head. 'Never mind. Just make sure that your Mr Lacy knows about his intended's goings-on. Play your cards right and you might still bag him.'

Mrs Turner hadn't felt so good for a while. Hurriedly she pushed some bread and corned beef across the table towards her niece. She had always liked Bonny, a nice, decent girl.

'You have that, luv, eat up . . . And leave Mr Lacy to me.'

A little while later Bonny went upstairs to Harris's bedroom. There was mess everywhere, her friend's party dress thrown over a chair, her shoes in the bin.

'Hey, you can't throw those away!'

'You have them,' Harris said sullenly, her arm across her eyes as she lay back on the bed. 'They didn't do me any good.'

'I can't fit them,' Bonny wailed. 'Not unless I cut my toes off.'

Ignoring her, Harris went on helplessly, 'Ben was at the

dance with some other girl. Some uppity piece called Clough.'

Bonny's eyebrows rose. 'Not Eve Clough?'

Harris sat up, her face puffy from crying. 'You know her?'

'Her and her mother come into Gorner's for tea. Sit there, surrounded by shopping, chatting away like a couple of harpies.' Bonny paused. 'She's rich.'

'I'm rich.'

'Yeah, but you have Saville. The Cloughs are respectable. Not a breath of scandal around them. And as for Sydney Clough, that creepy little dwarf –'

'He's a dwarf?'

Bonny shrugged. 'Well, not really, but he's very short – and he's worth a fortune. You must have seen him at the dance.'

'I didn't notice,' Harris said honestly. 'I couldn't stop looking at Ben and that woman.'

Sitting down at the end of the bed, Bonny sighed. 'I know you like him, but Ben Ramsey's not treating you well, Harris –'

'He *does* treat me well! He's always doing romantic things.'

'Yeah, like taking some other girl to the dance,' Bonny said. 'That was a right showing-up. You could do better for yourself.'

'But I want him!' Harris snapped, sitting up and staring hard at Bonny. 'I told you, I'm going to marry Ben Ramsey.'

'But –'

'I am!' Harris insisted. 'He loves me, he does.'

'Has he said so?'

'Of course he has! He says it all the time. And he's very loving –'

'Oh God,' Bonny said, her shoulders slumping. 'You haven't slept with him, have you?'

'Bonny!' Harris snapped. 'What kind of a girl d'you think I am? I don't do that kind of thing. I've more sense.'

A long moment passed between them, Bonny picking the fluff off the coverlet, Harris immune to the pain she was causing.

'He wouldn't respect me if I slept with him. Which man would? Like Irma always says, who'd buy the cow if they could milk it for free?'

Stung, Bonny looked up, then said simply, 'Moo.'

'What?' Harris replied, then flushed, her dark eyes fixed on her friend. 'Bonny, you haven't! *Have you?*'

She nodded.

'With the American?'

Bonny nodded again.

'What was it like?'

'Painful at first. But it improved.'

Curious, Harris swung her legs over the side of the bed. 'Do you love him?'

Laughing bitterly, Bonny shook her head again.

'So why . . . ?'

'Did I do it?' Bonny finished for her. 'Because I wanted to. Because I was stupid. Because I wanted to please him.'

Another long silence passed before Harris spoke again.

'Is he still around?'

'No.'

'But he'll be back?'

'No.'

'Oh well,' Harris said lamely, 'I suppose if you didn't love him, it's not so bad. I mean, no one will know, will they? No one need ever know.'

'Me having a baby in August might tip some people off.'

Her eyes wide open, Harris stared at Bonny incredulously. 'You're pregnant?'

'Well, it's not wind.'

Shaken, Harris searched for words, but couldn't find anything to say. Her mind reeled from the news. It was terrible. Bonny had ruined her life.

'Are you going to have it?'

Stunned, Bonny turned on her. 'Of course I am! I'm not going to murder a baby just to get myself out of trouble. I'm surprised at you, Harris! I never thought you'd say anything like that.'

'I just wondered if it might not be the right thing to do,' Harris blustered. 'You know, for you. Think about it – you can't have a baby. It would spoil everything. You'd have ruined your chances –'

'My chances for what?' Bonny replied, getting to her feet and looking down at her friend with contempt. 'I don't think the be all and end-all of life is catching some man. Marriage isn't everything, Harris. You might think so, but I don't. And, anyway, you can look at me with pity, but I pity you more – running after some bloke who treats you like a rubbing rag.'

Harris was on her feet instantly. 'You know nothing about it!'

'I know plenty. And I know what people are saying round town. How they're laughing at you. You've been seen with him, Harris. In his car, up on the Bloody Mountains, walking about late at night. You might fool your aunts, but I come from the wrong side of the tracks, remember? And having some hole-in-the-corner affair is nothing new to my sort.'

Without thinking Harris struck out, slapping Bonny hard across her face. Then, as soon as she had done it, she was ashen with remorse.

'Oh God, Bonny, God. I'm sorry, I'm so sorry. I didn't mean it . . .'

But Bonny wasn't about to be placated. Her tone cold, she moved to the door and then turned.

'You think you're so much better than me, don't you? You always did. Thought you were being kind, even as a child, by being friends with a couple of poor kids. But I'll tell you one thing, Harris, you're a spoiled bitch with no real feelings. Otherwise you'd never have said what you just did. Or pant after some man who'll never marry you. Ben Ramsey's marked his spot and it's not here. You watch, he'll marry Eve Clough and you'll look a right fool –'

'Get out!'

'I'm going!' Bonny hissed. 'I didn't plan this baby, but I'm glad I'm having it. You're trying to plan your life and it's all going to go belly up. You want to know why? Because you've picked the wrong man. I did, but I can face up to it. You can't. That's why I'll always be better than you, Harris. I may be poor, but you're the stupid one.'

THIRTY-ONE

'Darling, listen to me –'

Harris pushed away Ben's hand. 'I don't want to listen! You went to that dance with someone else. You never asked me. And you never even said you were going. Why was that? You expected me not to be there, I suppose?' Her tone was bitter, Bonny's words still ringing in her head, three days later. 'If Eve Clough is so fascinating, why bother to see me any more?'

Ben wanted to know the answer to that question himself. It was all so simple really. He could win over the Cloughs and marry Eve, securing himself a good future with all the contacts an ambitious medical man could ever want. There was only one problem – Eve wasn't Harris. And he loved Harris.

'Sweetheart, calm down. I just went with her because her parents asked me to. They're my patients – how could I offend them?'

'*We're* your patients, but you never worried about offending us!' Harris snapped back.

Her temper was heightened by humiliation. She had no doubt that what Bonny had said was true – people *were* laughing at her. But she couldn't stop herself, couldn't tell Ben Ramsey to go to hell. She wanted him too much. Probably as much as Eve Clough did.

'You made me feel so stupid!'

'I never meant that,' Ben replied, looking at her lovely face and feeling the old rush of passion. She was more attractive than he had ever seen her before. All stewed up she lost her doe-eyed devotion and was more of a match for him. Gently he took her hand.

Immediately she snatched it away. 'No!'

'I want you so much,' he said, irritation building. He could always manage her; she would settle down in a minute. 'Harris, look at me.'

'I don't want to look at you! I fell out with my closest friend because of you.' She turned to him, her expression hot with fury. 'And you're not worth it. You don't love me –'

'I do.'

'And I suppose you love Eve Clough too?'

'She's nothing to me.'

'She didn't look like nothing! In fact, you looked like the perfect couple.'

Ben was tired of the argument and wanted it to be over. He was, if he admitted it, as confused as she was. He should stick with Eve Clough, marry well – but Harris had tied him up in knots. He wanted her more than he had ever wanted another woman, dreamed of her, found himself daydreaming about her persistently. Could he really pass up on a woman who fascinated him so much? Was Rodney Street *that* important to him?

Maybe not . . . Gently Ben touched her throat and then let his hand slide along her collarbone.

'Speaking as a doctor, I think you have a very interesting case, Miss Simons.'

Her skin tingling, Harris struggled to keep her anger fired up. 'What kind of case?'

'I'm not sure,' he murmured, leaning between the car seats and unbuttoning the top of her blouse. 'I'll have to examine you. Thoroughly, very thoroughly.'

Harris knew she should push him away. Who wanted soiled goods? Who married them? And yet she wondered if by letting him make love to her she might keep him. Perhaps Irma was wrong – after all, what did she know? If she had sex with Ben it might tie him to her for ever, keep him away from the Clough woman and the Clough money. It was a gamble, but she knew how much he wanted her – and she knew how much she wanted her triumph.

Slowly Harris allowed him to undo her blouse, his fingers lingering over her nipples. She sighed. Everyone in Wigan would see her catch her man; see her victory. She would have the big wedding her aunts wanted – and the man she wanted. Gently, Ben let his hand move from her knee upwards, his fingers toying with the edge of her panties.

Stop now, he told himself, stop now. But he couldn't. He wanted her so much it was impossible to resist. His plan, his plotting were fading to the back of his mind, his whole attention focused on the beautiful brunette who was now waiting for him to make love to her. Harris looked up, her eyes half closed in the dim light, her tongue passing for an instant over her bottom lip.

And then he moved on top of her and, quickly and almost violently, he entered her. She cried out, his mouth muffling the noise as his tongue found hers. Her skin was soon moist with sweat, hairs sticking to the side of her neck, his lips moving over the damp skin and then down to her breasts again.

Outside the car the night wound on. Below them the town slept, and for a while no air raid disturbed the tranquil sky. They made love and then parted, both staring ahead in silence . . . And night moths, like so many unspoken regrets, pelted the windscreen blindly before their eyes.

THIRTY-TWO

Chewing thoughtfully on a piece of toast, Birdie listened to the news on the radio. The German 'Gustav Line' had been broken at Monte Cassino and hundreds of German paratroopers taken prisoner. Maybe it was true this time, maybe soon it *would* all be over. And then the world would be different. There was a new time coming: a time to make new plans.

'I told you,' Sydney said, grinning as he listened to the German losses. 'I could see this coming.'

'You see *everything* coming, darling,' Birdie replied. 'I'm sure the Government should have asked your opinion long enough since.'

'I could have given them good advice,' her husband replied, immune to his wife's irony. 'You don't get as good in business as I am without looking ahead. The future is where we have to focus . . .'

Birdie stemmed the flow deftly by turning off the radio and holding her husband's gaze. 'What about *Eve's* future, darling?'

'What about it?'

'She's in love with Ben Ramsey,' Birdie replied, her tone composed. 'I told you in bed last night.'

He couldn't remember, but then every time Sydney's head hit

the pillow he was asleep instantly. His wife should know that by now, he thought. They had been married for long enough.

'Never tell me anything important at night!' he snapped, then modified his tone as he cut into a breakfast kipper. 'God, this is tough!'

'You can't get the same quality as you could before the war.' Sydney was off again. 'Well, I can look ahead and I can see –'

'About Eve,' Birdie interrupted him, smiling. 'What about her and Ben Ramsey?'

'Has he got money?'

'Don't be silly, darling, he's a doctor,' Birdie replied, finishing her toast and then dusting off her fingers. 'She loves him very much. She told me so. In fact, he's the first man she's ever been really keen on.'

'Hah! Since when did that count for anything? Love doesn't last if you're poor.'

'Eve will never be poor, Sydney, you and I will see to that. The real question is, do we think Ben Ramsey's the right choice for her?' She watched her husband picking at his kipper and leaned towards him. 'I thought fathers were supposed to be possessive! Aren't you supposed to be demanding what Ben Ramsey has to offer our only child?'

Sydney was more interested in the kipper. 'You do that, Birdie. You always see to everything at home.'

'Eve is not a cooker, Sydney, she's our child.' Smiling through gritted teeth, Birdie moved the half-eaten kipper out of her husband's way. His attention guaranteed, she continued, 'Ben Ramsey is personable, good-looking, smart and very ambitious. I introduced him to a few powerful people at the ball and I could see they took to him. He could go far – with the right help.'

'So?'

'So he could change from being a run-of-the-mill GP to having rooms on Rodney Street.'

Sydney blinked. 'Wasn't that where I went to see that man about my gout? He was no bloody good.'

'That's because it wasn't gout, Sydney. You had an ingrowing toenail.'

'Whatever.'

Birdie was not about to be put off. She knew that Sydney only had a limited interest in anything outside business so she had to move fast.

'Eve loves Ben Ramsey and I want her to be happy. I want her to have the man she's set her heart on. She should be married, time's getting on and we don't want a spinster on our hands. You know only too well how easy it would be for us to help Ramsey get on.' She paused, smiling to herself. 'Besides, having a *professional* son-in-law sounds nice. It's time we had a bit more class in this family.'

'There's nothing wrong with trade!'

'Of course there's nothing wrong with trade, darling. We both know that. But you don't have a nice brass plaque outside your door. And people *like* things like that. Besides, when Eve and Ben marry they might have children who would be doctors too – or even surgeons.'

Losing interest, Sydney reached for the kipper again, but immediately his wife slapped away his hand.

'Eve wants Ben Ramsey.'

'If you think it's right, Birdie, let her have him.'

'There's a problem.'

Sydney thought as much and sighed. Honestly, business was easy compared to real life.

'Ben Ramsey appears to be . . . attached to someone else.'

'Who?' Sydney asked, suddenly interested. How dare the man be fooling around with another woman when he was courting his daughter!

'Harris Simons.'

'And *who* is Harris Simons?' Sydney asked, although the name sounded vaguely familiar.

'She comes from a rich family –'

'How rich?'

'Not as rich as us, darling, don't panic,' Birdie teased him. 'They live at Deerheart House. Two spinster sisters and a poor imbecile of a brother.' She dropped her voice. 'He exposed himself in the park once.'

Sydney's eyes bulged. 'He never!'

'He did. I mean, Saville Simons's behaviour is no reflection on his niece, but on the other hand, it does cast rather a pall over her suitability as a doctor's wife.'

Sydney's eyes narrowed suspiciously. 'You mean that Ben Ramsey might just be having a bit of a fling with the Harris girl?'

'I sincerely hope so. He couldn't be fool enough to queer his pitch by marrying her,' Birdie replied. 'On the other hand she's a very good-looking young woman, quite unusual in fact. I pointed her out to you at the dance in April.'

'Good God, Birdie, I can't remember every woman you draw my attention to!'

His wife leaned forward and cupped his cheek with her hand. 'And that's why I love you so much, darling,' she replied lightly before leaning back in her chair again. 'What it comes down to is this – Ben Ramsey seems to be besotted by Harris Simons. Miss Simons is most certainly crazy about him. Dr Ramsey is also interested in Eve. And our daughter certainly wants to marry Ben Ramsey. You *do* see what I'm getting at, Sydney? We have to make sure that our daughter gets the prize – and not Miss Simons.'

'How do we do that?'

'Use your powers of foresight, Sydney, and look ahead. Ben Ramsey is ambitious. He might be in love with Harris Simons, but I'd bet money on his career coming first. He's been seeing Eve for a while.'

'As well as the Harris girl?'

Birdie shrugged. 'Why not? He's not married to either of them. *Yet.*'

'Go on,' Sydney said, looking at his dainty wife with admiration.

'I think he just needs to have his mind made up for him; have the advantages of an alliance with our family pointed out, which would highlight the disadvantages of marrying a woman with the Simons name. Personally I would like a good-looking doctor as a son-in-law. And besides, I was beginning to think that no one would ever take Eve's interest.' Smiling, Birdie got off her seat and slid onto her husband's knee. 'Don't say that having the house to ourselves would be so bad? And anyway, we would have grandchildren to look forward to. A little doctor for me – and a tiny tycoon for you.'

Laughing, Sydney kissed her. 'Birdie, you're wicked.'

'I know.'

'So we *buy* Ben Ramsey?'

'Got it in one, darling,' she replied, squeezing him. 'Got it in one.'

Dandy Gilburn was standing by the lockup behind Mill Yard, waiting for Madge. After a little while she came down the ginnel, her face set.

'Yer won't believe it!' she snapped. 'Bonny's in the club.'

Dandy had no interest in Bonny. He was too busy thinking about the way he had tried to outsmart his colleagues – men richer and cleverer than he was; men who were not prepared to let him get away with siphoning off some of the money he had made from booze and black-market cigarettes. And besides, the police were on to him.

'Madge, I need a favour –'

'Didn't yer hear what I said!' she snapped back, her voice almost sober. 'My girl's pregnant.'

'She's not the only one round here.'

With one quick motion, Madge smacked Dandy round the head, his teeth coming together with a satisfying clack.

'Hey, watch it!' he said, affronted, hugging his ear. 'That bloody hurt!'

'It were meant to,' Madge replied. 'Yer want to watch yer mouth, Dandy Gilburn. It'll get yer into trouble.'

He knew that much already. Normally he would, at this point, have walked off in a huff, but he needed help. Fast. And there was only one person who could give it to him.

'Madge, luv –'

'Don't "Madge, luv" me!' she hissed, knocking away his roving hands. 'I'm not in the mood.'

'Yer always in the mood.'

'Well, yer wrong about that! I've got other things on m' mind.' She paused, accepted one of Dandy's illegal cigarettes and leaned back against the wall. Her make-up was smeared, whether from sleeping in it, or crying, Dandy wasn't sure. But he knew one thing – she looked like a slattern.

'I could have a word with an old woman I know. Ask her to help Bonny with her trouble.'

'I'm not having my girl carved up by some bloody witch!' Madge replied. 'I know what them hags can do.' Dandy didn't doubt that for a second. 'Bonny says she wants to have the baby. God, some Yank's kid. And he's buggered off and left her high and dry.' She eyed Dandy up and down. 'Yer all married. All looking for some fun on the side.'

Dandy wasn't having that much fun at the moment. Smiling winningly he slid an arm around Madge.

'Look, luv, I'm in a spot of bother –'

'Who ain't?' she shot back at him, stepping away.

This was turning out to be harder than he had expected. Before long his colleagues would arrive and want to see just what he had secreted in the lockup. And when they found out . . . Oh Jesus, Dandy thought desperately.

'I'm sorry about yer girl –'

'Yeah.'

'– but I need a favour, Madge,' he hurried on, offering her

bait she couldn't refuse. 'I'll pay yer – ciggies and some brandy. How's that?'

Suddenly interested, Madge narrowed her eyes and then laughed. 'Yer in trouble? Serves yer bloody right.'

'Hey, now –'

'Been skimming the profits off the proceeds?' she asked, knowing at once that she had scored a direct hit. Still, what the hell, Madge thought, he'd been generous with her. She could help him out for some fags and a couple of bottles of brandy. 'I want three bottles of brandy.'

'Two.'

She shrugged, as though he had beaten her down. Little did he realise, Madge thought, she had another key to the lockup and – in her sober moments – had checked out exactly how much her lover had stashed away. If the truth be known, she didn't much care if Dandy got in trouble, but she *did* care about losing her booze and cigarette allowance.

'So, Dandy, what's the problem?'

'I have to move everything from the lockup.'

'To where?'

'Yer house?'

'M' bloody house!' Madge barked. 'And what if someone comes looking there?'

'They won't. No one knows about us.'

She thought about it carefully, her greed outweighing her caution. Besides, if anything happened to Dandy, she'd still have the goods.

'OK, yer can put them inside. But we have to hide them, yer hear me? I don't want Bonny finding anything.'

He nodded eagerly. 'Can we do it now?'

'Now?' Madge asked, irritated. 'What's the hurry?'

'There are some people coming over here soon.' He looked round, nervously. 'Yer know the type, Madge, people who don't ask too many questions, people who'd like to knock me about a bit.'

'Been cheating?' Madge asked, amused.

Dandy could have cheerfully slapped her then, but kept his temper. Slowly he let his hand run down her cheek and rest on her left breast.

'I only cheat in business, never in love.'

Appeased, Madge glanced over to the lockup. 'We better be getting on with it then,' she said.

Dandy moved hurriedly towards the crude brick building and unlocked the door. He ducked in, then ducked out again. 'Can yer keep watch?'

'Expecting the invasion?'

'Aw, Madge, come on, this is serious.'

Fifteen minutes later all of Dandy's black-market goods were moved. With a sigh of relief, he closed the door of the lockup and walked into Madge's sordid kitchen. She was eyeing up the hoard and slowly uncapping a bottle of gin.

'I said yer could have brandy.'

She stopped, took a long swig from the bottle and then fixed him with a steely look. 'Yer not in a position to argue, are yer, Dandy? I mean, I could shop yer good and proper, if I had a mind to.' Again she took a swig of the gin, then wiped her hand across the back of her mouth.

He watched her, realising with no little discomfort that she had him over a barrel. Let her drink all she wants, Dandy thought, Madge Baker was no good to him sober.

Smiling, he moved towards her. 'I'll tell yer what, luv, yer a life-saver, and no mistake.' He reached for the gin and then took a swig, pulling Madge towards him and letting the liquid run from his mouth into hers.

Laughing, she swallowed, and then he slung his arm around her. 'Let's hide this stuff and then we can relax. Get down to some serious drinking, hey, Madge?'

She nodded eagerly. He was welcome to hide booze under her bed any day.

*　　*　　*

Two of the summer months passed. The war *was* coming to an end; soon there would be peace again. Hopeful talk was everywhere. After all, there had been the D-Day landings and the Nazis were finally on the run. Driven out of Normandy, they suddenly looked vulnerable. Optimism began to rise. Families who had not lost loved ones prayed that they would continue to be spared, and those who had lost someone felt that maybe – *maybe* – the price would be worth paying after all.

In Scholes, Bonny was continuing to live with her mother and write to Richard. He assured her constantly that the war would be over soon, promising that he would be there for her when the baby came. As for Madge, her outrage had been temporary. She thought her daughter was a fool and should have aborted the child, but soon she accepted the situation. After all, Bonny was still working, putting on a brave face. Or a hard one, depending on your point of view. Thrown out of the snobbish Gorner's, Bonny was now working full time at the munitions factory, where no one cared what state their employees were in. As for the scandal, 'Who doesn't have a bloody scandal in their family?' Madge said to anyone who would listen. 'I mean, look at the Simonses. They have no reason to point the bloody finger. What with Saville, and now Harris running after that doctor and making a right fool of herself.'

Although she hated to, Bonny had to agree. Harris *was* being a dope . . . Their argument had driven a wedge between them that had grown, not lessened. When they were younger they had argued and then forgotten about it, but not now. This time neither of them could forgive the other's hard words.

Yet Bonny was determined to make an attempt at a reconciliation. One morning she waylaid Harris and Mildred on their walk to the salon, dropping into step with them and nudging Harris with her arm. Tactfully Mildred dropped back, watching the scene unfold before her.

'Still mad at me?' Bonny asked Harris.

Silent, she kept walking, staring ahead.

'Aw, come on, let's not fight.'

Her face set, Harris stopped. 'I don't want to talk.'

'You always want to talk!' Bonny replied, trying to cajole her. 'Talking's what you do best.'

For a moment Harris wavered, but then, stubbornly, she walked on. Bonny didn't bother to follow her.

Surprised, Mildred said nothing at the time, but the following day at breakfast she tackled Harris.

'You should think about what you're doing. Bonny's only trying to talk some sense into you.'

Fiddling with the morning paper, Mildred wondered just what she was going to say next. Rumours abounded of her niece's behaviour. She had been seen on the street, publicly brawling with Ben. He had looked very embarrassed, Nora Broadbent said. Other clients hadn't been slow to comment either. Mrs Barnsley had told Mildred that Harris was acting like a clown, and when Mildred snapped at her Mrs Barnsley took great pains to recall an incident that had happened only the previous evening.

'My husband was coming back from Manchester and he saw your niece in an embrace with Ben Ramsey. In his car.'

Mildred had bridled. 'Mrs Barnsley, this has nothing to do with you –'

'I think it has! It's an affront to public dignity to see things like that. Besides,' she had added meanly, 'everyone knows that Ben Ramsey's going to marry Eve Clough.'

Remembering that conversation, Mildred turned back to face her niece. 'We should talk.'

'About what?' Harris replied, on the defensive immediately.

'About you and Ben Ramsey.'

Her tone was sulky. 'There's nothing to say.'

'There's plenty to say!' Mildred snapped back. 'Harris, that man is no good for you. You should drop him now, save some face.'

'Drop him?' Harris replied, facing her aunt incredulously. 'Why would I do that? He loves me –'

'Rubbish!' Mildred snapped, her patience gone. 'Oh, it's not all your doing, Harris. Some of this is my fault. I've spoiled you. We've all given you too much of your own way and now look what's happened – you're mooning over some man who'll never marry you.'

'How do you know that?' Harris barked, her own unease making her brittle. 'You don't know anything about it!'

Mildred was unprepared for her niece's hostility. Harris obviously wasn't going to listen to anything she had to say.

'I know some things about men,' Mildred continued, trying to keep her temper, 'and the way Ben Ramsey treats you isn't right. And you shouldn't allow it.'

Flushing, Harris moved to turn away, but Mildred stopped her, pulling her round to face her.

'Look at me! This is Mildred, your aunt, the one who loves you, whatever you do. I'm not having a go at you, love, I just have to stop you ruining your life. This *has* to stop. You *have* to stop it.'

On the landing above, Saville was standing, listening. The air raids had shaken him to the bone, the sedatives wearing off rapidly, leaving his nerves shattered. Shrinking against the wall, Saville trembled as he heard Mildred's raised voice. Not *Mildred*, of all people. And she was arguing with Harris, his adored Harris.

The Harris who had changed so much of late. No more chats, no more secrets laughed over together in his room. No more confidences. After all, didn't he know about her and Dr Ramsey? Hadn't she told him? *Him*, stupid Saville. Not so stupid really, or his beautiful cousin wouldn't have confided in him.

'He loves me!' Harris shouted, her voice carrying upstairs through the half-closed door.

'If he loved you he would respect you!' Mildred replied shortly. 'And it's obvious he doesn't. I've heard all about it,

Harris. About how you sneak off to meet Ben Ramsey between seeing his patients. You've been seen in his car, kissing and –' Mildred stopped, embarrassed. She would look like a spinster fool of an aunt, talking about something she knew nothing about. At least, that was what her niece would think. 'Harris, listen to me, please.'

Upstairs Saville was still eavesdropping, hopeful that Irma, floored by one of her headaches, wouldn't wake and catch him. *Harris had been kissing Ben Ramsey . . .* Saville considered the words. Was kissing that bad? He hadn't thought so. Harris kissed him on the cheek and so did Mildred. What was so wrong about kissing?

Below in the morning room Harris's eyes were cold, her tone uncharacteristically mean as she stood up to her aunt. 'Ben Ramsey loves me.'

Ben Ramsey loved Harris, Saville thought blindly. That was OK, wasn't it? But what did it mean? That she would go away with him? Leave? Not Harris, please, not her . . .

Louder than usual, Mildred's voice echoed up the stairwell. 'You keep saying he loves you, but I see precious little to back it up! He should be taking you out, showing you off, introducing you to people. But he doesn't, does he?'

Harris looked away. 'It's private –'

'It's sordid!' Mildred snapped back. 'If a man really loves a woman he wants the world to know. If he just thinks of her as a girlfriend, a bit on the side, he doesn't want anyone to know.' She paused before adding the damning words. 'He's still seeing Eve Clough. There's a rumour that she's his intended.'

Harris sat down as though the wind had been knocked out of her. Upstairs, on the landing, Saville blinked slowly, trying to understand. The man Harris loved had another woman. That was wrong. He knew *that* was wrong. The doctor was a wicked man.

When she finally answered, Harris's voice was barely more than a whisper. 'He said he wasn't seeing her any more.'

'Well, he is,' Mildred retorted, hating herself for the pain she was inflicting. 'He's seeing her regularly. They were spotted at the town hall concert only last week.'

Shaken, Harris looked up at her aunt. Her expression changed from bewilderment to fury in an instant.

'I don't believe you! You just don't want me to have him. You don't want me to be happy, just because you're an old maid!'

The bitterness of the words stunned Mildred, making her wince as though they had actually cut into her. On the landing above, Saville also reacted, putting his hands over his ears to block out the shouting. His Harris was being cruel, his lovely Harris. She was never cruel before. What had happened to her? What was happening to everyone?

It took Mildred a moment to catch her breath. 'Harris, how could you say that to me? Your happiness is everything to me. Your life is everything to me –'

'So let me live it my way!' Harris replied. 'I trust Ben. He loves me. So what if he's seeing Eve Clough? Her parents have promised to help further his career. He's probably just taking her out to keep them sweet.'

'And that's all right!' Mildred bellowed, her tone shaking Harris. 'You could love a man who uses people? Who's playing with another woman's feelings? Think again, Harris. If he's manipulating Eve Clough and her parents so well, what's he doing to you? He's an opportunist. He'll make you suffer, Harris. And worse, he'll make you look like a fool in front of the whole town.'

On the landing Saville held his breath, fighting tears. The argument was unlike anything he had ever heard between Mildred and Harris. The words were vicious, their voices hard. And what had Mildred just said? 'He'll make you look like a fool in front of the whole town.' Saville knew something about that. About people pointing, staring – and he didn't want that to happen to Harris.

Slowly, he stumbled back to his room, his face running with

panicked tears. It was all horrible again. The house was full of shouting, people calling each other names and hating each other. Like before . . . Sobbing, Saville lay down on his bed, his face buried in his pillow, a painting of his father looking down at him from the wall above.

Meanwhile, the truth of Mildred's words had sunk their teeth into Harris. For the last month she had really believed that Ben would reject Eve Clough once and for all. And why? Because she had given him what he wanted. In the end she had let him make love to her, thinking that she – Harris Simons – would manage to catch Ben Ramsey that way. So what? she had told herself. So what if she had heard about other women who had been seduced and then left? She was different, wasn't she?

Or maybe she wasn't. Maybe she was like all the rest. And maybe she would be left too. Watching from the sidelines as Ben married Eve Clough, people pointing at her and laughing. 'Look at her, thinking she was special,' they'd say. 'No one decent will have her now. So much for all the Simonses' big plans . . .' A cold sweat pooled suddenly down Harris's neck and spine. Mentally she might deny the truth, but her body was having a physical reaction to the lies. Ben Ramsey *was* duping her. He was cheating on her. He didn't love her, after all.

But didn't she suspect that already? If she was honest, hadn't she suspected him for a while?

'Please,' Mildred said gently, reaching for her niece, 'think about what I've said, love. I don't want to hurt you –'

'Oh, leave me alone!' Harris replied, desperation making her strike out.

Shaken, Mildred stepped back, her niece glaring at her with something approaching hatred, her voice so loud that it reverberated around the house.

'I'll show you! I'll show you and everyone in this bloody town who's right. Ben Ramsey is going to marry me. Me. Not Eve Clough, but *me*. You wait and see. You just wait and see.'

THIRTY-THREE

Before Mildred could stop her Harris ran out of the house. Catching a bus into the town centre, she made her way towards Dr Redmond's surgery, arriving to find the reception area full. Surprised, Mrs Redmond looked up when she saw her.

At once her face flushed crimson, her voice unnaturally high-pitched. 'Hello there, Harris. Have you got an appointment?'

Purposefully, Harris walked by her, making for the surgery beyond.

'You can't go in there!' Irene Redmond said, the waiting patients watching curiously, Gladys Leonards putting down her copy of *Picture Post* and staring, through her thick glasses, at the scene in front of her.

'Let me through!' Harris snapped, beside herself.

She knew that people were watching her – but so what? She had to talk to Ben, had to see him. He was her life, her future, everyone would know that soon enough.

'Let me through!' she said again, pushing against Irene Redmond, who was blocking her way.

'I can't, Harris, go home. Go home now.'

But Harris wasn't going anywhere. She had come this far and was blind to reason. Everyone was wrong and she would prove it. Ben would come out and explain. He would put his arms around her and then the whole town would know that he loved her.

'Let me through!' she repeated, then saw the surgery door open and Ben walk out.

Smiling, she moved towards him, Gladys Leonards watching – as did all the waiting patients.

'Ben,' Harris said simply.

'What are you doing?' he replied, his tone cool. 'What is the matter with you?'

Harris could feel her legs weaken, but still wouldn't give up. 'Ben, I had to see you. Can we talk? We have to talk.' She touched his chest and Ben flinched. 'Please . . .'

And then she looked over his shoulder into the surgery. Eve Clough was standing there with an expression of triumph on her face, her arms folded, her jacket thrown onto the chair next to her hat.

Mortified, Harris looked at Eve Clough and then glanced back to Ben.

'She's just a patient, isn't she? She's just come for an appointment, hasn't she?'

Ben said nothing, the waiting patients all holding their breaths, watching.

Harris could feel herself drowning, humiliation welling up in her. And yet she still tried to save the situation. 'Ben, darling, tell me you love me.'

With a sigh of irritation he knocked away Harris's hand. 'Go home –'

'You love me!'

'I did love you, but . . .' He paused. God, he could hardly say the words, but he had to. His father had told him to marry well, and Ben had worked hard to plan his future. There was no choice. Harris was not wife material and the sacrifice had to be made. He would hurt her, and himself. But it had to be done. It *had* to be. 'Harris, it's over.'

Her breath stopped somewhere in her chest as she shook her head incredulously. 'But you said –'

'Mrs Redmond,' Ben said crisply, 'will you see to this?'

And then he turned away, just as Irene Redmond took Harris's arm. In that instant Harris reacted. Brushing off Mrs Redmond's hand, she flung herself at Ben and hit him hard across the head, her fist crashing into his cheek.

'I'll get you for this!' she hissed, watching his face pale. 'You've not got one over on me, Ben Ramsey. You marry Eve Clough, use her and her parents' connections, get to Rodney Street. But remember, I'll be watching you. And I'll pay you back one day.'

It was all over the town within the hour, the story growing more scandalous with each telling. Harris Simons had done it now; shown herself up good and proper, Gladys Leonards said. Blood will out, they say, and it's true. She's like her grandfather, common as muck, shouting and bawling like a fishwife ... On her way to the salon Mildred saw Gladys talking to the stout Mrs Ramsbottom and waved, the two women smiling with mock sympathy before they walked off.

Now what was that about? Mildred wondered, getting ready for her first client at ten thirty. She would sit down and have a cup of tea and a look at the paper, she thought, annoyed when she heard the bell sound. Putting her head round the door, she was surprised to see Bonny standing there.

'Well, you're a sight for sore eyes,' Mildred said, taking care not to glance at Bonny's distended stomach. 'What brings you here?'

'I skived off work, said I had to go to the dentist,' she replied, frowning. 'So you haven't heard?'

'About what?'

'Harris called in to see Ben Ramsey unannounced – and Eve

Clough was there.' She paused, sitting down, her hands folded over her swollen belly. 'Harris hit the good doctor in front of a room full of waiting patients.'

'Oh, my God! Harris hit him?' Mildred said. 'We had an argument this morning, a real set-to. She must have gone there straight after she stormed out of the house.'

'It's not your fault,' Bonny replied, getting to her feet and moving into the back room. 'I'll make us some tea. Everyone always says that when there's a crisis, so it must do some good.'

Without protesting Mildred sat in her chair, taking the tea that was offered her. How *could* Harris have lost control like that? she wondered. How *could* she have made such a fool of herself so publicly? Her beautiful Harris, reduced to a brawling harpy. And all for a man like Ben Ramsey . . .

'Where is she now?'

'I dunno,' Bonny replied. 'I just wanted to tell you before some of the bitches in this town did.'

'Thanks.'

'Don't mention it.'

Mildred sighed. 'I know you and Harris argued. I'm sorry about that.'

Bonny shrugged. 'She didn't want to hear any home truths.'

'From either of us,' Mildred replied quietly, looking at the young woman sitting in front of her. Bonny hadn't changed, still lanky, except for the huge round stomach. 'When's your baby due?'

'August, they said around the twenty-fourth.'

Mildred nodded. 'Are you coping?'

'Sure. Everyone always said I would turn out bad, so I've had an easy time of it. People like to be right.'

'You didn't turn out bad, Bonny.'

She laughed, almost slopping her tea in the cup. 'What d'you think this is, Mildred?' she asked, pointing to her stomach. 'Gas?'

To her amazement, Mildred didn't laugh, just looked at her quizzically. Embarrassed, Bonny glanced away, sipping at her tea. If the truth be known she was almost glad of the scandal because it gave her an excuse to call and see Mildred. The baby's birth was getting closer by the day and Bonny was feeling isolated. No man around, no brother and certainly no help from Madge. Suddenly she longed to be with someone kindly. Someone like Mildred Simons.

'You're very brave.'

Bonny laughed again. 'Stupid, more like.'

'No, brave.' Mildred sighed and glanced towards the door.

She looked weary, tired of arguments and problems. And she had aged, Bonny realised. For years Mildred had never seemed to grow any older and now, suddenly, the years were catching up with her. The plump smooth skin was still there, but it no longer hid the tiredness around her eyes and the strain about her mouth.

'Are you OK?' Bonny asked anxiously.

'I'm fine, love.'

'Harris will survive, she's tough.'

'And you, Bonny, will you survive? You'll have a baby to look after soon,' Mildred said quietly, 'your own family. And no man to help you. I don't want you to be a stranger any more, love. Spend some time with us.'

'Harris –'

'Bugger Harris!' Mildred said sharply.

Bonny jumped with surprise. Was this Mildred talking? Kindly, patient Mildred? Astonished, Bonny watched her put down the cup of tea and lean back in her seat.

'Let's talk about you, Bonny.'

'Not much to say.'

'I think there's a lot to say,' Mildred contradicted her. 'Stop being so brave and tell me how you feel.'

Bonny paused to consider the truth. 'Lonely.'

'It's frightening being pregnant, isn't it?'

Surprised again, Bonny studied Mildred. This was not a conversation she had ever expected to have with the innocent Miss Simons.

'It's scary, yes,' Bonny agreed. 'You feel responsible – you know, like you have to take care of this other person. Make sure you're doing all the right things. And no one seems to know much. If I go to the hospital, they get all snotty with me – "*Miss* Baker" they say. All smiles with the married women, but the ones that aren't, they can hardly be civil with. We're the rubbing rags.'

'I couldn't have done it.'

'Sure you could,' Bonny said without thinking.

'No,' Mildred replied, holding her gaze, 'I couldn't have done it. And I didn't. I didn't keep my baby.'

Bonny could feel the colour leave her face. 'You were pregnant?'

Mildred nodded. 'The man was married. You know how it goes. Well, I didn't then, but I do now. He was married and he didn't want to know when I got pregnant.' Mildred folded her arms across her chest. 'My father was a bully, a frightening bully – I could never have told him. Or my mother. Besides, she wouldn't have done anything . . . If I'd been brave I would have left home, gone off and had the baby on my own. Fought for it, worked for it. Made a life for it. But I didn't.'

Bonny took Mildred's hand and squeezed it tightly. 'I'm sorry.'

'I wasn't sorry enough,' Mildred said frankly. 'But now I'm getting on I keep thinking of that baby and wondering about how it could have been.' She paused, her eyes focusing on some point in the distance. 'I loved the wrong person. Once. I did one reckless thing. Once. One reckless thing in my whole life. The rest of the time I've been a coward.'

'No –'

'Oh, yes, I have. You're not a coward, and neither is Harris. She's stupid and wilful, but brave. You're alike, you two, and

I want you to be friends again. You'll need her, and she'll need you.' Getting to her feet, Mildred smiled, restored to her old self. 'And remember that I'm always here for you, Bonny. Remember that.' She glanced at her watch. 'Time to get ready for work. Thanks for coming. Oh, and what I said just now –'

'Was between us,' Bonny replied firmly. 'And always will be.'

THIRTY-FOUR

She had hit him! And in front of his patients, Irene Redmond, and Eve. Ben lit a cigarette and leaned against the window frame. How like Harris, he thought. Only she would get so passionate, so mad that she wouldn't give a damn what anyone thought and strike out.

And he had deserved it . . . Ben stared out of the window, not seeing anything other than his own reflection looking back. A handsome man, a professional man. A ruthless man . . . ? Harris's face floated before his eyes. Everyone had been so outraged, so eager to condemn her. And as for Eve, hadn't she gloated? In her well-bred, cool way she had comforted Ben afterwards, talking about Harris, about the lunacy of love. As if she knew something about it . . . Then Ben had felt her touch and realised that it was suddenly stronger, almost proprietorial. She had won.

But won what? Ben inhaled deeply. He had known for some time that a choice between the two women was inevitable, and in a strange way Harris had made it for him. Her behaviour told him – and the whole town – that she wasn't suitable. Not the kind of woman a doctor needed. She had shown her lack of breeding in public and thereby let him off the hook. Who could condemn Ben Ramsey for ending the relationship?

And who wouldn't expect him to marry the altogether more suitable Eve?

He didn't love Eve Clough, but he was going to make a go of the marriage. Ben sighed, oddly despondent. Eve was good-looking, rich and well connected. Eve was the perfect consort. Eve was in love with him. And yet all her virtues, piled house high, couldn't make a dent in the blistering, self-destructive passion of Harris Simons.

He *would* get to Rodney Street, Ben thought. But at what cost?

The following morning Harris woke very early. Her eyes opened and for an instant she didn't remember. And then she did – pulling the sheet over her face, her breath heated against her skin. It was over. Ben didn't love her. He was with Eve Clough now. He didn't love her. She rolled over onto her back, her hands clenching the bed sheet. She should have tried to talk to him, to reason with him, not lost her temper. Dear God, why had she hit him? *Why?* His face when he had been struck had been full of hatred . . . Tears pricked behind Harris's eyes, her teeth biting down hard into her bottom lip.

It would be all over town, she knew that much – another scandal from the Simons family. Guilt made her wince. Mildred would suffer. The hell with Irma, but Harris had never wanted to do anything to hurt Mildred. Her mind wandered back . . . Ben was lying on the grass, one arm under his head, Harris leaning over him.

'I love you,' she had said, Ben looking at her and smiling.

'I love you too,' he'd replied, touching her hair and pulling her to him.

And then another image came back.

Ben had been sitting in his car, his fingers drumming the steering wheel as she hurriedly climbed in. 'Where the hell have you been?'

'I was held up at the salon.'

'I'm busy, Harris. I can't hang around waiting for you to finish curling some woman's hair.' He had paused, not yet free of bile. 'I'm a doctor, you know. My time's precious.'

'Sweetheart,' Harris had urged him, resting her head on his shoulder, 'I had to help Mildred.'

'Mildred! That blasted aunt of yours always comes first. Whatever Mildred wants, she gets.'

Harris had laughed softly into his collar. 'Oh, Ben, you can't be jealous of Mildred.'

But inside she had been pleased, so pleased. A man only became jealous when he cared.

'I have to go now.'

As he said it, she had sat up, surprised. 'But I've only just come! I thought we could spend some time together.'

'You were late, darling,' he had answered sleekly. 'Make sure you're not late again, hey?'

Harris's attention was dragged back to the present as she heard footsteps sounding in the corridor outside. Irma – or Saville. God, she couldn't face Irma. The footsteps faded, Harris's thoughts drifting again. Sex with Ben had been disappointing at first, but later she had grown to long for it. He had a game. She would have to tell him exactly what she wanted him to do. And he would reply – telling her that he would do this, but not that. Or maybe he would. If she was good. If she pleased him.

And all the time she tried to please him, tried so hard, obsessed with her first, glamorous, older lover. Never realising that he had learned to manipulate her perfectly. That whilst she obeyed every command, she wasn't making him love her, but despise her. Her kind compliance became the stick with which he beat her. And soon the games became more strange . . .

Her face flushing, Harris closed her eyes. Had she really done some of those things? Had she? Had it been her – Harris Simons – who had allowed him to bind her hands and blindfold her?

And then leave her, in the darkness, waiting? Sometimes for a minute, sometimes for what seemed like an hour. Until he touched her, or laid his head on her bare thighs.

Oh God, Harris thought, turning over and burying her face in the pillow. I should hate you, I should hate you – but I can't. I want you so much.

And I don't know why.

August came in cool and quiet. News came that the Germans had withdrawn from the Channel Islands, but all hopes for a quick end to the war faded. Wearied by shortages, Scholes was sordid in the heat, Mill Yard overrun with rats, the outside lavvies filled with vermin as the nights came down.

Struggling at the end of her pregnancy, Bonny was getting too tired to work and spent most evenings lying on the top of her bed, listening to Madge's cheap radio. As for her mother, Madge was out. Madge was always out. The cheap booze she had been consuming for years had raddled her indifferent looks, and was now affecting her health. She ate little, and drank as much as she could buy, or beg. Or prostitute herself for.

And at Deerheart House the atmosphere was hot with guilt and resentment. Irma had heard about Harris's outburst and could hardly bring herself to look at her niece. As for Mildred, she had tried endlessly to talk some sense into Harris – but it was no good. Whatever she said, Harris was still trapped in some kind of loathsome obsession. Had she been an insect caught on a piece of flypaper she could not have been more helpless. Her absorption with Ben Ramsey had not diminished one jot. His betrayal had not turned Harris against her lover – but had done the opposite. She was now convinced that he had not let her down, she had failed him in some way. It was all her fault . . . And all Mildred could do was to watch her niece hopelessly and know that Harris was blind to sense.

She might want to shake her niece, but Mildred couldn't feel anything other than pity for Harris. She knew only too well how obsession festered in the brain, how it fed off its own misery. She looked at her niece and her thoughts went back to the first night she had come to them – a stroppy little kid, a fighter in short socks. And yet now, instead of using all that beauty and charm to make something of her life, Harris had squandered it on a man who didn't want her. A man who was committed to someone else.

There *has* to be a way to get through to her, Mildred thought. There has to be.

Irma had her own ideas.

'I can't face it! Not another scandal. That blasted girl needs a good slapping.'

'Irma, Harris is not a child.'

'She's acting like one,' Irma replied. 'Made herself cheap. Dragging herself and our good name into the gutter.'

'It's been in the gutter, on and off, for years,' Mildred replied tartly, putting down her reading glasses and staring at her sister. 'You really are a cow, aren't you?'

'What?'

'I said you're a cow. Harris is in real pain.'

'Hah!'

'Don't "hah" me! I remember you when you were goggle-eyed over Harry Delaney –'

'That was different!'

'It was no different!' Mildred snapped back, her patience exhausted.

She was tried of watching Harris suffer. Tired of seeing people snigger about her niece behind their hands. It was too much – and here was Irma, hiding away in the house, offering *advice*. Irma, who couldn't face the world. It was laughable.

'You make me sick, Irma! You make me want to knock your blasted head off.'

Glowering, Irma rounded on her sister. 'How dare you talk to me like that?'

'I have every right to talk to you how I please,' Mildred countered. 'You haven't a kind bone in your body. I thought you had, but now I'm not so sure. Harris acted stupidly, but she's confused –'

'*Confused!* What's there to be confused about? Ben Ramsey dumped her.'

Moving quickly, Mildred pushed Irma against the wall, Irma's eyes bulging as her plump, middle-aged sister glared at her.

'I hate you! I think I always have, really,' Mildred hissed, frustration making her cruel. 'I hate the way you think you're right, the way you think that everyone else is a fool. You've no compassion, no understanding –'

Knocking Mildred out of her way, Irma moved past her, smoothing down her dress.

'I'm not brawling with you. One fighter in the family is enough.'

'What family?' Mildred snapped. 'This isn't a family. This is a group of people crammed together under one roof, with only a name in common. You have nothing in common with me, or with Saville. And absolutely nothing in common with Harris –'

'Thank God for that,' Irma muttered sourly. 'It's no good taking this out on me, Mildred. Just because you're annoyed with Harris. It's not my fault that she's turned out wrong.'

'She's not turned out wrong!' Mildred almost screamed. 'She's just fallen in love with the wrong man –'

'And hit him, in his surgery, in front of half of Wigan! Good God, Mildred, what do you call wrong in your book?' Irma replied, her tone chilling. 'And as for saying that you hate me, so what? There's never been any love lost between us. We're here because that's the way life turned out for us. We both know that if things had gone differently we would have got out long ago.'

'You had the choice.'

'So did you,' Irma replied, staring at her sister evenly. 'You think I'm a complete fool, Mildred don't you? How typical of you to underestimate me. But then, your being the *nice* sister, it was easy to fool people, wasn't it?'

A cold sensation rippled down Mildred's spine. How had the argument got out of control like this? This wasn't just two sisters having a fight, this was different. The gloves were off. All the years of suppressed temper and bitterness were coming to the fore. Stop it, Mildred urged herself, stop it now.

'Look, Irma –'

'Always the sweet one, weren't you?' her sister taunted her, moving around the room to pause by the photograph of their parents. 'Remember Father? And Mother? Poor woman hardly ever said a word, did she? Only to name this house – and even then he contradicted her.' Irma picked up the photograph and then allowed it to slip from her fingers, the glass smashing on the floor.

'Irma!'

'Yes, that's my name. Irma Simons. It should be Irma Delaney, but Father put a stop to that, didn't he?' She stepped forward and then ground her heel into the photographic print of her father's face. A look of vicious triumph swept over her features.

'Irma, come on . . .'

'Come on *what*, Mildred? Come on, let's all be friends again?'

'This is bad for your heart.'

'What heart?' Irma replied. 'I don't have one, do I? I mean, you're always telling me that. How cold and uncaring I am.'

Shocked, Mildred could see her sister's heel still grinding the photograph into the floor.

'We're sisters, Irma. All sisters say stupid things at times.'

'No, sisters say *true* things at times,' Irma contradicted her, glancing down at the crushed photograph and then moving away. 'It's a very odd thing, the truth. Everyone sees it a different way – their truth, a little of the truth, the whole truth and nothing but the truth. The truth shall make you free –'

'Irma, please.'

'– but the truth is very ugly at times. That's why people avoid it. That's why we've always avoided it.' She looked Mildred up and down. 'God, I never realised you were ageing. I knew I was, but you always seemed so much the baby sister.'

'I'm going to get some tea.'

'That's your answer to everything, isn't it, Mildred? A cup of tea. Perhaps you should pop over to Germany and make a pot for the Führer. That should stop the war.'

'The war is not my fault!' Mildred said, folding her arms. 'I'm not taking the blame for that.'

But Irma was past cajoling. She had hidden away at Deerheart House, thinking there she could stay safe – but it had all gone wrong. The niece who could have restored their good fortune had turned out to be a clown and was now an object of ridicule, even pity. There was to be no way back to status for Irma. No road that would return her to the Mayor's Ball, no happy endings.

Tears were close – but bitterness won out.

'Mildred, I want to show you how kind I can be. After all these years, I want us to share something. Be real sisters. I want to show you how caring I really am.' She smiled and leaned over the sofa towards her sister, her voice low. 'I knew all about William Kershaw. *And I knew about the baby.*'

'Give us a kiss,' Madge said blearily, her heavily rouged lips puckered up grotesquely.

Gritting his teeth, Dandy planted a smacker on her mouth. God, he thought, that cheap lipstick tastes of bloody wax.

'Miss me?' Madge said, leaning against him as they moved towards Mesnes Park.

The railings had been taken for the war effort, the street-lamps turned off, the night cosy around them. Too cosy, Dandy thought.

'Hey, I said – did yer miss me?' Madge repeated, leaning even more heavily against her consort.

'Yeah, sure. Missed yer every minute.'

'Wot about every *second*?' Madge asked, coyly touching his shirt buttons.

'Yeah, that too.'

She stopped at once, her gait unsteady, but not unsteady enough to prevent her from standing, legs spread, arms akimbo.

'Yer playing me false?'

'Hey?' Dandy said, astounded. 'What the hell does that mean!'

'Yer fooling around, cheating on me?'

'Madge, we aren't Romeo and bloody Juliet! Besides, yer not exactly choosy who yer go with –'

'Hey, now, less of that!' Madge barked, her eyes unfocused. She blinked twice, slowly. 'I've given yer my heart.'

'And a dose of clap, I don't wonder.'

'Yer bugger!' Madge snapped, belting him one on the shoulder and sending him rocking backwards.

Dandy laughed, flinging his arm around her shoulder good-naturedly. Wouldn't do to fall out, not now, with all his stuff under her bed. Good thing he had kept their relationship quiet – on more than one account.

'Yer my girl, Madge.'

'Make sure I am,' she slurred. 'I don't take kindly to men playing fast and loose. I've got feelings, yer know. I can get hurt.'

'I know, Madge, I know,' Dandy replied, planting another kiss on her cheek.

'We could go round the back of the toilets,' she offered, instantly mollified. 'For a quickie.'

The idea had all the appeal of an enema. But then Dandy saw – with relief – someone blundering through the park gates.

'Hey, Madge, isn't that Saville? Saville Simons?'

She turned, focused, and then nodded unsteadily.

'Sure is. Wonder what he's doing here. Up to no good, I'll be bound.' She clung to Dandy's arm. 'Oh, wouldn't it awful if he flashed me?'

She laughed raucously, Saville seeing her and stopping in his tracks. He had run to escape his fighting sisters at Deerheart House, but gone far further than he had intended. Before he knew it he had entered the park. It was dark. He had thought he could sit and think – but now there were these two people standing staring at him.

There was nowhere he could go, Saville thought desperately. He was confused and just wanted – above everything – to get home.

'Hey, Saville Simons, what yer doing out? Looking for a girl?' Madge called to him, walking out from beside the bushes and beckoning to him.

'Aw, leave him alone,' Dandy remonstrated with her. 'He's a bit soft in the head.'

But Madge wasn't about to let a good thing pass.

'Hey, Saville, yer sister's looking for yer.' She could see Saville's interest perk up and continued, 'Come over here, I'll tell yer where she is.'

Hesitating, Saville looked at the dishevelled slattern in front of him, his gaze then moving to her foxy-faced companion. Instinct told him to run.

'Where *is* my sister?' he asked, his childlike voice at odds with the masculine walrus moustache.

'Come over here,' Madge said, beckoning him again, 'and I'll tell yer. I'm not shouting.'

'Which sister?'

'Yer what?'

Saville was hovering, moving from one foot to the other nervously. 'Which of my sisters is looking for me?'

Madge thought for a moment, then remembered that the nice one was called Mildred.

'Yer sister Mildred,' she said hurriedly. 'Mildred said to tell yer – Oh, come on, Saville, get over here!'

Slowly he approached her.

Dandy flicked some ash off his cigarette. Madge was obviously very drunk, and at such times she could get mean. He knew that, and watched her suspiciously.

At last Saville drew up level with Madge.

'Where's Mildred?' he asked, looking round fearfully.

'Why? Yer don't need yer sister to hold yer hand, do yer?' Madge asked him, stroking his arm. 'Yer a big boy now, Saville, yer should have some fun.'

'Let him be,' Dandy said quickly.

At once, Madge turned on him. 'Yer shut up! Yer want to watch what yer say to me. Remember it's not only yer shoes yer have under my bed.'

Duly warned, Dandy turned from protector to accomplice in an instant.

'She's right, Saville, yer need a bit of fun.'

Slowly, Madge leaned towards the helpless Saville. 'Like a kiss?'

He stepped back, horrified, Dandy catching hold of his arm tightly.

'Let me go!' Saville blustered. 'Please, let me go.'

'We're not going to hurt yer,' Madge cooed. 'I just want to see what yer made of. Word has it that our Saville here is only like a little boy. Wonder if that's true, eh, Dandy?'

Smiling wolfishly, Dandy joined in, holding on to the now struggling Saville.

'Aw, come on, just let Auntie Madge have a little look,' she said, reaching for Saville's fly.

Throwing up his arms, Saville tried to escape, but Dandy clung on.

'Hey, don't get all shy, Saville! After all, it's not something yer haven't done before,' Madge sniggered. 'This is just a private view.'

By this time Dandy had pinned Saville's arms behind his back, Madge grinning as she let her hand run over his crotch.

'Nothing much there.'

'Yer sure?' Dandy asked, now enjoying himself. 'Yer might surprise yerself.'

With one quick movement Madge unbuttoned Saville's fly and tried to pull out his penis. Desperate and frightened, Saville screamed and tugged himself free from Dandy, running down the path away from the laughing couple.

All he could think of was getting home. To keep running and get home . . . His feet banged on the dark pavements, his breathing fast, his face flushed. And then Saville had just rounded the bend of Bridgeman Terrace when he ran slap into a night watchman.

The man shone his torch on Saville. He took in his flushed face, his heavy breathing – and then he saw his unbuttoned fly.

THIRTY-FIVE

In her bedroom Eve Clough was talking to Birdie, her face animated.

'Ben wants us to get married before Christmas!'

'Good, darling,' Birdie said, looking at her daughter through the dressing-table mirror. 'But what about Harris Simons?'

Eve raised her eyebrows. 'Oh, that's over. She burned her boats when she came to the surgery like that. Imagine making such a fool of yourself? And then hitting – *hitting* – Ben! My God, some women act like idiots.'

That they do, Birdie thought. But not my daughter.

'You sure he's not still involved with her?'

'Positive,' Eve said. 'Why do you ask?'

'Because men are very complex, in a stupid kind of a way. They think they have it all worked out and then,' she clicked her fingers, 'a woman works her magic and they're all mixed up again. Did he sleep with Harris Simons?'

'Mother!'

'Oh, darling,' Birdie replied, 'you can't be that easily shocked. Men will be men.'

Eve looked down. 'Yes, he did. If you must know.'

'Silly Harris,' Birdie said thoughtfully, 'a woman should never let a man have what he wants before she catches him good and proper.' She caught her daughter's gaze in the mirror. 'You're not –'

'No!'

'Clever girl,' Birdie said approvingly. 'Let your wedding night come as a surprise, darling. To both of you.'

At the same time that Saville was being apprehended by the night watchman, Harris was standing round the corner from Dr Redmond's house. She had no pride left, only an overheated desire to see Ben again. If she could just talk to him she could explain. Automatically her hands went up to her hair and smoothed it. He liked her thick dark hair, and her red dress. The one she was wearing now, especially for him.

If only he would come home. Or come out. Harris didn't know if Ben was on a visit, or inside with the Redmonds. Just hoped that if she stayed there long enough she could catch him one way or the other. Sighing, she leaned her head against the stone wall. There was a foul atmosphere at Deerheart House – and it was all her fault. She had caused the argument between her and Mildred, and now the two sisters were fighting. She had heard them from her bedroom and had wanted to intervene – but what could she say?

So, with distorted logic, Harris had decided that she would try to win back Ben. If she did, she could go home and show everyone that all the arguments hadn't been for nothing. She could make everything all right again. Make peace. Stop the looks of pity and loathing from Mildred and Irma. She could make things right.

If she could just get Ben back. *If.*

'You knew about the baby?' Mildred asked, her face white as chalk.

Irma's eyes were unblinking. 'I knew about it all along. Wondered when you'd tell me. Confide. After all, I'd confided in you about Harry, hadn't I? And you'd been so understanding, Mildred, like you always are. So I waited. We were in the same boat then, you and I, we had both lost the men we loved. We could have had that in common. We could have shared our losses. But you never said a word.' She walked around the sofa, almost baiting Mildred. 'I wanted my sister then. I wanted to turn to you, to help you through. Just like you'd helped me. But you kept quiet, treated me like you treated our parents. Like the enemy.'

'*How* did you know?' Mildred asked, her voice low, shock making her limp as a glove.

'I knew about William Kershaw because I saw you two together once. As for the baby – that was a guess I made at the time. Call it sisterly instinct. I only knew for certain just now, when you didn't deny it.'

Stunned, Mildred stared at her sister. She hadn't told Irma because she didn't trust her. And that lack of trust had driven them further apart. She could imagine how much Irma would have brooded on it, how much she would have resented her exclusion.

'I didn't –'

'*Want* to tell me,' Irma finished for her. 'I understand. It's just difficult to think that you have an ally in a family and then find out that you haven't. That you're on your own.'

'Irma –'

'I have to say it changed me,' her sister went on, leaning against the sofa, her dark eyes challenging. 'If I couldn't trust you, who could I trust? Here we both were, in this damned house, our father terrorising us – why weren't we friends, Mildred? Why did you stop that?'

Blathering, Mildred tried to explain. 'Irma, believe me, I didn't think –'

'Yes, you did. You always think things out, Mildred, you

always have. I used to look at you and imagine what our father would say if I told him what you'd done. I mean, I'd been out in the open with my romance. But you'd been sneaking around, sleeping around, carrying some married man's bastard. I have to say you hid it well. I suppose being plump did you a service there. Oh yes, no one was on to you.'

Mildred slumped in her seat. 'Irma, stop it! This has to stop.'

'Why? It's been going on for decades, why stop now? In fact, it's out in the open now. The truth – that thing you're so afraid of.'

Inside Mildred's head she could hear her blood rushing, her heart speeding up. God, she should have kept the baby, should have got out when she could. And now this was her punishment, to be loathed by the very person who should have been her closest ally.

'I was sorry for you at first,' Irma went on, 'then I hated you. I used to watch you covering up your feelings as though nothing had happened. I couldn't even pity you, because what had you done? Nothing, to all intents and purposes. You were the *good* daughter. If you had played your cards right you might even have bagged Lionel Redmond.' She laughed hoarsely. 'A doctor, no less.'

'Irma, this is the past –'

'Not really,' her sister replied. 'Don't you see? Our histories are being repeated in our niece. Another Simons woman who fell for the wrong man. Another doomed romance. It could be the house: maybe all that heartache's got into the walls.' She hugged herself, shivering melodramatically. 'Maybe all the misery sinks into our bones at night.'

Unnerved, Mildred watched her sister. 'Harris has made a mistake, but she's not ruined her life.'

'You think not?' Irma asked. 'You think chasing a man who then dumped her isn't ruining her chances? Who decent will have her now? Mind you, I shouldn't be surprised, I

274

mean, with an aunt like you how *could* she have any real morals?'

Shaken, Mildred stood up. The blood rushed to her head, a pain started in her temples. All the bitterness of years was coming out, pouring from her sister's mouth like a poisoned spring.

'How dare you say that to me!' she roared. 'How *dare* you?'

'I didn't get myself into trouble with Harry Delaney. He was a slum boy, but I didn't act like a slum kid myself. I had some respect –'

'Respect!' Mildred shouted, her head pounding with fury and pain. 'What respect have you got, Irma? You're a laughing stock, a silly snob who used to suck up to the Mayor. You and your jumped-up ways. You and your ambitions. You're only sorry about Harris because she's messed up your plans, not because she's messed up her own life!'

'I WAS SOMEONE!'

'You were *never* anyone! You were a fool, a bitter, spiteful, frightening female copy of our father. That's what you were. And it's not my fault! It's no one else's fault that you didn't marry Harry Delaney or that I didn't keep my baby. We have only ourselves to blame, Irma, only ourselves.'

'You could have helped me.'

'*You could have helped me!*' Mildred countered. 'Why didn't you speak up? Why didn't you talk to me? Ask me if I needed help? You were my sister, my older sister. God, Irma, why didn't you swallow your pride and help me?'

There was a long sour pause.

'Because I didn't want to,' Irma replied finally. 'Because I wanted to keep your secret until the day I could use it against you. Until I could harm you the most.' She paused, Mildred staring at her, hardly breathing. 'The day finally came, Mildred. It was a summer day, hot, and our father was in the garden, reading his damned papers. I saw him and went over to him.' Mildred was watching her sister, horribly transfixed. 'I knew he would throw you out of the house for carrying some married man's bastard. He was very still when I got to his side, then he looked up. You remember how frightening he was, Mildred? He was that day too. He just said, "What is it?" and I opened my mouth to tell him all about you.'

Mildred could see their father sitting in the wooden chair outside, his expression unwelcoming, his tone distant. God, Mildred thought, he would have killed me if he'd found out what I'd done – and Irma would have given him the reason.

'Jesus, Irma, what did you do?'

'You're interested now, aren't you?' her sister asked, almost smiling. 'I have your full attention. Just like I had his – that summer day.'

Mildred was finding it harder and harder to speak. 'Irma, what did you tell him?'

'I said, "Father, I've got something to tell you."'

'And?'

'He stared at me.'

'And?'

'He told me to go away and stop bothering him. He said I was in his light.' Irma laughed. 'He said I was always getting in his bloody way.'

Mildred's voice was a whisper. 'So you never told him about me?'

Irma looked over to her sister and held her gaze. Then she nodded slowly.

'Oh yes, I told him all about you. When he was dying. When he was lying upstairs in that bedroom . . . I went in to see him. Mother had left him for a little while and I went in. I know he knew I was there. I could see his eyes flicker . . .'

Mildred was listening, terrified, and holding her breath.

'I wasn't afraid of him any more, Mildred, not then. He was ill, he was dying and he couldn't hurt me. He couldn't hurt anyone. So I sat down next to the bed and leaned towards him, Put my mouth only inches from his ear . . .'

Unblinking, Mildred stared at her sister.

'. . . and I told him about how much I had loved Harry Delaney and how my own father had made me into the bitch I was. And then I told him about Saville – how he wet himself with fear every time he heard his father's voice. I kept my voice steady, so he would hear every word. Then I told him about Gideon, and how stupid he had been to love the child who had hated him the most.' Irma paused, staring into the middle distance as though she could see herself bending over her dying father and whispering into his ear. 'And then I told him about you. Kind, good Mildred. Told him that you had been with a married man and got pregnant with his child . . .'

Her head swimming, Mildred slumped back down onto the sofa, her limbs leaden with shock.

'So in the end our father knew all our secrets. All the things we had hidden, I told him. When it was too late for him to do anything. Except take them to his grave.'

A shower had started as Harris watched the Redmonds' front door. Hurriedly she tied a scarf over her head and fretted about her dress getting water-marked. Come out, she willed Ben, come out of the house. But he didn't, instead she got wetter and colder. Her eyes never moved from the door, her ears straining for a sound. Which didn't come. She couldn't go home, Harris told herself, not until she had made everything all right again. *Then* she would go back, hand in hand with Ben, and show Mildred that she had nothing to worry about. If only he would come out.

Far away Harris could hear a car engine, but it passed the end of the street without stopping. Glancing up at the moonlit sky she wondered if there would be an air raid. The Germans usually picked clear, moonlit skies. An air raid would drag

Ben out of the house and into the shelter round the corner. Everyone knew that the Redmonds hadn't got their own shelter. But time passed and there was no air raid. No reason for Ben Ramsey to come out that night.

The first hour cleared, and then the second, Harris now huddled against the wall, bedraggled and bereft. The unexpected coolness of the August night had sunk into her bones, melancholic and sad. She was fooling herself, Harris realised finally. There was no way she could win Ben Ramsey back. He was gone. Already some other woman's partner. She had gambled and lost him.

The truth chilled her, Harris pulling her jacket around her shoulders, tears at the back of her eyes. Shame hit her, full force. Shame for what she had done, and for dragging her family with her. There was only one course of action left. She would go home and talk to Mildred, apologise to her. And to Irma. They had been good to her, taken her in, and she had shamed them.

And then, as she turned, Dr Redmond's door opened and Ben walked out. All her good intentions disappeared at once as she ran over, flinging her arms around him. He was rigid, but he didn't push her away.

Instead – Harris saw hopefully – his look was tender, almost sad.

'Ben, I'm so sorry, so sorry –'

'Harris, listen to me.'

'I'll be better,' she pleaded. 'Just let me have another chance. Please.'

'Harris –'

'Ben, we can work this out –'

'Harris!' he repeated, his tone sharp, all pity gone. 'Your aunt's just died.'

Stepping back from him, Harris shook her head. 'Oh, no. Poor Irma.'

'It's not Irma,' he said, his tone flat. 'It's Mildred.'

PART FOUR

And, as the cock crew, those who stood before
The Tavern, shouted – 'Open up the Door!
You know how little while we have to stay,
And, once departed, may return no more.'

The Rubáiyát of Omar Khayyám

THIRTY-SIX

I had taken her for granted, and I knew it. Too late. All the little inconsequential things – her handbag by the door; the white nightdress still smelling of her; the old calfskin notepad with the stamps still in it – they were all there, waiting for her. Each inanimate object Mildred had ever touched seemed poised for her return.

She wasn't meant to die. It was supposed to be Irma. Another of life's freak happenings. Shock had caused Mildred to have a stroke. I found out later that it wasn't just what Irma had said, but the fact that Saville had been returned home, apparently up to his old tricks. And then there was me, and what I had done – which played no little part. In fact, it was a bitter soup of all our stories – mine, Irma's and Saville's, that pushed Mildred from Deerheart House into some other place where none of us could reach her to apologise.

I had broken her heart. And her dying broke mine.

THIRTY-SEVEN

All through the funeral, Bonny held on to Harris's hand. If the people of Wigan had wanted something to take their minds off the war, then Mildred Simons's death did just that. Irma, stiff as a bamboo cane, stood in the pew and stared straight ahead, Saville sobbing beside her. Dry-eyed, Harris looked at the coffin, her fingers closing over the locket that had once been Mildred's. The locket she had always worn. The locket that didn't open.

In respect for Mildred's memory the night watchman promised that he would never tell anyone how he had found Saville. 'Just keep him in, or have him put away,' the man said. 'He'll get too old before long to get into any more mischief.'

Lionel Redmond had told Irma all about it, standing close to her as though he had expected her heart to give out. Which it didn't.

And standing alone by the window of the morning room had been Harris. Her obsession with Ben Ramsey seemed suddenly wicked to her. What did a man like him matter when she would have given him up at a minute's notice to have Mildred alive again? And what did dreaming about impossibilities do to help? Mildred was dead. That was the horrible truth. The truth Harris would have to live with for the rest of her life.

In the days that followed, preparations were made for the funeral by Irma and Harris, Saville in his room, comatose with grief. 'Mildred's dead. Why?' he kept asking repeatedly. 'Why?' And Irma would look at Harris, and Harris would look at Irma and both of them wondered just how responsible the other was. Or if their share of guilt was equal.

And so the morning of the funeral arrived. At St Catherine's church many people came to pay their respects, Bonny ready to give birth at any moment, but defying anyone to comment. Sitting next to Harris, she could feel eyes boring into her back. Go on, she wanted to shout, have a bloody good look! I'm in the club and Harris has been dumped by her man.

But she said nothing, just kept holding Harris's hand and thinking about the last time she had seen Mildred, and the conversation they had had. About how Mildred would be there for her. And about babies. Dead babies and live babies . . . Bonny closed her eyes for a moment to block the tears. I'm calling the baby Mildred, she thought suddenly, *Mildred Baker*. It sounded good. We need more Mildreds in such a bitter world.

'We have to go,' Bonny urged Harris a minute or so later. 'We have to follow the coffin out.'

Slowly, Harris got to her feet, her delicate features gaunt. For an instant her eyes rested on the coffin in front of her and she wavered, then began the long walk to the graveside. It was still cool for August, weather melancholic, the service over quickly. Soon the churchyard was as empty as a turned-out pocket.

'I'll miss her,' Bonny said, looking down at the grave.

Harris's voice was hardly audible. 'I should have brought flowers.'

'You sent a wreath.'

'Mildred would have liked *fresh* flowers,' Harris said tonelessly, looking round. 'I didn't even do that right.'

Bonny squeezed her hand. 'Come on, let's go home.'

'No,' Harris said, shaking her head. 'I'm not going back to Deerheart House to talk to people who are only coming to gawk. They're the same people who ostracised Mildred before. Let Irma see them – but not me.'

'People will talk.'

'People always talk! Anyway, Mildred would understand. She couldn't bear any of them.' Harris turned suddenly as Bonny's hand gripped hers. 'What is it?'

'I've started.'

'Started what?'

'Jesus, don't be daft! I'm having the baby!'

Incredulous, Harris looked at her. 'You *can't* have a baby in a cemetery.'

'Well you push it back then!' Bonny snapped. 'I tell you, *I'm having my baby*.' Suddenly she sat down on the grass, panting, Harris calling out to a couple in the distance. But they were too far away to hear her.

'Bonny, come on, get up!' she urged her, panicking. 'I've got to get you home.'

'I can't get up,' Bonny replied, gasping and gripping her stomach. 'God, it hurts!'

Hurriedly, Harris took off her coat and put it over the ground under Bonny's legs.

'I thought it took hours to have a baby. I thought you had contractions.'

'I did,' Bonny wailed. 'I just wanted to be at the funeral so much I thought I could manage it. They weren't coming quick at first.'

She screamed suddenly, the sound sending a flock of summer birds out of the trees, Harris looking round desperately.

'I'll go for help.'

Fiercely, Bonny gripped her arm. 'No! Stay here, I don't want to be alone.'

'But I could get help and be back in a few minutes.'

'And I'll have had my baby by then.'

'You can't have your baby here, Bonny!'

'I've not got a choice. Anyway, it'll be fine. Mildred's here, she's with us.'

Touched, Harris stroked Bonny's forehead.

'There's a phone in the pub down the road . . .' Bonny bit down on her bottom lip hard. '. . . After the baby comes, get help there.'

'You would know where the pub is,' Harris teased her.

A flicker of amusement came into Bonny's eyes, followed quickly by another scream. It was piercing – and it carried. Looking up, Harris glanced across the graveyard and saw a man in the distance. He stopped, looked over to where they were, and then began running.

'Someone's heard us!' Harris said, relieved. 'He's going for help.'

'I hope he's a bloody fast runner,' Bonny gasped, 'because this baby's waiting for no one.'

Mildred Baker was born precisely twenty-seven minutes after Mildred Simons was buried. In the same cemetery. Life coming full circle. Death and birth. For the rest of her days Bonny would say that Mildred had managed to keep her promise and been there for her.

Even after death.

THIRTY-EIGHT

My dearest sister –

Well, I was so sure that I would be home and with you when the baby was born, but Hitler had other plans. Do I have to say how pleased I was that Harris was with you? As for having a baby in a churchyard – oh, Bonny, only you could have done that!

I'm glad you called the baby after Mildred – she was a wonderful person and I know full well how she saved my skin. I suppose I'm not the only one thinking that it should have been Irma who died. They do say that's the secret of happiness – dying in the right order. I'm home on leave at the beginning of October. Kiss my niece for me, my little Mildred.

Your loving brother,
Richard

Dear Dope –

Thanks for your letter. Milly (Mildred) cries all night and even manages to wake Mam. She looks like pickled beetroot, but everyone says she'll improve. The midwife – when she could bear to talk to me – said Milly was a good weight. Mam got her some baby clothes off the black market – eat this letter now! Trouble was, they're too big, the poor little sod's drowning in pale blue wool. I can't say that I'm a natural mother, but I'd kill anyone who touched my baby. So make sure there's no invasion, right?

See you in October. And Harris sends her love. No, not the kind you think. Sisterly love. OK? Keep dodging the bullets, and come home to your niece and everyone else who loves you.

Bonny

When Churchill arrived in Moscow for talks with Stalin, Mr Lacy told everyone in the Bishop's Finger that they shouldn't be fooled. No one could trust the Russians.

Looking on, Mrs Turner glowed. Nelly Fisher had been routed at last. Her promiscuity hadn't caught her out – Mr Lacy's back had. It was one thing to rely on being with an older man for his pension, it was quite another thing to expect to spend the rest of your life looking after some crock. Besides, Mrs Barraclough had had enough of Nelly's sloppy housekeeping and so she was finally sent packing, Mrs Turner watching over the wall as her rival departed.

'Good luck,' she had called out cheerfully, Nelly Fisher turning and glaring at her.

'You're welcome to him!' she had snapped. 'What good's an old fool to me? I'm after a younger man.'

'You've been after a few younger men, if what I hear is true,' Mrs Turner had replied smartly, walking away.

And now here she was, safely back with Mr Lacy. A ring on her finger too. Not a good ring – he wasn't rich, after all. But he had realised that marrying a mature widow would be easier on his pocket – and his vertebrae.

Having finished his diatribe about the Russians, Mr Lacy turned back to his companion.

'What about Harris? I heard she were taking Miss Mildred's death badly.'

'She should – she were part cause of it.' Mrs Turner sniffed. 'You've no idea what it's like in the house now. I mean, you could go a month without a laugh before, but now . . . Miss Irma looks like she'd bite anyone who came close, and as for poor Saville, he never comes out of his room any more.' She dropped her voice for effect. 'That salon of theirs is shut up. No one's been there since Miss Mildred died. Shame, that; it were a nice little business.'

'I thought Miss Irma –'

'Oh, she won't go back there!' Mrs Turner interrupted him. 'Besides, they don't need the money. Not like the rest of us. I suppose it'll just sit there until they sell it.'

Mr Lacy digested the information thoughtfully. 'Must be nice to have money and not have to work.'

'You reckon?' Mrs Turner replied. 'I don't know about that. Keeping busy has saved many a man from madness.'

Sitting in the seedy kitchen at Mill Yard, Bonny looked at her mother. Madge had fallen down the steps at Wigan station and cut her lip. Moaning to herself, she held a piece of blood-soaked towel over the wound and reached for her gin.

'Leave it!' Bonny said, holding Milly in her arms. 'That won't help.'

'It helps the pain!' Madge snapped back, looking her daughter up and down. 'We have to talk. Yer been off work long enough, Bonny. Yer have to get some money coming in.'

Her mouth hanging open, Bonny took a while to reply. Then: 'I've just had a baby –'

'We all know about that – except the father!' Madge replied sharply.

'Why don't *you* work, just for a while? I mean, get a proper job.'

'I'm too old,' Madge said, her expression shifty.

'Aw, come on, Mam, let's not lie to each other. I know what you've been up to. You make a nice bit on the side – especially with the Yanks from the camp. You've been on the game for years.'

'What if I have? I've kept this bloody place going –'

'With my rent helping you.'

'Which isn't coming in now!' Madge exploded. 'Christ, I can't carry yer *and* that kid.'

Holding her child tightly to her, Bonny looked at her mother with loathing. 'I've never asked you for anything. I wouldn't have bothered to anyway, because I wouldn't have got it. But now I thought, for once, you might want to help me out. I was wrong.'

She looked around the kitchen, the sink piled high with dishes. Madge was doing no housekeeping; Bonny had been clearing up the day after Milly was born. Suddenly she could smell the odour of the mean house – cheap fat and worse, bugs. No place for a baby. Did she want to see Milly grow up here? With Madge around? Did she want her child to think this was all her life could amount to?

'I'm *going* to get a job, Mam –'

'When?' Madge asked, pressing the bloodied towel to her face, her lip swelling.

'Tomorrow. The same day after I leave here.'

It took Madge a moment to respond and then she swivelled round in her seat. The grate in front of her was full of ash and cigarette butts, an empty beer bottle holding up one leg of the rickety table.

'Yer what?'

'You heard me. I'm leaving,' Bonny repeated, walking to the door with her baby in her arms.

Drunkenly Madge staggered to her feet. Her face was bloody, her eyes unfocused, her dress torn at the hem. She was a drab with no future, and a past so sordid it showed in every line of her face.

'Yer leave here and yer don't come back! Yer hear me!'

Exasperated, Bonny turned. 'What in God's name would I come back for?'

At precisely the same moment Harris arrived at Mill Yard to see Bonny. Surprised, she watched as her friend struggled to pull an old pram out of the front door, Madge hurling a cardboard suitcase after her.

'Yer get out and bloody stay out!' she screamed. Then, turning to her neighbour: 'And what the fuck are yer looking at?'

Running over to Bonny, Harris took Milly from her and they both hurried out of the street, Bonny pushing the old pram in front of her. Its wheels squeaked as they walked, half of Bonny's clothes dangling haphazardly over the hood.

'Bitch.'

Harris didn't have to ask who she meant. 'What happened?'

'I'll be fine. Me and Milly, we'll get on just fine.'

'Bonny, what *happened*?'

She stopped at the top of Baldwin Street, sweating from the heat of wearing as many clothes as she had managed to put on before she left.

'I've left home.'

Harris moved Milly in her arms, the baby sleeping peacefully. 'To go where?'

'I dunno, yet.'

'I could help.'

Bonny took off a couple of layers of clothing and piled them on top of everything else in the pram.

An old man, curious, passed by staring.

'How do, Mr Rimmer?' Bonny called out.

'How do, Bonny? Yer doing a flit?'

'Something like that, Mr Rimmer,' she replied, jerking her head towards the pram. 'Me and my baby, we're off to seek our fortune.'

'Good luck, luv,' Mr Rimmer called back. 'Yer doing right, getting out of 'ere.'

Harris watched the exchange thoughtfully, Bonny turning back to the pram and then loading the cheap suitcase on the top. The rusty wheels squeaked under the weight.

'You can't wander off into the distance with a new baby,' Harris began. 'Be sensible.'

'You think living with that slag of a mother is sensible!' Bonny snapped back. 'You think seeing my child grow up in that filthy house is sensible? Well, I'll take my chances, but I reckon I can do better for us than that.'

Annoyed, she started walking again, the pram wheels making a high-pitched whine as they rattled over the cobbles.

'Can you cut a straight line?' Harris asked, hurrying behind her, Milly still asleep in her arms.

'What?'

'I said, can you cut a straight line?'

Bonny stopped walking. 'Yeah, I can cut a straight line. So what?'

'Then you've got a job.'

'Cutting straight lines?' Bonny replied, her head on one side. 'What the hell are you talking about?'

Harris took in a deep breath. She had needed something to jolt her back into life, and here was her opportunity. Heaven-sent. Besides, she knew that Mildred would have approved.

'I'm going to reopen the salon, Bonny, and I need someone to work with me.'

'I can't do hair!'

'If you can cut a straight line, I can teach you the rest. Mildred always used to say that it all started with a straight line. If you have an eye for it you can learn easily enough.'

Suddenly Bonny burst out laughing, walking on again.

'You're mad!'

Falling into step beside her, Harris continued, 'Why? You

291

need a job and I need a partner. There's a flat above the shop. It's not much, Bonny, but it's small and clean and you could make it nice for the baby. Think about it – your own place. Just you and Mildred.'

Bonny stopped walking again and looked at Harris. 'I'm calling her Milly for short. Mildred's for when she gets older, you know, when she's a woman.' Bonny's head was bowed, her voice very low. 'We have to get one thing straight, Harris. I'm not going to be grateful. I'm not going to spend the rest of my life saying thank you. I've never needed help from anyone before and I don't now. You and me aren't meant to work together, we're from different sides of the tracks. It would be a disaster and you know it.'

'I know you're selfish,' Harris said, her tone stinging.

Bonny's eyes blazed. 'Selfish!'

'Yeah, selfish. You have a chance to get yourself a good job and a nice home and you're putting your pride first,' Harris replied.

'Give me my baby!'

'No!' Harris replied, walking off, Bonny hurrying behind with the creaking pram.

'Give me my baby!' she hissed as she drew up beside Harris.

'No! I know what's best for this baby and for you. I might have made a complete fool of myself and buggered up my own life, but I won't stand by and see you do the same.'

'You're right, you did make a right ass of yourself,' Bonny agreed, fighting to keep the pram going in one direction as she pushed it along hurriedly. 'The whole town thinks you're a bloody fool. I'm not sure I'm in your league.'

'You could learn,' Harris teased her. 'Working with me, some of my lack of judgement might rub off on you. After all, you *did* pick the wrong man, so there's hope for you yet.' With that, Harris stopped walking.

Smiling wryly, Bonny took Milly out of Harris's arms and looked into her baby's face.

'What d'you think, kiddo? Fancy working for a crazy woman like this? A woman with a past.'

'Takes one to know one.'

Bonny was still looking at her baby. 'I can't crawl to you, Harris. I just can't. If you want a lackey, that's not me. I'll do my best and keep the place nice, but I can't stop being who I am – and saying what I think.'

'I don't want you to change.'

'You know what you're getting, don't you?' Bonny went on, looking directly at Harris. 'I'm crabby and blunt. I don't get fooled that easily by life. And I tell it as I see it. Do you *really* need that in an employee?'

'No,' Harris said frankly. 'But I need it in a friend.'

THIRTY-NINE

The streets of Wigan were buzzing with the news. The war was over, the war was over! No official announcement had been made, but Harris and Bonny sat by the radio in the back room of the salon, and waited. Then, finally, at 3.00 p.m., Winston Churchill announced that the war in Europe was at an end.

Outside the salon window they could hear cheers, people in the street hugging each other and whooping as they ran down into Market Place. Picking up Milly, Bonny clung to her child and then looped her other arm around Harris.

'We made it.'

'Sure we did,' Harris said, smiling.

'Richard made it too. *And* he's bringing a medal home. That's one in the bloody eye for some people.' Bonny paused, suddenly overcome as she buried her face against her child's shoulder.

Over Bonny's head Harris could see people hurrying past, running towards a future that had to be better. A new time was beginning, with new chances. Her gaze wandered and then came to rest on the photograph she had kept over her desk. A picture of Mildred dressed in a fussy summer suit, her magnificent froth of hair a luminous halo around the well-loved face.

Who would have believed that the end of the war would see Mildred dead? It was incredible . . . Harris stared back into the street. She knew she should be full of hope, but she felt nothing. Even working with Bonny hadn't lifted her melancholia. Mildred was dead; the one security, the one constant in her life, was gone. And she was partially to blame.

'We can really make a go of things now,' Bonny said excitedly. 'There's only one way for us – and that's up.'

Harris turned and smiled. Of course Bonny was right, but somehow no achievement would ever be enough if Mildred wasn't there to see it.

There really wasn't much point keeping an eye on Saville, Irma thought. Whatever had happened to him that night had changed him irrevocably. He would now sit in his room, cutting out pictures from magazines and papers, and spend endless hours pasting them into albums. To her eyes, they made no sense, but maybe they did to Saville. Maybe a lot of life made no sense to her, but did to others . . . Irma sighed, smoothed her already tidy hair and walked towards her own room. So it was over, she thought, the war was finally over.

And what exactly did that mean to her? She stopped dead, looking round. At the end of the landing was a large oval window, looking out over the garden, which was a mess, neglected, the squat Anderson shelter grinning up at her like an ugly troll. Memories followed: her and Mildred in the shelter, with Saville. Then her and Mildred arguing . . .

It was all her fault! Irma thought despairingly. She hadn't meant to say so much, but she was so tired of everyone's damned secrets. God, *why* had she said it! Irma wondered, clenching her hands together. She knew what everyone in Wigan was thinking – poor Mildred, what a loss. *It should have been Irma.* Well, who could blame them? They were right, it should have been her.

But it wasn't. Mildred was dead and she was alive. And somehow she had to make sense of it. She could see what Harris was thinking, but what right had *she* to judge? Hadn't she broken Mildred's heart? Upset the whole family? And as for Saville . . . Irma stopped. It was no good trying to blame others. It had been *her* words that had killed Mildred. Her fault. Shared with others, but primarily hers.

Harris had asked her repeatedly what had gone on the evening Mildred died, but Irma had dodged the questions. Apparently Saville had told Harris about the argument, but thankfully he hadn't heard what had been said. He had run away and hidden. As he always did. Harris could think what she liked, Irma thought, but she wasn't going to find out the enormity of what her aunt had done. It was enough to be hated for living, it would be too much to be hated for being Mildred's killer.

'WELCOME BACK' the banners said at the stations and hanging from the streetlamps. Gradually the army, navy and air force sent home their men, towns filling again, families complete again. The ones that were lucky. In other homes there were blank spaces at tables, and sombre visits to graves. But the living were welcomed home to a land fit for heroes. No more unemployment, the men were told; you've fought for your country and now it will reward you with a safe future.

Then, on 26 July, Winston Churchill was usurped as Prime Minister by Labour's Clement Attlee in a landslide victory. Churchill had been a great leader in wartime, but there was no room for a warmonger now. New times were here, new brushes sweeping clean. Everywhere there was a sense of optimism. Rationing might still be on, but there was no fear of being killed in your bed. It was time to be normal again.

Smiling, Richard stood at the end of Market Place and looked round. He was free, and alive. And full of the kind of news every man wants to share. He smiled again, unable to stop himself, and then began to walk towards Simons Coiffeuse.

Who would have thought that Bonny would have ended up being a hairdresser? The idea cheered him. That was one in the eye for all those people who had looked down their noses at his sister. Bonny wasn't like Madge, after all. She had gone wrong once, but made the best of it, and never repeated her mistake.

Walking along, smiling to himself, Richard's thoughts turned to Harris. It had hurt him to hear about her and Ben Ramsey. But then again, Harris had always been headstrong. But to show herself up, to *beg* some man to have her . . . it was incredible. Slowing his steps, Richard glanced at his watch. Bonny had told him that Harris went home for lunch – primarily to see Saville – and that one o'clock would be the best time to come to the salon.

It was precisely ten past one when Richard walked into Simons Coiffeuse. Suddenly three pairs of female eyes looked up from basins, or from under dryers. Dear God, Richard thought, that can't be Mrs Brewer, can it? She looked like a mummy in curlers.

'Richard!' Bonny flung herself into his arms, the three pairs of eyebrows raised in unison. 'I'm so glad to see you!' Knowing full well that everyone would talk, she added loudly, 'So, where's your medal?'

He flushed. 'Bonny!'

'Come on!' she teased him. 'Let's have a look. I want to brag about my hero brother.'

Dodging the subject, Richard looked round. 'Where's my little niece?'

'Asleep upstairs. You can see her when she wakes. *Please* don't make me get her now. She screams like a bloody siren if she doesn't get her sleep out.'

'I'll see her later,' Richard replied, looking around him. 'You're busy – I don't suppose you can get away for a bit?'

'It's OK, Harris is here,' Bonny replied, hurrying on. 'She didn't go home. For once. I know you wanted to tell me something in confidence, but I couldn't ask her to leave, could I?'

Richard didn't have time to reply as Harris walked in at that instant. She hadn't seen him for several months and smiled warmly. God, she thought, he looks so grown-up now. So different. Like a man who had found his feet. Nothing like the poor lad who had once tried to kill himself. And he was a hero too. Her old friend, *a hero*.

'Richard!' she said, moving over and kissing him on the cheek. 'God, it's so good to see you. We're all so proud of you.'

He wanted to smile back and say something light, but for an instant words failed him. God, she was beautiful, the resemblance to Vivien Leigh all the more pronounced. The same dark colouring, elfin expression, the same pert sexuality. *I loved you once so much I wanted to die for you*, he thought. *I hope you never know.*

'Harris,' he said at last. 'You look good.'

'Amazing what work does for you,' she answered, lightly, but with some trace of bitterness under the words. 'That, and public humiliation.'

'From what I heard Ben Ramsey wasn't good enough for you.'

'Next time I'll let you choose who I fall in love with,' she replied, turning away.

Wincing, Bonny looked at her brother, but although she had expected to see the same longing in his eyes, it wasn't there. He looked sorrowful instead, pity in his face as he watched Harris.

'Go on, you two,' she continued, turning back to them. 'I'll hold the fort here.'

Bonny looked round at the customers. 'I can't leave you on your own . . .'

'Get out!' Harris teased her, winking at Richard. 'And I want to see some more of you now you're home.'

In silence Bonny walked across the town, linking arms with her brother. She felt safe again, now that Richard was back. The old feeling between them hadn't changed. It was odd, she thought, despite everything we could still be kids. Before Harris, before the baby, before the war.

'She looks wonderful.'

Bonny nodded. 'Harris is beautiful, always has been.'

'I haven't seen Mam yet.'

'No loss there,' Bonny answered coldly.

'You two really fallen out?'

'For good.'

'I'm sorry . . .'

'Oh, forget it, Richard! You haven't seen our mother lately. You don't know what she's like. I couldn't stay in that house with her. It was bad enough for me, but my baby's not living like that. She was no grandmother, she didn't give a damn about Milly. If she'd had her way, I would have been up Ma Denham's and had the knitting needle treatment –'

'Bonny!'

She turned to look at him, amazed. 'Jesus, Richard, I wonder about you! You're so naïve in some ways. Did you grow up with your eyes closed? Didn't you see the squalor we lived in? Or know about Mam?'

'I knew,' he said quietly.

'I don't think you really did,' Bonny answered, folding her arms across her chest. 'I don't think you ever *really* knew. You weren't around much during the war to see how far she sank. Or who she ran around with. Or what she did. I didn't want to be near her in the end. Didn't want it to rub off. Everyone thought I'd turn out like her, I know they did. Especially when I got pregnant. "Just like Madge," they said. But I wasn't going to let myself down. I might be an unmarried mother, but I'm no scrubber. I had one man, and only one.'

'Bonny, you don't have to explain –'

'I do!' she contradicted him. 'I do, Richard, because it's important. No one can point the finger at me and say I turned out like Mam. *No one.*'

'Is she at home now?'

'How would I know?' Bonny replied, walking on. 'Before I left she was hardly ever there. If she's got herself in trouble I wouldn't be surprised.' She looked at her brother seriously. 'I don't mean my kind of trouble – police trouble.'

'You're joking!'

'Nah, I wish I was. Anyway, enough of our mother,' Bonny replied, changing the subject. 'Where's the medal?'

He paused, then passed it to her in its case. Smiling, Bonny opened the box and stared at the medal as it caught the sunlight. '"For valour",' she said, reading the words inscribed on it. 'God, aren't you going to wear it?'

Shaking his head, Richard closed the box and pocketed it. 'It means a lot to me.'

'So wear it.'

'Not like that, Bonny . . . I mean, if it hadn't been for you I wouldn't have been alive to win any medal.'

'I only saved you for that,' she teased him.

'I won it because I wanted to redeem myself. Is that the right word – *redeem*? You know, I wanted to make good after acting like a bloody coward and trying to top myself.'

'You weren't a coward, you just weren't thinking straight.'

'But I left no note, nothing to explain why I did it. Everyone would have thought I was scared to go back to the war, that I *was* a coward.' The thought made him shudder. 'Jesus, Bonny, what if you hadn't come home and found me?'

'Then I would be walking along the road talking to myself,' she said, nudging him with her elbow. 'I was *supposed* to find you, stupid. Someone was looking out for us that night.'

'I think about Mildred Simons a lot,' Richard continued. 'How she covered up for me. How she organised it with Dr

300

Redmond that no one found out what had really happened. What she did made sure I wasn't thrown out of the army and my name ruined.' He stopped, looking down at his sister. 'I was so lucky to have you, and her. So lucky Mildred kept my secret.'

'Mildred was good at keeping secrets,' Bonny replied quietly. 'Anyway, enough of the past. What's this big news you've been waiting to tell me?'

Smiling, he steered her sister towards a bench and sat down. A bus passed, Vimto advertised on the side, and at the corner of the street a woman called for her child. Normal, everyday life.

'I'm engaged,' he said at last.

'As what?'

'Oh, Bonny! I'm engaged to be married.'

She put her head on one side and stared at him. 'You kept that bloody quiet!'

'I wasn't sure you'd want to be involved, after the last time. Anyway, I wanted to be sure.' Richard paused, wanting to get the description just right. 'She's incredible.'

Well, Bonny thought, I had you for all of a few minutes and now you're off again. Soon you'll be someone's husband, someone's father before long. Damn it, she thought, why was she so selfish? She should be glad for him. Glad that he wasn't in some cemetery with a slab over his head. Dead by his own hand, or some German's.

And yet envy ate into her.

'That's great.'

'You sound disappointed.'

She squeezed Richard's hand. 'She better not bugger you about. I don't want anyone flighty as a sister-in-law.'

'Penny's perfect.'

'Penny Perfect,' Bonny repeated drily. 'Sounds catchy.'

'You'll love her. She's sensible, caring . . .'

'How did you meet?'

'She's the sister of one of the men I was billeted with. We started writing and then it went from there. Her brother was killed a couple of months ago . . .' Richard paused. 'It's quick, I know, but it's right to marry her.'

'You *have* met her?'

He nodded. 'Of course I have! A couple of times. She lives in Oldham.'

'Well, someone has to.'

'Oh, Bonny!'

She turned and kissed her brother on the cheek. 'I'm glad, honestly I am. When are you getting married?'

'In a while, no rush.'

'It's not like she's pregnant.'

He gave her a slow look. 'Bonny, what is it?'

Shrugging, she looked down at her hands. Another bus passed, a boy following on a bike. The sun was warm on her back, the street dry and flecked with pigeons.

'I'm just jealous, that's all,' she replied honestly, looking over to her brother and screwing up her eyes against the sun. 'Aren't I a bitch? Always thinking of myself. It's just that I'd have liked to be able to tell you that *I'd* met someone.'

'You will, in time.'

'Sure. With another man's kid in tow.' She grinned mischievously. 'You let me down, brother. All those men in the army – couldn't you find *anyone* for me?'

He put his arm around her, and Bonny laid her head on his shoulder. Richard had been worried about telling her, realising how easy it would seem for him. Bonny had had a child and was raising her alone, with no man to help . . . But that would change now. He might have a fiancée, but he would find more than enough time for his sister.

'I'm not going anywhere far away.'

Bonny mumbled, 'Except Oldham.'

'Listen, Bonny, I promise I'm not going off and leaving you again. I'm back home and I'll always be there for you.'

'You said you'd be there when the baby was born!' Bonny chastised him. 'I can't believe a word you say. How do I know you won't run off and be a mercenary somewhere? Leave me *and* Penny Perfect.'

'You'll like her a lot.'

'No, I won't!' Bonny teased him. 'I shall hate her and we'll be enemies. You'll never see Milly again and I'll never nurse your children.' Sitting up, she punched his arm when she saw his expression. 'You are a clot! Did you believe me?'

'No – but I was thinking of cutting my wrists again.'

Bonny laughed loudly, looking out over Market Square. 'I'm glad you can make a joke of it now.'

'You never let me take it seriously. You were merciless in your letters.'

'I didn't want you to get soft.'

He paused, let a moment hang. 'Did I ever say thank you?'

'Never in person.'

'Well, thanks.'

'You're welcome. Does Penny Perfect know about you and Harris?'

He shook his head vigorously. 'Only that I loved someone and it didn't work out.'

'Nothing else?'

'No.'

'Good,' Bonny said at last. 'It's in the past. No point letting it colour your future.'

'That's very wise.'

'I read it on the back of a matchbox.'

'Good to see you keeping up your education.'

Laughing, Bonny leaned heavily against her brother. 'I want Milly to get fond of you. It's important to me, Richard. There are no other men in her life. I want her to have a good example, someone to look up to. I don't want her growing up thinking all men are stupid sods.'

'Even if it's true?'

'*Especially* if it's true.'

The stitch in his side was really hurting now, Dandy gasping for air as he kept running. Jesus, he was scared. That bloody Fleming had sent a couple of heavies after him, and not just to frighten him either . . . Slumping against a wall in the back streets of Scholes, Dandy tried to get his breath back. That was the trouble, you drank too much and smoked too much and then you had no bloody air when you needed it.

Gingerly he peeked round the corner. No one in sight. He would wait a little until he knew they had gone and then double back, catch a bus out of Wigan and head for Manchester. Then keep quiet for a while until things blew over . . . It had been his own fault. Greed had made him dupe Fleming again. Why didn't he learn? But war was over now, the glory days were gone. Before long rationing would be finished and no one would need the likes of him.

No more dealing in booze, cigarettes, stockings. Anything you wanted, Dandy Gilburn could have got it for you. He had been so popular for a while – especially with the ladies. Breathing heavily, Dandy thought of Madge. Rumour had it that she had been admitted to hospital with liver failure. And where was his stuff? Under her bloody bed, that's where.

It was obvious that he would break in and try to get it out. What was also obvious was that Fleming's boys had been watching him. They had seen him take what was left and waited until Dandy was ready to go before they jumped him. Typical that, let the poor sod work like a bloody navvy and then grab him.

But Dandy had broken away and given them a right run for their money. They didn't know Wigan like he did, or they would have caught up with him. And now here he was, round the back of Vauxhall Road, his lungs rattling like nails shaken in a tin cup.

'Oi, Dandy!'

He turned, white-faced, and then tried to make for the end of the street. But there was another man waiting for him there.

'You've been a naughty boy,' one said, staring Dandy in the face. 'Running off like that. Trying to make us look bad in front of our boss.'

'You can have what you like!' Dandy blustered. 'Take what you want!'

'We want you . . .' the second man said pleasantly.

'. . . to give us . . .' the first man continued.

'. . . what you owe us.'

Dandy was shaking like an aspen leaf. 'I haven't got any money. God, I haven't got a bean left.'

'Oh, dear.'

'That's a pity.'

'It certainly is,' the first man concluded. 'So what *can* you give us?'

'An apology?' Dandy offered, with what he thought was a light touch.

The first fist smashed into his solar plexus, making him throw up, the second striking him full under the chin. Dandy Gilburn went down like a sack of coal, the first man kicking out and catching him on the side of the head with the toe of his boot. Blood spurted from Dandy's ear, an excruciating pain spearing through his brain as he screamed and rolled on the ground.

'Jesus!'

'– isn't listening,' the first man finished for him.

Hauling Dandy to his feet, they propped him up and then beat him against the wall, a semiconscious Dandy finally slipping down onto the pavement again, his face coming to rest in a pile of dog muck.

'Enough,' Dandy croaked, his lips puffy, 'please, God, enough . . .'

'OK. OK,' the first man said, turning away and then turning

back. 'But you can have this as a goodbye.' And then he swung back his leg and, with all his force, kicked Dandy fiercely in the kidneys. 'That should have you pissing blood for a month.'

The war was over. And so was Dandy.

By the time Richard reached the cemetery the sky was cloudy, threatening rain. He looked up, then pulled his coat collar high around his neck. In the distance a flurry of late summer birds made for the scuttling clouds, the far landscape mottled with green and gold. Breathing in deeply, Richard looked around, then entered the cemetery.

It took him only a little while to find the grave.

Mildred Agnes Simons
1890–1944
Loved and missed in equal measure

Bending down, Richard brushed away a few drifted leaves and rearranged the flowers that someone had recently left. Harris, no doubt, as Irma never left the house. For a moment Richard wondered if he should say a prayer and then thought better of it. He had never been a religious man and doubted if Mildred had had much truck with any faith. She just lived well, and honourably, always standing up for her own. Or those she considered her own.

Moved, Richard touched the white headstone. He could remember Mildred clearly; the mass of soft hair, the plump figure, the quizzical look she had when anyone was trying to fool her. She had been kind when he and Bonny were children. The foul Irma had always made them feel their place, but not Mildred. She had even stood by Bonny when she was pregnant. A spinster lady, an innocent – and yet she had never judged his sister. Amazing that.

'I would have liked to see you to say thank you,' Richard

said, talking to the white headstone and feeling a little foolish, but pressing on anyway. 'You saved my good name and I'll always owe you for that. I would have been done for, if it hadn't been for you. And you never brought it up, did you? Never held it over me, or asked for thanks. You just wanted to help, without even pausing to wonder if it would rebound on you. And it could have done – if anyone had found out. You were so brave. I was going to take the coward's way out, but that wouldn't have been your way . . . So I want to thank you, Mildred, the only way I know how. The only way that matters and I know you'll understand.'

Looking round to check that no one could hear him, Richard reached into his pocket and drew out the medal. Then, carefully, he dug a little hole in the marble chippings that covered the grave, and laid the box there. Finally he scattered the loose chippings over the top, the box disappearing from sight.

'That's for you,' he said, straightening up. 'For valour, Mildred Simons. *For valour.*'

FORTY

Wigan, two years later

Dressed in a heavy winter coat, Eve Clough walked out of the back door of her house, the rain falling on her head and wetting her hair in moments. She should go back for a hat, but she didn't care. What was the point? What would it matter if she got a cold? Ben wouldn't give a damn. She stopped at the thought of him, the rain splashing over her expensive leather court shoes.

Let your wedding night be a surprise for both of you – her mother's words had come to haunt Eve over the years. Oh yes, it had been a surprise. If not for Ben, at least for her. Shivering, Eve walked on. He had his own practice now, on the outskirts of Wigan, and was making good money. On his way, everyone said. 'Darling,' Birdie assured her repeatedly, 'Ben will be on Rodney Street within ten years.'

It hadn't always been bad. At first she had loved him, and he had *tried* to love her. Eve was sure of that. She was also sure that Ben had been desperate to fit in with her, her family and the ambitions they had for him. After all, he was ambitious too. But after a few months Eve noticed little changes in her husband. He was generous, but the presents he bought her weren't to her taste. And she told him so – expecting him to be indulgent, like her father.

Ben saw it otherwise. His wife was criticising him. His taste wasn't good enough for Eve Clough. There were other things that began to fester between them. She liked to go out, but her husband was always tired. 'We have to socialise,' Eve had said to Ben repeatedly. 'It's important to have a busy life.'

'I *have* a busy life,' he had replied. 'I work all the time and come home exhausted. I just want to relax. Is that too hard to understand?'

Yes, Eve thought, it was. Because she needed to be busy, needed to have other people around. That way she wasn't alone with her husband; that way they weren't forced into a false cosiness. Ben wanted to sit reading or listening to music, but Eve wasn't comfortable relaxing with him. She couldn't loosen up, couldn't lay her head on his shoulder, couldn't tease him. The closeness wasn't there.

And he knew it too. So as time wore on Ben found more and more excuses to stay late at work. He encouraged Eve to visit her mother, even though he was getting worn down by Birdie's constant interference. He told Eve that he felt as though – slowly but inexorably – his life was being repossessed by the Cloughs. And it made him overreact.

Rubbing her arm, Eve winced then paused under a streetlamp to look at the bruises. Love games, he called them. *Let me tie you up, sweetheart . . . Come on, relax, you're such a prude . . . People do these things everyday . . . Christ, if you weren't so bloody frigid, you'd enjoy it . . .* Eve doubted that. Doubted she would ever enjoy her husband's lovemaking, or his manipulation. And then, just when she made up her mind to leave him, he would change, as if he knew he had gone too far and needed to win her back. Then he would be tender, romantic, pay her compliments. Undress her, look at her with longing. Try to please her. For a while . . .

And so she would stay; pray that the good times would last, that he wouldn't slip back. And he wouldn't. Maybe for a week, or a month, once for three months. Three whole months. And then he had changed, of course. Coming home one night late and irritable, without a word he had woken her up and pulled up her nightdress.

'I'm tired, Ben –'

'I don't give a fuck.'

She hadn't known which had shocked her most – the action or the word. Grunting on top of her he had had trouble coming to climax, blaming her, shouting at her, ordering her to dig her nails deeper and deeper into his back. As if somehow he had expected the pain to relieve him. And then finally, it had been over.

Thank God they hadn't had any children, Eve thought. If there had been children to consider she could never have left him. She had been clever there. Let him think that it was her fault, that she was barren, never suspecting that his wife was using precautions. But if he ever found out, if he ever knew that she was lying to him, preventing the birth of a son and heir . . . Eve's footsteps echoed on the road. A car passed, Eve automatically turning away.

Why? Because she was afraid it might be him in the car; she was afraid of her own husband. And she had reason to be now. Ben Ramsey wasn't a normal man. He might look and sound normal, might behave normally outside, but she had seen him at other times and wondered.

Just like she wondered why she hadn't already left him. It would be easy just to go home to her parents, start again . . . Eve paused, her breathing rapid. But life without Ben would be more intolerable than life *with* him. And then she knew just how trapped she really was. An unwelcome image came into Eve's mind at that moment – Harris Simons.

Had she liked Ben's lovemaking? Had she revelled in it? Made him feel good? Made *herself* feel good? Eve remembered how desperately Harris had been in love, making a complete fool of herself, running after Ben like a whipped dog. Eve had laughed at her then – but she wasn't laughing now.

310

'I love you, darling,' Ben had reassured her. 'I never think of Harris Simons any more. And you have to make sure I never do. You can do that, darling, *can't you?*'

Rooted to the spot in thought, Eve stared ahead. How the tables had turned. Harris Simons was free. Alone, yes, but rid of Ben Ramsey. Harris had her own business, which was thriving. She was more attractive than she had ever been. And rich. It was true that she had thrown herself into work, but so what? In time she would find herself a new man.

With a prickling sense of unease, Eve thought back to the day in the surgery when Ben had slammed the door in Harris's face. How smug Eve had been when she had finally usurped her rival; how she had gloated, looked at Harris with pity. How she had crowed over getting her man.

But she hadn't got him. He wasn't hers to get.

Coming in from the salon, Harris put her handbag down on the hall table and slowly pulled off her gloves. On the landing above, Irma stood watching. She had been restless for some time, and was now heading for a crisis. Her chosen exile had become increasingly irksome over the three years since Mildred's death, and now she was haunted by the realisation that at any moment everything could end for her. She had come to realise how short life was, and know that in an instant it could be over.

And what would be her epitaph? That she had been a bitter lonely woman, guarding her brother? But what had she *achieved?* No husband, no family, not even a career any more. It wasn't enough, Irma realised. It wasn't anything like enough! In fact, unless she did something about it soon, she would look back on a wasted life.

But there was still time to do something about it. Still time. If she was quick . . . Irma watched Harris in the hall below. Her niece had changed: better-looking than ever, but stern. Was she like that with everyone, or just at home? Irma wondered, walking downstairs towards her.

Hearing her footsteps, Harris looked up. 'Evening, Aunt Irma.'

'I think you should call me Irma now. You're a little old for Aunt.'

'Whatever you say,' Harris replied, walking on into the drawing room.

Emotionless, Irma followed her, Mrs Turner bringing up the rear.

'We've got some chops,' she said. 'Not the best quality, but an improvement to what we've been having.'

'Good,' Harris replied absent-mindedly.

'Dinner in fifteen minutes then,' Mrs Turner added, walking off, her eyes raised to Heaven.

'You would think they would have come to some understanding by now,' she'd told Mr Lacy. 'I mean, it's over three years since Miss Mildred died and there's still the same chill over the place. Like a couple of strangers living together in a posh boarding house, barely able to look at one another.'

Back in the kitchen Mrs Turner jumped as she saw a shadow move outside the window.

'Dear God!' she said, as Richard walked in. 'You gave me a jolt.'

'I just called by to show you the little one,' he said happily, holding up his son, Tom. 'He's a grand boy.'

'He is that,' Mrs Turner cooed appreciatively. 'Can you wait until I've served dinner, luv, and then I can have a right good look at him?'

Nodding, Richard stared at the fine china and serving dishes. 'Are they having guests?'

'Oh, there's no guests come here, luv. This is how they have their dinner every night.' Mrs Turner wiped her hands hurriedly and looked at the dishes on the tray. 'I'll be back in a minute. Wait for me.'

Sitting down beside the kitchen fire, Richard looked at his son, pulling faces as the baby laughed. How could anything in life be so perfect? he wondered. His sister might have called his wife Penny Perfect for a joke, but it had stuck and Penny Perfect had now given him Perfect Tom. Contentedly, Richard leaned back into the old armchair. He could remember the kitchen from childhood, the year that Madge had been ill and he and Bonny had come to Deerheart House. It had all been so long ago, when he had believed he would be important someday.

The hell with that, Richard thought happily, who needed money when you had a family you loved and who loved you? He wasn't rich or successful, working at the gas works, but he wouldn't have it any other way. Thoughtfully he stared into the flames, watching a few sparks fly up the dark chimney. He could have missed all of this – Penny, Tom – he could have just disappeared like one of the sparks, flying off to God knew where.

'That's it for now,' Mrs Turner said, returning and flopping into the chair next to Richard. Smiling, she reached for the baby. 'Come here, little one, and let me have a look at you.'

'I said I'd take him off Penny's hands for a while, give her a break.'

'I never trusted my husband like that,' Mrs Turner replied. 'He didn't know which end to feed and which to wipe.' She wiggled her finger in front of the baby, who was staring at her, mesmerised. 'He's like you, Richard.'

'Everyone says that.' He studied his aunt. 'Don't you ever think of retiring?'

'What for? I like work and work likes me. We get on.'

'But you're engaged to Mr Lacy.'

'Engaged but not wed!' Mrs Turner replied heatedly. 'That man has an allergy to marriage.'

Smiling, Richard looked back to the fire. 'How's Harris?'

'Reserved, serious, successful,' Mrs Turner said, summing

it up and then studying her nephew curiously. 'You don't still carry a torch for her, do you?'

'No!'

'Good thing. What with a lovely wife like yours and this little lad . . .' She jiggled the baby again, Tom's eyes closing as he slipped back to sleep. 'She's making a right go of that salon, Richard. And opening another –'

'She's not!'

'Oh, she is. If you ask me, Harris Simons has her heart set on being one of these career women. I blame the war. Women had to do men's work then, and some of them discovered they liked it.'

'Where would she open another salon?'

'Bonny said Manchester.'

'Manchester!' Richard replied, aghast. 'She's aiming a bit high, isn't she?'

'Harris Simons can't aim high enough,' Mrs Turner replied, rocking Tom in her arms. The firelight illuminated her face, and made the shadows around her mouth darker. 'If you ask me, that hairdressing business is becoming Harris's whole life. She's no man, no child, no home of her own. And she's not looking for a family either. No, she's set on making money. *Money* – the one thing that can't answer you back, let you down, or run away with another woman.' Mrs Turner paused, firelight pooling over her face and that of the sleeping child. 'She's obsessed with being successful and making more and more cash to put in the bank. Our Harris is falling in love with money like she fell in love with Ben Ramsey. And I can't see it doing her any more good.'

'I think we should talk about Saville,' Irma said, laying down her knife and fork.

'What about Saville?' Harris replied, looking up, her face troubled.

314

'He should be in a home, with people like him. I know he's not running off any more – I mean, you can't even get him out of the house now – but he might benefit from being around other people.' She paused, but Harris didn't say anything. 'I don't need to watch him all the time. Besides, I could be doing other things with my time.'

'Such as?' Harris asked calmly, helping herself to some peas. Mr Lacy had done them well all through the war and was still providing the best produce in the area. 'Why not?' he'd said to Mrs Turner. 'The Barracloughs hate veg.'

'I have an idea,' Irma replied, eyeing up the mound of peas on Harris's plate. 'It would be better for Saville –'

'To be put away with the crazies?'

Irma's eyes narrowed. 'I never said that!'

'No, but he does. Frequently. He's heard you mention it often enough over the years. Anyway, I don't agree. I think Saville should stay here.'

'I should remind you that this is my home!'

'Maybe Saville and I should *both* go and live with the crazies then.'

Sniffing, Irma began to cut into a chop. Harris was impossible, and getting worse. She had thought that time would mellow the bitterness between them, but it had intensified instead. Harris told her nothing, not a word about the salon, or her life.

And how Simons Coiffeuse was flourishing! Irma thought, hanging on to every word Mrs Turner threw her way. It wouldn't do to be seen to be reliant on information from an employee, but it was the only way Irma was going to find out anything. Harris was doing well, the salon was getting busier and busier and now her niece was talking about opening another salon – in Manchester!

But had she told her aunt about it? Had she hell as like.

'I hear you're busy at the salon.'

Harris glanced up. 'Always busy.'

'But even more so now.'

'Women like to look good. I think it's a lot to do with the war ending. Ever since then they can't seem to spend enough time on themselves. They want to be glamorous, like the film stars.'

Harris took a mouthful and began to chew. Behind her, Irma could hear the sonorous ticking of the grandfather clock. If she was honest she found conversation with Harris difficult and preferred their usual silent meals, Harris lost in her own thoughts only a yard away. But now Irma was impatient with silence. After three years she wanted more than a few chilly words. She wanted to talk.

'I heard that you were thinking of opening a salon in Manchester.'

Harris paused, a forkful of food halfway to her mouth. 'I'm thinking about it.'

'That would cost money.'

'We have money. I've made a success of the salon and tripled the income.'

Tripled the income! Irma was impressed. She had enjoyed doing the accounts before, but it had always been little more than a hobby, a way of keeping busy. She was bored with her life, but *this* was really interesting.

'Tripled the income!' Irma repeated, her tone for once animated. 'You've done well.'

It was Harris's turn to be surprised. Her aunt never usually praised her. 'Thank you.'

Is that it? Irma wondered, watching her niece lapse back into silence. For a moment she wanted to lean forward and push Harris's pretty face into the blasted peas. But instead Irma kept her patience.

'About Saville –'

'We could convert the lodge house,' Harris said evenly, 'and get a nurse to look after Saville. He would have his own place then, next to us, but small enough to feel safe. I think he'd like that.'

It was quite a thought, Irma realised. The lodge house was compact, but big enough for Saville and a nurse. And having her brother out of the main house would free her up nicely, give her a life back.

'Maybe Saville *would* like the lodge. That's a good thought, Harris.'

Two compliments in one conversation! This was quite something, Harris thought. Finishing her chops, she laid down her knife and fork. It was unsettling to be with a silent Irma, but this loquacious, agreeable version was far more unnerving.

'Sweet!' Mrs Turner said, walking in with a pudding and slapping it down on the table, where it glowered from its dish. 'I've had this recipe for years and I've been dying to try it.'

The pudding looked at Harris, Harris looked at the pudding, then caught Irma's eye. Her aunt's expression was a classic. She was regarding the pudding with a hostility usually reserved for foreigners.

'What is it?'

'Apple and cinnamon suet,' Mrs Turner replied, beaming. 'You really feel like you've eaten something when you've had that.'

I don't doubt it for an instant, Irma thought, waiting for Mrs Turner to leave before she plunged her spoon into the pudding. Steam rose up like a geyser as she ladled some into a dish and passed it to Harris.

Slowly, she then tasted some for herself and winced. 'I can't believe we pay that woman to poison us! Eating the blasted sofa would be easier.'

Manfully Harris struggled with a mouthful, then swallowed, the suet grinding down her throat and seeming to take a film of skin with it.

'I can't eat this!' Irma said at last, her head bent down over the offending dessert. 'No one could eat this. You could sharpen a razor on it.'

It had been a long time since Harris had really looked at her aunt, but now she did and realised, with no little surprise, that Irma was dyeing her hair. It was a very subtle shade of dark brown – and there wasn't a grey hair amongst it. How long had she been doing that? Harris wondered. Usually Irma displayed no vanity. And why would she bother, when no one saw her?

'So,' Irma said, pushing away her plate, 'you're going to open another salon in Manchester?'

'Maybe.'

'Well, are you, or aren't you?'

'Why? You're never interested in what I do,' Harris countered truculently.

'I'm interested now.'

'Why?'

'Because I am,' Irma replied, sipping her glass of water and wondering how Mrs Turner could even make water taste bad. 'Whereabouts in Manchester?'

'There's a tiny place off St Anne's Square –'

'Expensive!'

'I'll rent it.'

'No one of any breeding rents! It's throwing money down the drain.'

'I'll rent it for a while to see how it goes. Besides, I can't afford to buy there yet.'

'Renting is for peasants.'

Smiling bitterly, Harris looked away. 'Stupid old fool,' she muttered under her breath.

'Silly bitch,' Irma replied, also *sotto voce*. But both had heard the other and found – to their amazement – that they were amused.

'You'll need more staff,' Irma said coolly. 'Who'll run the Wigan salon if you're in Manchester?'

'Bonny.'

'Ah.'

'*Ah* what?' Harris countered, her tone defensive.

'Just *ah*,' Irma replied, poking her pudding with her spoon.

'I don't want you interfering.'

'I don't *want* to interfere,' Irma countered, 'even if you are about to make a mess of things. Again.'

'A mess of things?' Harris retorted. 'How d'you make that out?'

'Because no one rents. Anyone who wants to make a real business buys their premises. That's what Mildred and I did. And we did well enough.'

'I'm putting money aside. You know that, you encouraged me. When I have the money, I'll buy.'

'*When* . . .' Irma said, her tone disbelieving. Prodding the pudding peevishly, she leaned back in her seat. 'How much?'

'Huh?'

'Don't say "huh"!' Irma snorted. 'It's common.'

'You are the end, aren't you?' Harris replied, her tone hostile. 'And where did all your ridiculous snobbery get you? Locked away in this house, bored out of your mind, with no friends and nothing to do with your time. You don't even want to look after Saville any more.'

'Saville isn't a baby, he doesn't care who looks after him,' Irma replied. 'Anyway, he doesn't like me.'

'You amaze me.'

'You don't like me either, do you? I know you'd give anything for it to be Mildred at this table.' Her eyes fixed on the locket around Harris's neck. 'Whilst she was alive my sister never took that off, did she? I always wondered what was in it – guessed it would be a picture of a man. I have to say that I never bought Mildred's story about it not opening.' Irma paused, looking at her niece steadily. 'So before I gave it to you, I tried to open it myself. But my sister was right – it doesn't open. It suits you, Harris – but I don't suppose that you'd have worn any locket *I* left you. I don't imagine you'd want anything of mine.'

Sensing trouble, Harris tried to calm her aunt down. 'Don't get upset. You'll have an angina attack.'

'I don't care!' Irma replied, her voice raised. 'No one would give a damn if I had a heart attack and expired in that bloody pudding.'

'Mrs Turner might.'

A flicker of unexpected humour lit up Irma's eyes. 'You can be such a bitch!'

'I can't think where I get it from,' Harris replied, watching her aunt as she left the dining room.

Alone, Harris leaned back in her seat, Irma's footsteps fading as she moved along the corridor above. For the first time in her life she felt pity for her aunt, and something else, curiosity. Had there been a bond between them for a moment? Or had she imagined it? Further footsteps overhead told Harris that Irma was returning, her footfall determined and surprisingly quick.

'There!' Irma said, walking back into the dining room and slapping an album down on the table in front of her niece.

'What's this?'

'Open it and find out.'

Obediently Harris did so. Inside were photographs of hair-styles Irma had done years before. The pictures were old-fashioned, almost quaint.

'You kept photographs?' Harris asked, looking at her aunt in astonishment.

'Some. What do you think?'

'They're old-fashioned –'

'I know that!'

'– but you were a good hairdresser.'

'Not *were*, am. I *am* a good hairdresser,' Irma corrected her, hurrying on: 'Oh, I know what you're thinking. What would you want with some disagreeable old trout working at the salon? And I kid you not, I *am* disagreeable, but that never stopped clients coming before. And it won't again.' Harris was goggle-eyed, unmoving. 'I can look after the Wigan salon.

Don't look at me like that, Harris! I don't want to take over, I just want to be busy.'

'You're sixty. You're old.'

'You're rude!' Irma snapped.

'You're sick.'

'You're joking,' Irma retorted hotly. 'I've got many years left in me. Good years. You need me, Harris, and if you had any sense you'd snatch my hand off. I can run that salon as well as I ever could. And you could turn your attentions to the new place. It would free you up, take a load off your mind.' She wiggled a forefinger at her niece. 'Look in the back of the album. Yes, there. In that envelope. Open it.'

Sighing, Harris did so, her mouth falling open as she saw the stack of notes.

'Good God, how much money is there here?'

'Enough to buy those premises off St Anne's Square,' Irma replied, flushing slightly. 'It's a bribe, Harris. You see, I have no pride really. Not when I want something. The money is a way of buying my way into your good books. You don't have to like me, but you *have* to employ me. Besides, I could pull rank and say that the Wigan salon is mine anyway.' She paused, her dark eyes fixed on her niece. 'Take the money and buy that salon in Manchester. It's a nob area, with plenty of moneyed people around. Take the money and buy it. Mildred and I did the same once. We took a risk and we were successful, despite what anyone thought. It felt good to prove them all wrong, to make money. *Our money.* Mildred spent hers, but I invested mine, and put some aside.' She waved the money in front of Harris's face. 'This is what I saved. And I never knew what I saved it for – until now. I want to be useful again. I want to be busy. I miss the old days with Mildred, just like I miss her.'

'I miss her too,' Harris admitted, her voice low.

'Do it for her then,' Irma said, her tone remote. 'If you can't do it for me, do it for Mildred . . . Oh, think about it, Harris! I can bring in custom, people of class. Snobs, like me. You might laugh, but snobs are important, they send other snobs and news travels. I might not be young any more, but I can always make a woman look her best. That's why they all came to me before.' She leaned towards her niece, her voice compelling. 'I haven't been a good aunt, or a confidante. I won't be a nice kind old lady – it goes against the grain with me. But I *can* be useful. And that's what you need.'

Staggered, Harris looked at her aunt for a long instant before finally finding her voice again.

'Irma, tell me one thing, will you?'

'Yes?'

'When did you start colouring your hair?'

FORTY-ONE

From his office looking out over Market Place, Jimmy Henshaw watched the rain coming down. To avoid the downpour, passers-by ducked into doorways or jumped on passing buses, the October light fading past four o'clock. Stretching his long arms, Jimmy yawned and then settled down to some paperwork. But his heart wasn't in it.

It wasn't as though he missed the war, but he missed the excitement. Civilian life was good, but where was the challenge? He had been one of the élite, in the air force, a young man with no fear of the enemy, or death. And so, luckily, both had missed him, if only by a hair's breadth. Then he came home, to parents who had prayed daily for him, and a younger brother who never stopped asking – 'What was it like? Weren't you frightened up in the sky on your own? What were the aeroplanes like?'

If Jimmy had said, 'Noisy, smelly and held together with glue and spit,' it still wouldn't have put Hugh off. His big brother was a hero and he was going to make sure that everyone knew about it. *A hero* . . . Jimmy thought about the word and wondered how two syllables could mean so much to so many people. He had been doing his duty. Just like everyone else. His medal was no bigger or brighter than the others, and meant no more.

So he had put it to the back of his top drawer and returned to work at his father's practice, Henshaw, Crabbe and Henshaw. Jimmy's elevation to partner had been part reward and, he thought mockingly, part thank you to God. *I'll make the boy a partner*, George must have said, *if you spare him*. As though God needed another solicitor.

He would go home soon, Jimmy thought, spinning round on his new swivel chair and then slamming his feet on the desk. His long legs in their dark business suit looked like another man's. An older man's. But then he *was* older. Sensible now. An honest-to-goodness citizen. A professional man in a solid family practice.

And bored.

A knock at the door made Jimmy look up. Quickly he took his feet off his desk as his secretary walked in.

'A message for you, sir,' Joanie said, passing him a note. 'I'll be off now, if there's nothing else you want.'

'No, you go home. And thanks.'

Smiling, Joanie left, picking up her coat and waiting for the lift in the corridor outside. No one could say that Jimmy Henshaw was handsome – too tall and thin for good looks – but there was something about him. He moved quickly, but talked slowly, drawing out his words for emphasis. And then, just when you'd decided that he was a dope, he would wink or smile and you were sunk. She liked Jimmy, did Joanie. When he first came back to work she liked to imagine that he had noticed her. After all, Jimmy was no snob. She even expected him to ask her out. But she was disappointed. Jimmy was shy around women and never made a move.

Suddenly the lift jerked to a halt on her floor and Joanie stepped in – then jumped out again immediately. Re-entering the office she picked up her gloves she had left behind and then paused. Was that the sound of an engine? Was it? Carefully she crept towards the noise, looking through a crack in the door of Jimmy's office. He was sitting at his desk, his hands around some imaginary plane's steering wheel, the *rat-a-tat-tat* of gunfire coming from his mouth. Mesmerised, Joanie watched him and then, laughing silently, left the office again. What a kid he was, she thought as she stepped back into the lift. But nice. Childish, but nice.

Jimmy was just flying over the Ruhr Valley when the phone rang next to him.

Coughing, he answered, 'Henshaw, Crabbe and Henshaw –'

'I want to talk to George Henshaw,' a woman's voice said sharply.

'He's not in the office today. Can I help?'

'Who are you?'

Slowly, Jimmy answered, 'I'm his son, James Henshaw.'

Irma wasn't impressed. 'I don't want to talk to some beginner –'

'I'm fully qualified, madam, and have been for some years.'

'How old are you?'

'How old are you?' he asked, his slow voice amused.

'Well, you've got your father's nerve!' Irma replied shortly. 'I need a solicitor. Fast.'

'How fast?'

'Today?'

Jimmy paused, looked at his watch. Well, why not? He was in no hurry to go home. 'Where are you?'

'What does that matter?'

'I just wondered,' he slowed down his speech even further, 'how long it would take you to get here, Mrs . . . ?'

'*Miss* Simons.'

'Oh, Miss Simons, it's a pleasure to talk to you.'

'I wouldn't be too sure about that,' Irma replied, with her usual charm. 'I could be over to your office in about ten minutes.'

Jimmy nodded. 'And I'll be waiting for you.'

True to her word Irma Simons walked into Henshaw, Crabbe and Henshaw nine and a half minutes later. As she entered reception a lanky man came out to meet her, his hand extended.

'I'm James Henshaw.'

She shook hands with him firmly. 'Pleased to meet you. You're very young.'

'Thirty-two.'

'Like I said, young.'

'Not if you're twenty-two,' Jimmy replied languidly, guiding Irma to a seat in his office.

The redoubtable Irma Simons's reputation had preceded her. Nicknames like 'Medusa', 'Hitler's Bride' and 'Irmastein' were frequently bandied around town. Working at Simons Coiffeuse, Irma looked out of place in her dark suit, the severe brown hair drawn back from the high brow, the pitiless eyes black as sloes. Whilst her niece and the young assistant laughed as they worked, Irma glowered at the clients' heads, as though, at any minute, she might bite. But then she worked her magic – and the clients kept coming.

'What can I do to help you, Miss Simons?'

'I – we – need some advice on buying a property in Manchester. Are you sure you're up to this?'

Jimmy had faced the Germans with less anxiety, but he kept his voice slow and even. 'I'm sure. Please, go on.'

'It's not difficult. My niece and I are buying a salon just off St Anne's Square. Do you know it? It's a very nice part of the city. Very upmarket. Anyway, we need someone to do the conveyancing – in a hurry. The premises seem suddenly to be very popular and I don't want to be caught out.'

Who would dare? Jimmy thought to himself. 'If you give me all the details, Miss Simons, I can work this out for you.'

Irma sniffed. 'Well, I'll give you a try. I just hope you work faster than you talk.'

* * *

Tucking a sleeping Mildred up in bed, Bonny turned back to the mirror. Then she took off all her clothes and, luxuriantly, touched the new underwear she had just bought. For years she had been wearing Utility underwear, brought in when the clothing industry was regimented. It was ghastly stuff, the Utility wear, or 'Futility', as it was called. Pink rayon camiknickers worn over a cotton Kestos-type bra. If you were unlucky and couldn't even get that, you had to make your own brassiere out of triangular pieces of cotton and bits of elastic. But now there was new underwear, gorgeous soft, peach-coloured bits of silliness . . . Bonny ran her fingers over the satin and smiled to herself, slowly putting on the bra and then slipping the camiknickers down over her body. Then she turned and looked in the mirror.

Not bad, she thought, patting her stomach. That was the one good thing about being gangly, no lumpy stomach. And no bust . . . She sighed, ah well, you couldn't have everything. The underwear had cost her half a week's wages, but for once Bonny had been extravagant. She needed some luxury. It was all right being careful, but she was a woman and she wanted to feel like one again.

Which brought her to Howard Waring . . . Bonny sighed. Howard was a bus driver, working the route round Wigan, a thickset, no-nonsense, sexy-looking man. She had never made love with anyone like Howard. Not the sex act, but the cuddles, the frequent loving looks, winks and touches. Oh yes, he was quite a man. *And* he had good teeth. Bonny liked men who smiled and had good teeth. Teeth that didn't come out at night. Mind you, she didn't know about that yet. They were only just starting to date. It was early days. Too early to buy underwear . . . Smiling mischievously to herself, Bonny glanced at Milly. Howard had said that he didn't mind about the little one. That's good, Bonny had replied, because I'm not getting rid of her. And then he'd laughed, not put off a bit by her bluntness.

Sitting down carefully on the bed, Bonny stared at her child. So much time had passed that it wasn't easy to remember Milly's father in any detail, but the little girl obviously resembled him far more than she resembled her mother. Gently Bonny touched Milly's dark blonde hair, letting the curls rest against her palm. I never had blonde hair, or curls, she thought. Or a little snub nose. She was overcome with love for a moment, longing to pick up her sleeping child and hug her. But she resisted. No good spoiling her. That wasn't the way to bring up a child. Milly was going to do well in life brought up properly. Not like Bonny herself had been.

At the thought of Madge, Bonny shuddered. Out of hospital she spent her time trawling the streets and begging for drink. All Richard's offers of help had been rejected. For some reason Madge seemed to want to blame her children for her fall in life. It had to be someone's fault, so why not theirs? Well, Richard might try to help, and good luck to him. But Bonny was way past trying.

Looking back at her child, Bonny stroked Milly's plump little forearm, resting on the embroidered coverlet. Everything she had ever given her baby had been the finest. Every bit of clothing, of food, had been of the best quality she could afford. Nothing was too good for Milly. And when she let her, Harris had helped. Not in an obvious way, but in simple gestures. The milk was delivered and paid for. Not by Bonny, but by Harris. Bread the same. After all, Harris said, it's for the salon really. And when it was Christmas, there were always presents of clothes and toys – enough for four children. Harris should have her own, Bonny thought, but had always been touched by her friend's generosity. And tolerance.

It hadn't been easy for Harris at first. Bonny might be able to cut a straight line, but she was hopeless at setting hair. Rollers seemed to take on a life of their own in Bonny's hands. They fell out, or slipped at rakish angles, or she stuck in the pins too hard, usually straight into the client's scalp. At the beginning, her disasters far outweighed her triumphs.

328

But Harris was always there to make it right. Never critical, always discreet, she corrected Bonny's mistakes and never once made her feel like a cack-handed fool. Then gradually Harris discovered Bonny's real strength. No more rollers for her – but plenty of perming.

In fact, Bonny thought, she had probably permed more than a third of the heads of hair in Wigan. After a while she could spot her work from the back, without even seeing her client's face. And she was proud of that. Not bad, Bonny told herself, not bad for slum fodder, with a kid and no husband to help. Not bad at all.

And now she was in her own little flat, with her own beautiful child and wearing glamorous underwear. Sighing, Bonny stretched out on the bed next to Milly and smiled up at the ceiling. It was a good life, after all.

Carefully cutting around a photograph of a dog, Saville concentrated, his brow wrinkled. It was nice in the lodge; he liked it there with Mrs Biddy. He wasn't sure if that was her real name, but he'd heard Irma say she was a biddy so many times that it stuck. And Mrs Biddy didn't seem to mind. It was a good thing she was small too, Saville thought, because there wouldn't be much room in the lodge for him and another person – if she'd been big. Luckily Mrs Biddy was built on Toy Town dimensions, no taller than five feet, and weighing little more than seven stones. And always whistling, humming, or chatting.

She was in the poky kitchen now, making sandwiches. Saville liked sandwiches, almost as much as he liked order and safety. And Mrs Biddy was certainly safe. She had had two children: two boys, all grown up now. It had seemed after a couple of weeks and a thousand stories that Mrs Biddy's boys became surrogate brothers to Saville. He never tired of Sam and Percy – what Sam had done, how clever he was and how he had his own newsagent's shop now. Percy, however, was not that bright. Saville liked Percy for that. There were too many clever people in the world.

'Percy's gardening now,' Mrs Biddy said, walking in with a tray of sandwiches and milk. 'I'll take you to see him at the park one day.'

Saville dropped the cutting in his hand and started to shake. Anxious, Mrs Biddy put down the tray and sat beside her charge.

'What is it, luv?'

'Not the park!' Saville blundered. 'I don't want to go to the park.'

Inwardly cursing herself, Mrs Biddy remembered the story of a much younger Saville exposing himself in Mesnes Park.

'We don't have to do anything we don't want, Saville. I don't want to go to any stupid park, anyway.' She passed him some sandwiches and a glass of milk. 'Percy can come here and see you.'

Saville relaxed and nodded. 'I'd like that.'

'Then that's what we'll do,' Mrs Biddy answered. 'Did I tell you that Percy had a new girlfriend?'

'No!'

'Oh yes, she's called Sally and she's very pretty.'

Saville put his head on one side, chewing thoughtfully. 'Will they get married?'

'What a thing to ask!' Mrs Biddy laughed. 'Why does that matter?'

'Because people *should* be married,' Saville replied, swilling down his sandwich with a mouthful of milk. 'My sisters never got married and it made Irma mean.' His gaze travelled to the collection of photographs on the windowledge, the collection that kept getting knocked over in the cramped space.

'But your brother married,' Mrs Biddy went on, looking at the glossy Gideon. 'Do you remember him?'

Saville closed his eyes. 'Gideon wasn't what they thought.'

'No?'

He shook his head. 'No, he wasn't.'

There was a long pause, Mrs Biddy noticing Saville's discomfort and changing the subject deftly. 'Sam was going to marry this young lady from Stockport –'

He cut her off: 'People are like animals, Mrs Biddy. I can look at a person and know what animal they would be. Gideon would have been a stag, Mildred would have been a Koala bear and Irma's always been a crocodile ... And Father was a *pig*.'

The word was spat out, coming from under the thick walrus moustache like a bitter pip from some rotten piece of fruit. She had never seen Saville anything but childlike, scared or meek, never hostile. Until now.

'A big rough pig, something that snorts and snuffles in the muck.' Saville then glanced over to Mrs Biddy, colouring. 'I'm sorry, I shouldn't have said that! You won't tell anyone, will you?'

'Saville,' she replied, perfectly calm, 'there's no one to tell. You're safe with me.'

His eyes were wide, then relaxed, his breathing regulating. 'I know things. Lots of things. People think I'm stupid, and I am – but I *know* things.'

Mrs Biddy looked at him curiously. 'What things, Saville?'

'Secret things,' he replied, his voice hardly more than a whisper. 'I know who's in the locket, Mrs Biddy. Mildred said it didn't open, but it did. Once. And I saw who was in it.' He tapped his nose, comically knowledgeable. 'Saville's not as stupid as they think. Oh, no, he keeps lots of secrets.'

Dr Redmond walked in and stared at his wife, transfixed. 'Irene, what *have* you done to your hair?'

She touched her coiffure, beaming with pride. 'I had it changed.'

'I can see that.'

'The colour's called Midnight Seduction.' She sidled over to her husband and looked up at him lovingly through her thick glasses. 'It's supposed to bring out the beast in a man.'

Yeah, Lionel thought, a hyena.

'It's very . . . different,' he said tactfully, staring at his wife's newly dark locks. 'It makes you look younger –'

'More seductive?'

He studied her homely print dress and slippers and chose his words carefully. 'Well, it makes you look more . . . appealing.'

'It's the same colour Joan Crawford has her hair done,' Irene went on, clasping Lionel's arm and steering him into the sitting room. '"A brunette has the power to change her man for the better. To make him feel powerful, virile."'

Lionel flushed. Oh God, he thought, Irene was trying to seduce him again. He hated that. He had no sexual drive whatsoever, but every couple of months Irene planned an ambush, a means to have her way with him.

'Easy, girl, it's just hair dye.'

'But that's it!' Irene exclaimed, reiterating what the beauty book had said. Goggle-eyed, she had read it under the hair dryer, a mischievous Bonny watching her from the sidelines. 'Colour dictates who we are, Lionel, and how powerful we appear to others. "A brunette holds all the mystery of the dark in her sultry looks."'

'Have you been reading those women's magazines again?' Lionel replied, collapsing into his chair and sliding off his shoes.

She wasn't going to give up, Irene thought. Her dear husband might think that the romance had gone out of their marriage, but he had another think coming. And he was completely fit now, no excuse – apart from his bay window of a stomach. They were married, and by God, she was going to get her conjugal rights. Whether he liked it or not.

Leaving the room, Irene went upstairs, Lionel breathing a sigh of relief and resting his head back against the chair. Was it true what he had heard earlier? Could it possibly be true that Ben Ramsey was coming unstuck? He thought of how Ben had been when they'd worked together: a smooth operator, a man women loved, and a good doctor. But the arrogance that had always been Ramsey's Achilles heel was now finally threatening to undermine him. Lionel had said as much to Irene, but she had put it down to jealousy.

'Lionel . . .'

He opened his eyes and then blinked. He was dreaming, he must be! In front of him stood Irene with her new dark hair loose, and wearing a pair of red camiknickers.

'Bloody hell, old girl!'

'It's new.'

'It's not you, though, is it? I mean, it's a bit . . .'

'Revealing?'

Mesmerised, Lionel couldn't drag his eyes away from his wife's little thin legs projecting from the red lace.

'Oh, do cover up, Irene. You'll get cold!'

Silencing him, she slid onto his lap. 'You can keep me warm. You great big handsome man.'

He was mortified, desperate. 'I've got some work to do –'

'You certainly have!' she teased him, her unusually red lips coming at him like a puffer fish. 'You and I have some very *hard* work to do.'

Gasping, Lionel tried again to rise, Irene pressing down on him, her mouth next to his ear. 'Say you love me, *little kiss kiss lips.*'

'I need to eat!' Lionel croaked, trying to get up.

'Then make a meal of me!' Irene replied, kissing him full on the mouth. 'I'm all yours.'

Oh God, Lionel thought as she swamped him, why hadn't he gone home via David Lewis's? Dressing a leg ulcer was better than this.

FORTY-TWO

Well, he still liked the look of her and no mistake, Jimmy thought, walking down the path from Deerheart House. What a stunner. Whistling, he opened the gate and then looked back. But there was no sign of Harris at the door, or at any window. Ah well, Jimmy thought, pulling his trilby over to one side, he would have to win her over slowly, that was all.

Still whistling, Jimmy jumped when a man leaped out in front of him as he passed by the lodge. A large man with an old-fashioned walrus moustache, he stared for a moment and then shrank back.

'Hello there.'

Without responding, the man ran back into the lodge, Jimmy moving on. So that was Saville Simons, was it? Jimmy went over what his father had told him: the Simonses had money, but they were odd. Very odd. Well now, Jimmy thought, his dad had been part right, but there was nothing odd about Harris. Apart from her name.

He thought it was actually the kind of name that would look good carved into a tree trunk, or a windowledge, encased in a heart, with an arrow going through it . . . Jimmy stopped walking. No, that was no good! Too corny. What about Harris written in the snow? Or what about hiring a plane and skywriting it? Now he could do that. If he had the money. And the plane.

Wow, boy! Jimmy said to himself. One thing at a time. She might not even like you. Oh, yes, she did, he answered himself, she was smiling on both occasions he had visited and looking interested. But was that *attraction* interest or *friend* interest? He started walking again, whistling under his breath and thinking back to what his mother had said.

'Harris Simons is fast. Ran around after some doctor, and then he dumped her and married another woman! A few years ago Harris Simons made a total fool of herself.'

'But she's doing well in her business,' Jimmy had offered.

His mother nodded. 'She is that, becoming very successful. Which has put some people's noses out of joint. They thought she would never amount to anything, but she proved them wrong. And I admire her for that, if nothing else.'

'And what about men?' Jimmy had asked, his mother staring at him cautiously.

'To Harris Simons's credit, she's lived a very quiet life since the affair with Ramsey. Calmed down a lot, never even had a boyfriend since – not one anyone knows about, anyway.' Mrs Henshaw had paused. 'But she's not a respectable girl, Jimmy. She's one that will always be trouble. A man would have his work cut out being married to Harris Simons.'

'I dare say he would,' Jimmy had said slowly, raising his eyebrows. 'But would it be worth it?'

Warfare had been a way of life for Bonny and Irma ever since Irma had begun working in the Wigan salon. Both confrontational, they clashed repeatedly, Harris the peace-maker at first. But now she'd opened the salon in Manchester they were left alone for most of the time, and the real tussle for power began.

Living above the salon, Bonny opened up every morning,

Irma arriving later. Chilling politeness marked their every conversation, each waiting for the moment to strike and gain a point.

'Morning, Irma,' Bonny said, opening the appointment book. 'Your first client's cancelled.'

'Clients don't cancel on me!' Irma retorted. 'And she can't just come back and think I'll fit her in when it suits her.'

'I doubt she will,' Bonny replied smartly, moving into the back. 'She's dead.'

Stung, Irma studied the appointments book. Now she would have to find another client, or she'd be down on her numbers. Taking off her coat she looked at her reflection in the mirror and then put her starched white overall over her business suit. If the truth be known Irma was enjoying herself enormously. She had heard the nicknames about her – particularly liking 'Irmastein' – but it suited her to be reviled. Being feared meant she hadn't got to be nice and mollify people. She could be a complete swine and people expected it of her. How lucky could you get, Irma thought, to be yourself, in all your nasty glory?

'Morning, Irma,' Mrs Broadbent said, walking in and sitting down in front of the mirror. 'I thought we'd have a change. Let my hair grow a bit longer.'

'You'd look like a skittle with a wig on,' Irma replied, Mrs Broadbent glancing down at her bag, embarrassed.

'If you say so.'

'I do say so – and you know I'm right,' Irma replied, putting on her glasses and peering at the woman's scalp. 'Oh . . .'

'What?'

'Uh huh . . .' Irma went on, holding Mrs Broadbent's head steady as she scrutinised her scalp.

'What is it? Is it serious?'

Finally Irma straightened up, slipped her glasses back into the pocket of her overall and spoke: 'You have something we call . . . Well, never mind that. It's not serious, nothing we can't cure. So don't panic.' She dropped her voice. 'I do a very prominent lady solicitor's hair, and she has it.'

Oh, so that was all right, Mrs Broadbent thought. If you had to have something, it was good to share the disease with the right sort of people.

'Is it catching?'

Irma clicked her teeth. 'No, no. You just rub in the lotion I'll give you and you'll have no problem. It's a little expensive, but what's money when you want to keep your hair?' She turned away and then turned back. 'Tell no one, though. I mean about the lotion – or your condition. We wouldn't want people thinking the wrong thing, would we?'

Mrs Broadbent's lips were sealed.

Satisfied, Irma walked into the back room and took down a bottle from the shelf.

Watching her, Bonny frowned. 'Who's that for?'

'My client.'

'What for?'

'Her condition,' Irma replied, writing the sale down in the ledger. One up on you, Bonny, she thought. You haven't sold any lotion for weeks.

'There's nothing wrong with Mrs Broadbent's hair.'

Irma raised her glossy black eyebrows. 'I'm the judge of that.'

'It's just dandruff!' Bonny persisted. 'She doesn't need to spend all that money on lotion.' Her eyes narrowed. 'You're just trying to beat me on the sales, aren't you?'

'Good Lord,' Irma replied loftily, 'there's no need to be jealous. You know only too well that I'll teach you all I know. All you have to do is ask. I'm sure even *you* could learn the basics of salesmanship.'

Stung, Bonny folded her arms and glowered at Irma. 'You don't care! You'd sell snake oil, wouldn't you?'

'Bonny, my dear, I could *make* it.'

*   *   *

337

Well, it was impressive service and no mistake, Harris thought as she watched Jimmy Henshaw climb the stairs up to the salon. He had taken off his trilby, his dark hair floppy as he combed it through with his fingers hurriedly.

'Well, hello there, Miss Simons.'

'Call me Harris.'

'Harris,' Jimmy repeated, his voice slow and steady. 'You can call me Jimmy. Or James, whichever you prefer.'

'Jimmy it is,' Harris replied, walking into the salon and waving her arm around proudly. 'This is it. My new salon. Small, I know, but a good start.'

Slowly Jimmy paced the long narrow room and then glanced out of the window, turning his hat in his hands. From the side window the view was over St Anne's Square, with the church on the right-hand side. Admittedly the salon was high up a flight of steep stairs, but it was a good address, bought with Irma's money. And Harris's.

Turning back, Jimmy looked around at the basins and the mirrored stands, twirling one chair round and laughing awkwardly.

'You've done well, for someone your age.'

'Thank you, *sir*,' she replied, mocking him.

Just who was this Jimmy Henshaw? Harris wondered.

For years she hadn't been interested in men. No one had been able to coax her out of the carapace she had built around herself. After Ben Ramsey, Harris had shut down. The hurt had been intense, but the humiliation had nearly killed her. And then the death of Mildred – the loss of someone she had loved *so* much, coming with the loss of someone she had loved *too* much – it made Harris think of love as dangerous. As unhealthy. It had made a fool out of her, and worse, it had turned her into someone she couldn't recognise. Who *was* that girl who had done all those things? Who had acted so recklessly? Who *was* the stupid scrubber who had crawled to a man who was no damn good?

Love wasn't what they said. It wasn't beautiful, selfless, noble, enduring. It was sex, degradation and borderline madness. Or at least it was for her, with the wrong man – a man like Ben Ramsey. But maybe not with *every* man. Harris sighed. She couldn't stay alone forever. Not like Irma. And she couldn't cut herself off from what life had to offer. She was too young. Too sexual, if the truth be known. Work was good, but it wasn't a lover. It didn't put its arms around you in the night. Bloody-mindedness had made Harris succeed. At last she was finally winning back some respect – so was it now time to risk loving again?

But what if it went wrong? What if he left her? God, she couldn't face the pitying looks again, the humiliation ... Harris walked around the salon, apparently thinking about her business, but inside she was wondering about the solicitor. He was single and from the right family. He was gangly, almost gauche, but he had charm in his own way. And he was kind, because kindness became him.

'These are for your records,' Jimmy said, handing Harris some papers, fidgeting with his hat. 'I thought I'd drop them in. I was just passing.'

'From Wigan?' she countered, her face turned to the window, the light falling on her.

Taking in his breath, Jimmy stared. 'Has anyone ever told you that you look like Vivien Leigh?'

'Now and again.'

'Any Rhett Butler around?'

Surprised, she laughed, Jimmy blushing.

'Gosh, I'm sorry, that's not like me to be so personal.' His confusion was genuine, his voice hesitant. 'I mean, what I wanted to say, was – would you like to ... Well, I could ... we could ...'

'Yes,' Harris said simply.

He looked over to her, the hat finally still in his hands. 'Yes, what?'

'Were you asking me out?'

'Well, yes . . . I mean, yes, yes, I was.' He smiled, running his hands through his hair again. 'This is great! You'll go out with me then?'

She nodded, smiling too. 'Only on one condition.'

'Name it.'

'Let me cut your hair.'

Laughing, Jimmy moved from foot to foot, then sat down in the chair Harris pulled out for him. Briskly she put a cover over him and tucked a towel around his neck, Jimmy watching her in the mirror.

'You know, I normally go to a barber.'

'I can see that.'

'No good, hey?'

'I can do better,' she replied, beginning to comb his hair.

Soothed, Jimmy found himself transfixed by the action, his eyes watching Harris in the mirror as she began to cut. He could see how slim she was – and then noticed the full curve of her bust. Flushing, he shuffled under the cover.

'Hey, keep still! You want this to be even, don't you?'

'That *would* be nice,' Jimmy replied, as Harris flipped the front of his hair down over his forehead and began to cut again.

'I'm amazed you can see where you're going half the time.'

'I just stumble about,' Jimmy replied. 'I'm clumsy anyway, so no one notices.'

'You're not clumsy, just tall.'

He wasn't clumsy, just tall . . . Hell, Jimmy thought, that sounded better.

'Keep still!' Harris commanded him, bending down to clip the back of his hair.

Her hands worked deftly, the comb running through his hair rhythmically, the action intimate. And then Jimmy suddenly felt Harris's fingers brush against his scalp, his skin tingling at the touch. Go on, he willed her, don't stop.

Bending lower, Harris rested one hand on his shoulder as she trimmed the back of Jimmy's hair. She could feel the heat of his skin under her hand and she left her fingers resting against his shoulder longer than she would normally have done. Surprised that she was attracted to him, Harris looked up – and caught Jimmy watching her through the mirror.

For a moment she expected him to bluster, even flush, but he didn't. He held her look, and then reached up. Gently he laid his hand over hers, and then winked.

She smiled, amazed at the electricity between them.

'So, what d'you think?'

'You're amazing,' Jimmy said, his eyes never leaving her face.

Still smiling at him in the mirror, Harris said, 'I meant the haircut. What do you think of the haircut?'

Reluctantly Jimmy looked away from her and studied himself in the mirror. If she had tarred and feathered him he would have sworn it was an improvement.

'Wonderful.'

'You like it?' Harris said, intrigued to discover how much his approval meant to her.

'I like my haircut. And I like you, Harris Simons.' Jimmy's hand tightened over hers as he spun round in his seat and faced her. 'I can honestly say that I like you a lot.'

And then he kissed her.

FORTY-THREE

Climbing the steep stairs up to the Manchester salon, Harris walked in and looked around proudly. It was early in the morning, before everyone else had arrived, St Anne's Square still quiet outside.

She had done it – with help from Irma, but using her own money too. And her skill, the talent that had kept the old clients and brought her new ones. All the products that had been newly marketed sat on the shelves behind the counter, their labels turned to the front. And on the desk sat a phone and a pristine appointments book.

Lovingly Harris ran her hand over the cover. This was more like it, she thought. She was in control of her life now. No silly little girl any more. She was focused, successful and still young. Glowing, she read the advertisement in the *Manchester Evening News* – 'NEW ERA HAIR SALON'. It had been running for a while now, drawing in new customers. She knew she wasn't the only female who had carved out a career for herself, but she was still in a minority, one of a few who had taken on the men, and were determined to make their mark.

Smiling to herself, Harris glanced into the mirror and studied her reflection, dressed in a fitted green suit with a white blouse. The cut of the jacket accentuated her small waist and full bust.

Her eyes travelled up to her face, approving of the make-up Irma deplored, and the thick, dark head of hair. No point being a hairdresser if your own hair looked a mess.

'Hey!'

Harris turned, pleased to see Jimmy walking in. 'These are for you,' he said, passing her a huge bunch of flowers.

'What's the occasion?'

'No occasion – I just wanted to give a beautiful woman flowers.'

I love you, Harris thought suddenly, but not like I loved Ben Ramsey. A shock of longing ran through her at the thought of him, but she pushed it away.

'These must have cost a fortune,' she said, hugging him.

'Only the best for you,' he replied, looking round the salon. 'You've done so well, Harris. Quite the businesswoman now.'

She was momentarily vulnerable. 'Will it last, Jimmy?'

'Of course it will! You're young and glamorous and you're the best.' He paused, touching her cheek. 'You can do anything, Harris. *Anything* you set your mind to.'

She took his hand and kissed the palm. 'Thanks.'

'Thanks for what?'

'For always being there when I need you. For caring about me. And for your support.'

I want to marry you, Jimmy thought. But now is not the time to ask. I have to know you better, know that you feel the same. The shadow of Ben Ramsey was still between them. Harris might never have mentioned him, but Jimmy knew how much she had loved the man and also knew that she didn't love *him* in the same way. How could she? He wasn't handsome or exciting. He was Jimmy Henshaw, a good guy, without guile. But was that enough to make Harris love him? And *keep* her loving him?

'I'll see you tonight,' Jimmy drawled, kissing her on the cheek and moving to the stairs. 'Oh, and you look good in that suit.'

She raised her eyebrows. 'You like green?'

'If you're wearing it, I like any damn thing.'

The sun was high, a few birds flying over the Wigan streets as Richard carried his son on his shoulders, whistling as they walked up Market Place. An old friend of his aunt's was walking towards him, obviously without recognising him.

'How do, Mrs Riley?'

She turned and looked at him, frowning. 'Well I never! Richard!' she said, surprised at his impressive weight gain. The tall rangy young man she remembered had changed into a burly, bearded figure, grinning like a lunatic. 'Yer looking pleased with yerself.'

'Life's good,' Richard replied. 'I've been promoted. Back at the gas works here.'

'I thought you were Oldham way?'

'We were,' Richard replied, Tom wriggling on his father's shoulders. 'But I'm home now.'

'Bonny'll be glad,' Mrs Riley replied, wondering about Madge and unable to resist a comment. 'What about yer Mam?'

Richard's bearded face clouded over. 'Not good.'

'Still in hospital?'

He didn't like the turn the conversation had taken. Madge wasn't at the top of his list of priorities. Today he wanted to celebrate his good fortune, not think about his mother, holed up in the Bootle Hospital with alcoholic poisoning.

'Mam's . . . well, she's Mam,' he said, then moved off, calling over his shoulder, 'Good to see you, Mrs Riley.'

'Oh, and you, Richard. Good to see you too.'

Well now, what a turn-up! Fancy Richard coming back to Wigan. And carrying more than his son too. Must be four stones heavier, if a pound. That wife of his must be a right good cook . . . Quickly she hurried off to find someone to pass on the piece of gossip. It wasn't much, but the offspring of Madge Baker were always worth talking about.

Arriving at his new home, Richard stood on the pavement and admired the small terraced house on Wood Street. The windows had been scrubbed clean, the door newly painted. Smiling with barely contained pleasure, Richard swung his son down off his shoulders and pointed to the house.

'See that, Tom? That's our new home.'

Not in Scholes, he wanted to add. Not a slum. Not much, admittedly, but better than anyone would have expected from the Baker lad. Oh, he was a happy man, Richard thought, scratching his beard as he looked round. Not a filthy drain in sight. No smells, no piled-up rubbish, no brooding menace – as there had been in the streets where he had grown up. This was simple, but respectable. And *he* had done that. He had got his family to Wood Street. Bloody hell!

'You coming in, or going to stand out there all day?' Penny asked, standing in the doorway.

'Stay there!' Richard shouted to her.

'What for?'

'Because I want to keep that image for ever.'

He stared at her lovingly, taking in the pale red hair, the soft round face with its large eyes. She was – at that moment – his ideal, in her dark blue dress with the floral apron on top, a string of fake amber beads around her neck. *His wife*.

'Oh, come on, you big softie!' she teased him, flushing and walking back into the house.

He followed her, Tom running ahead into the kitchen. On the table was a white cloth, and clean white pots from the market. Not expensive, but new. And from the oven came the smell of pastry cooking, a pot boiling on the hob. A memory came back to Richard in that instant – his mother's kitchen when he had last seen it. A kitchen where nothing was ever cooked, the table propped up on its broken leg, the windows covered with torn blinds. Dark greasy lino had covered the floor, cigarette butts in the unemptied grate, a cold water tap dripping into a Belfast sink, where a slimy cloth hung over the rim.

And then he remembered that dreadful night he had climbed the dark stairs up to his room. He could see himself – as though he was watching another person – pick up his razor. Outside someone had called out a woman's name, and then passed on. The quiet had crouched down on him, despair overwhelming. Slowly he had extended his arm and then drawn the razor across his wrist . . .

The memory bit into him, then lifted – and he was back in Wood Street.

'Are you all right?' Penny asked anxiously, walking over and touching his hand.

'I was just . . .' he struggled for words. 'I was just remembering something.'

She laid her head against his chest. 'Whatever it was, don't ever think of it again. Your face changed, Richard. I was afraid.'

I could have died. I could never have loved this woman and my child. I could have missed all this happiness . . . Breathing in deeply, Richard let the memory pass away. It slid from him like dirt under water. Happiness cleansed him as he held on to his sweet wife in their clean home. No more slums, he told himself. No more slums for you, or your family. The bad is over.

Once and for all, it's over.

Whistling to get her attention, Mr Lacy looked over the garden wall and then beckoned for Mrs Turner. Fully aware that Irma was in the breakfast room and might see her running down the garden, Mrs Turner sidled over to the outhouse and then ducked behind the wall.

'What's up?' she said, popping her head over the gap and startling Mr Lacy.

He blinked, looking round. 'Where the hell did you come from?'

'I didn't want Irmastein to see me, so I took a different route. What d'you want me for?'

Frowning, he leaned towards her. The autumn chill had made the ground hard.

'You know that man that Miss Harris were so keen on? You know, years back?'

'She's got a new man, a very nice new man. A man who treats her well,' Mrs Turner said, her tone insinuating. 'A man who looks set to make her into an honest woman.'

Mr Lacy wasn't taking it in. 'What were his name? Oh, you remember! You must.' He blew air between his lips, the vapour curling into the slate-grey sky. 'He were a doctor –'

'Ramsey!' Mrs Turner snapped. 'Ben Ramsey. Your memory not what it was, is it?'

'Nothing's what it was,' Mr Lacy replied, winking.

Pretending to be affronted, Mrs Turner glanced down. 'I don't know what you're thinking of, talking to me like that! I'm a clean-living woman –'

'Not like your sister.'

Mrs Turner's head snapped up, her eyes narrowed. 'Oh, if you want to talk about skeletons in cupboards, we could mention your uncle Desmond, who was no better than he should have been. The local abortionist, wasn't he?'

'Hush!' Mr Lacy said, looking round. 'I didn't know you knew about Desmond.'

'You'd be surprised what I know. And what I choose to keep to myself. *Or otherwise.*'

'You'll say nothing about Desmond?' Mr Lacy blathered on. 'I mean, if the Barracloughs heard about him . . . You know, it'd not do me a bit of good, and I'm not as young as I was. They might like an excuse to fire me for a younger man.'

Satisfied that she had him temporarily over a barrel, Mrs Turner continued smoothly, 'So what were you going to tell me about Ben Ramsey?'

Blinking, Mr Lacy returned to his first theme. 'Oh, yes, right.

347

Well, that Ramsey fella, I've heard all kinds about him. Like he's been drinking and taking stuff –'

'Snuff? What's wrong with snuff?'

Mr Lacy stared at her blankly. 'What about snuff? Who said anything about *snuff*?'

'You did!'

'I never. I said stuff – Ramsey's drinking and taking *stuff*.'

'What kind of stuff?'

'Medical stuff, I guess.'

This was real gossip. Leaning closer, Mrs Turner pulled her cardigan around her tightly. Even the cold wasn't going to drive her away from this news.

'You mean drugs?'

Mr Lacy nodded. 'Well, sounds like that. I mean, what else do doctors take? They have all kinds on tap, just ready to take a bit when they fancy it. They could be taking anything they liked and no one any the wiser. Remember that doctor who was taking arsenic?'

'He was poisoning people! He wasn't taking it himself.'

Mr Lacy carried on gamely, 'Word has it that Dr Ramsey were seen in Manchester, staggering around. Well, he wouldn't do it round here, would he? No one shits on their own doorstep.'

'Mr Lacy!'

He flushed. 'Sorry, Mrs Turner, I forgot myself there.'

'He might get struck off.'

'He might at that . . . But it could just be gossip. Dr Ramsey's a handsome man, and people get jealous.'

'He was a pig!' Mrs Turner replied shortly. 'And I don't want you mentioning this to Miss Harris, you hear me? It took a long time for her to get over that toerag; no point raking up the past. He led her a right dance, he did. Not that that's something peculiar to doctors. There's lots of men who lead women on, saying one thing and meaning another.'

This was too subtle for Mr Lacy and he made no response. Frowning, Mrs Turner continued, 'Ramsey's married to Eve

Clough . . . I bet her mother won't be laughing about this. That little Irish songbird's as tough as a navvy. If Ben Ramsey's on the skids he'll have wrecked all Birdie Clough's careful plans. And she won't like that. She won't like that a bit.'

Her head thrown back, Harris watched the tightrope walkers, her mouth slightly open. It had been Jimmy's idea. A kid at heart, he had thought that it was worth a visit to Manchester to see Billy Smart's Circus. 'They've got lions, tigers, the lot,' he'd told Harris. 'We could take Saville.' She had been touched by the offer, but Saville never left the lodge now. So she and Jimmy went to the circus alone.

It was a freezing night, Harris bundled up in a heavy coat and fur hat, her hands in thick gloves. By the time they had got into the main tent her nose was red, her eyes watering with cold. Taking off his scarf, Jimmy wrapped it around her neck and put his arm round her, Harris leaning against him in their cramped seats.

But when the acrobats came on Harris forgot all about the cold. Mesmerised, she watched the men on the high wire, a woman in her pink tights twisting and turning under the paraffin lights.

'She could fall!' Harris said, peering through her fingers.

'She doesn't think so,' Jimmy replied, all too aware of the small boy next to him guzzling down a bag of chips, and the smell of cooked onions drifting into the tent.

Well, he hadn't planned it, but *this was the moment,* Jimmy thought. Now. Do it now. But what a hell of a place to pick, a damned circus. Was that a proper venue for a proposal? Maybe he should take Harris out for dinner instead, buy her roses and drop on one leg by candlelight. The thought mortified him. Oh no, there was to be no kneeling down. He'd look too stupid. He couldn't afford to mess this up.

'Harris,' Jimmy began, his mouth close to her ear, 'I want to ask you –'

The small boy next to him suddenly jumped as the acrobats made a flying leap – and sent half his chips over Jimmy's trouser leg.

'Hey, watch out!'

The boy gave Jimmy a defiant stare. 'Yer nudged m' arm!'

'The hell I did!' Jimmy replied, the boy's stocky father suddenly leaning forwards and fixing him with a basilisk stare.

'Yer frightening m' boy?'

Jimmy looked the burly man up and down and answered slowly. 'He dropped his chips over me.'

'Yer nudged 'im!'

Her eyebrows raised, Harris glanced over to Jimmy. 'What did you want to say to me?'

'Yer made m' drop m' chips!' the kid wailed, the acrobats flying overhead, Harris as serene as an angel, looking at Jimmy expectantly.

'What was it?'

''E wants some more chips!' the giant father said pugnaciously, staring at Jimmy.

'With vinegar,' the kid added.

'What was it?' Harris asked again, Jimmy feeling the hot chips burning through his trouser leg.

'Harris, I wanted to ask –'

'Yer buying 'im them chips, or what?' the giant said, leaning across his son and tapping Jimmy on the shoulder.

'Here!' Jimmy snapped, chucking a half-crown at the grinning kid. 'Get yourself enough to choke on!' Then he turned back to Harris. 'I want to marry you. I love you. God, I love you so much. Harris, will you marry me?'

But before she could answer the giant slapped Jimmy on the back of his head, acrobats, chips and Harris all mingling together in a soup as he slumped, unconscious, back into his seat.

FORTY-FOUR

'We could have a double wedding,' Bonny said, deliberately antagonising Irma. 'Me and Howard, and Harris and Jimmy.'

For once Irma was not going to be provoked. Her niece had come through. At last. Oh, she had been proud enough of Harris's business skill, and the Manchester salon, which was slowly, but surely, taking off. But this was a real triumph. Harris Simons was marrying James Henshaw. *A solicitor.*

Smiling to herself, Irma mixed up some hair dye and turned back to Gladys Leonards.

'What's this about weddings?' she asked, looking avidly for gossip.

'My niece is marrying a professional man. A solicitor. James Henshaw.'

'Oh, really? I heard they were courting,' Mrs Leonards replied, unable to resist adding, 'I hope this turns out well for her. Poor girl, she had such a disappointment before.'

Without blinking an eyelid, Irma applied the dye and mentally made a note to leave it on a few minutes longer than necessary. A good stinging of the scalp should remind Gladys Leonards to watch her tongue.

'Will you be having a big wedding?' the shrill-voiced Mrs

Hardman asked, joining in, leaning closer from her seat on the other side of the mirror.

'I think marrying a professional man calls for it,' Irma replied, revelling in her triumph. 'The reception's going to be at Deerheart House. I shall ask the Mayor and Mayoress, of course.'

'Oh,' Mrs Hardman replied, 'are you having caterers?'

'I hardly think Mrs Turner would be up to catering for the *crème de la crème*,' Irma answered her briskly.

Oh, this was sweet, she thought, looking round. All you smug little women will be desperate to come to Deerheart House, where you can have a nosy round, and look at what the Simonses' money has bought. I bet no one mentions Saville now that the family was about to be elevated to social sainthood. The past couldn't take the sheen off *this* triumph.

'Harris will make a lovely bride.'

'We're going to have the dress made,' Irma offered, unusually loquacious. 'Raw silk, ivory.'

Could hardly be white, Gladys Leonards thought churlishly. Well, it was quite something to hear that Harris had caught one of the most eligible bachelors in town. And with her past . . . Wonders never ceased. You'd have thought that Jimmy Henshaw would have picked a nice decent girl. Perhaps he didn't know about the scandal! she thought suddenly with excitement. Perhaps someone should tell him. It wouldn't be fair for a man to be bowled over by Harris's beauty and trapped into marriage without knowing the full facts.

'He's a wonderful young man,' Irma continued, Gladys suddenly feeling the dye bite into her scalp. 'So understanding of people's failings.' She fixed her client with a challenging stare as though she had tuned into Mrs Leonards' thoughts. 'Mind you, Harris is quite a catch –'

'I think this dye has been on long enough.'

'A little longer,' Irma replied, glancing back to Mrs Hardman.

'We're having some food sent from Kendal Milne. Smoked salmon from Scotland, fruit from –'

Her eyes widening, Mrs Hardman tried to memorise every detail. The war might be long over, but there was still food rationing – but not for the Simonses, obviously.

'And flowers, of course.'

'I think this dye has been on long enough –'

Irma ignored Gladys Leonards – and her large, reddening ears – and carried on with her conversation.

'Oh, yes, many flowers. And a wonderful bouquet for Harris to carry. I always say that you can tell when a person has breeding by looking at the flowers they choose.' She hustled Mrs Leonards out of her chair, the woman's eyes smarting from her stinging scalp. 'Oh yes,' Irma went on, as she instructed Iris, the junior, to wash off the dye. 'This will be a wedding to remember. There won't have been another like it in this town. You mark my words – no one will ever forget Harris Simons's wedding.'

Fast asleep, Harris sat in the rocking chair in front of the fire at Wood Street. On her lap was the sleeping Tom, his head resting against her chest. She was a beauty, Penny thought, a woman who would have handsome children – even if Jimmy Henshaw wasn't that good-looking. But a nice person, thoroughly nice. And no side about him.

For the last few weeks Harris and Jimmy had visited the Bakers at Wood Street often. Jimmy knew that Richard was one of Harris's oldest friends and accepted him as such. Only Penny wasn't so sure that the friendship had always been entirely innocent. It was obvious to her that Harris had no designs on her husband, and she doubted if she ever had. But as for Richard . . .

Making herself some tea, Penny thought about the woman sleeping in her kitchen. Richard had told her all about Harris's childhood, and about her disastrous love affair – but he had left out one thing. *The fact that he had loved her*. Drying her hands, Penny moved over to the fire and sat down in the vacant seat next to Harris. I should be jealous of you, of your beauty, your career, your money, but I'm not. I am Richard's wife. He loves me. He might have loved you once, but I have him now. And I have his child.

Stirring suddenly, Harris opened her eyes and caught Penny looking at her.

'Good sleep?'

'The best. I was exhausted.'

Penny kept her voice low, to avoid wakening Tom. 'I saw the article in the *Manchester Evening News* about the salon. You're getting well known.'

Still drowsy, Harris smiled, then said suddenly, 'I love Jimmy a lot.'

'I know.'

A silence moved between them, an understanding.

'I envy you your family, Penny. Your happiness. I want that. But I'm scared sometimes that Jimmy might regret marrying me.'

'Why?'

'Because of my past. Because of Ben Ramsey.'

'Do you still love him?'

Harris opened her eyes wide, holding Penny's gaze.

'I think of him every day. But I don't love him any more . . . I look back and wonder how I could have behaved like that, how I could let him treat me so badly. But I was obsessed by him. Some part of me still is . . .' She stared into the firelight now, avoiding Penny's gaze. 'I love Jimmy because he's *worth* loving. Because he's good, funny, kind. Honest. Jimmy loves the best of me, and brings out the best *in* me. Ben Ramsey brought out the worst, the dark side. The bit we all try hard to hide.' Harris turned her head, looking straight at Penny. 'Do you understand?'

'No,' she answered honestly, 'but I know that Jimmy loves you very much, and that you love him. That's all that counts in the end: knowing there's someone in your corner who'll be there for you. A person you feel safe with.' She paused, smiling to herself. 'You know, if Richard told me to jump off the roof, I'd do it. Not because I'm stupid, but because there would be a reason. And because I trust him.'

At that moment Richard walked in, blowing on his hands. 'My God, it's bloody freezing out there! You remember when Bonny and I came over to Deerheart House that first winter?' He smiled at Harris. 'Irma used to try and keep us in the garden, even when it was below zero. But Mildred used to sneak us back in again as soon as her sister had gone out.' He crossed the kitchen, then stood behind Penny's chair and rested his hands on her shoulders. 'I suppose Irma's organising the wedding?'

Harris nodded, Tom waking slowly in her arms. 'Hello, little one,' she said tenderly. 'You back in the land of the living, are you?'

It was the tiniest pressure, but Penny felt it. It came from Richard's heart right down into his hands: the reaction as he looked at Harris with his son.

'Tom adores you,' he went on, still studying her. 'I guess you'll want children of your own.'

'At least four,' she replied, laughing at Tom. 'All as bad and wicked as this one!'

Later, when Harris had gone home and Penny was clearing up, Richard settled Tom in bed and then came back downstairs. Lighting up a cigarette, he put his feet on the fender and reached for his wife's hand.

'She was the one,' Penny said quietly, 'wasn't she?'

He said nothing, just kept looking into the fire and smoking.

'How lucky am I,' she went on, squeezing her husband's hand, 'to beat a beauty like that to marry you?'

Her hand slid up his forearm, her fingers resting on his wrist and then, gently, stroking the faint scar there. She said nothing, and didn't need to. It was her way of telling Richard that she had seen her rival, and understood.

Dropping Milly off at prep school, Bonny walked across town, stopping at the tea shop where she used to work. With no little pleasure she ordered tea and a cake, making sure to spend time eating it, her old manageress watching balefully from the kitchen door. Not bad for a slum kid, Bonny thought, dropping another sugar lump into her tea.

She had shown them all. She had her regulars at the salon, people who asked for her specially, and who tipped her. Tips she put aside, tips which were growing into a tidy little sum. Not bad for an unmarried mother, a woman the nurses would hardly talk to when she had her baby. They would all talk to her soon though, when she became Mrs Waring. *Mrs*. Hah! Bonny thought. I'm going to be respectable at last. It was almost a shame. She had grown to love the little flat over the salon, had made it a palace for Milly.

Bonny stirred her tea, fully aware of the fact that the manageress was hoping she would choke on it.

She might have been an unmarried mother, but she had done well by her child. Milly didn't talk with a broad Lancashire accent, Bonny had seen to that. Don't listen to me, she would tell the little girl, listen to Auntie Harris. If Milly had to have an example, make it Harris Simons, not Bonny Baker. It was one thing to give birth to a child, but quite another to give that child a head start in life.

Smiling to herself, Bonny thought of her wedding day. She had half a mind to wear white, just to get everyone going. But no, she would wear something elegant, a suit perhaps, or one of those New Look designs from Dior that were so popular. Dear God, the fuss the New Look had caused, and was still causing. Women had been up in arms at the amount of material wasted, people tearing the clothes off the poor model when it was first shown. There had even been talk of the Government regulating the length of women's skirts. Fat chance, Bonny thought. No damn politicians were going to get their hands on the best thing that had happened to fashion for a decade. She could even get one of those Shaplies she had read so much about: mass-produced false busts made of rubber sponge. Coupon free.

'So how are you, Bonny?' the manageress asked, finally walking over to her table.

'I'm getting married.'

'Not before time,' the woman replied, her thin face overwhelmed by her large false teeth.

Nothing was going to spoil Bonny's pleasure. 'I think I'll have another cake, *Miss* Hicks,' she said, 'that nice chocolate eclair.'

Smarting, Miss Hicks put the cake down in front of Bonny. 'I must say I never thought I'd see you sort yourself out, Bonny Baker. You were a badly spoken, raw-boned little runt when I first gave you a job.'

'I remember,' Bonny replied, putting down her fork and looking at her old tormentor. 'You hated me, made me feel really small. Couldn't stop talking about my mother. And always loud enough for everyone to overhear.' Bonny paused, played with the eclair and then left it. Just to show that she could afford to buy and reject a fancy cake. Then she got to her feet. 'I'll pop in with my husband next time I'm passing, Miss Hicks. Oh, and I've left a tip under the plate.'

FORTY-FIVE

'Stand still!' Irma barked as Harris stood for her second fitting. 'You want this dress to be made right, don't you?'

Tapping her toe, Harris looked over to her aunt. Irma was dressed up in her finery, her hair newly dyed and crowned with an extravagant hat. My God, Harris thought, whatever happened to that dull spinster? It looked as though it was Irma getting married, not her.

'The wedding's not until the middle of February,' Harris said patiently. 'I don't know what all the rush is about.'

'These things take time to arrange properly,' Irma countered. 'We should look for your shoes next.'

Taking in a deep breath, Harris stood still whilst the seamstress altered the dress on her left shoulder. It was a glorious confection of ivory silk, the weight making it fall to the ground in a straight line, the waist nipped in with a boned basque.

'I can hardly breathe in this,' Harris said, wriggling. 'You'll have to let it out.'

Irma shot her an savage look. 'Cut down on the cakes, Harris! You don't want to go up that aisle like a galleon in full sail.' She glanced at the seamstress, anxious to make it known that the increase in weight was down to overeating, and not pregnancy. 'Honestly, you'd think my niece would want to look her best! Anyone of any breeding *loses* weight before they get married.'

Impatient, Harris sighed. 'I've got other things on my mind, Irma. The Manchester salon's doing really well now. I was even wondering if I might expand –'

'Keep still!' Irma countered, glancing up at her niece. 'Expand! Are you crazy?'

'There's a tiny place in Hyde which would do. They don't have a good hairdresser there.'

'Harris, concentrate on getting married, will you? You can think about your career afterwards.'

'But the shop might have gone by then.'

Waving the seamstress away, Irma waited for the woman to leave the cubicle and then turned back to her niece.

'You don't *need* another salon. You've got more than enough to think about. Anyway, what does Jimmy say? Most men don't like their women to work. And a well-off man doesn't like people to think that his wife *has* to work. It doesn't look good.'

Incredulous, Harris slipped out off her wedding dress and stood in her underwear, her hands on her hips.

'I'm not going to be some stay-at-home wife!'

'You'll have to be – when you have children,' Irma replied. 'Really, Harris, do you think James Henshaw wants his wife working day and night? He'll want someone who can keep his home nice and entertain his friends.'

'Then maybe he should get a housekeeper instead of a wife.'

'You really can be stupid!' Irma snapped. 'You want to get married, don't you? Men don't like career women – they never have.'

'But you had a career.'

'Yes, and I'm alone! You don't want to end up a spinster, do you? I had a career because I had no family,' Irma said impatiently. 'If Mildred and I had married do you think we would have opened that salon?'

Surprised, Harris sat down. 'You always said you liked working.'

'Because I had nothing else on my mind,' Irma retorted, the tulle for Harris's wedding veil on her lap. 'If I'd married, I would have put all my energies into my husband's career, not my own. It's the natural way of things.' She stroked the tulle thoughtfully, then realised what she was doing and stopped. 'Make your man happy, Harris. James wants you to put *him* first, not your career. Besides, the business doesn't matter that much to you, does it?'

Incredulous, Harris stared at her. 'Of course it matters! When I took over the salon and made a go of it I was thrilled. I felt as though I had really achieved something. And then to get a place in Manchester, and see *that* work . . .' She shook her head. 'Times have changed, Irma. Women have different ideas about life.'

'Nonsense!' her aunt snapped back. 'Men are men and they like one thing and one thing only – to have a woman's full attention. They want clean sheets, ironed shirts and food on the table when they come in.'

'But –'

'But nothing! If you want to keep a man like James Henshaw you have to behave the way he expects.' Irma dropped her voice so that no one would overhear them. 'This is a chance you might never have got, Harris. With your background, it's a miracle a solicitor looked at you twice. Don't mess it up. You're not the kind of woman who wants to live alone, fighting battles with the world. You need a man and a family. You need stability. You might think otherwise, but I know differently.'

It wasn't what Harris wanted to hear. 'Jimmy likes to know all about my work. He's always asking about what I'm doing –'

'You're not married yet,' Irma interrupted her. 'Things will change.'

'Why?'

'Because they do!' Irma retorted hotly.

'I don't know how you can be so sure. You've never been married!'

Flinging the tulle to one side, Irma stood up.

'I *could* have been. I was in love once, with an unsuitable man. Yes, Harris, *even me*. Even dried-up old Irma. I didn't have the courage to stand up for myself and after he left I wouldn't let another man close – and that's how I became what I am today. Bitter to the bone. You think you're the only one who's ever been in love? You think you're the only one who's ever been mad with longing?' Her face moved closer towards her niece's. 'I'm no fool, Harris, I know you still think about Ben Ramsey now and again –'

'Rubbish!'

'Oh, come on, Harris. We're both women, and I understand these things. I haven't stood on the sidelines watching people for years without learning something. I know you wanted Ramsey with all your heart – and if you're honest some part of you *still* wants him.'

Annoyed, Harris turned away, but Irma pulled her round to face her again.

'It's nothing to be ashamed of. You're rid of Ben Ramsey now. It's over. It would have been a disaster anyway. He did you a favour marrying Eve Clough. But now you have the one thing I never got – a second chance. Take it and make the most of it.'

A timid voice suddenly cut into their conversation. 'Are you ready to carry on with your fitting now?'

'We'll call you when we're ready!' Irma shot back, the woman jumping and hurrying away again. 'Harris, listen to me. I'm a cow, I know that, but if Mildred was alive she would say the same. Take your good fortune and hold on to it.'

The memory of Mildred cut through Harris and she glanced down at her hands, moved.

'Why didn't she ever marry?'

A moment tingled between them. Irma stared at Harris and was tempted to tell her all about her sister's past. It would be the right time – if there ever was one. But what purpose would it serve, making Mildred look human? Harris needed to think of her aunt as someone extraordinary, not a woman as faulted as everyone else. She needed a figurehead to admire and emulate. So Irma gave her one.

'Mildred wasn't interested in marriage,' she lied. 'My sister was happy with her lot. She liked looking after Saville, me, and the house. And she liked working at the salon.' Irma paused, seeing Harris accept the untruth. 'Mildred gave all her love to her family.'

'She would have made a good wife and mother.'

God forgive me, Mildred, Irma thought to herself.

'Maybe so, maybe not,' she hurried on. 'But my sister would still say what I'm saying to you – make James Henshaw happy and you'll have nothing to fear from life. You'll have a good man with you. You'll be a married woman, *Mrs Henshaw*, someone with status. A wife.' She snorted derisively. 'And that would be a first for the Simons women.'

Harris looked Irma straight in the eyes. Their relationship had always been strained, but that moment Harris knew that Irma was genuinely trying to protect her. And so, for the first time in her life, she kissed her aunt on the cheek.

Startled, Irma flushed and then touched her face, her eyes – to Harris's horror – filling.

Then she rallied. 'Hello!' she shouted loudly into the shop. 'Is someone coming to fit this dress, or not?'

It was Howard Waring's idea of romance, a winter wedding. What he hadn't counted on was the weather. Snow was falling heavily on 8 December as he hurried up the steps to the registry office, a queue of people already waiting. In his stiff, rented suit, he looked round awkwardly, spotted Harris and waved.

She walked over, placing a carnation in his lapel.

'Bloody hell! Where did you get that in this weather?'

Smiling, she tapped the side of her nose. 'Ask no questions, told no lies.' Beside her, Jimmy suddenly materialised, Richard and Penny bringing up the rear.

'Nervous?' Jimmy asked.

Howard shook his head firmly. 'No way! I can't wait to get wed.' Then he glanced at his watch. 'Have to hurry, though. I'm on the evening shift tonight.'

'You're working?' Richard asked, moving closer. 'What kind of honeymoon is that?'

'Bonny's kind,' Howard replied, shrugging. 'She said going away were a waste of money. Better to put it towards a deposit on a house.' Looking round, he asked anxiously, 'Where is she?'

'We're early,' Penny soothed him. 'Give her time.'

Almost as she said the words Bonny hurried in. She was wearing a pale blue wool suit, topped with a dark coat, her hair dishevelled.

'Good God, whatever happened to you?' Harris asked, moving over to her.

'Milly's poorly and I couldn't get anyone to sit with her,' Bonny explained. 'Nothing serious – a bit of a cold. But I didn't want her coming out on an afternoon like this. Winter wedding, my arse!'

Smoothing her friend's hair, Harris took out her own lipstick and offered it to Bonny. 'Put some on. Yours has worn off.' She watched her, then nodded. 'That's better. So who's babysitting Milly now?'

'Irma,' Bonny replied, rolling her eyes. 'I bet she'll have her sweeping the floors and scrubbing out the hand basins by the time I get back.' She glanced across the reception area to where the stocky Howard was standing. 'Oh, he looks grand, doesn't he?'

Harris agreed. 'Yes, he looks grand. And so do you.' Quickly she helped Bonny out of her coat and smoothed down her suit. Then stood back. 'Ready?'

'*Ready?* I've waited bloody years for this. Stand aside and let me at him!'

After the ceremony they came out into a five o'clock winter night, Bonny arm in arm with Howard, both grinning broadly. Standing on the steps, Richard and Penny threw confetti, Harris then pressing an envelope into Bonny's hand. Her face was puzzled, half lit by the streetlamp.

'What is it?' she asked Harris quietly.

'A wedding present.'

Slowly Bonny opened the envelope, then gasped. 'Hell's bells, how much is in here?'

'Enough to put a deposit on that house you were looking at,' Harris replied, snow falling onto her face and making white flecks in her dark hair.

'You're mad, Harris Simons,' Bonny said simply, tucking the envelope into her pocket, 'but I love you.'

With that, she turned back to Howard and hollered: 'Hey, husband of mine, we'd better get a move on or you'll miss your shift!'

FORTY-SIX

Her nails drumming on the arm of her chair, Birdie Clough stared at the wedding photograph on her dressing table. What a handsome couple they had made, she thought, the dark Dr Ramsey and the ethereal Eve . . . Rising to her feet, she paced the floor, ten steps one way, ten another. Then she paused. Was it true what she had heard about Ramsey? And if so, what could she do about it?

Now was not the time to talk to Sydney, she knew that much. Always better to plot, *then* tell him; let him think it was his idea. After all, as he always said, his little Birdie mustn't be troubled or upset. Well, she *was* upset! Birdie thought. Touching her stomach, she winced. The fish she had eaten for dinner wasn't sitting well on with her, or maybe she was just feeling nauseous about what she had heard.

Walking back to her dressing table, Birdie took out an antacid and sucked it thoughtfully. She had misjudged Ben Ramsey; had thought that he was so ambitious that he would stay on the straight and narrow long enough to get himself to Rodney Street. Once there, he would be powerful enough to indulge his weaknesses, but not before. Quickly Birdie bit into the antacid, a chalky taste filling her mouth. If *she* had heard about Ramsey then others would hear before long.

The doorbell ringing bit into her thoughts. Birdie walked downstairs to find Ben waiting for her in the drawing room.

'Good of you to call by,' she said, her lilting brogue all honeyed charm. Slowly she regarded her son-in-law. Handsome as ever, with his dark looks and big wide smile, but too arrogant. Too sure of himself.

'Always a pleasure to see you, Birdie,' Ben replied.

She waved him to a seat. 'Would you like a drink?'

'No, I still have some calls to make.'

'Sure you wouldn't like a little tipple?'

'No,' Ben replied, a little more forcibly.

'But I heard you were enjoying your drink,' Birdie went on, in her singsong voice. 'Heard you liked drinking a lot, in Manchester.'

Ben faltered, colour leaving his face. Birdie had put him on to the right people and he was near his goal – this wasn't the time to fall out of his mother-in-law's good graces.

'You shouldn't believe what people say, Birdie.'

'But I do, Ben. When I know it's true.' She touched her stomach and winced.

'Are you in pain?' Ben asked, eager to gain some points for being worried.

'Acid,' Birdie replied, her bright eyes hard. 'I seem to be having a lot of trouble digesting the things I eat. *And hear.*'

The fire in the grate suddenly shifted, blue flames licking the chimney. In the hall outside Ben could hear the hour strike. The snow was banking higher and higher against the windows.

'It's cold.'

'And it's going to get colder,' Birdie said ominously. 'How is my daughter?'

'Fine.'

'I don't see her much.'

'She's busy.'

'Too busy for her own mother? Too busy to visit the person who organised that lovely house of yours and bought that nice car?' Birdie's voice took on a metallic chime. 'I don't like wasting my time, Ben. I don't like lost causes either. If I believe in a person – promote them, introduce them to my friends and help them to get on – I expect some kind of return.'

'Birdie,' Ben blustered, leaning forwards in his seat. 'I don't know what you've heard, but it's exaggerated. I like a drink – who doesn't? But I've got it under control.'

As though considering his words, Birdie took out another antacid and sucked it thoughtfully. So her son-in-law was proving to be a liability. That wasn't what she wanted for her daughter. She wanted Ramsey on Rodney Street and a couple of grandchildren sitting round the fire with her. And she was going to get it.

'How much?'

Ben blinked. 'What?'

'How much are you drinking?'

'Not much –'

'How much!'

'More than I should.'

'And the rest?'

'What rest?'

'Don't play games with me!' Birdie snapped. 'I was born with more guile than you'll ever have. You might impress the ladies, but I can see through you like a windowpane. I always have. I knew what you were up to when you began courting Eve and I played you like a fish. And you took the bait so *greedily*.' She laughed lightly, as a child might. 'Such a hungry boy, you were. But now you're getting cocky, just when you're so close to our goal. Because, make no mistake, Rodney Street is *our* goal.' Her eyes flicked scorn at him. 'I think you need to remember just who has been helping you, Dr Ramsey.'

'I know how much I owe you –'

She cut him off mid-sentence. 'I made you, and I can just as easily *unmake* you.'

'Now, look here –'

'No, *you* look here!' Birdie countered. 'Get yourself off the booze and whatever else you're ruining your life with. Get Eve pregnant – and you can have my support back.'

He was rigid with anger and outrage. 'I can't do that!'

'You can, and you *will*,' Birdie replied evenly. 'Or you will pay the consequences. My husband loves me, Ben. One word and he'll have you thrown out of your practice and struck off without a second's thought. He has the connections – I think you already know that. And who would blame him? He would just be protecting his little girl. Which father – or mother – *wouldn't* act the same?'

Ben's eyes were cold, his voice sharp. 'What about Eve in all this?'

'Yes, *what* about Eve? I would like to see my daughter more. See if she's happy, healthy.' Birdie paused. 'And if I find out that you have made her suffer – in any way – I will *crucify* you.'

The flames in the grate spluttered again, a little puff of smoke coming into the room.

'Goodness me,' Birdie said lightly, 'just look at that, will you? The wind must have changed. I said we should have the chimney swept again, but Sydney hates workmen in the house.' She glanced out of the window. 'It's going to be cold. Very cold. The kind of weather a person wouldn't like to be stranded in.'

'I've got the hint,' Ben said sullenly. 'I don't need a weather report.'

'So I can count on you to get yourself back on the right track?'

Ben nodded, his temper suppressed. Jesus, he was being suffocated by this woman! By the whole bloody Clough family, in fact. Everyone knew everyone else's every move. It was unbearable. He took in a deep breath. Oh, he'd made a mistake, all right. His ambition had led him right up the garden path. Not that he hadn't *tried* to make the marriage work. He had tried to love Eve, to make a home with her, but it was impossible. They had nothing in common – nothing except bloody Birdie and their ambitions for Rodney Street.

I should have married Harris, Ben thought hopelessly. I should have taken a risk. He wouldn't have found reasons to work late then, wouldn't have needed the booze – and the rest. He looked at his mother-in-law suspiciously. How had bloody Birdie found out? Through Eve? No, Eve wouldn't betray him. She didn't want to admit that her marriage was failing. So it had to be someone else. Probably someone Birdie paid to spy on him.

'I'll get myself sorted out,' Ben said at last. 'It was just a blip, that was all.'

'I'm so glad,' Birdie replied, seeing him to the door. 'I would hate to see all your talent wasted. Now you hurry back to my daughter, and tell Eve I want to see her. And I want grandchildren, Ben. *Soon*. It's very easy really. You have only two things to concentrate on – getting to Rodney Street and making my daughter pregnant.' She kissed him on the cheek, like Judas. 'After that, you can go to hell in a hand basket.'

He flinched.

Birdie showed him the door. 'Lovely to see you again, Ben. I hope you know how welcome you always are.'

The roads into Wigan were almost blocked with snow, the ploughs out day and night to keep the routes clear. And in Manchester Harris sat by the window of the salon and looked down onto the empty streets. Beside her, she could hear the clock striking on St Anne's church and a moment later the cry of the newspaper vendor: 'Queen's son christened Charles!'

Charles, Harris thought, not a bad name, but a bit old-fashioned. When she had a son she would call him . . . The thought made her sit bolt upright. *When she had a son!* My

God, she was getting broody already and she wasn't even married yet. Content, Harris smiled to herself. It was a good sign. Maybe Irma had been right after all, maybe she wouldn't want to work when she was married.

She would certainly have a lot to do. They had already bought their new house, or rather Jimmy's parents had. No money worries for them, no scratching and scraping like Bonny and Howard. It was a fine house, up on Mesnes Park Terrace, where the well-to-do people lived. Irma, never one to be outdone, had then bought the furniture, lavishing money on the couple to prove that the Simonses were far better off than the Henshaws.

Her largesse probably impressed Harris's future in-laws, but what about *her*? Harris thought. Did *she* impress them? It was easy with Mr Henshaw. He was an even-tempered, well-read man with a comfortable practice and lifestyle. No deep thinker – he left that to his wife, and Mrs Henshaw certainly thought a great deal. *What* she thought was another matter. When Harris had first met her there had been an obvious reserve, a woman anxious to see if her son's choice was suitable. *I know about you,* her expression seemed to say. *Your past might not matter with Jimmy, but it does with me.*

Harris could hardly blame her. After all, what had she heard? That Harris Simons had run after a doctor, had an affair with him, and made herself a laughing stock, even hitting him in his own surgery like a common slut. The memory never failed to make Harris uncomfortable as she peered down into the street, looking for any sign of Jimmy.

Gradually she had won Mrs Henshaw over. But the day was never going to come when she pressed Harris to call her Mother. That wasn't on the cards. Still, Harris thought, she was marrying Jimmy, not his mother. And Jimmy loved her unconditionally.

But Jimmy hadn't made love to her. Frowning, Harris ran her finger down the windowpane, the frost settling on the other side of the glass. Now why was that? He knew that she wasn't a virgin any more, and yet he never tried anything on. Kissed her passionately, held her, made it clear that he loved her, but didn't *make* love to her. It was hardly something she could ask him about, Harris knew. It wouldn't be tactful to imply that she was frustrated, or that she wanted to control that part of their lives. Anything that reminded him that there had been another man was off limits. And yet . . .

Frowning, Harris peered through the window again. She would make a wonderful wife, make Jimmy happy. And they *would* be compatible in bed. After all, there was a real attraction between them, they both felt that. So surely she was worrying about nothing? But then again, what if they *weren't* sexually compatible? What if that incredible desire she had once felt became a memory? Would she find herself comparing Jimmy Henshaw to Ben Ramsey?

Flushing, Harris shook her head. Stop it, stop it now, she ordered herself. This is your chance, take it. You love Jimmy, and he loves you. Make this marriage work and don't look back. Sex is sex, after all, it wouldn't be the end of the world if Jimmy wasn't a great lover. She would simply learn to adjust. Sex had brought her nothing but heartache, shame, guilt. Why would she want to rekindle feelings that could lead to that?

Her eyes closing, Harris leaned her head against the cool glass. She had to stop thinking about sex, imagining herself with Jimmy and then remembering how it had been with Ben Ramsey. There was more to life, more to love, than sex. Her hand went up to her mouth, her fingers resting against her lips. Slowly she kissed them, then let her hand run down the line of her throat and rest on her collarbone. Time slid back. The snow wasn't falling, the cold wasn't biting into her. She was lying on her back, looking up at a naked Ben standing over her, his back against the sun. It had been summer, high summer, on one of their hurried meetings. Drowsily, Harris let her hand move down her breastbone and then cup her left breast.

A sudden sound below snapped her out of her reverie, Harris buttoning up her blouse, her face flushed. She could hear Jimmy whistling on the stairs. Running over to him, she pressed her face against his neck.

'Hey, there!' he said, laughing. 'What's the matter?'

'I've missed you,' Harris replied, her voice muffled as she clung to him.

'I've missed you too,' Jimmy answered her, pulling back and looking her in the face. 'Are you worried about something?'

'I was just . . .'

'What, darling?'

'Just wondering . . .' Her voice dropped, embarrassment obvious. 'Jimmy, do you *want* me? I mean, do you want to make love to me?'

There was a terrible silence. Oh God, Harris thought, had she ruined everything? Would he hate her now? Remember what she was? Would he leave her?

Unable to lift her head, Harris waited, her heart beating loudly in her chest. He was going to leave her – going to walk out. He was shocked, disgusted. She was no good.

And then he spoke. 'Harris?'

She didn't move.

'Harris, look at me. We have to talk about this.'

Slowly she met his gaze, her eyes wide with anxiety.

'I love you,' he said slowly. 'And I want to *make* love to you very much. But not until we're married. Then we can take all the time in the world to get to know each other.' He pulled her to him, stroking her hair. 'Did you think I didn't want you? Of course I want you! Jesus, who wouldn't? But I want it to be right, Harris. And it's not long until we're married now. We can wait a little longer. Can't we?'

She nodded eagerly, her face pressed against his neck, relief like a blood transfusion pumping through her veins.

FORTY-SEVEN

Mrs Turner was sipping her port and lemon in the Bishop's Finger, Mr Lacy beside her. It was a freezing night, the fire crackling in the pub grate, the landlord's cat dangling over the end of the counter and blinking, slowly, like a snake.

'Unhygienic, I call it.'

Mr Lacy looked up. 'What's that?'

'Letting that cat have the run of the place! Germs everywhere.' She eyed the animal suspiciously and frowned. As Mrs Turner was obviously out of temper, Mr Lacy regarded her cautiously as she carried on. 'Wedding, wedding, wedding! That's all I hear at Deerheart House. You'd think no one had ever been married before. And the money that Irmastein's chucking around ... *He's a solicitor, you know, this has to be done properly. Everyone of any importance will be there.*' Mrs Turner snorted. 'Hah! The wedding dress cost a king's ransom, and as for the food – my God, it's wicked to see such money forked out. And you'd think they would have wanted to be quiet about it – I mean, what with Harris having a reputation and all. Damn lucky she caught anyone.'

Mr Lacy felt trouble coming on and tried to change the subject. 'Did you see about Eva Peron –'

'What's Eva Peron to me? Another jumped-up woman with

no morals.' Mrs Turner downed her port and lemon and glared at the cat. It eyeballed her back imperiously. 'And they're getting married at night. *At night!* What's that about? I thought she was marrying a solicitor – not Bela Lugosi.'

Mr Lacy laughed.

'I'm glad you think it's funny! I don't. Here I am, engaged for God knows how long and no sign of a wedding. The Mayor'll bare his arse on the Town Hall steps before I'll get wed.' She stopped, tears close. Then: 'How *could* you treat me like this? I tell you, if my husband was alive he'd have something to say about it.'

'I wouldn't be engaged to you if he was alive.'

Mrs Turner let out a short shriek, the cat wiggling its ears, disturbed.

'You're a wicked man, Mr Lacy! I thought you were decent, but you've played me for a fool. And I've given you the best years of my life.'

'Hey, steady on –'

'Don't "steady on" me!' she snapped. 'You should be grateful that I've cared about you. But no, you don't give a damn about me.' Hurriedly she clutched her handkerchief to her mouth. 'You've broken my heart, Mr Lacy, broken my heart.'

'We'll get married –'

Her tears stopped immediately. 'When?'

'Soon.'

'Arrgh,' she moaned, sobbing again.

'I promise we will.'

'Promises, promises! That's all I ever hear from you!' she retorted, her voice carrying into the snug, where a few customers had started to listen avidly. 'It's not like you're such a catch – a broken-down gardener with a dicky back. You were glad enough to have me when that trollop Nelly Fisher moved on, but what have I got out of it?'

'I give you the best veg.'

Her eyes bulged uncomfortably. '*The best veg!* Is that all I'm worth to you? A cauliflower and a bag of King Edwards?'

From the snug came the sound of muffled laughter. Mr Lacy was acutely discomforted. 'Mrs Turner, you're shouting –'

'I mean to shout! It's time everyone knew about you. You're a lothario, a playboy.' Getting to her feet, she looked down at him. 'You're a bounder, Mr Lacy. A right bounder.'

The bounder was rooted to his seat, wearing his cloth cap and a tattered gardening jacket, a spool of twine poking out of the top pocket.

'Women should be warned about men like you!' she hissed. 'I'm going to make sure that everyone knows what you've done. You see if I don't.'

With that, she walked out of the pub, the landlord putting his head around the partition and grinning at Mr Lacy.

'Time for another pint, Errol,' he asked, laughter following, 'before Rita Hayworth calls for you?'

Having newly dyed her hair, Irma studied her reflection. Miss Irma Simons, aunt of Mrs James Henshaw, solicitor. Her mind raced on . . . The wedding of Miss Harris Simons and Mr James Henshaw was an extraordinary affair, with all the best people attending. The bride's aunt had organised everything to perfection, people agreeing that it was the finest wedding for decades. The bride herself was glorious in a very expensive gown, with a very expensive train, her hair arranged by Miss Irma Simons, well known co-owner of Simons Coiffeuse. The church was decorated by the best flowers money could buy, the bride given away by her uncle, *Saville*.

Irma winced. However many times she thought it, it was still a disaster. How *could* Harris insist on having Saville give her away?

'I don't care,' she had said over and over again. 'I love my uncle and I want him to do this for me. And he wants it too. We've talked about it at length.'

'Saville doesn't understand what it means –'

'Oh, yes he does!' Harris had countered. 'And he'll do it perfectly. I know he will.'

Reluctantly Irma had given way, even allowing Bonny to be a bridesmaid. As for little Milly, she was also going to be a bridesmaid. Dear God, Irma thought, why not invite everyone from the nearest mill too? Or perhaps they could have the miners from the pit to come and act as pageboys?

Smouldering, she looked back into the mirror and then smiled slowly. What did it matter? It was still going to be the best wedding that Wigan had ever seen. Something to make everyone sit up and take notice. A way of making the Simons name important again. And not before time, Irma thought, grabbing her coat and walking out into the street.

Briskly she moved along. Her angina attacks had all but stopped. Funny that, she thought. Perhaps she would make old bones after all. Nodding to a couple of people as she passed, Irma sailed on, the cold making little impression. She was important again. And it felt good. The only thing she missed was having someone to share it with. Harris was too busy, of course – the wedding was in ten days' time – and there was no one else apart from Saville. And she and her brother had never been close.

Irma continued to keep up a steady pace. She felt happy for the first time in years. She checked that no one was watching and then quickly kicked a loose stone along the pavement for several yards. Oh, do stop it! she told herself, giddy with suppressed excitement. Be serious now, this is not the place to be silly.

Pushing open the unlocked wrought-iron gates, Irma entered the cemetery and then walked over to Mildred's grave. For a moment she stared at her sister's headstone and then laid the flowers she had brought on top of the marble chippings.

'Well,' she said firmly, 'Harris has done it. In another ten days she'll be married.'

Irma looked round. It wouldn't do for anyone to see her talking to herself. They might think she was going the same way as Saville . . . Quietly she touched the headstone, then snatched away her hand as though it had burned her.

'I'm sorry, Mildred,' she whispered. 'I should have said it a long time ago, but I'm saying it now. I'm sorry for our argument, for what I said. I was cruel. You don't know how much I've regretted it since, how guilty I've felt.' She paused, rearranging the flowers unnecessarily. 'Harris is going to look so beautiful. I wish you could see her, Mildred. She's remarkable. We did all right – for a couple of spinsters. James Henshaw's a nice man and he'll make a good husband. I know that. Everyone likes him and he loves Harris.' Emotional and feeling awkward, Irma made to go and then turned back. 'Oh, and one more thing, Mildred, he's a solicitor.'

Above her head a rook cawed suddenly into the cold winter air. It sounded, to Irma's ears, like a woman laughing.

FORTY-EIGHT

Only three days before her wedding Harris left the Manchester salon and made her way home by train. I'm going to learn to drive, she had told Jimmy the night before. It'll make things so much easier. Staring out of the train window, Harris could see her own reflection staring back at her, and looked away. The train trundled along, stopping at all the minor stations en route, people getting on and off, a woman with a small child struggling to find her ticket.

All so normal, Harris thought, like so many other journeys she had taken. But this one was different: *The next time she travelled this line she would be a married woman.* The thought made her smile to herself and huddle further into her seat. Outside the lights of the houses flickered past, the train whistle blowing shrilly as it entered a tunnel. She was happy. Jimmy was loving and kind, the best sort of husband. And she had made it up to Irma too, made some amends for her past behaviour. Everyone was getting what they wanted. At last.

Looking down at her hand, Harris idled with the diamond engagement ring Jimmy had given her. It had been his grandmother's and was worth a fortune. Harris wished it was new. But it was such a small thing, why worry? And it meant a lot to Jimmy for her to wear it.

Rocked by the motion of the train, Harris found herself fighting sleep. Her eyes closing, she thought of Jimmy and slid into a doze . . . She was laughing, throwing his grandmother's ring up in the air and letting it fall a long way off, Jimmy turning to look at her with shock. The image faded. She was now running down a long tunnel, the sound of a train engine and the tat, tat, tat, tat, of the wheels on the tracks following her. And at the end was Jimmy waiting for her. Only it wasn't Jimmy, it was *Ben Ramsey*.

Startled, Harris woke up, a woman in the corner looking up from her knitting. Smiling half-heartedly, Harris glanced away and looked out of the window, her fellow travellers reflected in it – as was the man walking down the corridor beyond their compartment. Harris could feel herself tense, her breathing accelerating. She knew that man. Transfixed, she stared at the reflection and then saw the man turn.

It was Ben Ramsey.

Hunching down in her seat, Harris turned towards the window, her face averted. Let him pass, she thought, panic-stricken, let him pass. But he didn't. He paused, seeing her, and then he slid open the door of the compartment and walked in.

'So where is she?' Irma said impatiently of Mrs Turner, who was holding a tureen of soup in her hands at the dining room door.

'How would I know?' Mrs Turner countered, her patience at an end with everyone.

'I beg your pardon!' Irma retorted. 'You would do well to remember who pays your wages, and show some respect.'

Sulkily, Mrs Turner put the tureen down on the table. 'Leek soup.'

'Do you *always* have to introduce every dish like an execution?' Irma asked, also irritated.

379

'You want it, or not?'

Irma's expression set hard. 'What *is* the matter with you?'

'As if you'd care!'

Startled, Irma leaned back in her seat. She was going to be kind, she told herself. She was a changed woman now, she would be kind. If it killed her.

'Mrs Turner, can I help you in any way?'

'You could drop dead!' she replied, breaking into tears and running out of the room.

Exasperated, Irma lifted the lid of the tureen and took one sniff. Good God, it smelled ghastly! It wouldn't do for Mrs Turner to get upset too often, or she would wipe out the whole family.

A moment later, the housekeeper returned, looking sheepish. 'I'm sorry for the way I acted, Miss Irma. I'm a bit upset.'

That makes two of us, Irma thought, but smiled benignly. Or so she thought. To Mrs Turner it looked as though she was about to bite her.

'It won't happen again! I just had a falling-out with my intended.'

'Mr Lacy has been your intended for a long time, hasn't he?'

Mrs Turner nodded. 'Too long.'

'I hear that Mrs Barraclough is thinking of replacing him with a younger man.'

Stunned, Mrs Turner grabbed the back of a dining chair for support. 'Mr Lacy thought that too! But she hasn't said anything yet. Oh, my God, the poor man! It would kill him not to work. He's the best gardener in these parts.'

Irma's beneficence knew no bounds. It was time that people saw the nice side of her.

'Perhaps we could do a deal with your fiancé?' she began, the housekeeper still looking at her with suspicion. 'If he were to *marry you* he could come and work here. We don't want any single men at Deerheart House – apart from my brother, that is.'

Mrs Turner was staring at her, glassy-eyed. 'You mean you'd employ him?'

'If he was married, yes. But I'd expect him to work hard. I don't like idlers.'

Was this Irmastein? Mrs Turner wondered. And if so, what was the catch?

'You want Mr Lacy to work as the gardener here?'

Irma tried to keep her patience. How hard was it to understand?

'Mr Ford wants to retire, so we need someone. You want Mr Lacy, and I want a gardener. Seems like we could both benefit from the arrangement.'

'I don't know what to say –'

'Just get it organised, Mrs Turner,' Irma replied smoothly. 'Oh, and take the soup away.'

'Harris?'

She turned slowly, Ben sitting down beside her, the woman in the corner of the compartment watching them surreptitiously.

'I don't want to talk to you,' Harris said, her voice low.

'Harris, listen to me.' He leaned towards her, his breath warm against her cheek. 'I've been wanting to see you for a long time. I've been trying to think of a way to get in touch.'

Hurriedly Harris got to her feet and moved out into the corridor, Ben following. The train was moving at speed, Harris grasping the handrail as he faced her.

'You look beautiful –'

She glanced away from him, fighting panic. God, he was so handsome. How could she have forgotten that? Everything about him crackled with sexuality: his voice, the turn of his head, the expression in his eyes.

'I'm getting married, Ben.'

'I know,' he admitted, the train's whistle piercing the air

381

momentarily. 'I read it in the paper. James Henshaw, solicitor. I hear he's a nice man.'

'Nicer than you ever were,' Harris said coldly, trying to move past him. She had to get away as quickly as she could, had to stop the old memories and feelings flooding back. 'I don't want to talk to you, Ben.'

'Well, you can hardly get out, can you?' he replied, his expression full of longing.

She saw the look and felt the sexual *frisson* between them. But the feeling was followed by mistrust. This was the man who had caused her so much heartache and humiliation; the man who had rejected her to marry another woman. The man she had never forgotten.

'I've missed you, Harris,' Ben said, hurrying on. 'Sometimes I drive past the Bloody Mountains and think of the first time I saw you there. I was obsessed with you –'

'So much that you married Eve Clough,' Harris retorted bitterly. But her voice lacked conviction. She knew it, and so did he. 'Leave me alone, Ben. There's nothing you could say which would make me hate you less.'

'Hate is very close to love.'

She laughed in his face. 'Love! You've always been so sure of yourself, haven't you? So sure that you could do, or say, the right thing and it would all be fine again. Well, it won't this time. What we had was an affair, there was no love in it.'

The train picked up speed, Ben's profile lit by the light from the compartment as he slid the door fully closed, the knitting woman turning away, her eavesdropping thwarted.

'I'm so sorry for the way I treated you,' he said, his tone gentle. 'You don't know how often I've regretted my actions. If it's any consolation, I'm not happy. I married the wrong woman.'

'Am I supposed to feel sorry for you?' Harris replied, trying to work out how long it would be before they reached the next station.

382

Wherever it was, she would get off. Anything to get away from Ben Ramsey. If she talked to him much longer, if she *looked* at him much longer, she would forget what he had done to her. The obsession hadn't died: just lain dormant.

'Eve doesn't love me –'

'Well, Jimmy loves *me*!' Harris countered frantically, trying to convince herself as much as Ben. 'And I'm marrying him.'

'Do you love him?'

'I don't have to answer that!' she snapped, the knitting woman still watching them through the compartment window, irritated that she could no longer hear their conversation. 'You used me, you know you did, Ben. You were a bastard.'

He blinked at the insult, holding on to the handrail tightly as they were jostled by the speeding train.

'I was a lot of things, I know that now,' he said, his tone suddenly pleading. 'My life's a mess – and I deserve it. I was so ambitious that my career came first.' He touched her cheek, withdrawing his hand immediately. 'Jesus, Harris, I was such a bloody fool to let you go. Nothing went right after you –'

'I don't care!' Harris shouted, craving – against all logic – for him to touch her again. 'I loved you so much I would have died for you, I lived for you, for what you said, what you thought, how you looked. I used to do things and think – I'll tell Ben this, or I'll show him that – my life *revolved* around you. You were my happiness. I imagined us being together for ever. I longed for you, ached for you . . . Jesus, you tore my heart out.'

She stopped, overcome. The train was rattling noisily around them, the dim corridor light casting their shadows on the floor. He was suddenly overwhelmed by her, in as much turmoil as she was. They were meant to be together, Ben thought desperately, wasn't that obvious? How could they feel so much emotion, if they didn't still love each other?

'I never wanted to hurt you, Harris,' he said gently, 'I was confused –'

Her head snapped up. 'You weren't confused at all! You dumped me for a woman who was the perfect consort – and now you can live with the consequences.'

'It wasn't like that!'

'It was!' she hurled back. 'I might have been stupid then, but I'm not now. I made a fool out of myself for you. I was a laughing stock. But I've sorted my life out. People respect me now. I have a business –'

'I know.'

'Two salons,' she blurted out, trying to impress him and wondering why. 'Two salons! I did that. You left me flat and I got back on my feet. Whilst you were having a cushy time of it, swanning around with Eve Clough and her parents' influential friends, I was working to keep myself sane.'

'Harris, stop it –'

'No, *you* stop it!' she retorted, mad with fury and confusion. 'You're unhappy now? Good. Because I was unhappy then. And it was much worse for me because I was a woman. I lost my reputation because I slept with you. That wasn't something *you* had to worry about, was it? There wasn't a stigma hanging over *your* head. No, off you went and married some rich woman who you could use to get to bloody Rodney Street!' She stopped, out of breath, her head throbbing. 'Get out of my way, Ben Ramsey!'

But he blocked her path.

'Listen to me, Harris. Just listen! You know as well as I do that there's still something between us. I can feel it. And I know you can. Deny it as much as you like, but I can see it in your face, in your eyes. You still want me as much as I want you –'

'I don't!' she snapped, her voice breaking.

'You're lying! I've been wretched without you, Harris. Nothing matters now, not even Rodney Street. I can't stand my wife, or her parents. I'm drinking –'

'I don't care!'

384

'*You do care!*' he insisted. 'You don't want to, but you do. You care about me, just as I care about you. We were meant to be together. You can't deny it, neither can I. There's never been anyone for me like you. I love you, Harris, I always have.' He paused, staring into her face. 'I've left my wife.'

Shaken, Harris shook her head. 'No . . .'

'I have. I've left Eve. I couldn't stay with her any longer. I want you back, Harris. I have to have you back.' He leaned towards her, so close that his breath was warm on her cheek. She could feel his body brush against hers as the train juddered on the tracks. 'You might think you can marry another man, but you'll always be thinking of me. Just like I'm always thinking of you. You'll talk to him and hear *me* replying; you'll look at him and see *me* sitting there. You'll make love to him and see *me* –'

Lunging out, Harris drew back her arm to slap his face, but Ben fielded the blow and caught hold of her wrist.

'Look at me and say you don't want me,' he told her, his lips brushing against her cheek. 'Look at me and tell me to go away.' His lips rested momentarily against her forehead. Harris's skin burned with longing. 'Look at me and tell me that you can forget me. That you can forget us. That you can live for the rest of your life without our being together.'

He was leaning against her, his mouth next to her ear, Harris's whole body aching for him. She felt dizzy with confusion, longing to reach out for him, but resisting. He was no good; he would hurt her again. *He was no good . . .*

And then suddenly the train lurched as it entered a tunnel. Thrown into darkness Ben caught hold of her, Harris responding hungrily. In the dark they kissed each other desperately, urgently, as though they were drugged and beyond reason. As though they both knew they were hopelessly, undeniably, damned.

FORTY-NINE

Two days passed. Two nights before her wedding, Harris gave up trying to sleep and walked into the bathroom, rinsing her face in cold water. On the wardrobe door hung her wedding dress, her veil over the bedroom chair.

When the train had stopped she had run off, Ben following her out of the station and then stopping when he saw her get into a waiting car. Ducking back, Ben had watched Jimmy Henshaw kiss Harris on the cheek and then pull out into the traffic.

Shaking her head, Harris tried to dislodge the memory. But it came back, over and over – the noise of the train's whistle, the sound of the wheels on the track, and Ben kissing her in the darkness. She had wanted him so much her skin burned, her body pressed against his, both of them matching, their bodies in total unison. But then, leaving the tunnel and coming out into the light, she had broken away . . .

In the car Jimmy had noticed nothing, just kept talking about their honeymoon. They were going away to Scotland for a week and he was thrilled, describing the scenery he remembered from a boyhood visit. In silence, Harris had sat with her hands on her lap, guilt making her nauseous.

For the following two days everywhere she went Harris

saw Ben Ramsey. He was careful, not obvious, just letting her know that he was watching her. Stalking her almost. When she went to the salon, he passed in his car; when she went for her last wedding dress fitting he passed by the shop window. Her ghost, her shadow. She should have resented it, tried to stop him, but after a while she *wanted* to see him, wanted to know he was still watching her. That he still wanted her. But she wouldn't go back to him. Sexually she might be obsessed by him, but she wasn't going to ruin her life again.

Having rinsed her face, Harris walked back into her bedroom and looked at her wedding dress. She was going to marry Jimmy. He loved her and she loved him. He was a good man, everyone knew that. Everyone said how lucky she was to get him. She was envied. She was on the home run. And soon she would be safe.

A knock on the door broke into her thoughts as Irma came in.

'So you're up, are you? About time.'

'I was tired.'

'Well, you don't look very rested,' her aunt replied, walking to the window and looking out. 'I remember the day you first came here. I was watching you from this window, walking with Lionel Redmond. You looked so small.'

'Thanks.'

Irma turned, frowning. 'Thanks for what?'

'For everything you've done for me,' Harris said, her tone subdued. 'I won't let you down again.'

'Of course you won't!' Irma said dismissively. 'Tomorrow evening you'll be Mrs James Henshaw. I can't tell you what that means to me.'

In a daze Harris went to the last wedding rehearsal, the vicar going over the instructions, Jimmy taking her aside afterwards. The church was already decorated with flowers, the scent of lilies melancholy.

'Are you OK?'

'Just nervous,' she said, squeezing his arm. 'I love you, Jimmy.'

He laughed. 'And I love you, Harris. I always will.'

Desperately she clung to him, her head against his chest. 'I can hear your heart beating.'

'That's good,' he teased her.

'It's loud and strong.' She went on listening. 'I couldn't live without you.'

'You don't have to.'

'You won't leave me?'

'Harris,' he said suddenly, holding her at arm's length, 'are you all right?'

'Of course I am,' she said, laughing hesitantly. 'I just wanted to know how much you loved me.'

'More than anything. More than anyone. More than living. Nothing you ever did would stop me loving you.'

Taking in a breath, Harris began, 'But if I told you –'

'Excuse me, but I have to ask you to move on now,' the vicar said pleasantly, interrupting them. 'I have another wedding rehearsal in five minutes.'

Jimmy nodded. 'We're just going. See you tomorrow, Vicar.'

Urgently, Harris turned to him. 'Jimmy, there's something –'

But his attention was diverted, his thoughts elsewhere as he hurried them both out of the church and into the winter evening. The temperature was falling, snow beginning. Within seconds it was disguising the street with white, the illumination spooling out from the church entrance, making a long yellow tongue of light on the ivory snow.

All that night Harris dreamed fitfully. She rose often, walking to the window and looking out. He was there, she knew, somewhere in the darkness, in the cold and snow. Watching, waiting. Then around three Harris slipped out of her bedroom and moved noiselessly downstairs, opening the back door and glancing round.

The moon was half full, bright on the frosty night and making blue shadows on the lawn of Deerheart House.

'I knew you'd come out,' Ben said suddenly, moving into the light. 'Harris, darling –'

'I came to say goodbye once and for all,' she replied, pulling her dressing gown around her and shivering. 'Don't ever come near me again, Ben.'

'You don't mean it.'

'I do,' she said, her tone flat.

But did she? Harris wondered. If she hadn't wanted to see him again, would she have come downstairs to talk to him on the eve of her wedding? In her nightclothes? The cold sucked the warmth out of her, Harris shivering as Ben put his arms around her.

'Don't!' she said, backing away. 'I'm not going to let you mess up my life again, Ben. I don't deny there's something between us, but it's not good, not healthy. Go back to your wife and get yourself to Rodney Street. That's what you really want –'

'I want you,' he said, reaching for her again

She stepped further back, her dark eyes huge in the pale face. 'Get away from me!'

'You don't mean it.'

'I do.'

'No, you don't,' he persisted.

Harris had wanted to be firm, but her voice wavered. 'I'm marrying Jimmy Henshaw tomorrow night.'

He shook his head. 'You're not.'

Angrily she turned away, but Ben caught hold of her arm and turned her back to face him.

'Do you think it's right to marry him when you love me?'

'But isn't that what *you* did, Ben?' she countered, shaking off his grip. 'Isn't that what you said *you* did?'

He winced, the words hitting home. Desperation was making Ben vulnerable as he began to plead with her.

'But I've left Eve now. Dear God, Harris, please let's give it another try. You and I belong together. You know that. There's something between us –'

She paused. There *was* something between them; it had always been there. And it still was. The sexual attraction was in the air around them, in every touch, in every word. Whatever they did it would still be there. But it wasn't enough.

'Sex is all that's between us –'

'No!'

'Yes,' she answered, her voice unexpectedly tender. 'There's nothing to build on, Ben. Nothing to make a life out of.'

'I don't believe that! We *could* make a life, we could do anything together.' He moved close to her, his voice imploring. 'I want to marry you, Harris.'

The words rocked her. Ben Ramsey wanted to marry her. *Now* he wanted to marry her. Not when she was single, and he was single, but *now* when he was estranged from his own wife, and she was about to marry another man.

'You don't mean that!' she said, turning away, close to tears. God, why had he said it now? Why now? She would have given anything for his proposal before. But now . . . 'You're just saying it to spoil my wedding.'

'*Spoil your wedding!*' Ben exclaimed. 'What about your life? Our lives? *His life?* Are you going to walk out on Jimmy Henshaw later, Harris? Because you *will* walk out on him one day. In a month? A year? And how will that be for him then? Easier? I don't think so.'

Confusion was making her uneasy. Why had she come out to see him? He could always manipulate her, make her do what he wanted . . . But then hadn't she wanted to marry him before? Hadn't she wanted that more than anything on earth?

He could see her weakening, desperation making him push

her further. 'Come on, Harris, you've got guts. Why don't you have the courage to walk away now? Come with me . . .'

She shook her head, trying to think clearly. 'And if I did, Ben. Then what? Have you leave me again for some other woman?'

'There is no one but you.'

'Only because you can't have me now,' Harris replied, shivering in the bitter night air. She was chilled to the bone with unearthly cold. 'It's too late, Ben. You're not going to spoil my life.'

'No, *you are.*'

She rocked at the words. 'Oh no, I'm going to make the right decision.'

'Really. Do you *want* him, Harris?'

Flinching, she looked away.

'Well, do you, Harris?' Ben persisted. 'I mean, do you want him? Long for him? Think of him touching you? Could you live *without* making love to him?'

The words shook her. How did he always know what to say to unnerve her? How had he guessed that there was not the same passion between her and Jimmy? She knew the answer only too well – a woman deeply in love would never have spoken to him again. Only a woman who was wavering would let him so close.

But she wasn't going to give in.

'I've heard enough!' Harris snapped, turning to go indoors, then turning back to face him. 'You want me because I'm a woman in my own right now, not some silly kid –'

'It's not like that!'

'I think it is!' Harris retaliated. 'I think that if I'd stayed some little no one, you wouldn't have given me the time of day.'

'That's not true!' he begged, trying to make her listen, but she was past listening to him. Tomorrow she was marrying Jimmy Henshaw. A good man, who wouldn't hurt her. Tomorrow she would be safe.

'I know you, Ben, when you first came here and people told you about Saville and my grandfather you decided that I wasn't wife material. I was a fling, nothing more. You made that very plain to me – in public. And you think I would seriously take you back when I'm on the up?'

'This isn't a competition, Harris,' Ben replied, his face strained with fatigue. 'I was wrong. I was on the make, all right, I admit it. But I've changed. I haven't just come back into your life. I've followed everything that's happened to you. All your success . . . I know I was a bastard to you. But as time went on I realised what I'd missed.' He looked into her face, his voice faltering. 'Don't punish me for ever, because that way you'd punish yourself. I need you, I love you, Harris. I want you in my life, in my bed. I want to hear your breathing in the dark. You, no one else.'

She looked away, moved. 'So why did you wait so long to come forward? Why did you wait until I was about to get married?'

He sighed. 'It wasn't an accident that I met you on that train. I'd thought of staying away from you when I heard about the wedding. But I couldn't – so I got on that train knowing that I'd get the chance to speak to you at last.'

'You were following me?'

'Yes,' he admitted, 'I was following you. I followed you in my head and in my heart.'

Leave him and go inside, a voice said inside Harris's mind. Go in now. Yes, you want him; yes, you still long for him. For his lovemaking, the excitement, for his voice, his scent, his body. But it would amount to nothing. It would fade, go wrong again. He would lie, or leave you. Go inside, go to sleep and think of Jimmy . . .

And then another voice said – how can you marry Jimmy if you love this man? How can you do that to someone who is good and doesn't deserve to be second best?

Bowing her head, Harris shivered. And this time when Ben

put his arms around her she didn't shake him off. Instead, for one scintillating instant Harris felt his body against hers. She remembered their lovemaking and knew that if she turned to him then it would all start over again. Sighing, she rested her head against his chest and heard his heart beating, repeating an action she had done so often before when they had made love. Dear God, she thought helplessly, I still want this man.

Only then did she move away.

'There was a time when I'd have given a year of my life to hear you say you wanted to marry me.' His eyes fixed on her, his expression lost as she stepped back. 'I would have done anything you asked. *Then*. But not now. We were lovers. Once –'

'We can be *more* than lovers.'

'No we can't,' she replied, her voice even. 'We'll never marry. We'll never be lovers again. We'll never even be friends.'

FIFTY

Having organised everything with terrifying precision, Irma was not about to let anything go wrong. The day passed in a welter of flowers arriving, telephones ringing, cards and telegrams being sent, as Harris – cool and still as a rock pool – prepared herself for her wedding.

Every thought was centred upon Jimmy and their honeymoon. If she wondered about what their lovemaking would be like, Harris dismissed the reflection. She would find out soon enough. He would be kind, she knew that much, because kindness became him.

Almost as though she was watching everything through a pane of glass, Harris Simons lived the day of 16 February. Whilst everyone flapped and scurried around her, she remained the eye of the storm, serene as a ghost.

'Aren't you nervous?' Bonny asked, looking at the clock. 'We should start to get ready now.'

Calmly, Harris got to her feet and began to brush her hair. 'I love Jimmy very much.'

'I know that,' Bonny said, hairpins in her mouth, Milly crying fretfully on the bed. 'Hey, come on, little one, you're going to look like a princess in this pretty dress. This is the first time you've been a bridesmaid.'

'Bonny?' Harris said, suddenly curious. 'Did you ever have second thoughts about Howard?'

'Before? Or after the wedding?'

Smiling, Harris linked arms with her friend, looking down at Milly. 'She'll steal the whole show, you know. No one will notice the bride.'

'Yeah right,' Bonny replied, jerking her head towards the wardrobe. 'Time to get started, Miss Simons. You have precisely one hour and fifteen minutes before you leave for the church.'

'Now, don't show me up,' Irma said to Saville. 'You know what to do, don't you?'

His eyes fixed on his sister's outfit. 'What *are* you wearing?'

'The most expensive outfit in these parts. It pays to show people how it's done.'

Fiddling with his cuffs, Saville looked uncomfortable in his morning suit, his hair greying at the sides, his vast walrus moustache still darkly black.

'I feel silly.'

'Everyone feels silly in morning dress,' Irma replied. 'It's to make you look classy, not comfortable.'

'Is Harris wearing morning dress?'

'Yes, and a top hat,' Irma replied sarcastically. 'She's the bride, remember? The one you're giving away.'

'But we get her back, don't we?' he asked, frowning.

Irma took in a deep breath. 'Harris is marrying Jimmy at six o'clock. After they're married they'll live in another house – but not far away – and come and see us very often.'

Saville knew well enough what was going to happen, but it didn't make it any easier to swallow.

'I'll miss her.'

'We all will,' Irma said, pulling on her gloves and looking

at him critically. 'You look good, Saville . . . I'm very proud of you.'

That evening Saville Simons was walking on air.

He would cut himself shaving, Jimmy thought, he just knew he would. His hand was shaking so much he might even sever an artery and have to be married in hospital. Calming himself, he picked up the razor again. He could hardly go to his wedding with a five o'clock shadow, could he? Mind you, if they'd married in the morning – like most people – he wouldn't have had this problem. But then he might have cut his throat earlier . . .

Humming to himself, Jimmy wiped the condensation off the bathroom mirror. He was marrying Harris Simons! She was gorgeous, the best-looking woman in Wigan. No, the world, probably the universe. And he was going to love her to death. No, *until* death, Jimmy corrected himself.

All his mother's worries had been futile. Harris wasn't flighty, she was stable and kind. Nothing like the reputation she had once had. But then who didn't make mistakes? Rinsing out his razor, Jimmy grew thoughtful. He was going to make love to Harris tonight. Would he be as good as she expected? Or would he disappoint her? After all, she had experience. The thought unnerved him and made him momentarily depressed.

'Jimmy!' a voice called up the stairs. 'Jimmy, you don't have too long. Are you nearly ready?'

Shaking off his torpor, he shouted back: 'I'm fine, Mother. I'll be ready in plenty of time. It's my wedding day.'

'Wedding *evening*,' his mother corrected him. 'Although whoever gets married this late, I don't know.'

We do, Jimmy thought. *We do*. Me, and my wife.

*   *   *

Hardly able to believe the tremendous emotion she was feeling, Irma watched her niece walk down the aisle on Saville's arm. He was straight as a ramrod and proud, looking directly ahead as though he was an army general. Whilst behind them came Bonny, and the little figure of Milly, both dressed in azure satin, with silk flowers in their hair. As for Harris . . . Irma had heard the intake of breath when people first saw her and when she turned she knew why.

The church was lit overhead with ceiling lights, but at ground level there were hundreds of candles flickering, their light casting shadows against the walls and making moving silhouettes out of the congregation. And that same candlelight illuminated Harris's face as she walked up the aisle. Her skin was smooth, her exquisite features composed, her eyes luminous. She looked – people said later – like a statue come to life.

Transfixed, Irma watched Saville give Harris away, and noted the look of adoration from Jimmy. If ever a man loved a woman, Irma thought, he loves Harris. Outside, snow was falling again, edging the windows as the couple began to take their vows.

Irma never heard the door open at the back of the church. Neither did anyone else in the congregation. Only one person caught that faintest sound and she tensed.

'Will you have this man to your lawful wedded husband?'

The sound of the door opening echoed inside Harris's head and obliterated every other noise. Or word. Her focus blurred, her hand tightening around her bouquet, her mouth dry as ash.

'Harris?'

Someone was talking to her, prompting her. She could see the vicar's mouth moving, but nothing coming out. And then she could hear the sound of muffled talking behind her, and a rustling of uneasy movement.

'Harris?' the vicar repeated anxiously. *'Harris?'*

And then she turned. She turned in all her ivory silk, her skirt swishing over the floor. She turned and Jimmy frowned, Bonny staring into Harris's face and saying something. Which Harris never heard.

Because she was walking away. Away from the vicar, the altar, and away from Jimmy. Incredulous, he stood, immobilised, watching her as she moved towards the back door of the church, dropping her bouquet as she covered the last few feet.

And then everyone saw him as he stepped out from the back – Dr Ben Ramsey. Irma saw him and sat down heavily in her pew; Jimmy saw him and turned, his eyes questioning, to his mother. And then Bonny saw him.

She saw Harris break Jimmy Henshaw's heart, as she had broken Richard's. She saw Ben Ramsey's hour of callous triumph, and Irma's crucifying humiliation. As everyone watched Harris Simons and Ben Ramsey hurry out of the church, so Bonny watched them too.

You better run, she thought grimly, and *keep* running. Because there's no way back this time.

PART FIVE

There was nothing else to say:
But the lights looked dim, and the dancers weary,
And the music was sad and the ball was dreary,
After you went away.

Ella Wheeler Wilcox

FIFTY-ONE

I know what I did. And I did it before family, friends and before God. Bonny was right, there was no turning back. I knew it the moment we left the church. The snow was falling heavily and it was viciously cold. Ben put his coat around me, and rubbed my hands, but I knew I would never be warm again.

I had to be with him. It was as simple as that. It made no sense then, and none now. But there it is. I can't give you excuses, I have none. You see, I was so sure – until that moment I heard the door open – that I was going to marry Jimmy. And then I heard the door and knew I couldn't. Knew I would leave him later, or make him unhappy. Which is no comfort, I know that. I should never have let it go so far. That was my real cruelty – humiliating him.

It was no way to treat a man who was kind. Because kindness became him. And that was why I couldn't marry Jimmy Henshaw. Not because I wasn't good enough for him, but because I wasn't kind enough. The destructive part of me – my father's side – won out. I didn't want to leave him, but had to. I knew it was wrong, but couldn't stop.

Or maybe I could have done. Maybe I could have ignored

the opening door and said 'I will' . . . But then fate would have been changed, and there would have been no more to this story.

But there is.

FIFTY-TWO

'Get in,' Ben said hurriedly, opening his car door for Harris and pushing the train of her wedding dress round her feet as she sat in the passenger seat. Around her shoulders was his coat, but even so, the violence of her shivering was making her teeth chatter uncontrollably.

Drawing away from the kerbside, Ben pulled out into the quiet traffic, Harris stealing a glance at him. Dear God, she wondered, what have I done? He was staring ahead at the road, then stopped at some traffic lights and turned to her.

'Are you all right?'

She nodded dumbly.

'I put some clothes on the back seat for you to change into.'

He had known she would go with him. He had made plans, and she had followed them blindly.

'Whose clothes are they?'

'Does it matter? They'll do fine until we get you something else.'

Glancing over the seat, Harris saw a pair of slacks, a black jumper and a duffel coat.

'There are no shoes.'

'I'll buy you some.'

'I can't go anywhere in these shoes. They're my wedding shoes,' she said distantly, turning back and staring at the road ahead. Snow was falling heavily, visibility poor, the windscreen wipers battling against the onslaught. 'Where are we going?'

'I've sorted it all out,' Ben assured her. 'It'll be fine. Honestly, it'll be fine.' And then he squeezed her hand, flinching at the coldness of it.

The impact of what she had done came to Harris in that moment. She had left Jimmy Henshaw standing at the altar, left her family and friends to run away with Ben Ramsey. And was she happy? No, she felt like an animal that had run away from the hounds, straight under the wheels of a car.

Why had she done it? Jesus, why had she done it? Her eyes stared ahead. She had been so sure that she was over him, that she no longer wanted Ben Ramsey, but she had been wrong. Something had compelled her to throw her lot in with him. And she could never go back on that moment's madness. They were together now. The thing she had wanted for so long, denied for so long, was now reality.

So why did she feel sick with unease?

'I love you so much,' Ben said suddenly. 'God, Harris, I couldn't have seen you marry that man.'

That man is Jimmy, Jimmy Henshaw. That man never showed me anything but love and kindness.

'People won't like this, Ben.'

'They don't have to. We have each other.'

'But your practice might suffer,' Harris persisted, giving him reasons to regret what he had done. Perhaps enough reasons to turn round. 'What about your wife?'

'I've left Eve, I told you.'

'It'll be all over Wigan in hours,' Harris said, shivering feverishly again. '*God, what have we done?*'

He pulled over to the kerbside and turned off the engine. Looking at her, he touched her face and then kissed her hands, his voice low with emotion.

'We were meant to be together. I wasn't supposed to be with Eve and you weren't supposed to be with Jimmy Henshaw.' He leaned towards her, kissing her cold lips. 'We'll make this work out, Harris. We're together. Nothing can harm us now.'

Snow was falling heavily when they came to the commercial travellers' hotel, a grim, secluded place on the outskirts of Prestwich. Parking round a dark corner on some waste ground, Ben glanced over to Harris. 'You should change before we go in.'

She nodded, moving into the back seat and taking off her wedding dress. Oddly he stared ahead, not looking at her. It was difficult to change in such a confined space and her veil momentarily caught in her hair as she pulled it off and folded it on the top of her wedding dress. Hurriedly she then pulled on the slacks, jumper and coat, her feet still in her white satin slippers.

'I need some heavier shoes –'

'We'll get them.'

'But I need them *now*,' Harris persisted, close to tears.

'Why do you keep going on about the shoes?' Ben asked sadly.

'Because everyone will know. They'll all see my shoes and *know*.'

He turned to look at her, sitting in the back seat in the dark, the ethereal white vision of purity doused under the sombre day clothes.

'Harris, are you having second thoughts about this?'

She looked down. Why had she done it? What on God's earth had prompted her to run away?

'What we did – what *I* did – was cruel.'

He reached for her hand, taking it in his own and trying to rub some warmth into it. 'It will get better. This is the worst bit.'

'How do you know? Have you done it before?'

Hurt by the words, Ben got out of the car and walked round

405

to the back passenger door. Opening it, he helped Harris out and then pulled her to him, forcing intimacy. She was rigid in his arms and stayed rigid as he guided her up the hotel steps.

A flabby, middle-aged woman put down the book she was reading as they entered and walked over to the reception desk.

'Evening.'

'Mr and Mrs Court.'

She looked them up and down, staring for a long moment at Harris's satin slippers.

'Oh yes, you booked. No luggage?'

'I've got a small bag, but the rest will follow,' Ben said smoothly.

The woman nodded, then handed them a key, jerking her head towards the stairs. 'Second floor, third door on your left. We do breakfast, but you have to stay out of the hotel until six in the evening. Even if it rains.' She studied them curiously. 'You here on business?'

'My wife and I are looking for a property to buy,' Ben replied, the story obviously well rehearsed. 'We'll probably only stay for a couple of days – just to look around the area. See if there's a house we like.'

The woman nodded again, obviously not believing the story, and then turned back to her book. All the time Harris had kept her head down and only looked up when they were upstairs and Ben had unlocked the bedroom door. In silence they walked in. The room was sad, cool, the double bed taking up much of the space.

Hurriedly Ben pulled the curtains and then turned on a bedside lamp.

'It's not much, but it was all I could find in a hurry. We'll move on to somewhere better. Rent somewhere nice. Then we'll buy something.'

Numbly, Harris nodded, watching as Ben put his case on the bed and began to unpack. She had nothing, only the clothes he had bought her. The clothes he had chosen for her.

'Are you hungry?'

She shook her head, unable to speak, wondering what she was doing and why she was there. She should be with Jimmy now, at her wedding reception in Deerheart House, laughing and talking, eating the food Irma had paid so much for. *Irma* ... She would be shattered; maybe she would have a heart attack because of what her niece had done. Jesus, Harris, she told herself, you've hurt so many people.

'I have to go back!'

Spinning round, Ben stared at her. '*What?*'

'I have to go back.'

'You can't,' he said simply, taking hold of her. 'You can't ever go back. You've burned your boats, Harris. There *is* no turning back.'

And then he kissed her on the cheeks, the forehead and then on her lips, Harris crying silently as he undressed her and laid her down on the cold coverlet over the bed. Looking at him, she closed her eyes and then, as he touched her body and began to lick her nipples, she responded. Grabbing his hair, she pulled him towards her, her mouth open, her tongue finding his. Blindly they made love, frantically, in the cold bedroom, sweat pouring off them as she tried to forget what she had done. And then his teeth fastened for an instant on her breast, a cry coming from her lips: desire mingled with despair.

She was jinxed – and she knew it.

That terrible evening dragged for Jimmy Henshaw. When he returned home with his parents he poured himself a stiff Scotch and then walked out into the garden. The moon was high and bright, making the snow luminous – cruelly, thoughtlessly beautiful.

'Put this on,' Mrs Henshaw said, coming out with his overcoat.

'I don't feel cold.'

'That's shock,' his mother replied, putting the coat around her son's shoulders.

'Why did she do it?'

'I don't know, Jimmy.'

'She loved me. I know that. *I know she loved me*.' He stared up at the blind moon. 'I was supposed to be married tonight. I was supposed to be with Harris. *My wife*.'

'Jimmy, don't think about it –'

Uncharacteristically cruel, Jimmy turned away. 'Let me be, will you! I don't want a pep talk about how these things happen. Or how she wasn't good enough for me. I don't want to know what you think, or feel. I just want to be on my own.'

Smarting, she walked away, her bemused husband sitting slumped in his chair by the fire. Sitting down beside him, Mrs Henshaw stared ahead. She had never been sure about Harris Simons, but to be proved right like this . . . Dear God. Anxiously she glanced out of the window to where her son was still standing in the snowy garden.

'Jimmy should come in. It's cold out there.'

'He will, when he's ready,' Mr Henshaw said, his voice low. 'He'll take this hard. Jimmy loved that girl.'

'I know.'

'But he'll find someone else.'

Mrs Henshaw nodded, choked up with tears. 'I know that too. But he'll never get over this. Another woman will come along and he'll marry her, but Harris Simons will always be between them.'

Outside, Jimmy sipped his whisky and tried to regulate his breathing. He would get over the humiliation – that didn't bother him as much as realising that he had lost Harris for ever. Madly, he knew he would have taken her back at that instant if she had suddenly walked into the garden, the snow landing white on her midnight hair. Closing his eyes, Jimmy could almost see her, walking towards him, smiling.

'I'm sorry, Jimmy, so sorry. Forgive me . . .'

His eyes snapped open. The garden was empty. From now onwards, it would *always* be empty of Harris. Jimmy could see his life unfolding before him. He would meet other girls; people would *want* him to find someone. They would introduce him to women, some clever, some funny, some gentle. And all the pretty women would feel sorry for him and want to love him. They would be kind, because he was. And in every pretty face that turned to him he would find fault – eyes too pale, lips too wide, skin too dark. Every face would fade like an old watercolour into nothingness – because the one face, the one and only face he longed for, they could never replace.

Letting out a cry of pure frustration, Jimmy Henshaw – a kind man, because kindness became him – threw his whisky glass at the window, the pane smashing violently, broken shards of glass catching the moonlight and winking like so many malevolent, mocking eyes.

The following morning Mrs Turner walked into the drawing room and drew the curtains. Then gasped. Irma was sitting in her seat by the unlit fire, still wearing the clothes she had worn for Harris's wedding, her face blank. The room was chilled, the morning light draining every last breath of colour from her face.

'Miss Irma, are you all right?'

She said nothing, just stared ahead. 'I thought she was going to do a Miss Havisham,' Mrs Turner said later, 'she looked so scary just sitting there.'

'Miss Irma, say something!'

Slowly Irma lifted her head and then rallied. 'I think we'll have lamb for dinner. A nice lamb chop would be good.'

'I'm so sorry about what happened,' Mrs Turner blathered on. 'Poor Mr Henshaw, being left like that. It wasn't anything anyone expected of Miss Harris. I mean she –'

Moving surprisingly quickly Irma got to her feet.

'Mrs Turner, I'm sorry to have to curtail your obvious pleasure, but if you want to gossip about my niece you'll have to find someone else to talk to.' Taking off her hat, she smoothed her hair, colour returning to her face. 'I'm going to get ready now and then I'll be leaving for the salon.'

'You're never going to work today!'

'I have clients,' Irma replied, surprised. 'Life goes on, you know, whatever happens. I think a boiled egg would be nice for breakfast. I'll be down in ten minutes.'

Leaving Mrs Turner with her mouth hanging open, Irma walked upstairs to her room and closed the door. A memory of the Mayor's stunned countenance rose up before her, together with the expression on Mrs Henshaw's face as Harris hurried past her. Irma had said that Harris Simons's wedding would never be forgotten and she was right.

Having slowly taken off her clothes Irma washed and then dressed herself in a business suit, taking care with her hair. Finally she picked up the photograph of Mildred on her dressing table and stared at it.

'Well, I bet wherever you are you're enjoying this,' she said bitterly. 'I always knew you'd get your revenge someday, Mildred, and you did it in spectacular fashion. Harris has done a runner – turned out to be just like her father after all. And now I have to face the town *and* the gossip.' She put down the photograph and then checked the top for dust with her finger. 'Left Jimmy Henshaw flat. Went off with Ben Ramsey.' She was still having trouble believing it even as she said the words. 'And everyone saw it. The Mayor and Mayoress and everyone from the bridge club – not to mention Gladys Leonards. I suppose no one noticed the flowers, and they cost a fortune.' An unexpected, tight smile crossed Irma's features. 'Serves me right, doesn't it? Well, that's what you'd say if you were here now. There I was, bragging about the wedding, buying all those things, spending money like a Rothschild, all to impress. To make everyone envy the Simonses and talk about us again. Well, they'll be talking about us all right, Mildred. In fact they'll probably be talking about little else.'

A panicked voice came from downstairs. 'Are you all right up there? Miss Irma, are you all right?' Mrs Turner could hear Irma talking to herself and thought she was rambling.

'She thinks I'm going crazy,' Irma continued to her dead sister's image. 'Well, I'm not. I'm not going to hide this time *or* have a heart attack. That would be too predictable. And too common.'

'But I thought Harris was marrying *Jimmy*,' Saville said to Mrs Biddy for the fourth time that morning. 'Why did she go off with the doctor?'

'Miss Harris changed her mind.'

Saville frowned. Life was so complicated.

'Did I do it wrong? Was it my fault that she went off?'

Taking in a breath, Mrs Biddy put down the breakfast dishes and sat next to Saville, looking him squarely in the eyes.

'It had nothing to do with you. You gave your cousin away very well, Saville. Miss Harris just changed her mind, that's all.'

'But –'

'It happens.'

'But *why*?' Saville didn't understand, and no one was explaining it to him. 'But Harris was supposed to marry –'

Even the patient Mrs Biddy was growing tired of Saville, his questions, Harris Simons and Jimmy Henshaw. It was a sorry business, that was for sure. But there was nothing she could do about it.

411

'I don't know why Miss Harris did what she did,' Mrs Biddy began, in a last-ditch attempt to explain. 'These things just happen. And no one knows why. Life is like that sometimes, things don't make sense. *They just happen.*'

Satisfied, Saville let out a long sigh. At last someone had explained. Not only about Harris, but about all the other random events that happened in life. In everyone's life. *Things don't make sense. They just happen. And no one knows why* . . . So no one was any wiser than he was! No one knew any more than he did! Hugely relieved, Saville picked up his crayons and began to colour in his book again.

He wasn't so stupid, after all.

FIFTY-THREE

'So, is she coming into work, or not?' Bonny asked as soon as Irma arrived at the salon.

'I'm bearing up very well, thank you,' Irma replied tartly, taking off her coat and putting on her white cover-up.

Bonny shrugged. 'Sorry, how are you?'

'Thrilled. My cup runs over,' Irma replied acidly, glancing at the appointments book. 'First client in fifteen minutes. I doubt that anyone will cancel today. They'll be too eager to get all the gossip.'

Bonny's eyes widened. 'You're not coming in to *work*, are you?'

'No, I just thought I'd walk up here to stretch my legs,' Irma retorted icily. 'Of course I'm working! One Simons woman bailing out is enough.'

With grudging admiration, Bonny studied Irma. She was going to brazen it out, was she? Good on her, the old tartar.

'I have to say that the flowers looked good.'

Irma glanced over her shoulder, one eyebrow raised. 'They should have done! They cost a fortune. I don't suppose anyone else noticed them – with all the other excitement going on.'

'Why did Harris do it?'

413

'I was hoping you could answer that,' Irma replied honestly. 'I thought you might be privy to some inside information.'

Bonny shook her head. 'I thought she was going to marry Jimmy. Harris never said anything to me about Ben Ramsey. I didn't know she was even seeing him.'

'Well, she certainly is now,' Irma replied, glancing into the tea caddy and frowning. 'We need some more tea.'

Surprised, Bonny folded her arms. 'I must say you're taking this very calmly. Or are you going to go off your head in a week or two? I mean, if you are, I want to get my holiday in first.'

Smiling wryly, Irma glanced up. 'You're not the little tough nut you think you are, Bonny. I could see from your face in the church that you were shaken.'

'Weren't you?'

There was a long pause, Irma putting down the tea caddy and sighing. 'I was staggered. Then all last night I sat up, thinking. About my family, all our secrets . . .'

Bonny thought of Mildred's secret and winced.

'. . . about how strange we were. *We are.* Then I thought about Harris's background, and her father. Maybe her background worked against her; made her reckless.'

'You can't believe that!'

'Not of everyone,' Irma responded. 'I mean, look at you. You have a dreadful mother and you came out all right – when you got married, anyway.'

Bonny flinched. 'You always know how to give a compliment.'

'Think nothing of it,' Irma answered drily. 'To be honest, I had a hunch that Harris had never really got over Ben Ramsey. She was besotted by him, but I thought that his running off and marrying Eve Clough had cured her. I thought she had enough sense to stay away.'

Surprised, Bonny studied her. The Simons women were a revelation. First Mildred and now Irma, both revealing

414

that under their spinsterish, respectable exteriors they were unexpectedly worldly.

'Aren't you angry with Harris?'

'I don't know,' Irma replied, surprising herself and Bonny. 'In a way I admire her –'

'What!'

'– because she's got courage. Nerve.'

'You think that dumping some poor guy at the altar takes *nerve*?' Bonny snapped.

'Why are you so upset? Were you carrying a torch for James Henshaw yourself?'

'Oh, for God's sake!' Bonny replied hotly. 'I feel sorry for him, that's all! He's a nice guy and he loves Harris. And she loved him. I know she did.'

'But not enough,' Irma replied shortly.

'But Jimmy was so good for her!'

'Oh, come on, Bonny! Since when does anyone choose the things that are good for them? That's the certain way to a boring life.'

'Irma!'

'Yes, *Irma*! Aren't I a revelation to you?' She smiled an unreadable smile. 'You want me to be the enraged spinster aunt – *how could Harris bring shame on the family!* Dear God, how could she *not*, being one of us?'

Incredulous, Bonny stared at her. 'So what are you going to do about it?'

'What can I do? I don't even know where they are. Harris didn't leave me a map with an arrow on it.' Irma glanced over to the door, then back to Bonny. 'Maybe she'll turn up at the Manchester salon. I can't imagine her keeping away for long.'

'And if she doesn't? Then what?'

'I'll stay here and you'll go to Manchester and run the place,' Irma replied calmly.

'And it's OK that you do the work of two? You're not

exactly twenty-one, are you, Irma? And you've got a bad heart.'

'Bonny, my dear, I am quite capable, and you,' Irma said, her tone chilling, 'are not going to get control of these salons.'

'I don't want your bloody salons!'

'You came to work here eagerly enough.'

'I had no job, no home and a baby to look after!' Bonny hurled back. 'What did you expect me to do, *refuse*? Without this job, Milly and I would have been in real trouble.'

Eyeing her up and down, Irma sighed. 'So you agree that you owe Harris a lot?'

'I've never denied that,' Bonny replied cautiously.

'But you're not defending her, are you? You're her closest friend, Bonny, and all you've been whining on about since I walked in is your workload. You wouldn't *have* a workload if it hadn't been for my niece. You wouldn't have had a home either – or all the other help Harris gave you along the way.'

Flushing, Bonny looked away. 'I'm not saying I'm not grateful.'

'But you're not standing up for her!' Irma snapped. 'Look, you and I are the only people in this town who'll have a good word for Harris now. People who have envied her for years will be queuing up to call her names, you know that. Someone has to stand up for her.'

'What she did was wrong!' Bonny shouted, unable to stop thinking of Richard and the night she had found him with his wrists cut. All because of Harris. All because of loving Harris. And now Harris had hurt another man, cutting Jimmy Henshaw to the bone. 'It was wrong!'

'She was stupid, wilful, immoral.' Irma paused. 'And she's wrecked her life. You know that, and I know it. Isn't that punishment enough? You wail about your workload, about Jimmy Henshaw – well, think about my niece, will you? She's gone off with a man who'll break her heart as sure as I'm standing here. And whatever I think, however much

I might want to slap Harris senseless at the moment, I don't want to see her used and thrown away.' Irma looked away, unusually emotional. 'She is my beautiful, talented niece. I don't want her to end up in the mud, whatever she's done. And neither should you.'

Rebuked, Bonny flushed deeper. 'I still think what she did was cruel.'

'Because of Richard?'

Bonny's head jerked up in surprise. 'You knew about Richard?'

'Of course I knew,' Irma replied, glancing back to her. 'There are very few secrets I don't know, Bonny. You might do well to remember that.'

Almost doubled up under the weight, the two workmen hauled the large crate through into Sydney Clough's study, where he was waiting anxiously. Giving directions as to where it should go, Sydney asked them to unpack it. Gradually the large figure of a Japanese warrior was revealed, in its ancient battledress and helmet.

'Who's this? Fu Manchu?' one of the workmen asked, grinning.

Sydney regarded the figure lovingly. 'I've been waiting for this for years. I said long enough since that Japanese objects would turn out to be *the thing* to collect.' He grinned broadly. 'No bugger believed me. Thank God!'

His conversation was cut short by Birdie entering and steering him out and into the breakfast room.

'Birdie, I was just –'

'Shut up, darling,' she said lightly. 'We have to talk about Eve –'

'She's upstairs.'

'– and Ben Ramsey.'

'She's left him,' Sydney replied, desperate to get back to the warrior who had been left propped up against a bookcase. 'What's the problem?'

'Harris Simons jilted Jimmy Henshaw at the altar last night.'

Sydney frowned: 'What were they doing in church at night?'

'Getting married, darling,' Birdie replied, fighting to keep her temper. 'But Harris *didn't* marry Jimmy Henshaw.'

'She didn't?'

'No, she ran off with Ben Ramsey.'

It took an instant for the words to permeate Sydney's thoughts. 'Ben Ramsey! *Eve's* Ben Ramsey?'

'The same.'

'But why does it matter? I mean, Eve's already left him.'

'It matters because they're still married, darling,' Birdie replied, her tone even. 'Because we planned to get Ben Ramsey to Rodney Street. Because we were going to be proud grandparents.' Her voice had risen sharply. 'Don't you listen to anything I say, you moron!'

Unnerved by the outburst, he winced. 'Hey, Birdie, luv, steady on –'

'I've spent more time than you could imagine grooming that bastard –'

Sydney's eyes bulged uncomfortably. 'Birdie, language!'

'– don't tell me what I can say, or not!' she snapped back, her voice high enough to crack glass. 'Eve wanted that man, and I made it happen. Then he wasn't what she expected – well, who is? But he had potential.' She began to pace the room, irritated beyond measure. 'I helped Ramsey and he let me down. Drinking and taking all sorts – if what I hear is true.'

'You never said –'

'What would you have done if I *had* mentioned it! If someone isn't dressed in a suit of Japanese armour, you're not interested.'

'Birdie,' Sydney chastised her, 'you know I'm interested in anything that interests you.'

'Then do something about Ben Ramsey!'

'Like what?'

'He's not making a fool of me!' Birdie replied, carrying on her pacing. 'I told him I would get him to Rodney Street if he got Eve pregnant and mended his ways. But what did he do instead? Ran off with Harris Simons. Well, he needn't think that he can get away with that. I want you to see that his practice folds. Get him struck off, Sydney.'

'I can't do that!' he replied, aghast. 'It's not my business. And why does he need to be struck off? You'd ruin the man just for spite. Anyway, Eve's left him; she doesn't want him any more. So why don't we just forget Ben Ramsey and get on with our lives?'

Birdie stopped pacing and swung round. 'Let him get away with leaving our daughter and ruining his chances? Let him disgrace us?'

'If he's no good, Eve is better off without him,' Sydney said rationally. 'She can get a divorce. Marry again.'

'And let Ramsey off the hook?' Birdie screamed. 'Never! That man is going to rue the day he crossed me. When his practice fails we'll see how attractive Harris Simons seems then.' Her breathing was rapid with fury. 'We'll see if she's enough to make up for his ruined ambitions. We'll see how far Ramsey gets without powerful friends behind him. And a powerful, wealthy family.' Hurriedly, she moved to the door and then shouted up the stairs, 'Eve! Come down here. *Now.*'

A few moments later her daughter walked in, closing the door behind her. She was still sleepy, her slim form wrapped in a dressing gown.

'What is it?'

'Eve, I have something to tell you,' Birdie began, then launched in. 'Harris Simons jilted her fiancé at the altar last night. She ran off with your husband.'

Waiting for the explosion, Sydney tensed. But it never came. Instead Eve looked at her mother – and shrugged.

'Good, I'm rid of him.'

'Oh no, my girl, you can't pass it off that easily!'

For once Sydney was repelled by Birdie, seeing her in an unexpected, unflattering light. 'It's for Eve to react how *she* wants, Birdie. It's not your business.'

She turned on him, furious. 'Oh, but it is! You see, I made that man, I invested in him. And I don't like to see my money wasted.'

'You can't buy people.'

'Sydney, you can buy *anything*,' Birdie replied, with scorn. Her mask was off. All the years of letting her husband think she was superficial were over; fury had revealed the true Birdie Clough.

And Sydney didn't recognise her. 'You're upset, luv, calm down –'

'I don't want to calm down, you old fool!' She turned back to her daughter. 'And you, idiot! How could you let it go so wrong? I sorted it all out for you. All you had to do was to keep Ramsey happy and everything would turn out right.'

It was with a chilling tone in her voice that Eve answered her mother.

'You never asked me *why* I left him. I kept waiting for the questions, but they never came.'

Birdie tried to interject: 'But, Eve –'

'All I heard was what *you* wanted, what *you* did, what *you* had planned. Never what *I* wanted.' She looked down at her mother with obvious distaste. 'Well, I'm glad I left Ben Ramsey. He wasn't what he seemed. And – just in case you're interested – I was afraid of him.'

Knowing she had gone too far, Birdie snatched her daughter's hand hurriedly. 'Listen to me, darling, I wasn't thinking clearly. I was angry for you –'

'No, Mother. You were angry for yourself! I never had anything to do with it. You wanted to see me married, you wanted grandchildren. As long as I was the brood mare, you would have been happy.' Shaking off her mother's grip, Eve moved to the door. 'I don't care if Ben's run off with Harris Simons. She's welcome to him. In fact, I pity her. And if she has one half of the trouble I had, God help her.'

FIFTY-FOUR

Harris woke to find that Ben had already left for his practice. Turning over in bed she covered her face with her hands and tried to calm herself. The mornings were always the worst. When she finally slept she would wake, exhausted, images hammering into her brain. The wedding, Jimmy's face, Irma's . . . And what about home? Saville? Work? What about the salons?

Swinging her feet over the side of the bed, Harris stared through a crack in the curtain, the grey Prestwich street melancholic in the slush. They hadn't left the commercial travellers' hotel. But Ben had given her a ring to wear – *until we get married after my divorce comes through* – and Harris had put it on. Pretending that it was love; that it would lead somewhere . . . A pigeon landed on the windowsill outside, one red eye peering through the curtain at her . . . What about work? Harris thought again; she should go into work. But not Wigan, God, not Wigan. But what about Manchester? She had to work. The salons were her achievement – how could she just have walked away from them?

But if she went in, how would she explain? But if she didn't, how long would the business keep going with Irma running both salons? It was easier for Ben – he was a doctor, with his own practice. No one would dare question a *doctor*. Slowly

Harris rose to her feet, hearing Mrs Wilson, the landlady, calling for her dog in the yard below.

Sex was all that was keeping them together. At least that was what Harris believed. She didn't know *what* she truly felt for Ben any more; she was just obsessed, blindly driven to cling to him, to make some sense out of what she had done. Don't think about Jimmy, Harris urged herself, don't think about him . . . Checking that the corridor was clear, she moved down to the bathroom, washed and dressed herself in the same slacks and jumper Ben had first bought for her. Only the underwear and shoes were new. And a dress Harris hadn't worn yet.

People eloped all the time, she told herself. They were happy; they couldn't live without each other. But we just want each other in bed. And that isn't enough.

The rest of the time Harris looked at Ben with curiosity. He was still handsome, charming, loving – but there was no safety there.

Putting on her lipstick, she looked at her face in the mirror. It wasn't a bitch's face, although there was a hardness around her mouth that hadn't been there before. She would have made Jimmy unhappy, Harris told herself. It was better this way in the long run. She was meant for someone like Ben; someone she couldn't push around, someone who would stand up to her. Someone who made love to her and made her think of nothing else.

Throwing down her lipstick, Harris grabbed her coat and left the hotel.

'You can't come back before six,' Mrs Wilson called.

'I won't *be* back before then,' Harris called back. 'I'm going to work.'

Had it only been a few days since she had last climbed the steep stairs to the Manchester salon? As she turned at the top of the steps, several pairs of eyes fixed on her.

'Oh, hello, Miss Simons,' one of the assistants said, with barely concealed contempt. 'We were wondering when you'd manage to get in.'

Harris heard the tone in the voice and felt her palms grow sticky. But what could she expect? She had jilted her fiancé and was now living with her married lover. She wasn't anyone to inspire respect.

'How are things going?'

'OK,' the girl replied, finishing her client's hair and then jerking her head over to Joy, the other assistant. 'We heard you were busy, and thought we'd just get on with it until we heard from you.'

'Thank you.'

'Don't mention it,' Joy said slyly. 'We realised you were tied up.'

A snigger came from the first girl, Jenny, Joy covering her mouth and turning away.

I deserve this, Harris thought, I asked for it. And this will be my life from now on. Sniggers and a lack of respect – because I threw my reputation away. Again. For the same man.

Harris glanced at the appointments book for the following day. 'It looks busy.'

'What d'you expect?' a voice said behind her. 'Think we'd collapse without you?'

Surprised, Harris turned to see Bonny watching her.

'Can we talk?' Harris asked Bonny awkwardly. 'In the back?'

Stiff-necked, Bonny walked into the room beyond, Harris closing the door behind them. Someone had just made tea, cups and saucers laid out on a tray with bourbon finger biscuits. All so normal, so achingly familiar.

'Bonny, please don't be angry with me –'

'Don't be angry!' she barked. 'What you did to Jimmy was bloody wicked. And the thing that hurts me the most is that you never said a word to me. Not a bloody word about what

424

you were going to do. I didn't even know you were seeing Ramsey again, let alone running off with him –'

'Bonny, listen to me.'

'I don't want to listen to you!' she retorted sharply. 'You could have trusted me, we're pals. But no, you had to keep all your secrets to yourself.'

'I didn't know that I was going to run off with Ben.'

'Oh, really? What happened? He put something in your tea to *force* you to elope?'

Shaken, Harris sat down, her face turned away. Still enraged, and yet feeling reluctantly sorry for her, Bonny studied her friend. If this was elopement, you could keep it, she thought. Harris looked dead beat, and worse, she looked like someone who had just made the biggest mistake of her life.

'How *could* you leave Jimmy flat like that? He loves you so much –'

'I loved him.'

'Past tense, Harris! So you didn't love him as much as you loved Ben Ramsey? Well, if that's true, you're a bloody fool, because Jimmy's worth ten of Ramsey.'

Harris's voice was barely a whisper. 'I didn't want to hurt Jimmy –'

'That never stops you, though, does it?' Bonny hurled at her. 'You just railroad people's feelings. You've ruined two men's lives –' She stopped short.

Harris was looking at her quizzically. 'Two men? What are you talking about?'

Bonny had gone too far and she knew it. She also knew that the oath of secrecy she had given to Richard was suddenly under threat.

'I meant one man.'

'You said "two",' Harris repeated. 'Who was the other man?'

'It was a mistake.'

'No, it wasn't,' Harris persisted. 'You don't make mistakes

like that, Bonny. Who was the other man? You have to tell me!
You can't blame me for something I don't even know about.
Who was the other man?'

'Richard.'

'Richard?' Harris repeated, wondering for a moment who
she meant. And then she realised. Her Richard, Bonny's
brother, her old friend.

Discomforted, Bonny looked away. 'He was desperately
upset about you. He was in love with you for years.'

'But I never knew!' Harris said, getting to her feet. 'Why
didn't he tell me? Why didn't *you* tell me? You talk about
secrets – this was one you kept to yourself long enough.'

Guilt put Bonny on the defensive and she struck out.

'Don't try and make me the guilty party! You're the one
who nearly killed him.'

'What!' Harris said, baffled. 'How did I nearly kill him?'

Throwing down the towel she had been holding, Bonny
rounded on her. 'Because he tried to commit suicide. You
remember that, Harris, don't you? He came home on leave
and cut his wrists open. And why? Because he'd lost you.'

'But I didn't know . . . I didn't know he felt like that . . .'
Harris tailed off, her skin ashen.

Unable to stop, Bonny hurried on, 'Richard came home that
time, all ready to propose. But then he found out that you were
in love with someone else. He had left it too long to speak up
– and you were smitten with Ben Ramsey.'

Rigid, Harris turned to face her. 'Why didn't he say
something? Why didn't *you*?' Slow, silent tears began to
fall down her cheeks. 'You should have told me how he
felt.'

'It wasn't my business.'

'You should have made it your business!' Harris replied
helplessly. She had taken the news hard, her eyes flat with
shock. 'I wouldn't have hurt Richard for anything. I would
never have hurt him deliberately.'

Bonny had gone too far and knew it. Sitting beside Harris, she hung her head. 'I shouldn't have told you. Richard made me promise never to tell you.'

'Now I know why you're so angry,' Harris replied, her voice shaky. 'I didn't only hurt Jimmy, I hurt Richard too.'

'Harris, I shouldn't have told you –'

She interrupted Bonny immediately. 'If it's any consolation to you, I couldn't be more miserable.'

'Bloody hell, Harris!' Bonny said, all anger gone. 'Why did you do it? Why didn't you talk to me? We could have worked something out.'

Harris shook her head. 'It seems so unbelievable now, but at the time . . . Ben had been in touch with me a while before the wedding. He had left his wife and said he loved me and wanted me. I wanted him, I always did, Bonny. Something about him made me long for him, but I knew he was wrong. So I told him to go away. And he did. But he came back, kept following me. He was everywhere I was, watching me. He even came to Deerheart House the night before the wedding. I went out in the dark and told him then that I was going to marry Jimmy. He said I couldn't, that we were meant for each other. That it would be wrong to marry Jimmy and I'd be bound to leave him later.'

'And you believed him?'

'It sounded right.' Harris shook her head. 'Or maybe it was just what I wanted to hear. But something *still* held me back. Here was the man I'd been obsessed by, the man who had hurt me so badly – here he was offering me marriage. Telling me he loved me. But I didn't go with him. I told *him* to go instead. It was over, I said.' She bowed her head and her voice became a whisper. 'The following day I was at the altar, Jimmy beside me, and there were flowers everywhere, so many flowers at this time of year. I was about to say my vows when I heard the door open. I knew it was Ben – even before I turned round. *I had to go.* I had to be with him. It was meant;

it was supposed to be. He loved me, he wanted me. And I wanted him, longed for him so much. So I walked out of the church . . . It was snowing and Ben put his coat around me, being kind. Being kind because he'd won. And for a moment I wanted to hit him, to punch him, to dig my nails into his face and eyes and tear him apart . . . but I didn't. I went with him instead.'

'Oh God,' Bonny said simply. 'Do you know how he feels?'

'He's happy,' Harris answered. 'Ben has what he wants and he's back at work.'

'Is he going to get divorced?'

'He says so.'

'So you'll marry?'

Harris jerked up her head. *I'll never marry him!*

'But you left Jimmy for him. You can't just shack up with Ben Ramsey.'

'Don't tell me you're worried about my reputation? I put paid to that a long time ago,' Harris replied bitterly.

'You were in a mess before, but you got over it. You got the salons going, started to build up your own little empire. People were sick with envy because of your success – and that was just the start. Only the other day you were talking about opening another place.'

'What does that matter now? I let everyone down. Jimmy would *never* have hurt me . . .' She paused, turning to Bonny. 'Have you seen him? Is he all right?'

Bonny shook her head. 'I haven't seen him. I just heard that he moved out of his parents' house and into the new house. I bet it feels odd, without you.'

'But you haven't seen him?'

'I've been over here since Saturday,' Bonny replied, 'Irma told me to run the salon whilst you were away.'

Harris's voice dropped even lower. 'How *is* Irma?'

'Oddly enough, it's given her a new lease of life. She a bloody weird woman, your aunt. I thought she was sure to lock herself away again, or at least have a heart attack, just to spite you. But not a bit of it. She was talking about what you did as though she almost expected it.'

'*What?*'

'I know, I thought it was a bit strange myself. But there you go. She was talking about the Simons women and how your whole family is peculiar. I didn't argue with that. Anyway, Irma's at Simons Coiffeuse now, drilling holes in the scalp of anyone who so much as mentions the wedding.'

'I can't face her.'

'There are many who say the same,' Bonny replied, nudging Harris with her elbow. 'So the grand gesture turned out a bit flat, did it?'

Harris nodded.

'But the sex is good?'

'It's the only thing that is.'

'God, what a mess,' Bonny said sympathetically, 'you've buggered up your life good and proper this time. If you ever want to be respectable again, you'll *have* to marry Ramsey.'

'That would make it all right, wouldn't it?' Harris replied, her tone hardening. 'In time everyone would say that it *was* a love match and that we were destined to be together. But that would be the easy way out.'

'And you're not going to take the easy way out, are you?'

Harris shook her head. 'I don't know what I'm going to do yet, but I'm not going to kid myself any longer. I've been a selfish bitch. But there's going to be no more of that.' She breathed in. The tears had dried on her face. 'Maybe I *do* deserve Ben. Maybe Jimmy was too good for me.'

'Maybe you've been inhaling too much perm lotion,' Bonny replied drily. 'Jimmy was no better than you, Harris.'

'We never slept together.'

'Ah . . .'

'I wondered about that often,' Harris confessed. 'It shouldn't have been that important and yet I kept thinking about it.

429

Would he like me? Would I like him? And when I thought about sex –'

'You thought about Ben.'

'Yes,' Harris agreed. 'And then he turned up out of the blue and my stomach belly-flopped with excitement. The only thing I could think about was making love to him. Lying next to him, touching him . . .' She paused, flushing. 'And that's the only reason I'll stay with him.'

'Harris, no one can live like that.'

'I deserve it,' she replied, totally without self-pity. 'It's to be my punishment – getting what I wanted and finding out that it wasn't worth having after all.'

FIFTY-FIVE

On the third week of their elopement, Ben and Harris were still living in the commercial travellers' hotel. At his practice Ben was not bothered by questions, as Harris had supposed, because no one interrogated a doctor. As for herself, she was back working full time at the Manchester salon, Bonny relaying any information she had about Irma, Saville or Jimmy.

Ben had been kindness itself, his lovemaking tender, his attentions gentle. Almost daily he bought Harris something, or left her a note on her pillow. He loved her, showered her with attention, played her records, read to her, made a sensual womb out of that seedy hotel room – all to make her forget what she had done. But it wasn't working, and before long Ben knew he was losing her.

Not physically. Their equally passionate sexual appetites bound them inexorably, but emotionally he knew that Harris had already gone. There was nothing in her words or actions that he could have pointed out as an example, but the adoration in her eyes, the pure love she had had for him had disappeared. What held them together was guilt and sex. Nothing more.

In between patients, Ben sat in his surgery and told himself that he didn't care. He would divorce Eve and still make his own way to Rodney Street. After all, he was a clever man,

431

with charm. No one could hold him back. Except the wrong woman ... Exasperated, he held his head in his hands and stared at the blotter on his desk.

'You've another patient –'

'I know! Give me a minute!' he shouted, his secretary backing out of the office hurriedly.

He would have to calm himself down. His life had gone haywire, but he could put it back on track. Stop the drinking at least, and the other stuff. It was stupid anyway; he needed a clear head to impress people, to prove that he was someone to be reckoned with. He would show that bitch Eve that he wasn't a failure. How dare she walk out on him? How dare she leave him? He would pay her back, make her feel as bloody small as she had made him. As for her mother – Birdie Clough had helped him, that was true, but she hadn't *made* him. He was his own man, with his own talent – and he would create his own future. The people she had introduced him to would *still* help him, Ben was sure of that. After all, Birdie Clough didn't have that much power. *Or did she?*

One thing was certain: he would have to marry Harris otherwise it would look bad. If he married her, in time people would accept what had happened. She was a beauty from a rich family. And, anyway, who questioned a successful man's choice of bride? No, Ben thought, panic subsiding, he would recover from his setbacks. He would still get to Rodney Street – with Harris at his side.

'Sorry I shouted at you,' Ben said a moment later to his secretary. 'I was a bit preoccupied.' He smiled, glancing round the waiting room. 'You can send in the next patient now, if you would.'

Waiting until the door closed behind him, his secretary then turned to Irene Desmond, who had just dropped in.

'His temper's still up and down, but he's better than he was. He was on the way to a breakdown before.'

Irene Desmond's eyes widened. 'All sorts of rumours were

432

flying round a while back. Some said,' she dropped her voice, 'that he was drinking. Have you ever seen him drunk?'

The secretary shook her head. 'Never. Bad-tempered in the mornings –'

'That can be a sign.'

'– but not since he got back with Harris Simons.'

Irene Desmond considered the information carefully. 'I can remember the day she hit him. Slapped him across the face so hard I expected to see his teeth take a bite out of the mantelpiece.'

'She never!'

Irene nodded sagely. 'Oh, yes she did. Made a fool of herself over him. Then he went off and married someone else. And now they're back together –'

'And this time *she* was the one who was going to marry someone else.'

Irene nodded again. 'Seems like he can't let go of her.'

'And she can't let go of him.'

'It's romantic.'

'Like a film.'

'Yeah, like a film.'

Sighing, Irene stared ahead. 'Love's wonderful, isn't it?'

Penny had been watching Richard for over an hour. He would fill in one crossword clue, then pause, read another and then pause again. Thinking. Upstairs Tom was fast asleep. Penny banked up the fire and sat beside her husband in the kitchen.

'Our son's going to be tall, like you.'

Automatically Richard took her hand. 'And handsome, like you.'

'Women can't be handsome!'

'Well, I could hardly say he was going to be pretty, now could I?' he teased her, putting the paper to one side. 'I keep thinking about Harris.'

'I thought you were,' Penny replied, without jealousy. 'Everyone's talking about it. Everywhere you go, people have something to say.'

'Ben Ramsey doesn't sound like the right man for her,' Richard said evenly, 'Jimmy would have been perfect.'

'But she didn't want Jimmy.'

'She didn't *think* she wanted him,' Richard corrected her, squeezing Penny's hand. 'I know Harris of old: she always wanted to do the unexpected. To be different. And damn to what anyone thought. The excitement of Ben Ramsey will have blinded her. If he'd never come back on the scene she would have married Jimmy.'

Penny thought back. 'I'll never forget her face in the church. When she turned round and then just started walking. It was as though she was hypnotised.'

'Enough of Harris,' Richard said suddenly. 'If she needs us, we'll do what we can. Until then, we have to get on with our own lives.' A glint of mischief flared up in his eyes. 'Which brings me to our holiday.'

Surprised, Penny repeated the word. 'Holiday? What holiday?'

'The one I've been planning.'

'We haven't got the money for a holiday.'

'Correction, we *didn't* have the money for a holiday, but soon we will have,' Richard replied, overjoyed to see the pleasure on his wife's face. 'I got a bonus.'

'You never said!'

'I wanted to keep it a secret, until everything was arranged.'

Clasping her hands together, Penny was shaking with pleasure. 'We've never had a holiday before.'

'It's our very belated honeymoon.'

'But we've got a son now,' Penny said, laughing, 'I think we might be doing things the wrong way round!'

'Tom can come with us,' Richard replied, glowing with achievement. 'It's all arranged. I've booked us rooms in Blackpool for a week at the end of March next year.'

'A year away!'

He grimaced. 'I know it's a way off, but I want to save up a bit more first. You know, make it a holiday to remember. Have some spending money to buy things. Do it right.'

Penny's face was ecstatic. 'Richard, have you *really* booked a holiday?'

'Of course I have! I told you, we're all having a week in Blackpool next spring. Away from Wigan, in the sea air, just you and me and Tom.' He scooped her up from her chair, twirling her round in his arms. 'Happy honeymoon, Mrs Baker!'

The room spun around them, both of them laughing, their bodies becoming twirling, spinning shadows on the kitchen wall behind.

Another month creaked past, Irma calmly managing in Wigan, Harris in Manchester. She had sent Bonny back from time to time to help Irma, albeit reluctantly, as she found it difficult being alone with her sniggering assistants. Harris had even caught them watching her from the top window when she went out for lunch on the one and only day Ben had called for her. In the past she would have been so proud to be seen with him, but now she was ashamed. Not of him, but of herself. And the whole sordid situation.

'We need some setting lotion, Amami will do, Jenny. Can you go out and get it for me?'

Sullen, she took the money, exchanging a look with her co-worker before looking back to Harris. 'Is this enough?'

Harris's tone was cool. 'More than enough. And I would like you to address me as Miss Simons.'

'*Miss* Simons,' the girl repeated. 'Are you sure this is enough, *Miss Simons*?'

'I've told you, it's plenty. Please do what I ask.'

Turning back to her customer, Harris could feel her face

burning. The assistants were trying it on, treating her disre-
spectfully in front of the clients. And what could she do to
stop it?

'I wouldn't have anyone talk to me like that!' her customer
said suddenly.

Harris tried a smile. 'She's tired, that's all.'

'She's rude, my dear,' the woman replied, tucking the towel
round her neck. 'I'd get rid of her. You didn't hear what they
were saying about you when you weren't here.'

Anxiety made Harris unusually curious. 'What *were* they
saying?'

'About how you and your man friend wouldn't last. About
how they'd liked your other young man, and how you'd left
him flat.' She paused. 'It's none of my business, my dear, but
frankly I think you did the right thing. In this life, you have
to go where your heart takes you.'

Harris held her customer's gaze in the mirror: 'What if it
takes you up a blind alley?'

'If it takes you up a blind alley, you get a torch,' she replied
kindly, 'and you keep walking forward until you get back into
the light.'

Sleep was proving to be something of an adventure for Irma.
Some nights she slept like a dead horse for eight hours, other
nights she slept fitfully, waking many times, the water by her
bed tasting of dust. And now lately she had developed a whole
new pattern of sleep. She would doze until the early hours and
then wake up, full of life, about three. At first Irma had tried
to go back to sleep, but that was impossible, so she altered her
routine. At three in the morning she got up as though it was
morning.

It was, she discovered, another world. The earth was quiet,
only the sound of foxes, owls or the odd cat fight making much
impression on the stillness. And places looked so different. The

garden was no longer green, but inky black, the flowers grey and silver. And sounds were extraordinary: they travelled on the stillness in giant notes, making looping cuts into the night silence; the percussion of gravel and leaf noises sounding like a drum roll.

Stretching, Irma got out of bed. It was 3.15, one of the witching hours. Silently she walked downstairs into the kitchen and made herself some tea. Cocoa was for invalids. Then she walked into the drawing room and sat down, pulling a rug around her. If Harris was still in that dreadful commercial hotel in Prestwich she would be cold – Ben Ramsey being there or not. Irma sipped her tea. *A commercial travellers' hotel!* Who did he think Harris was? Some mill girl? If he was going to live in sin with her, it should have been the Midland, at least.

And she had taken no clothes. God only knew what Harris was wearing now. Although Bonny had said she was organised. How did a person like Harris Simons get herself organised in some seedy hole with a married man? A memory tickled the back of Irma's brain. *Mildred and William Kershaw.* Depressing the thought, Irma pushed her feet further into her slippers. Harris was not going to come home, that much was certain. Pride would prevent it. After all, how could she admit that she was wrong when she had bought her happiness at such a high price?

Deerheart House was too big for one person, Irma thought suddenly. Before there had been Mildred, Saville, Harris and her. Now there was only her – and Mrs Turner in the day. She would get a dog, Irma thought, then decided against it. The one dog they had adopted had been run over. Besides, dogs made messes on the lawn and left hair on the sofas. But Harris should have a dog, Irma thought suddenly, Harris should have her own dog, her own man, her own house and her own family.

'You fool,' Irma said out loud, in the cool, quiet room. 'You poor, silly fool. You were supposed to have it all, Harris – everything Mildred and I missed. I counted on you to make sense of everything. To show everyone that one of us could do it right. You would have been Mrs James Henshaw. You would have made it.'

Her mind slid back to the wedding – and then the flowers. Such lovely flowers, so expensive, and no one had said a flaming word about them. She could have put cabbages at the end of the pews for all it mattered.

And then Irma Simons – a.k.a. Irmastein, the scourge of Wigan – began, very quietly, to cry.

FIFTY-SIX

On 15 March Mrs Turner was having a drink with Mr Lacy in the Bishop's Finger. True to her word, Irma had told Mr Lacy that he would be employed as a gardener at Deerheart House – just as soon as he got himself married to Mrs Turner. He had balked at the idea at first – until Irma had pointed out that old gardeners with bad backs weren't in great demand. Besides, she threw in for good measure, there were more than enough strapping young men back from the war that needed work. So the wedding date had been set for 19 June: Mr Lacy sweating more as each day passed.

'I can't wait for tomorrow,' Mrs Turner said cheerily, sipping her port and lemon. 'There's going to be a big sale at the Co-op now that clothing rationing's finished. I might get myself a right nice costume. For our wedding, perhaps?'

He smiled wanly. 'What about men's?'

'Men's what?'

'Men's clothes, are they off the ration now?'

Mrs Turner nodded, taking this as a good sign. 'Oh yes, if we went together we could get something nice for you too, Mr Lacy.'

The thought of shopping with Mrs Turner was only marginally better than marrying her.

'I don't like shopping.'

'You men!' she said gaily. 'You'll have to get used to it when we're wed. A wife likes her husband to go out with her. It's seemly.'

'Would we have to shop together?'

'Of course!' she replied, laughing. 'That's what couples do. We'll have to get some new furniture too. And a new bed.' She sipped her drink, eyeing him flirtatiously.

'I thought we'd have twin beds.'

Her expression changed in a millisecond. '*Twin beds!*' she hissed, her voice low. 'No one has twin beds.'

'My parents had twin beds.'

'It's a miracle you were born then!' she snapped back. 'What's the matter with you? Newlyweds always have a double bed.'

'I'm used to sleeping in a single –'

'Well, I'm not!' Mrs Turner shot back. 'If you can't agree with me on this, we better call it off here and now. I'm not going to be spurned by you –'

'Hey, now, luv –'

'My late husband wouldn't sleep without knowing I was beside him.' She leaned towards Mr Lacy. 'You hear me? He wouldn't *sleep* without me. And you – *you* – suggest single beds. Well, the engagement's off.'

So was his new job, Mr Lacy thought, panicking. And his new home – living with Mrs Turner in her house off Stanshaw Street. And all his cooking, washing and ironing done for him in his old age. Suddenly marriage didn't look so bad. And if it took a double bed to ensure security, then so be it.

'All right, luv, get the new bed.'

'A double.'

He nodded. 'A double.'

Smiling, she rested her head on his shoulder. 'You're an old romantic at heart, Mr Lacy. You hide it well, but a girl can tell what a man *really* thinks.'

*   *   *

Well, everyone else could go to the celebratory sale at Lowes but Irma wasn't about to fight for a new dress amongst the riffraff. Gazing at the appointments book she could see that there were only two clients the following day, the rest having caught sale fever. Irma could picture the days to come – women arriving wearing impossible outfits just to show off, a whole bevy of hats hung up like so many Chinese lanterns on the pegs by the salon door.

As for Gladys Leonards – she would be the first there and the last to leave. And not one thing she bought would have any class. Who could forget the appalling ermine wrap she had been wearing round her shoulders for years? 'Ermine, my arse!' Mildred had said once. 'That's one rabbit that escaped a pie dish.'

Irma sighed to herself. Harris would have gone to the sale for sure, coming home with a mess of parcels, trying on everything and parading around. Mildred would have gone too; her surprisingly vicious elbow jabs parting the crowd as she passed through.

But not Irma. She didn't need any new clothes; the ones she had were still good. And any alterations could be done by Miss Lawson at Lowe's. Bored, Irma sat down at the reception desk and doodled on the pad before her. Her clients were either under the dryer or having their hair washed. Now was the time to think.

But think about what? How bored she really was? Time stretched out before Irma unappetisingly. A month had passed since Harris had left; four long weeks in which Irma had come to realise just how much she missed her niece. Of course, people had gossiped about the scandal, but not to her face – no one would have dared – although the phrases 'living in sin' and 'common as muck' reverberated constantly on the air. Irma also knew that people were remembering Gordon Simons – what he was and where he had come from – *and Saville*.

So many sticky little messes, never quite forgotten or cleaned up, were now resurrected daily. And yet if Irma looked back to how she had been in the past, she was almost amused. Had she *really* been that ridiculous snob? Had standing next to the stupid, overstuffed Mayor really been so important to her? As for the bridge club – she had been well and truly trumped there. Yet now she didn't give a damn. They had all been dull. And she had never really belonged amongst them.

The truth was that the Simonses belonged nowhere. They were outcasts. Money had brought them some regard, but money was not enough. The skin of respectability had been too thin to cover the unbalanced and unacceptable Simonses' bones. We are oddities, Irma thought to herself, and always will be.

But we're still a damn sight better than everyone else.

April wound in, days cool and rainy. In the commercial travellers' hotel the landlady, Mrs Wilson, watched as Ben walked down the stairs, then handed her his key.

'Not seen anythin' you like then?'

He looked at her, nonplussed. 'Sorry?'

'Your house, not seen a house you like?'

'Oh, no, not yet.'

'Your . . . *wife's* . . . not bin lookin'?'

'She's busy.'

'So it seems,' Mrs Wilson replied, picking a biscuit crumb out from between her front teeth. 'I thought you were only staying a few days?'

'Is there a problem?' Ben asked, suddenly on the defensive. 'I mean, we can move elsewhere.'

'Keep your hair on!' Mrs Wilson replied, resting her large bosom on the top of the counter. 'I just wondered. You two don't seem the type to like it round 'ere.'

'It suits us fine.'

'She were cryin' the other day.'

'Who?' Ben asked, knowing full well.

'Your wife. She seems upset about summit.' Mrs Wilson's small eyes narrowed. 'You two really wed?'

Ben could feel the pressure building up inside him. First there was his secretary always asking how he was, then yesterday Lionel Redmond had called by. To say hello, he had said, but in reality he was checking up on him. And Ben knew it. Then he thought he saw Birdie Clough pass by in her chauffeured car . . . His patients weren't as plentiful either. All the calls he had put through to Birdie's contacts had not been returned.

And he was back on the booze.

'My wife and I will be moving out very soon,' Ben said finally, his tone sharp.

'Look, I don't care if you're wed or not, we get all types 'ere.'

Disgusted, Ben moved away, then turned back. 'What d'you mean – you heard my wife crying?'

'She were cryin' fit to bust,' Mrs Wilson replied, her fleshy face expressionless. 'Seems like she has a lot on 'er mind. And none of it pleasant.'

Irascible, Ben walked out and got into his car. On the passenger seat was Harris's headscarf, her perfume still lingering on the wool. He had done it again! he thought angrily, beside himself with temper as he slammed his hand on the steering wheel. Hadn't he promised himself that he wouldn't get involved with the wrong woman? Hadn't he? And yet here he was, struggling – *and Harris was crying*.

Jesus, the bloody fool of a woman! He couldn't live without her, or with her. She was impossible; it was all her fault. If he just hadn't met her, if she hadn't flirted with him, slept with him, then he would have been free. He would have stayed married to Eve and been on Rodney Street by now.

The fact that Ben had started drinking before Eve had left

him was forgotten. As was the misery of his marriage. All he could see was his life unravelling and he had to find someone to blame. Reaching under the front seat, Ben pulled out a half-bottle of vodka in a brown paper bag and furtively took a sip. Then a bigger gulp. The liquid fired inside his throat and smoothed out his panic. Hurriedly he took another sip and then screwed the cap back on, pushing the bottle under the seat again. The road in front of him was greasy with rain, the day chill. He would go to the surgery and see his patients, show them that he was the best bloody doctor in town. Let Birdie Clough do her best, he wasn't scared of some t'penny h'penny Irish harpy.

As he pulled away from the kerb, a car horn sounded loudly, Ben jumping as he looked behind him. Jesus, that had been close! he thought, the van driver waving his fist as he passed. He had to be more careful, more controlled. Harris wasn't going to ruin his life. He would put her in her place, make her realise what *he* had given up by loving her. Make her realise what she had to be grateful for.

Couldn't she see that he was under threat, his enemies all around? Everyone was jealous of him, trying to pull him down. He needed support, Ben thought, self-pityingly. He needed to be loved. After all, *he* was the one with everything to lose.

What the hell had Harris got to cry about?

Howard Waring was sitting with Milly on his lap, waiting for Bonny to come home. The little girl was trying to read his newspaper and giggling, leaning her head back against his chest as he tickled her. Stealing a glance at the clock, Howard sighed. Honestly, Bonny was always late these days. And why was that? Because she was tied up at the damned salon all day. He didn't like the idea, his wife should be at home, spending time with him and Milly, not coming in at all hours, half dead, from Manchester.

And the worst thing was that Bonny enjoyed it. She knew that she had to underplay it to Howard, but he could see past her protestations. Bonny liked responsibility; liked the fact that she was Harris's right hand. And liked the extra money.

Oh, they had plenty to thank Harris Simons for: the deposit on their house, for one thing. But he would rather have saved up and got the deposit himself. It would have taken a lot longer, but he could have done it. As it was, he felt obliged to Harris Simons, and it made him feel indebted.

Immediately he was ashamed of the thought. He should be glad of the help Harris gave them – and pleased that Bonny was happy and bringing in such a good wage. But then again, what was money? He'd rather have his arms full of his wife than his pockets full of silver.

Poor Harris, Howard mused, her money hadn't done her any favours, had it? At the bus depot everyone had had a field day talking about how Jimmy Henshaw had been jilted. The women had all tut-tutted, whilst the men talked about Harris being 'a right goer, and no mistake.' It were hardly respectable, Howard thought, conveniently forgetting that he was nursing Bonny's illegitimate child.

''Lo there,' Bonny said suddenly, walking in and kissing Milly, then Howard, on the top of their heads. 'Sorry I'm late.'

'It's the third time this week,' Howard said, studying his wife. 'You look good today.'

Bonny grinned. 'I'll get us some supper –'

'I've fed Milly already.'

'I got some bargains at one of the sales – Kendal Milne.'

'Kendal Milne!'

'It was a sale,' Bonny replied, making some tea and cutting into a new loaf. 'How's my sweetheart?' she asked Milly, passing her a slice of bread and jam. 'Have you been good for your daddy?'

'I'm always good,' Milly answered, biting into the bread.

Howard watched the exchange between them, then looked over to Bonny again. 'Now that Harris is back at the Manchester place, I suppose you'll be able to get back to Wigan?'

Quickly making some sandwiches, Bonny shook her head. 'Harris wants me to stay with her for a bit.'

'In Manchester?'

''Course.' She turned to face him. 'What's up?'

'You're working all hours,' Howard said, adopting a pleading tone. 'I hardly see you any more.'

Smiling, Bonny bent down and patted him on the head. 'Feeling neglected, little lad?'

'I miss you.'

'I miss you too. But I can't cut back on my hours now.'

'So when can you?'

'Howard Waring, you are the end!' she teased him, sliding onto the arm of his chair. 'I've got a job to do. You don't mind watching Milly when she gets back from school, do you?'

He put his head on one side. 'Watching Milly's a pleasure, you know that. It's just that I'd like you working back in Wigan, so we'd both see more of you.'

She nuzzled his cheek. 'I'll be coming back, Howard, but not just yet. When things are more sorted out.'

'And what if Harris Simons decides that she'll run off with Ben Ramsey to Australia?'

'Why should she go to Australia?' Bonny replied, bemused.

'Why does she do anything? I mean, it's not as though anyone knows *what* she's going to do from one minute to the next. I doubt if *she* bloody knows. You want to look out, Bonny, you could get landed with that Manchester place.'

Biting his ear, Bonny cajoled him. 'I know it's been a bit hard on you lately, but things are getting sorted out. Before long, I promise, we'll have more time together.'

He put his arm round her. 'So you're bored with me?'

'Bored?' she exclaimed, then, smiling, took Milly by the hand and led her upstairs. Pausing on the landing, Bonny looked down, pleased to see Howard running up behind them.

'Give me just a minute,' she said mischievously. 'I'll settle Milly and then show you how bored I am.'

He grinned, showing his good teeth.

'How long?'

'Just a minute,' she repeated, moving into Milly's bedroom.

On the landing Howard waited. What the hell if he didn't see Bonny so much? When he did it was always good. And as for Milly – she was a smashing kid, no trouble. He should realise how lucky he was and stop bloody moaning.

The door opened, Bonny walking out onto the cramped landing.

'Still dressed?'

'Not for long.' Then, after kissing her passionately, Howard pulled back. 'I wish that we could be a real family. You, me, Milly – and a baby.'

Surprised, Bonny stared at him. 'We can't have a baby at the moment, luv.'

'Why not?'

'Because it's not the right time.'

'When will be? I mean, I'm older than you, Bonny, and I want to have a family.'

'You've *got* a family – me and Milly.'

He kissed her neck, whispering in her ear. 'I mean a child of my own.'

The thing about men, Bonny realised, was that you couldn't give them too much time to think. Obviously Howard had been brooding, feeling left out having to look after Milly. Maybe it was to be expected. After all, Milly wasn't his child and he had been an indulgent stepfather. But now he was making a point – *I'll play it your way, but you have to give me something I want.*

Life was all compromise, Bonny thought wryly.

'I'll tell you what, Howard Waring . . .'

'Yeah?'

'Why don't we fool around a bit?' She kissed him on the side of his neck, knowing he was ticklish. 'As for a baby, why not? In a little . . .' She kissed him again, Howard laughing outright and trying to duck out of her way. '. . . in a little while. But in the meantime . . .' again she kissed him, guiding him into their bedroom and kicking the door closed with her foot. Once inside, she pushed him back onto the bed and grinned. '. . . let's see what you're made of.'

FIFTY-SEVEN

It was a bitterly cold night when Harris left the Manchester salon. She had stayed on alone, doing the books, the dark coming down outside the windows. Finally, at 6.30, she had left, walking towards the station to catch a train over to Prestwich. Rain fell in a steady torrent, Harris ducking into a doorway and waiting until the worst of it had passed. Then she moved out onto the street again.

The town seemed depressing to her. Even the sale banners in the windows looked bizarrely grim. Several cars passed, a man riding by on a bicycle and throwing up rain from the road. She would get some food for their dinner, something better than the dross Mrs Wilson served. Not that Ben seemed to mind much; he didn't seem to care at all about food any more.

Nine weeks had passed since they had eloped. Nine long weeks, and they had never moved from the commercial travellers' hotel. All the promises of finding somewhere to live had evaporated, the ring on Harris's finger now looking like a sick joke.

As she waited at the traffic lights, a memory suddenly came back to her. Richard had been teaching Bonny and Harris how to cross the road.

'You look right and then left and then right again. Then you can cross.'

'But what if something had come whilst you were looking right?' Harris had teased him.

'Or when you were looking left?' Bonny had suggested.

Richard had sighed, perennially patient. 'That's why you look right, then left, then right again.'

'What if something fell on you from *above*?' Harris chimed in.

'How many flying lorries have you seen?' he had countered evenly.

'It could have been lifted by a crane,' Bonny added, 'and the chains could have broken. And then it fell and crushed you.'

'OK,' Richard had replied, still standing at the edge of the kerb. 'You look up, then right, then left, then right again – then you can cross.'

'You didn't look *down*,' Bonny had said suddenly. 'You've just walked into a huge crevasse –'

'Yeah,' Harris replied, laughing, 'but the lorry missed him.'

A car horn made her jump, Harris hurrying across the road and then stopping on the other side. Her eyes were staring ahead, as though she could still see the three of them as children, at some other street corner, laughing under the sunshine. I never knew you loved me, Richard, she thought, walking on. Why didn't you say anything? Then an image of Richard's home rose up before her. The sleeping Tom in Penny's arms, the simple house on Wood Street, always warm. I could have had that, Harris thought, I could have known what safety was like. I would have been secure with you.

Or with Jimmy . . . She leaned against the wall and stared down the rainy street. The lamps were on, making yellow splotches on the black road. She would get her train and go back to the hotel, pick up her key and walk to their room, using another name. Not his – Ben hadn't registered them as Dr and Mrs Ramsey. The thought hit her hard. *He had never meant them to be seen as man and wife.* He had been craven instead, hiding them away as though they were doing something sordid.

Which they were . . . Arriving at the train station, Harris walked to her platform and waited. Beside her, a young child talked to its mother, the woman tucking a scarf around the child's throat. I won't ever have Ben's children, Harris realised suddenly. We don't love each other enough to bring children into the world. She thought suddenly of Madge Baker, how her children had been neglected, dragging themselves up. And how she had ended up after a lifetime of booze and sex as a hospitalised drab with a smell.

Ben might talk of marriage and a family, Harris thought, but that's all it was, *talk*. Besides, lately he had mentioned marriage less and less. And was spending more time away from her. They met not to live together, to eat, to chat, to plan a future – they met to make love. That hellish hotel room had become a place where they fought to hold their relationship together. Not with words, or actions, or even guilt, but with sex.

Only in the moist, heated turmoil of desire were they suited. After that – sweaty with effort and empty with regret – they lay next to each other and stared blankly at the ceiling . . .

Hearing the train approach, Harris walked forward and then boarded it. Finally reaching Prestwich, she walked the remainder of the way to the hotel, Mrs Wilson looking up as she entered.

'May I have my key, please?'

'Your husband's got it, luv,' Mrs Wilson replied, jerking her head up the stairs. 'Came in a bit ago.'

'I thought he was going to be late tonight,' Harris said. 'He must have changed his mind.'

'No law against that – or we'd all be in trouble, hey?'

Her footsteps slow, Harris moved upstairs. The landing light was on, the low wattage bulb giving little illumination. Didn't Ben see how depressing it was? For a moment she didn't want to see him, or enter the sordid bedroom again.

Then she walked in quietly. His back was turned to her, his head bent down. The room smelled of dust and damp. Ben hadn't seen her, that much was obvious, as Harris moved round to face him. Slowly she approached and then stared. His left arm was extended, the sleeve rolled up. And he was injecting himself.

'Jesus!' she said simply, backing away.

In one movement, Ben jumped to his feet and slammed the door shut behind her. 'What are you doing?'

'What am *I* doing! What are you doing?' Harris asked, watching as he snatched the needle out of his arm and tossed it onto the bedside table.

'I don't do it often –'

'*What?* What don't you do often?'

'It's only when I'm under pressure,' Ben went on, moving towards her, Harris backing away. 'Oh, come on, it's nothing.'

'What are you taking?'

'It's only like having a drink –'

She put up her hands to stop him talking. 'You need help.'

'I need help!' he snapped back. 'What a fucking nerve! I need help, do I? What about you, Harris? You're so messed up you don't know what you're doing half the time.'

He was enraged; the injection hadn't yet taken effect. How dare she question him? He was a bloody doctor and she was some half-witted hairdresser! Who the hell was she to think she could tell him he needed help? He wouldn't be in this mess if it wasn't for her. She had dragged him down; it was her fault. All her bloody fault.

'Don't look at me like that!' he snapped, Harris backing against the wall.

'Ben, calm down, please.'

'You make me so mad!' he went on, approaching her, Harris cringing. 'You've ruined my life –'

'What about mine?' she snapped back defiantly. 'I left Jimmy Henshaw for you –'

'Then go back to him!' Ben hurled at her. 'Go on – not that he'd have you. You're washed up, Harris, no decent man would want you now.' He stopped, suddenly mellowing. 'Hey, I'm sorry . . . Come on, let's not fight. We're just overwrought. Come here, sweetheart.'

But she stood her ground. 'What are you taking?'

'Loads of doctors do it,' Ben replied, grasping her arm and pulling her towards him. 'It's to help my nerves. You know, calm me down. You like it when I'm calm, Harris, don't you?' He leaned down towards her, his tongue running down the side of her neck. 'When I can take my time to please you. Take it nice and slow –'

Abruptly she pushed him off. 'I want to know what you're taking.'

'No, you don't,' Ben replied, reaching into his jacket pocket and taking out a bottle of vodka. 'Come on, have a little drink with me.'

'I don't drink –'

'You should, Harris, it would take the starch out of your knickers.'

Aghast, she watched him down an inch of vodka and then put the bottle on the bedside table.

'You could be struck off for this, Ben,' she said, trying to sound calm. 'You need to see someone about it. You're a doctor –'

'I know I'm a doctor,' he replied, walking over to her and leaning down, his lips an inch from her ear. 'And I can diagnose that you're in love with this doctor. And what you need is some private attention from your personal medical advisor.'

She pushed him off, revolted. 'I'm going out.'

'The hell you are!' he snapped back, grabbing her arm and twisting it.

'Ben, don't! You're hurting me!'

'Isn't that a shame? I'm hurting you.' He twisted her arm further, Harris crying out. 'You hurt *me* all the time.'

'Ben, stop it!'

'"*Ben, stop it*",' he parodied. 'You like it well enough when you're in the mood. Like a bit of rough sometimes, Harris, or don't you like talking about it? We could have sex now, would you like that? Kiss and make up . . .'

Enraged, she pushed him away and moved to the door, wrenching it open.

But he slammed it shut again. 'Harris, cut it out! You're not going anywhere, and neither am I. We're in this together, you and me.' His hand reached round and cupped her left breast. 'Come on, let's forget all this fighting. We can make it up. Come on, Harris –'

'Get off me!' she snapped suddenly, ducking out of his grasp. 'I hate you! I loathe the sight of you! I wish I'd never met you. You've ruined my life –'

And then he struck her. His arm went out and he caught her, back-handed, across the face, her top lip driven into her teeth. As she fell to the floor he then kicked out, one blow landing in her stomach, the other in her kidneys as Harris tried frantically to roll out of the way. In a daze he stood over her, burned up with fury.

'You're so ungrateful, Harris. You don't know what I gave up for you!'

She stayed silent, not daring to speak.

After another moment Ben returned to the bedside table and took another drink of the vodka. Outside Harris could hear a car changing gears as it braked. Then she heard Ben move again. Slowly he walked back to her. She was lying still, her face turned away.

Kneeling down, Ben grabbed Harris's hair and jerked her

head back. 'Have a drink,' he said, emptying the vodka into her mouth.

Almost choking, she spat the liquid out, Ben losing his temper completely and throwing the bottle against the wall.

'You,' he said, lifting Harris's head by her hair, 'are a no one!' With real force, he slammed her head against the floor and then lifted it again. 'You're a stupid cow, you hear me?'

She could hardly breathe, the blood pouring from her mouth, her head jerked back so far that she thought her neck would break. All she could see clearly was Ben's face, only inches from hers, his voice suddenly calm and reasonable.

'Now you get yourself cleaned up. And don't make me have to do anything like this again. You hear me?'

She nodded, blood bubbling from her nose.

Exasperated, he let go of her hair, Harris's head falling to the floor. Without moving, she lay on the ground, hearing his footsteps walk round her. The pain from her kidneys was excruciating, her mouth swelling. Get out, Harris told herself, just get out, or he'll kill you . . . Her eyes focused on the door, her vision blurring. Don't pass out, she told herself. He's a doctor. He could talk himself out of this – whatever he does to you . . . Stay awake, stay awake. It's your only chance.

'Harris,' Ben said quietly, as he stood over her, 'can you hear me?'

She nodded, pain exploding in her temples.

'Then get up!'

Panting with the effort, Harris tried to rise, but only managed to get on all fours. Blood was dripping from her mouth onto the cheap linoleum.

Ben laughed. 'You should see yourself – not much like Vivien Leigh now. Come on, get up! I want you over here, next to me.' His voice softened, suddenly crooning as he lay down on the bed. 'Ben's really sorry, baby. So sorry.'

'I can't get up,' Harris replied, her voice thick.

'Then crawl, sweetheart,' he told her. 'You can crawl, can't you?'

But she wasn't going to crawl to anyone, least of all him. Shaking with the effort, Harris pushed herself upright, her legs finally holding her up as she leaned against the dressing table. Ben was watching, enjoying himself, his hand patting the cheap coverlet beside him.

'Come over here, sweetheart, I'm sorry.'

Slowly Harris dragged herself across the floor, the pain so intense that nausea swamped her, blood still pouring from her mouth. He was watching her, smiling, his arms outstretched as she approached the bed. Then, pulling her to him, he began to make love to her. The world stopped, Harris unresponding, pain burning her body, her mind blank.

It took ten more minutes for Ben Ramsey to fall asleep. When he did so, Harris crept out of the bed and pulled on her clothes, terrified that she would wake him. Pain made her gasp several times, and once he stirred, Harris tensing as she stared at him. Please God, don't let him wake. Please God . . . When she was sure he was still sleeping she picked up her shoes and crept out of the room, locking the door behind her and throwing the key out of the landing window.

Waiting until Mrs Wilson moved away from the desk, Harris then hurried out into the street. It was still raining, the fresh air making her dizzy, her mouth bleeding again. But she kept moving, putting back her head momentarily to let the rain cool her. Several people stared as she passed, but no one stopped her. Finally reaching the railway station, she covered the bottom half of her face with her scarf and boarded a train to Wigan.

Stay awake, Harris willed herself, stay awake . . . Not for one moment did she dare to close her eyes. Her face turned to the window, her reflection alien to her. Every bump on the tracks punched her in the kidneys and stomach, every tiny jolt making her sweat with pain. I have to get home, Harris told herself. Please God, let me get home . . .

The journey was marked in waves of pain, Harris's eyes opening and closing, the blood drying around her mouth, hidden behind the scarf. When they finally pulled into Wigan station, Harris got off and stood on the platform, letting the night air slap her alert. She was nearly home; she was going to make it. Walking on stiffly, Harris made her eyes focus on the station exit. Then on the street, each yard marked out before her.

She would never forget that long walk home. The rain was incessant, but it kept her alert and cold, her legs dragging along the pavement as she crossed Market Place. Someone saw her and told someone else that they had seen Harris Simons, or someone who looked liked her, in a bad way. But no one approached her. And she kept walking.

Finally Harris reached Wigan Lane and stopped. For a moment she nearly panicked, thinking she was going to pass out, then slowly she began to walk again. Willpower gave her the strength for the last desperate effort to get home. She could see the lights on downstairs in Deerheart House and a figure passing across a window. Irma . . .

Keep walking, she told herself, delirious now, the drive changing, turning into the way it looked that first evening she came to Deerheart House. Her legs were rubbery, the wet azalea bushes brushing her as she passed. Suddenly Dr Redmond was there, with Mildred, then Bonny and Richard . . . Under her feet, the gravel was rising and falling. But Harris Simons kept walking. I just have to get home, she told herself. When I get home I'll be safe . . . The house was so close, but every time she got within reach it seemed to slip further away from her.

It took four minutes and forty-nine seconds for Harris Simons to make the last yards home.

FIFTY-EIGHT

As he frequently was at times of trouble, Lionel Redmond was summoned to Deerheart House. He was puffing, out of breath, as Irma opened the door and hustled him in.

'Thank you for coming. I trust this visit is in the strictest confidence?'

'I have . . .' he puffed, 'a partner . . .' again he gasped for breath, 'who makes house calls.'

'I dare say you do, Lionel, but I don't want anyone else,' Irma snapped. 'Anyway, you have poor taste in partners.'

Lionel ignored the barb. 'What is it?'

'You'll see,' Irma replied, showing him into the drawing room. On the sofa was a woman, her face badly bruised and bloody, a blanket over her legs. Lionel Redmond never thought for one moment that it was Harris.

'Dear me, you've been in the wars,' he said, walking over to his patient and then glancing at Irma. 'Has she been in an accident? We should call an ambulance.'

'Harris doesn't want an ambulance.'

'*Harris!*' Lionel Redmond repeated, looking back to the injured figure. 'Oh, my dear girl, whatever happened to you?'

'Ben Ramsey happened to her,' Irma replied, walking over to Harris and standing next to her. 'He beat her up.'

Kneeling down awkwardly, Dr Redmond examined Harris's face, then paused.

'Are you injured anywhere else?'

Her voice was muffled. 'I've been kicked in the stomach and kidneys.'

'I need to take a look at you, dear,' he said kindly, glancing at Irma. 'Give me a few minutes, will you?'

'No,' Harris said quietly, 'she can stay.'

Very carefully, Lionel Redmond examined Harris, her back bruised from her waist to her buttocks. As she rolled over, she winced, Lionel Redmond examining her stomach thoroughly.

'Does that hurt?'

'Yes.'

'And that?'

'Not too much.'

Irma's voice was metallic. 'How bad is it, Lionel?'

'Nothing too serious, thankfully. But she'll need a lot of rest and good food.'

'So much for Mrs Turner then.'

Despite herself, Harris smiled, Irma touching her niece's shoulder briefly.

'I'm just going to have a word with Dr Redmond outside, Harris. I'll be back in a minute.'

In the hallway, Irma's voice hardened as she turned to Lionel. 'No one does this to my niece and gets away with it! Harris doesn't want to press charges, but I want Ben Ramsey stopped. He's a doctor, for God's sake; he should be struck off for this.'

Lionel stared at the floor tiles. 'I can talk to some people I know –'

'Well, you should know the whole story before you do. Ben Ramsey was injecting himself with something, a stimulant of some sort. That's what Harris told me.' Irma added, 'And he was drinking. Vodka. Now I ask you, Dr Redmond, would you let a doctor like that loose on his patients?'

'We've been watching Ben Ramsey for a while –'

'Well, you weren't watching him close enough!' Irma retorted. 'Get him run out of this town, as soon as possible. You and your colleagues can manage that, Lionel. I know you wouldn't do it as a favour to me, but Mildred loved Harris. *And you loved Mildred.* So do it for her.'

She held his gaze as he winced. God, Lionel thought uncomfortably, did the woman know *everything*?

'I'll do what I can, Irma.'

'Yes, I know you will,' she replied evenly. 'I'm not a malicious woman – contrary to popular belief. I just want to see Ben Ramsey's life ruined. I want to see him where he should be. In hell.'

The news travelled around Wigan within twenty-four hours. Naturally Irma hadn't told anyone, but Mrs Turner did. And suddenly the reviled Harris Simons was an object of pity, not scorn. As for Ben Ramsey, no one could find him. He hadn't turned up at his practice and had left the commercial travellers' hotel without leaving a forwarding address.

'They say he's ruined her looks,' Mrs Hardman gabbled on, eagerly passing the information to Mrs Broadbent.

This was real news; the beautiful Harris Simons who had jilted Jimmy Henshaw had been disfigured. What she had done was terrible – but this was an awful retribution, even for jilting a fiancé.

'Poor girl, but there you are,' Mrs Hardman said, with mock sympathy. 'If you will run around with the wrong type –'

'But Eve Clough *married* Ben Ramsey. She obviously didn't know what he was like. And neither did Birdie – or she would never have let her daughter marry the bugger.' Mrs Broadbent paused, considering. 'Fancy, *a doctor*. Makes you reluctant to go in about your corns, doesn't it?'

* * *

Harris insisted that she was not going to stay in bed. I can get around, she told Irma, stop fussing. Slowly, painfully over the next days she walked around Deerheart House, trying to make sense of what had happened. To have sacrificed so much, for nothing . . . She would start again, she told herself, but how? Her mood vacillated between despair and optimism. The whole town would be talking about her again, Harris knew only too well, and she dreaded facing people. How could she get back from this?

Her security came in the unlikely shape of Irma. Stony-faced, her aunt would go to the salon early and come back late in the evening, full of news.

'Mrs Holden's pregnant. I mean, at her age, you'd think she'd have more sense.' Taking off her hat and coat, Irma continued, 'I wonder how they could tell she was carrying anyway – the woman's the size of a barn door.'

It was comforting for Harris to listen to her. She had been tense, expecting a confrontation with her aunt, an argument, bitter recriminations – but they never came. Instead Irma acted as though nothing had happened. As if Harris had never left home. Almost as though the whole episode with the wedding, Ben Ramsey, and the beating-up had never taken place.

As though Harris was a child again. If only we could walk back in time, Harris thought. Mildred would still be alive, and she would be young, naïve, before Ben Ramsey walked into her life. Before their affair clouded everything and pulled them into blackness. God, why did I go with him? Harris thought hopelessly. I knew it was all wrong, I knew he was bad. But I did it anyway.

As Irma continued talking, Harris followed her aunt into the dining room.

'Bonny's doing well in the Manchester salon,' Irma said cautiously. 'She's not family, but the girl's surprised me – considering her background. And her mother . . .' Rolling her

461

eyes, Irma continued. 'Madge Baker's back in that hospital again. I imagine they'll want to keep her body when she dies. After all, it'll be in perfect condition, pickled like a walnut.'

Smiling dimly, Harris watched her aunt as she sat down at the table, opposite her. On the wall behind, the grandfather clock ticked as it had always done; the tablecloth, cutlery and dishes unchanged for decades. It was all so safe, Harris thought, like being a child again. The shock of the beating had affected Harris deeply, and Irma's kindness – when she had expected hostility – was proving unbearable. I'm not worth it, Harris wanted to shout. Scream at me, curse me, but don't be kind.

'I'll be back at work soon,' she said finally, her voice low.

Irma's eyebrows rose. 'No rush. You can get back to the salon when you're ready.'

Mrs Turner walked in with their dinner. 'Chops,' the house-keeper announced, Irma waiting until she had left before lifting the lid on the serving dish. 'Dear God! Look at these – if she'd cooked them any longer I could sketch with them.'

Suddenly overwhelmed, Harris covered her face and began to cry.

'Oh, come on,' Irma said sympathetically, 'things aren't that bad, Harris. If we put some salt on them they might still be edible.'

FIFTY-NINE

*I inched back into life. And of all people Irma became my ally.
It's strange how life works out. Instead of hiding from scandal,
as she had done in the past, she faced it, and, I believe, enjoyed
it. I can still see her now, standing with her hands on her hips
and that look on her face – Come on, I'll take you all on.*

*The physical bruises faded much quicker than the internal
marks. Did I miss him? Of course I did. We can't change
overnight, however insane our behaviour seems. As for Ben
Rumsey – well, more of him later . . . For myself, I clung to
Deerheart House, Irma, Saville and the salons, like a falling
man clings to a rock face. They became my bolt holes, and all
the other people I had given up so easily rallied round.*

*Like Bonny and her family; Richard and his. They let me
share time with them, and they let me share their children.
Because I wasn't going to have children. I wasn't the right
kind of woman. And besides, I wasn't looking for a man. Any
man, any more.*

*My work would be the centre of my existence. Why not?
The war had changed everything; it was suddenly possible
for a clever ambitious woman to take on a man's world. So
I did. I didn't want the complications of love or the sordid
manipulations of sex. I wanted to remain alone, fixed for all*

time. Like Rosalia, the little girl in the crypt in Sicily. No man would change me, or touch me again. I was removed from that part of life for ever. As emotionally dead as it was possible to be, and yet still be alive.

And so for the next six months everything was calm. That peace – so hard won – enveloped everything, taking us all into 1950. A new decade, a new start.

I remember one spring day particularly – Bonny and her family, Richard and his, and me, all went to Mesnes Park. It was one of those dozy, warm days, the women turning out in their best clothes, men hanging around the bandstand, children throwing sticks off the bridge into the lake below. The band played a Glenn Miller dance tune and then – unexpectedly – a piece by Debussy.

Those electric, shimmering notes floated with the dust motes on the warm afternoon air. They seemed to hypnotise the people in the deck chairs, and even temporarily mesmerise the children by the lake side. Then, as the last notes faded into the four o'clock afternoon, a breeze blew up suddenly, snatching Bonny's hat from her head, Howard running after it.

But it wasn't only the weather that had changed. The figures in the landscape altered in an instant from then to now. And fate, so capricious and envious of happiness, lobbed another grenade into our steady lives.

SIXTY

Combing out her last client, Bonny glanced over to Harris. 'I think Richard's mad, taking them off for a break in Blackpool. Bloody Blackpool, it'll be freezing!'

'But very quiet,' Harris replied, looking up from the appointments book, which was pleasingly full for the next week. The little salon in Manchester, up the steep steps, had finally proved itself.

'I wouldn't want to go to Blackpool now,' Bonny went on, finishing the woman's hair and holding up a mirror to show her the back of her head. 'Is that how you want it?'

The elderly lady beamed at her. 'You do it so nicely, my dear. I wouldn't come to anyone else.'

Smiling, Bonny helped her on with her coat, took her offered tip and then watched her leave. Putting the money into the till, she then turned back to Harris. 'Those stairs will kill her one day. I expect her to keel over every time she comes in.'

Preoccupied, Harris kept staring at the appointments book. 'You remember how I was talking about opening another salon?'

Bonny nodded. 'In Hyde?'

'Yes, in Hyde,' Harris agreed. 'What d'you think? You could run this place.'

'No.'

'Why not?'

Grinning, Bonny leaned towards her. 'Because I have a husband who wants me home more. I promised Howard months ago that working here was temporary. He wants me back at the Wigan salon, and it's only fair. Anyway, he's right, I want to spend more time with him and Milly.'

Sighing, Harris closed the book and leaned back in her seat. 'Yeah, of course you do.'

'You could hire someone else.'

'I could,' Harris agreed, 'but they wouldn't be family.'

'I'm not family!'

'Don't be daft. You're part of the family, always have been.'

Touched, Bonny perched on the edge of the desk, her voice eager with excitement. 'I'm pregnant.'

Harris was momentarily stunned. 'What!'

'I'm having another baby. That's another reason why I can't take on more work.' She beamed at Harris. 'Howard's wanted us to have a baby for ages. He's great with Milly, but he wants his own child. You know what men are like.'

'Are you pleased about it?'

'Sure I am,' Bonny answered, although her tone wasn't as certain as she would have liked. 'I want to make my husband happy, and besides, Milly needs a playmate.'

'You could have bought her a dog,' Harris replied, teasing her, then winking. 'It's wonderful news. Really wonderful.'

'I want you to be the baby's godmother.'

'Me?' Harris looked at her in amazement. '*Me*, a godmother! Isn't that a bit risky? I mean, am I really the best person to guide a child through life?'

'Seeing as how you know most of its pitfalls, I'd say you were perfect,' Bonny replied drily. 'One day, Harris, when you have kids of your own –'

'Never!'

'In time you'll think differently,' Bonny assured her. 'It's still early days for you. Too soon after Ramsey. But some day you'll meet someone you can trust.'

Uncharacteristically sharp, Harris cut her off. 'I don't want another man. Not now, not ever.'

'I saw Jimmy Henshaw the other day,' Bonny replied, the words pulling Harris up short – just as she knew they would. 'He's seeing someone else now, a girl from Manchester way. Someone was saying it was getting serious, but who knows? Jimmy's still living in the house you two were supposed to move into after you got married.'

'Did he ask after me?'

Bonny shook her head. 'Nah. Still smarting, I guess.' Waiting for Harris to respond, Bonny paused, and then carried on hurriedly, 'He heard about what happened with Ramsey, though. Seemed angry about that.'

'I'm surprised he wasn't gloating. Saying it served me right.'

'Jimmy's not the type,' Bonny said flatly. 'I think he still cares about you – despite himself. Despite what you did to him.'

'I know what I did, Bonny, I don't have to be reminded of it.'

Rebuked, Bonny's voice softened. 'I just wondered if you wanted to talk about it. You know, if you minded that Jimmy had someone else.'

'I don't mind,' Harris lied, surprised by the scorching sensation in her heart. 'He should be married. Jimmy would make someone a good husband. She's a lucky woman, whoever she is.'

And she could have been me.

Excitedly, Penny was packing, trying to cram some of the toys Harris had bought for Tom into the overstuffed case. Pressing down on the lid, she pulled out a teddy bear and then tried to lock it again. Still no luck. Finally Penny took out a stuffed toy monkey Harris had given Tom for Christmas. This time the locks closed with a satisfying click. Almost guiltily, Penny looked at the monkey discarded on the floor. It was one of Tom's favourites, but then again, he had so many favourites. And they would buy him some more in Blackpool.

A holiday, she thought, excitement welling up again. She hadn't been on holiday before. Having no parents and no siblings left Penny had never experienced the usual celebrations. Richard was her life. And Tom. And it was enough. Just the three of them on holiday. God, she could hardly wait.

'You finished packing?' Richard asked, walking in at the back door, home from work early.

She looked up, her hair dishevelled. 'Almost.'

'This time tomorrow,' he said cheerily, 'we'll be in Blackpool. Fresh air, sea, sun –'

'Sun?'

'Well, maybe not that much sun. But fresh air certainly.' He looked at the packed cases and the tidied kitchen. 'Bonny said she'd call round and see that everything was all right whilst we were away.'

'She's busy enough with her own family,' Penny answered him. 'And she has the baby she's expecting to think about. Howard's glowing.'

'I know, I saw him this morning,' Richard replied, looking round. 'Where's Tom?'

'In bed. I put him down early so he would get some sleep. He was getting overexcited.'

'He's not the only one,' Richard teased her, sitting down and pulling Penny onto his lap. 'We've got the world on a string, Mrs Baker. Our little family off on holiday, to a *hotel*. Things are looking up.'

'You know something, Richard?' she said softly. 'Things began to look up the day I married you.'

* * *

468

Having had a run-in with Mrs Biddy, Irma headed for the salon, fuming. The woman was impossible! You'd think she owned the lodge *and* Saville. Still, she was devoted to her charge and made sure that he kept on his medication. That was certainly something to be grateful for ... Scurrying along, Irma crossed over at Market Street and nodded towards the butcher as she passed.

Saville, she thought suddenly, was looking older. They all were. But that was life. At least it meant that he hadn't got the energy to get into trouble again. That was the one good thing about age – the absence of desire. But Harris was too young to suppress that part of her life, Irma decided firmly. She might believe that she would never want another man, but time would tell. Perhaps – in the years to come – her niece would meet someone – a lawyer, or a businessman – and settle down. Have children, even. Irma liked that thought. If Harris had a child the family line would continue. She would inherit Deerheart House, run the salons and make a name for herself as a businesswoman *and* a wife and mother.

All this silliness about never getting married and having a family was just a reaction to her past. Irma checked her reflection in the Electricity Board window. Not bad, she thought, admiring her trim figure and glossy, tinted hair. There were many in the town who never imagined *she* would still be around. Many who thought she would have remained a recluse – or died of a heart attack long enough since. But not Irma Simons.

To be honest, she was enjoying her life and her work, even encouraging Harris to open another salon. Well, why not? When her niece *did* marry – and Irma was sure she would one day – Harris would need someone to run the new place. And why not her aunt? Oh yes, Irma thought, life was good. The plans she had laid for her niece so long ago had been thwarted – but only temporarily.

The best plans, like summers, always came round again.

* * *

'I don't care!' Eve shouted, her voice reverberating around the house as she faced her mother. 'You should have stayed out of this!'

'I did it for you!' Birdie replied, as Sydney walked in to see what the commotion was all about.

'What's going on with you two?'

'Ask *her*,' Eve said viciously.

Sydney turned to his wife. 'What is it, Birdie?'

'I was doing it for her own good.'

'For your own satisfaction, you mean!' Eve snapped. 'All you ever do is for yourself –'

'Eve, be quiet!' her father said. 'Now, Birdie, what's going on?'

'Ben Ramsey's finished,' Birdie said, trying hard to conceal her satisfaction. 'He's going to be struck off. No more *Doctor* Ramsey.'

For a long moment Sydney stared at his wife. He had refused to be a part of Ramsey's downfall, at his daughter's request, but did Birdie have a hand in it? He had seen his wife in a whole new light recently and was uncomfortably aware that she had a mean streak when she was crossed. But without his help, *had* she had enough power to cripple the man who had failed to live up to her expectations? The thought was an uncomfortable one.

'Birdie, what did you do?'

She was about to protest that she hadn't done anything, but saw the looks on her husband and daughter's faces. So they thought she had brought Ramsey down, did they? Thoughtful, Birdie turned away. Eve had been very vitriolic, accusing her of never caring, of doing everything just to further her own ends. What an ungrateful child, Birdie thought, smouldering. And as for Sydney, did he *really* think that she would do as he said? That just because he told her to leave well alone, she would obey? Fat chance! If she had obeyed Sydney every time he told her to they would never be where they were today. Didn't the

470

fat fool know that *she* was the real brains behind their success? That it was down to *her* skill and manipulations that Sydney Clough was the richest man in Wigan?

Slowly Birdie looked from her husband to her daughter. It had been Irma Simons and her cohorts who had turned the screw on Ramsey, Lionel Redmond exposing him to his medical cronies. But did Sydney and Eve have to know that? Perhaps, Birdie thought, it was time that they took her a little more seriously. Especially her husband – who even thought she was too stupid to know about his little dalliance with his secretary.

'I did what I thought was right. We have no room for liars and cheats in this family.' Sydney flushed, unnerved, as his wife continued, 'I just got rid of a useless husband and a disreputable son-in-law. What good was Ramsey to you, Eve? And what credit was he to you, Sydney?' She let her voice fall, as though she was hurt by their criticism. 'You two are my *life*. Why would I do anything to harm either of you?'

'Birdie, luv –' Sydney began, already trying to placate her.

But she cut him off, enjoying her borrowed triumph. 'I'm going to my room now . . .' she said, allowing her voice to break for effect, 'and when you've had time to consider what's happened, I think you'll both realise that you owe me an apology.'

There was a new moon that night, high in the dark sky, riding a cluster of stars. Curled up together in bed, Richard and Penny dreamed of their holiday, the journey beginning only a few hours later, when they would set off by coach in the early morning, before dawn.

As she turned in her sleep, Penny dreamed of the dark sea, the moon reflected on its surface, the lights from the promenade making yellow flecks in the blackness. Beside her, Richard turned over and rested his hand on his wife's stomach. He could feel her breathing, and hear the soft beating of her heart.

Out on the coast the night slid over the sea and rested, waiting for the morning hours. The town of Blackpool slept on, only a few night birds and foxes disturbing the quiet. Then, finally, dawn broke silent and sweet.

'It's time,' Richard said, smiling as he turned to his wife in bed. 'Come on, sweetheart, it's time to go.'

SIXTY-ONE

At quarter past six in the morning a lorry swerved on a greasy patch of road and smashed into the side of the holiday coach, heading for Blackpool. Richard and Penny Baker were killed instantly.

Their son, Tom, was the only survivor.

SIXTY-TWO

Jimmy Henshaw sighed to himself, trying to concentrate. But his attention soon wandered again, thinking of the terrible news and then remembering the conversation he had overheard months earlier. His secretary and the clerk had been talking, in whispers, about Harris being beaten up by Ben Ramsey. His first reaction had been to go to her. But he had resisted, still smarting. After all, hadn't his jilting been the talk of the town for months?

But despite the public humiliation, Jimmy felt no triumph at Harris's downfall. Everyone else talked about how Harris Simons had got her just deserts. And *how* they enjoyed her fall! She had been too beautiful, and had cocked a snook at society for too long not to make many a jealous enemy.

Then something no one expected happened – people were suddenly sympathetic. 'Poor Harris, Ramsey had given her such a beating she would never be the same again. She was crippled,' someone said. 'Her face was wrecked,' someone else trilled excitedly. It was Dr Redmond who told Jimmy the truth: Harris was badly beaten, but she would be fine.

She would be fine . . . How many times Jimmy had thought about her he couldn't remember. He even considered sending a card. But what *could* he say that wouldn't sound wrong?

Harris would be sure to think he was gloating, whatever he wrote. Because he would have thought the same. So the weeks passed, and then it became too late to send any card or message.

His parents' relief was palpable. After all, Harris Simons had become single, a free agent again. And their son had loved her very much. If he went back to Harris now she would snatch his hand off, Mrs Henshaw said, concerned. I never liked the girl and I don't want him ending up with her sort.

But Jimmy *didn't* end up with Harris, and Harris never contacted him. Instead he continued to see Lydia Owen and pretend to himself that they might have a future. But Harris was always on his mind. Everywhere he went he seemed to hear her name mentioned, the scandal thrilling Wigan. *Harris Simons was always a slut, what could she expect? Running around with Ben Ramsey, a married man, what decent girl would do that?*

It seemed to Jimmy that Harris would never escape her past, or the universal criticism, and when he felt moved to defend her people looked at him with pity. *Poor lad, you'd think he would have got over her by now . . . Some men just can't see reality when it stares them in the face.*

And so it went on, Jimmy aware that the love of his life was back in Deerheart House, only a few miles away. Near enough to visit, near enough to phone, but as distant emotionally as someone on another continent.

Then, as people finally began to forget, news came that the Bakers had been killed.

Jimmy shook his head with disbelief. He had liked Richard and now he was dead. And they had been about the same age . . . Who would have believed that something so shocking could happen so suddenly? And who would have believed the outcome of the tragedy?

Thoughtful, Jimmy leaned back in his seat. No one would have expected that Harris Simons would have turned out to be the one who saved the day – Bonny ill, and Harris taking over not only the care of her child, but Tom as well. Jimmy smiled to himself, then felt suddenly foolish. Why the hell was he so pleased? Harris had nothing to do with him any more. What did it matter that she had behaved so well? What was it to him that she had turned her life around, and would now tear public approval from the very people who had despised her before?

But despite himself, it *did* matter. It mattered that the woman who had jilted him, the woman who had been vilified, the woman who had made the blood run just that bit hotter through her veins, was coming back from the wilderness. The same recklessness that had been Harris's downfall would turn out to be her saving. It was just like her to look after Bonny, and her child. Just like Harris to give a home to Tom . . . She didn't have to, she didn't need to, but she did. Because, rightly or wrongly, she acted from the heart.

Sighing, Jimmy turned back to his papers and then stared at them, incredulous. He had been doodling whilst he thought, letting his pen run over the paper aimlessly. And there on the blotter was just one name – 'Harris'. Scribbled over and over again.

But it was too late, he thought helplessly, screwing up the paper. Way too late.

Under heavy sedation, Bonny lay unconscious in one of the spare bedrooms in Deerheart House. She had received the news of Richard and Penny's death with disbelief, then collapsed. Howard had been at a loss to know what to do and had phoned Harris. At once she had arranged for Tom to be brought to Deerheart House, along with his aunt, Howard confused, unable to think clearly.

'Why don't you come too?' Harris asked him.

But he refused. He had seen the effect the news had had on

his wife and was rigid with distress. So, unable to console a hysterical Bonny, he had led her into Deerheart House and left her there. With Milly.

'Brandy,' Irma said firmly, when Bonny was settled upstairs.

'She's out like a light,' Harris replied. 'She doesn't need a drink.'

'Who said it was for Bonny?' Irma replied, pouring herself a generous measure and then passing one to Harris. 'Go on, drink it. You'll need it.'

Downing half of it quickly, Harris glanced over to the sofa. Wrapped up in a blanket and eiderdown was Tom. He was sleeping, as though nothing had happened. That was the one blessing of being two years old: he was too young to understand.

'What do you think he saw?' Harris asked, her voice low.

'Maybe he slept through it,' Irma offered, sitting down heavily.

'Richard and Penny. Dead . . . I can't believe it.' Images of Richard loomed up before Harris: Richard trying to teach her and Bonny how to cross the road; Richard seeing off the bullies; Richard in his army uniform . . .

'They were so young,' Irma said suddenly, banking up the fire and jabbing it with a poker. 'What a time of the morning to travel! No one sets off so early for a holiday.'

Unmoving, Harris stared into the feeble flames. For some reason she couldn't remember Penny's face clearly, just hear her voice.

'Bonny's in a bad way.'

'I know.'

'She adored Richard.'

'I know that too. Are *you* all right?'

Again, Harris nodded. 'I just can't believe it. They were so excited about going away. They'd never been on holiday before . . .' She paused, watching a flutter of sparks leap up the chimney. 'What about Tom?'

'He's got his aunt,' Irma replied. 'Thank God he didn't have to rely on his grandmother.'

'But Bonny's so upset,' Harris said dully. 'She can't look after him at the moment.'

'No,' said Irma evenly, 'but we can.'

Surprised, Harris turned to look at her. 'You don't know anything about children.'

'I helped bring you up!'

'Tom is only two years old! I was much older when I came here.'

Irma sighed, fiddling with her hairnet impatiently. 'We can manage together, Harris. At least until Bonny's back on her feet.'

'Then what?'

'She'll take Tom on, of course. He's her nephew.'

'But she's already got Milly and she's having another baby.'

Irma sighed. 'Well, it's got a brother now, hasn't it?'

Lapsing back into silence, Harris rubbed her hands together to warm them. The morning was cold, without comfort.

'I still can't take it in. I can't believe they're dead.'

'You will,' Irma said, her tone emotionless. 'Even the worst news gets through in time.'

An hour later Tom woke and cried for his mother, Harris picking him up and nursing him. Unwilling to be soothed, he struggled in her grip, his face reddening as he screamed.

'He's wet,' Harris said, touching his pants. 'He needs changing.'

'Don't look at me,' Irma replied, stepping back. 'All his things are over there.'

'Can you find me a nappy?' Harris asked, laying Tom down on the sofa.

How hard could it be? she thought as she took the clean nappy from Irma. Hadn't she watched Bonny change Milly a hundred times? But putting a nappy on a screaming baby was more difficult than it looked, Harris jabbing the safety pin into her forefinger twice before finally getting Tom comfortable. Then she decided to feed him, Irma making up a mushy concoction and passing it to Harris triumphantly.

'Go on,' Irma said, folding her arms and watching. 'Give it to him.'

But Tom was still too upset to feed, his cries echoing around the house.

'He's still crying,' Harris said, trying hopelessly to rock him to sleep. 'Why is he still crying? I don't know what to do for him.'

'Rubbish!' Irma said emphatically. 'That baby knows and loves you. Just do what you think's right. He's been in an accident, Harris. Even a baby can suffer from shock.'

With that Irma left the room, her footsteps echoing down the corridor.

Holding on to Tom, Harris looked into the child's face. Life was so bizarre, she thought. Here she was now looking after a child who had lost its parents suddenly. Just as *she* had. Once. A long time ago.

'Tom,' she said softly, 'I don't know how much you understand, but I'm going to talk to you anyway. I know you're upset . . .' she looked into the toddler's face, Tom's cries lessening as he watched her. '. . . but it's going to be OK, baby. You've got us. Bonny and Irma and me. And we'll love you, Tom. We'll all love you.'

Watching him, Harris's heart shifted. The fire crackled in front of them, the old clock chiming in the dining room beyond. This is your son, Richard, she thought, and I don't know how to help him. I don't know what I'm supposed to say. But I promise you one thing – I'll look after him, as you always looked after me. I'll be there for him and for Bonny. This house is theirs for as long as they need it. I owe you that much.

Slowly, as Harris continued to rock him, Tom's cries died down, his eyelids closing as he slid into an exhausted sleep.

Overhead she could hear the soft muffle of voices, then silence again. The house held its breath, the walls waiting, the garden transfixed in those sad morning hours.

Later would come the questions; the police inquiry. They would discover who was to blame for the accident and act accordingly. Then the tiny house on Wood Street would be visited by the family. The sickening duty of sorting out Richard and Penny's possessions, clothes and furniture would be undertaken. And the photographs – the achingly sad mementoes of two young lives – would be put inside an album. For Tom, when he was older.

The grim housekeeping of death would continue to its inevitable end, Harris knew only too well. There were the funerals to face, the grief. Later. And then the realisation that they would never see Richard and Penny Baker again. The thought brought back memories of the death of Harris's own parents and the loneliness that followed. And now it was all to come again. It would all have to be dealt with and faced. Later . . . Gently she stroked Tom's cheek. There was no point thinking about what was to follow.

Later would come soon enough.

SIXTY-THREE

'And then he . . .' Harris paused, puffing out her cheeks, Milly and Tom watching her, spellbound, '. . . blew the house down!'

With one huge puff, Harris let out her breath, Milly rocking backwards, giggling.

'Again! Again!'

'No, you have to go to bed now,' Harris replied, her tone mock serious.

'*Please* . . .' Milly begged.

As she always did, Harris wavered, Tom's large brown eyes fixed on her imploringly. His devotion was obvious. Milly loved Harris – and always had – but for Tom, Harris was rapidly becoming his surrogate mother.

'OK, one last story, and then you both have to have a nap.' Harris paused. 'Once upon a time there was a frog –'

'Ugh,' Milly said, pulling a face.

'Oh no, don't say that! He was a very good-looking frog,' Harris offered. 'And he wore a green velvet suit –'

'Frogs don't wear clothes,' Milly replied smartly.

Beside her, Tom was staring at Harris. He didn't care about frogs, or even understand about them, all he wanted was for Harris to stay with them.

'This frog,' Harris said emphatically, 'wore clothes. Because it's a magic frog –'

'Can it do tricks?'

Harris raised her eyebrows. 'It can stay very quiet when people are telling stories.'

'That's not a trick!' Milly persisted. 'Anyway, I don't want to hear about him. Tell me about the princess.'

'The princess comes into the story later. She owns the frog.'

Mildred folded her arms, pouting: 'Aw, it's not the one where she kisses the frog and it turns into a handsome prince, is it?'

So you've heard it before, Harris thought, changing tack immediately. 'No – it's the one where she kisses the frog and it turns into *a car*.'

Stunned, both children watched her.

'A very *fast* car,' Harris went on, making engine noises as she turned a pretend steering wheel. 'The princess could drive fast, very fast, in this car. Everyone watched her in the town and she waved as she passed them. She sounded her horn too.' Depressing an imaginary horn, Harris made a loud honking noise, Tom grinning and immediately imitating her.

Soon the noise was deafening, both children caught up in the story, both driving in the imaginary car. Then – unexpectedly – Harris stopped. Surprised, both children watched her.

'What's the matter?' Milly asked, eyes wide.

'She ran out of petrol,' Harris said neatly, getting to her feet. 'Now, go to sleep. I'll play with you later.'

Walking out of the room, she leaned against the door, smiling. Mildred had done her best, but had never played with her when she was little. As for Irma, she had hardly spoken to her niece until she was virtually grown up. In fact the only person who had played with Harris when she first arrived had been Saville. A mature man, playing children's games, but too big to run around with. That had been the Baker children's province.

Harris pushed herself away from the door. The closeness she had with Milly was obvious to everyone. But with Tom she had a special bond. Was it because she had so much in common with him? Harris wondered. Because he, like her, had lost his parents in a freak accident?

At least Milly had her mother . . . Harris sighed. As a direct result of her brother's death, Bonny had lapsed into an unshakeable depression. Sitting with her endlessly for the first weeks, Howard had done his best to comfort her, but it was no good. He took Milly out and they both came back with presents for Bonny – flowers, chocolates, anything. But when Howard kissed her she was unresponsive, gazing blankly into the distance.

After a while, he came to Deerheart House less often. He was working late, he told Harris. Besides, Bonny didn't know if he was there or not. So why shouldn't he build up his overtime? The money would be useful – after all, Bonny wasn't working. And anyway, as Howard said repeatedly, it wasn't going to be for long.

But he was wrong. Weeks passed and Bonny showed no sign of recovery.

Confused, Howard became defensive.

'Why doesn't she talk to me?' he asked Harris, his broad-featured face baffled. 'We used to talk about everything before. Have some right laughs. She doesn't even like me to cuddle her, and she used to love our cuddles before. Said they made everything all right.'

'She *still* needs you,' Harris replied. 'She'll come out of it. In time –'

'Oh, come off it! She doesn't know I'm even here!' he retorted, pulling off his bus driver's cap. 'I never thought Bonny would take it like this. I mean, Richard's death were a shock, but I never thought it would get her this bad.'

'She loved him very much,' Harris replied, sitting down beside him. 'Give her time.'

Rubbing her eyes, Harris suddenly realised how tired she actually was. Work had always been busy, but now she was looking after Milly and Tom as well. Aware that her niece needed support, Irma was holding the fort in Wigan, but before long Harris had had to hire a manager for the New Era. It was only temporary, she said when she hired Catherine Wells, only for a short while . . .

'Howard, I need your help,' Harris said evenly. 'I have to look after Tom now. Bonny can't manage him yet, and she can't look after Milly either.'

'Well, I can't,' he said hurriedly. 'I mean, I would if I could, but Milly's not a baby, she's nearly six, and I were only used to minding her for a few hours a day.'

'Couldn't you help a bit?' Harris pushed him, wondering why he was being unreasonable. 'I mean, Bonny is going to have your baby in a few months' time –'

'She'll have to be better for that!'

'Howard,' Harris said, her tone cool, 'what's *really* the problem? Your wife's sick, but she's being looked after here. And she can stay for as long as she likes. But I don't understand why you're not around more, trying to help all of us.'

He looked down, his voice low. 'Bonny's changed so much. I can't bear to see her so sick.'

'Bonny isn't sick! She's depressed because of Richard's death.'

'But he were only her brother!' Howard snapped. 'I'm her *husband*. And anyway, why didn't she turn to me? Why did she come 'ere, to you, bringing Milly?' His heavy features were flushed with anger. 'I love that woman, and her little 'un, but a man doesn't like to come second to anyone.'

'*Second*? Who's second?' Harris said, astonished. 'You're not coming second to me. It's just that Bonny and I have known each other a long time. And I knew Richard too –'

'Does she talk to you?'

'No, Bonny's not talking to anyone much.'

He looked down, baffled. 'I don't understand it. It's like I can't reach her, whatever I do. To be blunt, I don't know what I *can* do any more. That's why I don't come round so much. I'm no bloody help to anyone.'

Harris moved her chair closer to his. 'Howard, listen to me. Bonny *will* get well in time. She's had a bad shock, that's all. Some people react like this. But she'll recover. And she needs to know you're around. She's carrying your child –'

'Maybe it would be better if she weren't,' he said, his tone weary. 'I mean, what kind of life would it be for a kid with a crazy mother?'

'Now you listen to me!' Harris said, enraged. 'You're lucky to have Bonny as a wife and even luckier to have her bear your child. Don't sit there feeling sorry for yourself, Howard Waring, think about *her*. And about that baby of yours she's carrying. She needs you – don't you dare let her down. Because if you do, you'll have me to contend with.'

As the aunt of Richard and Bonny, Mrs Turner *could* have offered to look after Tom herself, but she was more than willing for Harris to take over that duty. 'I mean,' she said often, 'the Simonses have money to burn, and besides, it would be best for the little one's future.' As for her poor niece – well, what could an elderly widow like her do? Bonny was in the best hands with Miss Harris and Miss Irma. Best leave her where she was . . . It wasn't that Mrs Turner didn't care, but she couldn't handle so much trouble and was more than willing to pass it over.

'It's like it was meant all along,' she told Mr Lacy that evening. Even though they were finally married, she couldn't refer to him by his Christian name. He would be Mr Lacy to his grave. 'It's turned Miss Harris into another woman. She's looking after Tom like she was his real mother.'

Mrs Turner thought of Richard. Life was awful – so many

ups and downs you never knew where you were. People had expected the young to die in the war, but not in peacetime. It was cruel. Bloody cruel.

'And Miss Harris is minding Milly too, until our Bonny gets better and up and about again.' A twinge of guilt made her hurry on. 'I do help them all I can. You know, keeping the house nice, doing the washing. Oh, there's lots of that now. And I make good food for all of them.' She was relieved that she didn't have to pay for any of it. 'Milly loves my apple tart, and the little lad's getting a real appetite.'

'He likes your cooking?' Mr Lacy asked, wondering if Tom would ever see maturity.

'He *thrives* on it,' Mrs Turner replied, her thoughts shifting. 'I thought Bonny would have rallied by now. But she and Richard were that close it's like she's lost a part of herself. Not said more than a few words for weeks. And she was always talking before. Giving everyone lip . . .' Mrs Turner thought of her hated sister. 'Of course, Madge cares nothing about it! I dare say she can't even remember having children. If it doesn't come in a bottle with a label on the front, she's not interested.'

'It said in the paper that the driver of the lorry were responsible for the crash,' Mr Lacy offered. 'Bang into the side of that coach, he went. No one stood a chance. It's a miracle that little lad survived . . . Makes you wonder what it's all about, don't it? You're going off on holiday and something like that happens.'

'Will they put him in gaol?'

'I dunno. Maybe. But put in gaol or not, I'd not like to have all those deaths on my conscience.' He took a sip of his beer. 'What a world. You've just got to try and get through it with the least knocks you can.'

'You're a deep thinker,' Mrs Turner said, looking at her new husband with admiration. 'A deep thinker and no mistake. That's what working in the fresh air does for you.'

*   *   *

Having put two large balls of cotton wool in her ears to try to reduce the noise level, Irma lay on her bed and then tensed again. She was too old for all of this, she thought, hearing Tom's crying reverberate along the landing. Why did children cry so much? A moment later she could just catch the muffled sound of Harris running into the bedroom. A second later, Tom stopped crying.

Taking out the cotton wool, Irma stared up at the ceiling. Harris was proving to be a wonderful mother, Milly responding to her naturally, and Tom relying on her more as each day passed. What had seemed to be a disaster had turned out magnificently. But what was going to happen when Bonny got well again? The thought made Irma sit up in bed, her arms folded over the sheet. How would Harris respond when Bonny took over the care of her daughter again? And her nephew, Tom?

After all, that would have been what Richard and Penny expected. Damn and blast it! Irma thought, hearing the sound of a radio playing loudly from below. Didn't Harris realise that some people had to sleep? Jamming the cotton wool back into her ears, Irma looked at the clock: 11.15. 'The radio settles Tom if he wakes up again,' Harris told her repeatedly, 'that's why I put it on late.' She should try hitting him over the head with it, Irma thought. That would keep him quiet.

Realising that she wasn't going to sleep, Irma got out of bed and pulled on her dressing gown. Pottering down into the kitchen she paused on the landing and looked down the drive. There was a light on in the lodge. Saville would be drawing – pictures of his now fighting for space alongside Milly's. It had been a hard decision, but Irma had made sure that her brother was not allowed time alone with the children. It wasn't as though Saville was a danger, it was just that you could never be too sure . . . Thoughtfully she went to put the kettle on.

'Are you making tea?'

Frowning, Irma took out her ear plugs and stared at Harris. 'What?'

'Are you making tea? If you are, I'd love a cup.'

Nodding, Irma ladled more tea leaves into the pot. Her hair was pressed flat under her hairnet, thin ankles sticking out from under the heavy dressing gown, the cotton wool poking out of her pocket.

'Did Tom wake you?'

'Me, and most of the North of England,' Irma replied sarcastically, putting down the teapot. 'Harris, how long are you going to keep this up?'

'Keep what up?'

'Looking after two children and running your business?'

'I've got Catherine Wells managing the New Era now.'

'Is she any good?'

'She seems OK.'

'And when did you last go into Manchester, Harris?'

She shifted her feet awkwardly. 'Last week . . .'

'The week *before* last actually.'

Harris flinched. 'I thought you were the one who was always going on about me having a family –'

'*Your own family!*' Irma boomed. 'I didn't expect you to clog up the house with a selection of waifs and strays.'

'These *are* my family now,' Harris replied stiffly.

'And when Bonny recovers? When she wants Milly back, and when she takes over Tom?'

'But she won't want to take them back,' Harris replied half-heartedly, the dark shadows under her eyes. 'Bonny won't be able to cope with Milly, Tom *and* a new baby. She'll need me. Besides, Howard's not much help.'

'What d'you expect from a bus driver?'

Bemused, Harris shook her head. 'Bus drivers have children all the time, Irma. There isn't an unwritten law that says all men can have families except those who work for the Wigan Bus Company.'

Turning back to her tea, Harris stared into her cup. She was drowsy with tiredness, the last weeks more exhausting than any she had known. But she had relished every minute. Something in her had shifted; after the first anxious days she had begun to relax, her attention absorbed by the children in her care. They had become her life. Even when Milly was difficult, it was a challenge.

Beside her, Irma sipped her tea, thinking of the previous day. She had come home from work exhausted and decided on an early night. It was Harris's turn to do the accounts. Going upstairs, Irma had knocked on her niece's door, expecting to find her hard at work with the books. But Harris hadn't been there. Surprised, Irma had made her way to the makeshift nursery, opening the door and looking in.

On the large couch under the window Harris had been fast asleep, one arm round Milly, the other round Tom. Her usually immaculate make-up had worn off, her hair was dishevelled. Intrigued, Irma had studied her. So much for the accounts, she'd thought. Bookkeeping was obviously the last thing on her niece's mind. Frowning, Irma had looked from the sleeping children, back to Harris. So this was the high-flying career woman, was it? This was the woman who planned to open salons all around the North-West? Like hell, Irma thought.

Putting down her tea cup, her thoughts returned to the present. 'What about Bonny? When she gets better?'

Harris winced as though she had been pinched. 'What about her?'

Irma knew only too well that Harris didn't want Bonny to get better – to recover, of course, but not to get better enough to take the children away. All the disappointment of Harris's past had been annulled by them. They needed her and she was willing to give herself completely. But would she ever be ready to give them up?

'I want to call in a specialist,' Irma said suddenly. 'Someone to take another look at Bonny.'

'Why?' Harris asked, alerted. 'She'll come round in time. She's only depressed.'

'Bonny has been depressed for far too long,' Irma insisted. 'Do you really think that she's ever going to recover without help?'

'Dr Redmond said to leave her alone. Shock takes its own time,' Harris said emphatically. 'Bonny will recover when she's ready.'

'And then again, she might not,' Irma countered. 'Lionel Redmond doesn't know everything. I admit that I thought she'd snap out of it at first. But not now.'

'He said Bonny could recover any time. Tomorrow, any time –'

'Be that as it may, I've got Dr Samuels calling at the end of the week.'

Getting to her feet, Irma refilled their cups, then sat down again, the kitchen light draining all colour from her face.

'It's time to get Bonny well. Time to sort out the future for all of us.'

'But what if the future's bad?' Harris asked, her voice tight. 'Couldn't we leave it a little while longer?' she pleaded. 'Just a little longer?'

'No one can live in a make-believe world, Harris. You have to build on firm ground or nothing lasts. Bonny has to get well – and then we'll go from there.'

Harris was finding it hard to speak. 'And what happens if she takes Milly and Tom away? What if she goes back to Howard, and has her new baby? What then?'

'Then you carry on with your own life.'

'I don't want my own bloody life!' Harris snapped. 'I want to be part of their lives! I want to share my life with them. No one has ever needed me like those children do. Haven't

I done a good job? Well, *haven't I*? Bonny would be happy to know how well they are. Don't look at me like that! I never tried to cut her out. Every day I take Milly in to see her mother. It's not my fault that Bonny doesn't want to know!'

Hurriedly Irma moved over to her, but Harris stepped back.

'Those children need me! I've looked after them; they love me now. How can you talk about them going away? About losing them as easily as losing a couple of teeth? Milly and Tom mean everything to me. I can't let them go. Ever. Ever!'

And then Harris realised that Irma wasn't looking at her – but over her shoulder. Slowly, she turned and then turned away again, sitting down heavily.

In the doorway stood Bonny.

SIXTY-FOUR

Irma was the first to speak. 'How are you feeling, Bonny?'

'What d'you mean, you want my children?' she snapped at Harris, ignoring Irma completely. 'Milly's my child –'

Harris was on her feet in an instant. 'Bonny, I didn't mean it. It just sounded like that. I meant that –'

'You want my children!' Bonny repeated, her face chalk white, one hand clutching the back of a chair for support. 'You can't have them! They're mine. Tom's as much mine as Milly. Tom's Richard's child.' She stopped talking, the steam going out of her as she sat down. 'Where is he?'

'Who?' Harris asked softly.

'Richard.'

Taking the seat next to Bonny, Harris answered her. 'Richard's dead.'

'I know that! I mean, where's he buried? I don't remember the funeral.'

Frowning, Irma poured Bonny some tea. 'Drink that. It'll help.'

'Help *what*?' Bonny queried. 'My memory?'

'Well, if it doesn't help your memory, it'll flush out your kidneys,' Irma replied smartly, walking out of the kitchen.

A moment passed, Bonny sipping her tea, her bony hands

tight around the cup. Always thin, she was now gaunt, her cheeks hollowed out. And it was obvious that she was more than a little confused.

'Where's he buried?'

'St Anne's churchyard,' Harris replied. 'Penny's with him there.'

Nodding, Bonny sipped her tea again. 'I kept dreaming about him. It was a long time ago, and he had come home on leave, walking up the stairs at Madge's house . . . He was cutting his wrists and I was at the bottom of the stairs, trying to get to him in time.' Her voice shook. 'But I couldn't! I just kept running and running, but I never got to the top.'

'Richard died in an accident, Bonny. You couldn't have saved him.'

'He always said he would be there for me,' she replied distantly, 'but he wasn't. Like most men, he wasn't reliable. And he was my big brother; he should have looked out for me. But it was always me, looking out for him. He said he'd be there when Milly was born, but he wasn't. Held up somewhere. In the war . . .' She faded away, thinking about the past, then rallied. 'How long have I been here?'

'Six weeks.'

'Six weeks,' Bonny repeated, distantly. 'Where's Milly? Is Milly OK?'

'She's fine.'

'And Tom?'

'He's fine.'

'Milly must be on school holiday,' Bonny went on, rubbing her forehead as though she was trying to clear her thoughts. 'I should have been there for her. Was she upset? She must have thought I was crazy. But I was . . . I *was* crazy.'

'You're better now,' Harris replied cautiously, watching her. 'Soon you'll be back to your old self.'

'Why do you want the children?'

'Bonny, I just wanted to take care of them –'

'You can't take them from me –'

'I don't want them!' Harris assured her. 'I just got so fond of them.'

'But you can't have them!' Bonny snapped, moving away from Harris. 'You're always taking other people's things. Ben Ramsey was married to someone else and you took him.'

'I didn't!' Harris replied, stunned. 'He told me that he'd already left Eve. I only know now that *she* had left *him*.'

'He was still married to her, though,' Bonny countered, her eyes unfocused as though she was half asleep. 'And after all that, you couldn't keep him anyway. Poor Harris, you can never hold on to anything, can you? Not Jimmy, not Ben, and not the children. Milly's mine and I'm going to look after Tom. He's my nephew; I should look after him.'

Shocked by the verbal attack, Harris stared at the drowsy woman in front of her. 'All right, Bonny, whatever you say.'

'Well, I *do* say.' Her head rocked with tiredness. 'Tom is Richard's baby – Penny would want me to look after him.'

'I'm not going to fight you,' Harris replied, her tone rigid. 'I just wanted to do the best thing at the time. You needed help and I gave it to you.'

'But at what price?' Bonny replied, her blurry eyes accusing.

It was then that Harris realised Bonny was drugged, that the sedatives hadn't worn off. She was still half asleep, talking in a daze. Saying all the things Bonny would never have said normally. All the things Harris didn't want to hear.

'Well, *at what price*, Harris? If you'd married Richard, then the baby would have been *really* yours. But it's not – it's Penny and Richard's and *I'm* going to look after it. You'll have to find your own man and have your own children, Harris. Because you're not having these!'

Cowed by the attack, Harris stared down at the table. Bonny was right: she couldn't fight her for the children, and she wasn't going to. Her temporary contentment had been merely a greedy grasp at something that wasn't rightfully hers. The realisation was damning.

'You should get back to bed,' she said finally. 'You need sleep to get better, Bonny. And you have to think of the baby.'

'*The baby* . . .' Bonny repeated dreamily, looking round. 'Where's Howard? Why isn't he here?'

'He's working.'

'But he should be here now. I don't remember seeing him. Why isn't he here?'

'He'll come later.'

Rubbing her eyes viciously, Bonny looked round, bewildered. 'What happened? *What's happening to me?*'

'You're dreaming, Bonny. You're still asleep and none of this is really happening,' Harris lied, guiding Bonny upstairs and talking to her all the time. 'You and I are in a dream –'

'We're dreaming?'

'Yes,' Harris assured her. 'We're talking and walking in a dream. Soon you'll be back in bed and then you'll wake up later and you won't remember a thing. It will have gone from your mind, like so many dreams do.' Gently she settled her sick friend in bed. For a moment Harris stood in the doorway, her figure silhouetted against the light. 'Go to sleep now. We never had this conversation. We just met in a dream that wasn't real. Now, go to sleep and forget. In the morning you'll be with your children. But you have to rest now . . . It was just a dream, Bonny, that's all.'

Along the landing, hidden from sight, Irma was listening. She knew what it had cost Harris to let go, and admired her courage. And Bonny would never know what had happened. She would recover and take over the care of the children and never realise that – in a sedated haze – she had crucified her closest friend.

SIXTY-FIVE

At the New Era salon, the priggish Catherine Wells had managed to increase the takings by a quarter. She had also hired a junior and had the walls repainted. To her surprise, Harris wasn't annoyed by her actions. She had needed someone to whom she could delegate for long enough. Oh yes, Harris thought, the Manchester salon was in capable hands with Catherine. Now she could open another one.

Over the last fortnight Bonny had recovered steadily. Her depression had shifted, and although she was still weepy about Richard, her irritation with Howard jolted her back into life. What the hell was he playing at? Bonny had asked Harris only a week earlier. I'm having his child. He should be helping me out more.

As predicted, Bonny never remembered their conversation and was always telling Harris how grateful she was for her help. You've been a hell of a friend, she said often. I would have folded without you. God, I owe you so much . . . And Harris never said anything that implied that losing the children would tear the heart out of her. Instead she tried to reorganise her life. She had been a businesswoman once, she would be again. And it was not as though she wouldn't see Milly and Tom; she would always be a part of their lives. Just not as large a part as she had hoped.

Her thoughts returning to work, Harris watched as the efficient Catherine polished the mirrors, two clients sitting under dryer hoods.

'Harris?'

Turning at the sound of her name, she saw a man standing at the top of the stairs. For a moment Harris thought her eyes were deceiving her – but it *was* Jimmy, turning his hat round in his hands as he always used to.

'Jimmy!' she said, with pleasure. 'How good to see you.' Then she stopped. What a stupid thing to say. How could he possibly be pleased to see her?

'I came with some papers about this place. Some letters you should have had for your files.' He paused, then added awkwardly, 'I was just passing and thought I'd drop them in.'

I was just passing . . . How *could* she have jilted this man? How *could* she have left him for Ben Ramsey?

'Come into the back, Jimmy,' she said, showing him through and closing the door. 'How have you been?'

'Fine,' he mumbled, offering her the papers. 'I *really* was just passing.'

Harris could tell at once that he wasn't comfortable.

'I've wanted to say something for a while, Jimmy. I wanted to apologise.'

His voice was the slow drawl it always had been. 'There's no need.'

'Yes, there is,' she said awkwardly. 'I treated you so badly and you didn't deserve it.'

'You hurt me a lot, Harris,' he admitted, 'but life goes on. It's all in the past now.'

He paused, his hat still in his hands. The easiness between them had gone. *She* had done that, Harris realised. She had thrown away a good man – and a friend. For nothing.

'Would you like a cup of tea, Jimmy?'

He shook his head. 'No, I should be going.'

What could she expect? Harris thought. It was a miracle that he was even talking to her.

'What happened with you and Ben Ramsey – I'm sorry,' Jimmy said, his tone strained. 'No man should hit a woman. You should have prosecuted him, Harris. I'd have given you advice. Even taken the case on for you.' He smiled wryly. 'You see, always touting for business.'

Returning the smile, Harris glanced away. 'I didn't want to prosecute. Anyway, Ramsey's been struck off now and he's on his uppers. I just wanted to move on, wanted to put it behind me. People had talked about me enough.' Her words were all coming out wrong, as though the whole episode had been a bit of unpleasantness that was quickly dismissed. Looking back to Jimmy, she held his gaze. 'God, Jimmy, I'm so sorry. Running off like that was –'

'The past,' he said firmly, moving to the door. 'I just wanted to say that I'm glad you're all right. And I admire the way you've helped Bonny out.'

'Richard's death shook us all.'

'It shook me too, I liked him,' Jimmy replied, Harris eager to keep the conversation going.

'How are your parents?'

'Fine.'

'I hear you're seeing someone. Is she nice?'

There was a momentary pause before Jimmy answered, 'Lydia's good fun.'

Nodding, Harris pointed towards the kettle. 'Are you sure you don't want some tea?'

'No, I have to be going.'

'Of course.'

Not knowing what else to say, Harris hesitated, Jimmy turning to leave.

'Jimmy . . .'

He turned back to her. 'What?'

'Thank you,' she said simply, struggling to find the right

words. 'Thank you for bringing me the papers. And for being so kind ... I just want to say thank you. For everything.'

He looked at her, and then, unexpectedly, he winked.

'We had some good times, didn't we? Let's leave it at that, hey? Look after yourself, Harris. And be happy.'

Recovery for Bonny was rapid. Her sedation had been reduced and her crying jags were now infrequent. She had begun to look after Milly again, surprised to find that Tom cried fretfully for Harris whenever she went into work. But there was always Mrs Turner to help out, her aunt relieved by the prospect that soon life would return to normal. Less worry, less work, less laundry. As ever, Irma kept her distance, the children realising early on that the strange thin woman wasn't a ready playmate. But Bonny would never hear a word against Irma. She had let her into Deerheart House willingly; Harris and Irma Simons coming up trumps when her husband's devotion had been erratic.

'Well, hello there,' Bonny said sarcastically when Howard walked in in his driver's uniform one afternoon. 'Look what the cat dragged in.'

'Now don't start –'

'Don't start!' she snapped. 'Where the hell have you been, Howard Waring? You're my husband – not that anyone would know it.'

'I came to see you yesterday.'

'And stayed for twenty minutes.'

'I had to go to work –'

'Hah!' Bonny snorted.

Howard paused, then grinned, showing his perfect teeth. 'You're a bit cranky, aren't you? More like your old self.' He slung an arm around her shoulder. 'You're better now; you can come home soon.'

'Now that Irma and Harris have got me better –'

'Oh, let it drop!' Howard said, exasperated. 'I did what I thought was the best. How many times do I have to apologise?'

Mollified, Bonny stared at him. 'I missed you.'

'I missed you,' Howard replied, kissing her on the cheek as Bonny rested her hand on her stomach.

'We have to think about the future now, Howard, not the past. Richard's death was terrible, but there's a new baby coming. And there's Tom to think about.'

Tom . . . Sitting down, Howard took off his bus driver's cap and ran his hands through his sandy hair.

'Is Tom coming to live with us?'

'Of course he is!' Bonny replied, surprised. 'He's my nephew – where else could he go?'

'But we've already got Milly and there's the new baby on the way. We haven't room –'

Stunned, she stared at him. 'Howard, I know this is going to be a bit difficult for you, but I can't abandon Tom. He's my flesh and blood.'

'But he's not mine,' Howard replied quietly. 'Look, I took Milly on and that were fine, but another kid that's not mine – well, it's pushing it, Bonny. We've got our own baby coming in a few months. Isn't that enough?'

'Tom's not a bloody stray!' Bonny shouted. 'What am I supposed to do with him? Jesus, Howard, we *have* to look after him.'

Bowing his head, Howard mumbled something inaudible.

'Oh, speak up!' Bonny snapped.

'I were just wondering how all this might affect us . . . you know, our marriage.'

The threat slid across the wooden table and jammed Bonny under the ribs. So that was it, she thought. Her husband was asking her to choose. Leaning back in her seat, she sighed, her eyes closing momentarily. It had been so bloody hard bringing up Milly alone. She had thought when she married Howard that the bad times were over. But now here she was being forced to make a choice – to save her marriage and give up her nephew, or to keep Tom and see her marriage fold.

'You're a bastard, Howard.'

'Hey!'

'You're a bastard,' Bonny repeated, her tone dull.

She loved the man sitting next to her, and he had been a great stepfather to Milly. So was it fair to ask more of him? But then again, was it fair of him to ask her to choose? I like being married, Bonny thought desperately, I like having my own man, my security. But Tom's my nephew, Richard's child. I can't give him up . . . Years of lonely motherhood stretched out before her. Struggling to bring up Milly, Tom and the new baby. Alone. Wasn't she entitled to some happiness? *Some* bloody peace?

'I've got to go, luv,' Howard said, getting to his feet. 'I have to get back to work. Just think about it.'

'About what?' Bonny asked, hoping that he would explain and show her that she had misunderstood.

But she hadn't.

'Think about our marriage . . .' He stroked the nape of her neck gently. 'I love you and I love Milly. And I *really* want our baby. But Tom's not mine and I don't feel that I have to take him in too.' He hurried on, 'We don't have enough bloody room, for a start!'

Immobile, Bonny stared at him, disappointment etched in her face.

'We don't have enough money either, luv. Kids cost money, they need things. Three kids would break us.'

Her voice fell. 'Jesus, Howard, what if they had been *your* three kids?'

A long instant passed before he answered her.

'But they're *not*. Are they?'

SIXTY-SIX

Sitting by the front window of the lodge, Saville looked out longingly. During the past weeks he had seen children around, usually with Harris. A little girl and a toddler. This was incredible! he thought. Soon he would have new friends. It was like the time when Harris arrived at Deerheart House all those years before . . . But the weeks had passed and although Harris had visited often, the children never came.

His attention centred suddenly on the entrance to the drive, Harris walking through the gate and waving to him. Ducking past Mrs Biddy, Saville ran outside. The honeysuckle was in full bloom, the garden perfumed, heavy with leaf.

'Hello there, Saville,' Harris said, kissing him on the cheek. 'I was going to call in later to see you.'

'Where are they?' he asked, his dark eyes darting round.

'Who?'

'The children,' he replied, his voice still a boy's voice, although his hair was now grey, his walrus moustache white-flecked. 'I've seen children around. Playing in the garden. I knocked on the window once, to ask them in, but they ran off.'

From the start, Irma had made sure that Mrs Biddy under-stood her orders. On no account was Mr Simons to be allowed to play with the children. Why? Mrs Biddy had countered bravely. Mr Simons is no risk to anyone, including children. He's still on his medication and, besides, he's getting old.

Harris put it more bluntly. 'Irma, how could you even think it? Saville's never hurt children, you know that. He's harmless. He just exposed himself once –'

Irma expression was pained. 'Don't mention that! I am well aware of his little . . . adventure.'

'But it wasn't to do with children.'

'I don't want to talk about it!'

'But children weren't involved,' Harris had retorted vehemently. 'Saville's never been interested in children. You know that.'

'Maybe so, and maybe not,' Irma had replied. 'But I'm not risking it. Saville's not normal –'

'He's just retarded, Irma. He's like a child. Besides – not that I think he even needs it any more – he's medicated.' Her tone softened. 'You know how much he loves children. He was so good with me. Oh, let him see the kids, *please*.'

But Irma had been adamant; 'You visit him and I'll visit him. But the children stay away from Saville.'

Harris remembered the conversation only too well as Saville looked at her expectantly, waiting for her answer. It was all right for Irma to lay down the law, but it was never her aunt who had to impose it.

'The children are just visiting,' Harris told her uncle finally. 'They'll be going soon.'

The words pained her as much as they pained him. But for different reasons.

'But I drew some pictures!' Saville blurted out. 'I could show them to the children.'

'I'll show them to the children before they go.'

He paused, then said sadly, 'I'm not going to see them, am I?'

Harris hesitated, shaking her head. 'No, Saville, you're not.'

Disappointed, he nodded, then looked at his niece again, his expression serious. 'If you had a child, could I see *your* baby?'

'Oh, Saville,' Harris said, reaching out for his hand and squeezing it. 'Of course you could see *my* baby!'

Relieved, he smiled and then moved off, satisfied. In a moment he would forget their conversation, Harris thought. If only she could forget so easily.

Having walked back into Deerheart House she took off her jacket and moved into the drawing room. Irma wasn't home, that much was obvious from the selection of children's toys all over the carpet.

'Oh, it's you,' Bonny said, walking in and picking up the toys. 'I thought it was Irma.'

'Just me.' Harris sat down and kicked off her shoes. 'I saw Jimmy today.'

'Oh . . .' Bonny said, letting the toys drop from her hands and flopping down on the sofa. 'How was he?'

'He was nice, but a bit remote. Told me that I had nothing to apologise about. The past is the past. But he managed to infer that there could never be anything between us again. Just in case I'd wondered. He's toughened up, has Jimmy . . .' she frowned. 'He's seeing someone.'

'I told you.'

'I know. Now he's told me too.'

'Do you mind?' Bonny asked.

'How could I? I have no claim on him.' She looked over at Bonny, suddenly alerted. 'Are you all right?'

'I saw Howard today.' Harris said nothing, Bonny hurrying on, 'He's finding all of this very hard. You know, men. They can't handle things as well as women . . . He . . . Oh God, I don't know what to do.'

At once, Harris leaned forward. 'What is it?'

'I love him.'

'But?'

504

'I don't want to be alone again,' Bonny said, averting her eyes. 'I know it's selfish, but I don't want to be alone. I like being married, being respectable. He's looking forward to the new baby so much . . .'

'But?' Harris said again, frowning.

'I should pop up and see to Milly —'

'No, Bonny, talk to me,' Harris urged her. 'There's something on your mind. Tell me.'

'I owe you so much, I can't ever repay you for what you've done. You and Irma.' Her eyes rolled. 'I mean, who would have thought your aunt would have been so supportive? She didn't *have* to help me.'

'Irma always surprises people. It's one of her best traits,' Harris answered. 'You don't have to thank her, or me. We did what was right. You would have helped us.'

'But men don't think like that, do they?'

'Is this about Howard?'

'He was . . . he *is* so good with Milly,' Bonny hurried on. 'He took her on and helped me look after her. Never a word about how she wasn't his. Not many men would have done that. All he wanted was for me to have his child.'

Anxiously, Harris reacted. 'Is the baby OK?'

'Fine . . . fine . . .' Bonny's thin fingers toyed with the cuff of her cardigan. 'But Howard doesn't think he can take on Tom. I want to! He's my nephew and Richard's child, but Howard will leave me if I do.' Bonny kept talking frantically. 'Jesus, what kind of cow am I? Tom's my flesh and blood, I should tell Howard to bugger off. But I can't. I love him. I want him. I want to stay with him for the rest of my life . . .' Tears were beginning, falling down her hollow cheeks. 'I wanted to say – clear off, you sod, you're not making me choose – but I couldn't. What kind of woman does that make me?'

Frowning, Harris put her arm around Bonny's shoulder. 'Give him time. He'll come round.'

'No, he won't,' Bonny said quietly. 'I know Howard. He's

not going to budge. If I take Tom on, he'll leave.'

Don't think it! Harris urged herself, don't even think it. Tom is not your child. *Tom is not yours.*

Embarrassed, Bonny wiped her face with the back of her hand and sat up. 'I'm sorry, you don't need any more bloody nonsense from me. I'll sort it out –'

'Let me have him.'

The words were out of Harris's mouth before she could stop them.

'What?'

'Let me have Tom. Please, Bonny, let me take him on. I love him and he cares for me, I know he does. You said how he cries when I go out to work. Please.' She grabbed Bonny's hands tightly. 'I'll be a good mother, I won't let you down. I'm not stupid any more. Let me help you.'

Hesitating, Bonny looked at her. She had hoped beyond hope that this would happen, but now it had she was stuck for words.

'I was going to ask you to take him,' Bonny said at last. 'I was so hoping you would. God, Harris, *would you*? Would you really? Richard loved you so much, if he'd not been such a bloody fool he would have spoken up earlier and you two would have married. Tom would have been your real son then.' She swallowed, looking down at her stomach. 'Am I doing the right thing? God, Harris, *am* I? But this baby has to have its father. It needs Howard. Milly never had a father. I have to give *this* baby the best chance.'

'And you have to give Tom the best chance too,' Harris said firmly. 'Let me adopt him, Bonny. He'll always be your nephew, but I could make him my child legally. Oh, please let me! It would make up for so much. For all the lousy things I've done, for not loving Richard, for hurting him. Please, let me do one good thing. I have money, this house, I can give Tom the best education, the best start in life. And I can love him, Bonny, *I can love him so much.*'

A moment passed before Bonny spoke again.

'Would he be called Thomas Baker, or Thomas Simons?'

Hardly able to reply, Harris said softly, 'You choose.'

SIXTY-SEVEN

Mr Lacy was leaning on his shovel when Mrs Turner ran down the garden, waving a tea towel to get his attention. Wincing as he straightened up, he smiled a greeting.

''Lo there.'

'You'll never guess what's happened!' Mrs Turner said, beside herself with excitement. 'Miss Harris is going to adopt Tom!'

'Tom who?'

'My Tom!' she said impatiently. 'Richard's lad. Isn't it wonderful? I mean, look at this place, the Simonses are worth a fortune, the little lad will want for nothing.'

'But Miss Harris isn't wed. She's not got a man.'

'Oh, what's she need a man for!' Mrs Turner said dismissively. 'A woman like her doesn't need a fella. She's got the hairdressing salons, money, and now she'll have her own son. Why does she need a flaming man?'

Mr Lacy frowned. 'Why did you need a man then?'

'That's different!' Mrs Turner snapped back. 'Miss Harris has never had any luck with men. Everyone knows that. She'll end up like her aunts, a spinster –'

'She's too bonny for that.'

Mrs Turner sniffed. 'Bonny or not, I reckon Miss Harris is

508

off men for life. Besides, she doesn't need a man to look after her. She can look after herself.'

'So she'll be Tom's mother?'

Mrs Turner nodded. Oh, this was good news. One more worry off her shoulders. As for Madge, well, she'd gone to tell her all about it at the hospital, but her sister couldn't take anything in. She had looked bad, had Madge . . . Still, that wasn't going to stop her from getting her money's worth out of this bit of good fortune. One of her relatives ending up a Simons! Hell's bells!

'Think of it. Miss Harris will be Tom's mother. Our Tom, one of the Simonses –'

'I thought you said they were an odd bunch,' Mr Lacy offered cautiously. 'What with Saville and all –'

She cut him off. Money made everyone respectable. 'They're good enough for me! Oh yes, to see our Tom living the high life . . . that's good enough for me.'

The news that Tom was going to be adopted by Harris Simons was all over town by the weekend. Harris Simons, some said, was she the right person? Others were delighted. A single Harris Simons was a threat; as a mother she was somehow suddenly sexless.

Even Gladys Leonards was magnanimous. 'She proved herself when she took in those children. Everyone should have a second chance. Personally, I always liked the girl.'

'She's not exactly a girl,' the stout Mrs Ramsbottom replied, dropping her voice so that Irma wouldn't hear her in the back of the salon. 'I mean, she must be coming up for thirty before long. An old maid, like the other two. No man wants a woman with her reputation, or at her age. I reckon Harris Simons has decided that motherhood is the most she can get out of life.'

'Motherhood without the stretch marks . . . Can't be bad,' Mrs Leonards replied, looking up as Irma walked over to her.

'We were just saying that it was wonderful news about Harris adopting the little Baker boy.'

'He'll be Thomas *Simons* soon,' Irma replied, knowing full well that everyone was gossiping again. Well, let them, she thought. Life hadn't turned out the way she had planned for Harris, but at least she had a child. Who would have believed *that* a while back? 'We need some new male blood in the Simons family.'

'Well, you would. With Saville being –'

'How's that tint doing?' Irma replied, cutting off Mrs Ramsbottom in mid-flow. 'You did want to be red, didn't you?'

Mrs Ramsbottom panicked at once. '*Red!* I never said red, Irma. I don't want to be a redhead.'

'Lucky I used a blonde rinse then, wasn't it?' Irma replied, delighted to see the flush spread over Mrs Ramsbottom's fleshy jowls. 'I was just joking. You know me – always one for a joke.'

Smiling wickedly, she walked away again. There was a male in the Simons household, *an heir*. Now that was more like it. There hadn't been a proper heir since Gideon left. After all, Saville was hardly a credit to the family name . . . Irma had to admit that the toys, the broken nights and the dug-up garden plants weren't to her liking, but still, childhood only lasted so long. And Harris was looking after the boy, not her.

For the first time in years, Irma hummed under her breath. *Thomas Simons, heir to the Simons fortune.* Thomas Simons, surgeon. Thomas Simons, solicitor, Thomas Simons, Admiral . . . oh, it was all satisfying.

So much to look forward to. At last.

It was a boiling hot May afternoon when Harris took Tom down to Mesnes Park. A crowd of people were collected around the bandstand to listen to a selection of dance tunes, several couples dancing on the grass. In his pushchair, Tom kept calling out to Harris and she would stop to point out the ducks. Or the water. Or the trees. The world seemed fresh to her again.

She didn't need a man, Harris told herself, she was content for the first time in her life. *Alone*. Guiltily she remembered that she hadn't been into the salon for two days. Well, Catherine could cope, Harris thought. She didn't need to go in everyday, did she? But it hadn't been *that* long ago that Harris had been obsessed by work. In the days after Ben Ramsey, and the days before Tom.

Stopping to put the brake on the pram, Harris sat down on a park bench, the music from the bandstand lilting on the warm air.

'Lovely child,' a woman said suddenly, looking at Tom and then glancing back to Harris. 'He looks like you.'

A rush of pride threatened to choke her as Harris smiled and readjusted the canopy over the buggy. *He looked like her* . . . A memory came back unannounced: Richard and her walking through the same park many years earlier. Bonny had just fallen off a wall and was sulking behind them, Richard talking about how he would get a car one day. But he never did. Richard never got his car, or his shop. *But Tom would.* Tom would have everything his father hadn't had. Money, status, opportunity.

Oh yes, Harris thought to herself, I'm going to make sure your son has everything, Richard. *Everything*. Who needed a man to make a child feel secure? Hadn't she grown up with two women? Men were unlucky for her – better to leave well alone. She had Tom now. *He* was her life.

'Well, fancy seeing you here.'

Shielding her eyes from the sun, Harris looked up. 'Hello there, Jimmy.'

Without asking, he sat down next to her. A male friend she *would* like, Harris thought. And what better male figure to have around than Jimmy Henshaw? Jimmy, who was promised to another woman, Jimmy who had no interest in her any more. Jimmy, who was safe.

'I saw you walking Tom around. You looked like you'd been doing it all your life,' he said, tipping his head back to catch the sun. 'It's hot today. Wonder how long it'll last?'

'They said it would break in a couple of days,' Harris replied, offering Tom a biscuit. 'What are you doing here?'

'Walking.'

'Why?'

'I like to walk, it keeps me in shape,' Jimmy replied, teasing her. 'Sitting at a desk all day can ruin a man's figure.'

She laughed, totally relaxed.

'How's Irma?'

'Terrifying.'

'Nothing changes then,' Jimmy retorted, looking at Tom. 'You're a fine lad. A really fine boy.' Then he turned back to Harris. 'I'm going to get working on the adoption papers next week. It shouldn't take too long – I mean, no one's opposing it.'

Harris sighed, looking down the slope to the bandstand. 'I can't wait for the day when I can say that Tom is mine. *My son . . .*'

'Sounds good.'

'You'll have your own children soon, Jimmy.'

'I guess I will,' he replied, his gaze still fixed on the horizon. 'After all, I'm getting engaged.'

She winced at the words, but kept the shock out of her voice. 'That's wonderful, Jimmy.'

He nodded, staring ahead. 'I was wondering how to ask her. Thought I'd have a word with you. You know, womanly advice.'

Was he taunting her? Harris wondered. No, not Jimmy. What they had had was over. In his eyes he was Harris Simons's friend now, nothing more. And friends ask advice of each other. Just as he was doing now.

But it was still agonising.

'Should I take her out for a meal?'

Harris could hear the sound of the circus as if it was yesterday – and the kid wailing about his chips. Who would have imagined that years later she would be sitting on a park bench, giving advice to Jimmy about how to propose to another woman?

'You *could* take her out, Jimmy. Or just pick a quiet spot and surprise her,' Harris replied, fiddling with the blanket on Tom's pushchair.

'Maybe I could take her out for a walk. The weather's good at the moment . . .' He paused, then mercifully changed the subject. 'I heard that Madge Baker had died.'

Harris nodded.

'How's Bonny taking it?'

'She's OK. She wasn't close to her mother,' Harris replied. 'No one was close to Madge.'

'She was a rough woman. Working the streets like that, you need a thick skin.'

'And she certainly had that,' Harris agreed. 'God, I can remember her when I was a kid. All that make-up she used to wear and then later I'd see her touting for business on the street corners.'

'My mother used to tell me stories about Madge Baker,' Jimmy said, taking off his jacket and laying it over the back of the bench. 'It nearly killed her when she knew I was friendly with Richard!' he laughed. 'It all seems so stupid now, doesn't it?'

Frowning, Harris turned to him. 'What does?'

'How people judge other people. Who are the right people to know, and who you're told to avoid.'

'Like me?' she teased him.

A moment passed between them, Jimmy not replying, Harris looking at the dancing couples on the bank below them.

'D'you want to dance?' he said suddenly.

'What!' she laughed. 'Here?'

'Why not? Other people are doing it.'

'They're kids.'

'Well, let's show them what the old folk can do!' Jimmy said, laughing as he hauled Harris to her feet.

Taking her hand, he then slid his other arm around her back and pulled her to him. Their bodies touched, but innocently, Jimmy staring over Harris's head as the music lulled them. He had danced with her like this a long time ago, when they were engaged. In his arms, Harris suddenly wanted to cry and break away. To say – keep your distance, you're with someone else now. I might deserve it, but don't hurt me. Please don't hurt me.

Any day now he was going to propose to another woman, and then any link between them would be severed for ever. He might think they could stay friends, but Harris doubted it. Wives come before friends, always. She would never dance with him again. Never hold him again. She would just hear over the years about how the Henshaws were doing, and how their children were growing up. She might even pass Mrs Henshaw in Market Street, or watch Jimmy draw up at the traffic lights in his car. Someone else's husband, someone else's father. Out of her reach. Forever.

For an aching moment Harris wanted to hold on to him, to prevent the inevitable. But then the music stopped.

She stepped back, suddenly embarrassed. 'I should go home now.'

Jimmy nodded. 'So should I.'

Flicking the brake off the pushchair, Harris glanced over her shoulder and forced herself to smile. 'I forgot how well you danced.'

And then she turned and walked off. In the opposite direction, without looking back.

SIXTY-EIGHT

Harris looked out of the window, shivering. 'If there's one thing I hate, it's wind.'

'Eat fewer sprouts,' Irma said drily.

'You're very chipper,' Harris replied, glancing over to her aunt. 'I thought Tom's crying kept you up most of the night?'

'It did. But then an old vampire like me hardly needs sleep,' Irma responded, picking up her hat and coat. 'I think we should get a car, Harris. Mildred always wanted a car, but she would have been a terrible driver. You could learn to drive. I mean, when I look at all the idiots on the road, it can't be that hard.'

'It would make life easier and that's a fact,' Harris agreed. 'I could take us out for days.'

'No, you could take *Tom* out for days,' Irma corrected her. 'Having the house to myself would be a treat for me now.' Walking to the door, she pulled on her hat and coat.

'You're not going out in this?'

'Of course I am, Harris. A bit of rain never hurt anyone,' Irma replied dismissively. 'But don't take Tom out, he's too little.'

Smiling, Harris watched her aunt walk down the drive, an umbrella pulled low over her head. Irma should retire, she thought, take it more easy. After all, Catherine Wells was running the New Era and Harris could manage the Wigan salon if she employed some more help. As for getting another salon, time would tell . . . It would be nice for Irma to put her feet up and have a rest, instead of running around at her age. They might not have Bonny around for much longer, but there were plenty of women looking to learn a skill; never a shortage of hairdressing trainees.

Stretching, Harris then let her arms fall by her sides. Tom was in the kitchen; she could hear Mrs Turner talking to him. Yes, she thought, she would advertise for some youngsters, start to get things organised . . . Suddenly Harris remembered how important the salons had been to her once.

She remembered the weeks before she had opened the New Era in Manchester. The hours she had spent in Kendal Milne, agonising over the colour of the towels and the blinds. No curtains for her – she wanted the new look. Blinds. No one else had blinds; she was to be the first. Just like no one else had navy-blue flooring. 'You're mad,' Irma had said. 'It'll show every mark.' And it did. Then there had been the machinery . . . Harris smiled at the memory. She had cajoled every manufacturer from Wigan to Bradford to get the most efficient hair dryer. I want the best, she had said repeatedly. Only the best.

So many hours had passed in that salon, preparing, scrubbing, polishing. Then there had been the opening, the new clients, the buzz of success. Harris had created her own little empire. And she wanted to *keep* that empire – but it wasn't the most important thing in her life any more.

Now there was Tom. Hadn't she heard only the other day that you had to put your child's name down early for a good school? She would have to look into that. Tom was to have the best education available. If it was important for a woman, it was vital for a man. Would he be bright? Harris wondered suddenly. Richard had had common sense, but he hadn't been intellectual. As for Penny, she hadn't been interested in anything other than being a wife and mother.

Still, there was no rush. She had all the time in the world with Tom. Soon the adoption papers would go through and he would be hers in the eyes of the world. Who cared if he was brilliant or downright stupid? He was hers. And that was all that mattered.

Putting down the phone, Jimmy Henshaw was thoughtful. Normally his father looked after the Cloughs' legal matters, but this time he asked his son to cover for him, pleading an unshakeable cold. Jimmy doubted the story – his father wasn't one to let a cold get in the way of business. Still frowning, Jimmy looked at the photograph on his desk. An attractive young woman smiled out of the frame at him, Lydia Owen. Just the kind of woman his parents would love as a daughter-in-law. Just the kind of woman to make a good wife and mother.

Over the months they had been seeing each other, the hints had become more and more obvious, Jimmy's mother pressing him to bring Lydia round more.

'She's so pleasant, such a straightforward girl,' Mrs Henshaw had said. 'A girl any man would be proud of. When I looked at you the other day, I thought what a lovely couple you made. Honestly, Jimmy, I wouldn't hang around. A girl like that gets snapped up quickly enough.'

She was right and, besides, Jimmy had grown to be very fond of Lydia. The proposal, however, hadn't quite come off. They were supposed to meet the previous evening, but Lydia had cried off with a sore throat. Fine, Jimmy thought, he'd ask her at the weekend. What difference did a few days make? They were going to spend their lives together – what was the damn rush?

Turning back to work, Jimmy picked up the Clough file and began to read, preparing himself for the coming appointment. He had expected that it would be Sydney who was coming, but had been told that it was Birdie on her way.

'Did she say what she wanted?' Jimmy asked his secretary, the ever-smitten Joanie.

'No, just that she wanted to have a talk with you. And you had a spare half-hour. Are you ready for her?'

'Ready and waiting,' Jimmy replied, taking his feet off his desk and then nodding. 'Show her in.'

The first thing Jimmy noticed about Birdie Clough was how much she had changed. The Cloughs had been acquaintances of his parents for many years and Jimmy had seen Birdie often, but never, until that moment, had he realised just how old she was. Much of her preening prettiness had soured, even the light colours she had once favoured had given way to grey. But the mechanical charm hadn't changed.

'Jimmy, how lovely to see you,' Birdie sang in her lilting brogue. 'So kind of your father to put me in your capable hands.'

Guiding her to a seat, Jimmy moved back to his own.

'What can I do for you, Mrs Clough?'

'Well.' She paused, her crafty mind working overtime. Her confusion had to look convincing. 'Much as I like you, my dear boy, you might not be the right person to talk to about a very delicate matter. I mean, it does, in a way, affect you. And you might find yourself – without meaning to be, but being, none the less, biased.'

'I'm a solicitor,' Jimmy replied evenly, 'I can't be biased.'

'Unless you had some interest in the parties involved.'

Jimmy frowned and leaned across the desk. 'I'll tell you what, Mrs Clough, why don't you tell me what this is all about and I'll tell you if I'm the right person to help you.'

'But then you would know all –'

He cut her off at once. 'Anything you tell me in this office is in the strictest confidence, Mrs Clough, I won't breathe a word of it to anyone.'

Smiling, she seemed to relax. Time to settle a few scores, Birdie thought. This was going to be very enjoyable.

'You know that my daughter married Dr Ben Ramsey?' Jimmy flinched at the name, but said nothing. 'Of course you do: everyone in the town knows about that monster. Well, Eve left him when she discovered he was using drugs of some sort . . .'

Jimmy could feel the collar around his neck begin to tighten. He didn't want to hear any more, but he knew he couldn't back out.

'He was a vile man and my daughter was afraid of him.' She paused to check Jimmy's response, amazed that his face was expressionless. 'As you also know he went off with Harris Simons. Well, to cut a long story short, Ben Ramsey has been struck off by the Medical Council and my daughter is getting a divorce.'

'And?'

She was relishing his discomfort. 'Look, Jimmy, this really is *very* difficult. I think I should talk to your father when he's better.'

But Jimmy wasn't going to let her escape. There was something about Birdie Clough that infuriated him. He knew from his parents how angry Birdie had been when the marriage went bad: the fact that Ben Ramsey had let Birdie down being more important than anything he had done to Eve. But what did she want now? Ramsey was finished – surely even Birdie had had enough revenge?

'Mrs Clough, please go on.'

'But, Jimmy –'

He was suddenly impatient and about to snap at her when the telephone rang.

Watching Jimmy talk, Birdie smiled to herself. No one knew she had come to Henshaw, Crabbe and Henshaw, and if she played her cards right, no one would ever know. Sydney might be happy with the way things had turned out, but she wasn't. Her daughter was back home, with a failed marriage behind her, and little chance of making a good match as a divorcee. The dream of Birdie bragging about her son-in-law, the *consultant*, and her grandchildren was over. Her son-in-law had shamed her, and there were no grandchildren to soften the blow.

Birdie could have just about endured the showing up if there had been a child to compensate. But there was no grandson. All she had was a sulking daughter back home and a life of unbearable tedium stretching before her. Birdie didn't care much for Sydney and she actively disliked Eve now – her daughter had let her down. And Birdie was tired of people letting her down.

The only high spot had been Harris Simons coming to grief. 'Serves her damn well right,' Birdie had told her husband at the time. 'The bitch had it coming, breaking up Eve's marriage.' It was no good Sydney telling her that the marriage had already been over – the truth was not what Birdie wanted to hear. Neither had she wanted to hear – a few months later – that Harris Simons had turned into a saint.

The woman everyone had been so eager to despise, was suddenly an angel of mercy. Nobly, she was going to adopt the orphaned Baker boy. The news had ripped into Birdie like a razor blade. Harris Simons had won again. The bitch had recovered her reputation and was now going to adopt a child. It was plain to see what Harris Simons was up to. What a perfect home for him at Deerheart House, and a perfect mother in Harris. After all, hadn't she proved herself now? And hadn't the Simonses enough money to give the boy a wonderful life? No one questioned Harris any more. She wasn't the smitten fool any longer, or the woman who had been beaten senseless by her lover – she was a saint.

A bloody saint! Birdie thought, fury threatening to choke her. How stupid could people be? Well, she wasn't going to sit around and see the woman who had been a thorn in her flesh for longer than she cared to remember triumph over her. She wasn't going to let Harris have everything – money, respect *and a child*. Birdie was going to stop her, once and for all, using whoever – and whatever – was needed.

Finishing his call, Jimmy put down the phone. 'Sorry about that. You were saying?'

'That I should go,' Birdie replied, knowing he would stop her. 'I really would like to wait until your father recovers.'

'But didn't he tell you that I'm taking over your family's affairs now?' Jimmy said smoothly, astonished by the lie that had escaped so easily from his lips. He wasn't deceitful by nature, but something told him he had to fight fire with fire now. 'Please tell me what's troubling you.'

Feigning anxiety, Birdie looked at him. So you want to hear it, do you? All right, Mr Henshaw Jnr, we'll see what you're made of.

'I am very anxious about something. You know I'm on a number of committees – charity work and other social concerns – well, we aim to look out for everyone in the community. Especially children.' She paused, Jimmy watching her. 'The deaths of Richard and Penny Baker were tragic, an awful thing to happen. But we were wondering about their son. To be blunt, Mr Henshaw, many of us feel that Harris Simons is not the best person to bring up a child.'

'I disagree with you,' Jimmy replied coldly.

'You surprise me. After all, she ruined your life. But then again, maybe marrying her would have been worse. Besides jilting you, she also wrecked my daughter's marriage –'

'Mrs Clough –'

She cut him off immediately. Jimmy Henshaw was a no one; she could eat him for breakfast.

'Whether you agree with me and my associates about Miss Simons or not, there's another matter that you can hardly dismiss. *Saville Simons*.'

Shaken, Jimmy stared at her. What the hell was this all about? Perhaps Ramsey's downfall *wasn't* enough for Birdie Clough. Perhaps she would only be satisfied when she had her revenge on the woman she supposed had wrecked her daughter's marriage. And if Harris's past wasn't enough to damn her, Saville's reputation was.

'Mrs Clough,' Jimmy began evenly, 'Mr Simons hasn't been in any trouble for many years. And besides, he's retarded, a danger to no one. He's medicated and he never leaves the lodge.'

'Only because he's watched all the time!' Birdie replied adamantly. 'Is Deerheart House really the best place for a child to be brought up?'

'Harris Simons was brought up there –'

'Yes, and look how she turned out.'

Enraged, Jimmy put down his pen, struggling to keep his voice calm. 'Mrs Clough, the best interests of the child are of the most importance here. And I believe – as does his aunt – that Thomas would be in the best of hands with Harris Simons as his adopted mother.'

'We think otherwise,' Birdie said, her twinkling eyes suddenly cold as a stone. 'We think that Thomas should be removed from Deerheart House and placed with proper adoptive parents, a married couple, without a known sexual pervert in the family.'

'Don't do this,' Jimmy said, his tone threatening. 'You just want revenge –'

'How dare you!' Birdie snapped. 'I just want what's best for the child!'

'No,' Jimmy replied, 'you want to ruin Harris Simons. You want to take the child away from her for your own spiteful reasons.'

'Now, look here –'

'No, *you* look here,' Jimmy interrupted her. 'I have more than enough reason to hate Harris Simons, but I don't. I could have let what she did to me ruin my life, but I didn't. Anyway, she paid for it. She took a beating that would have floored most men.' He paused, loathing the woman sitting in front of him.

'You think Harris Simons broke up your daughter's marriage? Well, she didn't. Eve threw Ben Ramsey out long before. You know it, and so does everyone else. Your daughter never made a secret out of it. Besides, Mrs Clough, why would you want your daughter to *stay* with a man like Ramsey?'

'This has nothing to do with you!' she barked, suddenly as enraged as he was.

'This has everything to do with me!' Jimmy hurled back. 'Ramsey was an evil man, Eve's better off without him –'

'Hah! What chance has she got now to get married again? Who wants a thirty-year-old divorcee?'

'You would rather she had stayed with him?' Jimmy asked incredulously.

'Yes, I would!' Eve snapped back. 'Ramsey was a bastard well, most men are. But she could have handled him. But no, she had to let Harris Simons get him.' Bitterness was making Birdie talk, and now she couldn't stop. 'And what happened? Harris Simons walked out on him – and then managed to redeem herself. She became an icon in this town. *Her!* She was a slut once, and she always will be –'

'Get out,' Jimmy said darkly.

'*I* was supposed to have grandchildren. A son-in-law on Rodney Street.' Birdie's voice trembled with self-pity. 'And what happened? I lost it all! And that bitch Harris Simons is back on easy street *with a child*! A son! No, it's not going to happen –'

'I want you to leave.'

'Oh, I'm leaving, Mr Henshaw,' Birdie said, her voice deadly as she stood up. 'But I'll have my way. I always do, because I know the right people and grease the right palms. Harris Simons is a scrubber, a woman with a past. And if that's not enough to stop this adoption, her uncle's reputation will.' She walked to the door and paused. 'No one will let an unmarried woman adopt a child. Maybe a woman without her past – but Harris Simons? Never.'

SIXTY-NINE

Grinding a cigarette out with the heel of his shoe, Jimmy ducked his head down against the wind and began to walk on. He was enraged. What a bitch Birdie Clough was! What a devious, lying, manipulative bitch she was. His fury unsettled him – and then he wondered why he was so angry. Because she had wanted to ruin Harris? Or because she had rekindled feelings he had thought were gone?

But Harris didn't matter to him any more, did she? He was going to propose to Lydia. Jimmy stopped walking. If he had been madly in love, would a sore throat have stopped him? The hell it would! He wanted Lydia because she was safe, bound to accept his proposal. No worries with Lydia . . . Jimmy felt his mouth drying and hurriedly lit another cigarette. It was over with Harris. There was nothing left.

She had hurt him too much, and he didn't trust her. How could he? He hated her. Yes, he hated her for what she'd done to him. Made him look a fool, running off like that. The bitch. Well, he was over it now. He was over her for good.

Who the hell was he kidding . . . ? Jimmy started walking again quickly. He might rage against Birdie Clough, but in a way he was as bad as she was. The only difference was that he was lying to *himself*.

Harris was lying on her bed next to Tom when she heard the doorbell ring. A moment later came the sound of voices from below, Mrs Turner's and a man's. Sighing, Harris snuggled closer to the sleeping child, hoping that the housekeeper would send the caller away. But only a moment later, there was a tap on her door.

'Miss Harris, there's someone to see you.'

'I'm asleep,' Harris called back. 'Tell them to go away.'

'I can't,' Mrs Turner replied. 'He's –'

Without allowing her to say another word, Jimmy walked in, his expression enraged.

'I have to tell you something!' he said angrily, Harris sitting up on the bed and staring at him in astonishment. 'I have to talk to you. It's important.'

Gathering Tom up in her arms, Harris handed him to Mrs Turner. 'Can you feed him for me? I'll be down soon.' Then she closed the door and turned back to Jimmy. 'Well, this is a surprise.'

He looked round, as though suddenly aware that he was in her bedroom. 'Do you want to talk downstairs?'

Harris shook her head. 'No,' she said, walking over to the window seat. 'We can talk here. I was just dozing with Tom; I haven't woken up properly yet.'

Sitting next to her, Jimmy began to twirl his hat in his hands nervously.

'Why do you do that?'

'What?' he asked.

'Twirl your hat in your hands,' Harris answered, smiling. 'You always used to do it and you still do.'

'Harris,' he said urgently, 'I have to warn you about something important. About Tom –'

She was instantly awake. 'What about Tom?'

'Birdie Clough is trying to oppose the adoption. She's going to say you're an unfit mother. You're not married and Saville's got a record.'

Harris stared at him in horror.

'Harris, do you understand what I'm saying?'

'She can't!' Harris said at last. 'She can't take him away. No one can!'

'She's going to try. She wants to get her own back on you – and she has a lot of power in this town.'

'Tom's mine!' Harris said fiercely. 'He's my child. I'd kill that bloody woman rather than let her take him away. Tom's the one good thing I have left. The best thing I ever did in life was take him in. Without him, I wouldn't care if I lived or died –'

'Harris, don't, please,' Jimmy said firmly. 'I have an idea.'

'She can't do it!' Harris said again, hardly hearing what he said. 'Why would anyone hate me that much?'

Jimmy kept his voice calm. 'Listen to me. I think I have a way out. A way for you to keep Tom.'

She turned to him. 'Of course, you're a lawyer! You know about these things.'

'I don't know how you'll take it.'

'Tell me!' Harris said desperately. 'I'd give my life for that child. Just tell me what we can do.'

'It might work –'

'*What?*' Harris urged him frantically. 'Tell me, I'll do any-thing, *anything* to keep Tom.'

'Then marry me.'

'Don't joke!' she retorted bitterly. 'I want to know what we can do about Tom.'

'I'm serious,' Jimmy went on. 'They might have a case if you're a single woman wanting to adopt, whatever Bonny says in your favour. But if you're married, if you've got a husband and a normal family life, they can't stop it. Birdie Clough isn't as smart as she thinks she is.'

Dazed, Harris stared at the man in front of her. This was

Jimmy Henshaw, the man she had humiliated and hurt. The man she had betrayed. The man who was now big enough to stand by her, fighting her corner with her.

'Jimmy, you can't do this!'

'I can do what the hell I like.'

'But you're getting married to –'

'I'm not getting married to anyone!'

'Don't tell me she turned you down?' Harris replied, wickedly.

He looked at her, a moment passing between them and then he laughed.

'You don't change, do you?'

Slowly she shook her head. 'No, and I never will. Listen to me, Jimmy, I know you want to help. But think about what you're suggesting. Think about what it would mean. You don't *have* to marry me –'

'Jesus, Harris!' Jimmy replied, throwing down his hat in exasperation. 'You drive me insane! I don't want to love you, because, frankly, you're hard work. But trying to make myself fall in love with someone else isn't the answer either. I don't want to *risk* loving you, because you could hurt me again. And I wouldn't be able to take it. Not a second time.'

'Jimmy, listen –'

'I don't want to listen to you!' he said firmly. 'And I don't want to get hurt. But I don't want to miss out on something good because I was too much of a coward to have another go.' He paused, shaking his head. 'When I listened to that Clough woman trying to ruin you, I couldn't believe how angry I was. How much I wanted to protect you. To be with you –'

'Jimmy –'

He put up his hands to stop her talking. 'Harris, I don't want you to say anything except *one word*. One tiny word and we'll be back together, and Tom will be safe. The word's "yes", Harris. All you have to do is say it.'

SEVENTY

Three years later
The hard-won peace that Harris had wished for came finally with her marriage to Jimmy Henshaw. Needless to say, Irma was delighted, although it was decided that a big wedding was out of the question. No one wanted any bad memories to colour the occasion. So they married in the registry office, Bonny and Howard invited, with Irma and Saville, of course, and the children – Bonny's Milly and the new baby, and Tom, the adopted son of Jimmy and Harris Henshaw.

They then went to live in the house they had originally bought; the one Jimmy had occupied all the years he was alone. And Harris *did* buy a new salon, bringing in more staff, Irma finally retiring after she broke her hip.

On the other side of town, Birdie Clough raged at the failure of her plans. For so long her manipulations had shaped the lives of everyone around her, but no longer. The revenge she had been so eager to inflict on Harris failed miserably. Instead she had to watch her enemy marry Jimmy Henshaw, *solicitor*, Eve getting her divorce from Ben Ramsey a year later. There was to be no glamorous son-in-law for Birdie, no grandchildren, and only months after her divorce Eve moved out of her parents' house. The result of all Birdie's machinations was a lonely old age with Sydney – who never saw that one coming.

Where Eve Clough went to, no one knew. Some said she moved abroad, others that she eventually married a widower in Stockport. But no one was ever completely certain about what happened. As for her former husband, *everyone* knew what happened to Ben Ramsey. The addict, drunk and wife beater, moved from Wigan, to Manchester, then on to Liverpool. No longer able to practise, he spent his days as an alcoholic, roaming the city, sometimes sleeping rough – and always within sight of Rodney Street. He told anyone who would listen that he had been a doctor once, and that the most beautiful girl in the country had been obsessed by him.

Irma's hip healed, but she was never the same again. Prone to falls, she barked irritably at anyone who implied she was too old to live alone. Then, one cold winter night, she slipped on the front door step of Deerheart House and broke her arm. The arm healed, but her age was against her and she developed pneumonia, Harris and her family moving back into Deerheart House to look after her.

'I'm not dead yet!' she snapped at her niece. 'This place will be yours soon enough.'

'Oh, dry up and drink your soup,' Harris replied, teasing her. 'You'll be up and about in no time.'

But she wasn't. Irma had no reason to live any more – she had seen all her hopes fulfilled. What point was there in hanging around? Harris was successful, married, and a mother . . . The thought made Irma smile: her niece had shown them all. After so many struggles and ill luck, Harris had come up trumps. And the triumph wasn't just hers, it was Irma's too.

'Sit with me a while, will you?' she asked Harris one night, eager for company. 'That family of yours can spare you for an hour.'

Sitting next to her aunt's bed, Harris looked at her anxiously. 'How are you feeling?'

529

'I'm dying – how d'you *think* I feel?'

'You're not dying.'

'Don't contradict me, Harris!' Irma snapped. 'If I say I'm dying, *I am.*'

A moment passed between them, Harris laying her hand on the bed, *alongside* Irma's. Too much sentiment wasn't her aunt's style.

'I've organised everything, Harris. My funeral, the will, everything –'

'I don't want you to go,' Harris said, genuinely moved.

'Well, I am, so get used to the idea,' Irma replied, moving uneasily against the pillows.

Her face was lined, still handsome, the aquiline nose long. But the grey roots of her hair were showing, and that told its own tale.

'Are you hungry?'

'No,' Irma replied, her voice losing a little of its strength. 'I want you to stay here – until I've gone. I don't want you crying all over me, but I want you around. And don't let that idiot Mrs Turner come in. I reckon it's her food that's done for me.'

Smiling, Harris clicked on the bedside lamp. 'The nights are drawing in.'

'It's winter. I won't see Christmas,' Irma replied, in complete command of herself, as always. 'Now you look after that family of yours, and this house. Come and live here permanently, will you? I'd like that.'

'Don't, please –'

'Do listen to me!' Irma interrupted her. 'I don't want to have to repeat this, Harris – I haven't got the damn time, for one thing. Live here and bring up your children here. I imagine you'll have more children. My will is all sorted out, so no problems there.' She paused, suddenly tiring. 'I think I could sleep for a while.'

And she did, sliding off into a doze, Harris beside her.

The winter evening turned into night, Harris hearing Jimmy downstairs and Tom running across the hall. I remember when I came here, she mused, how big the house seemed. How impressive the garden was. And I remember you, Harris thought, looking at her sleeping aunt. I was so afraid of you. You were so cruel. I loved Mildred, not you. And yet you were the one who stuck by me, through thick and thin.

I should have loved you more, Harris thought guiltily. But you were so difficult to like, and Mildred was so affectionate, so easy to love. Gently, Harris tidied the bed clothes around Irma – then she leaned down and gently kissed her aunt's hand.

'Is there a fly in here?' Irma asked, teasing her. 'I could feel something crawling over my hand.'

'You're awake,' Harris replied, smiling. 'Do you want something to eat?'

'No.'

'Drink?'

'No.'

'Can I do anything for you?'

Slowly Irma opened her eyes. 'You've already done it. You've made me very proud.' Unable to reply, Harris looked down, Irma continuing quickly, 'There's just one thing I have to tell you. Mildred left you a letter. In the event of her death she asked that I give it to you. But I didn't.' Irma's voice was weakening with the effort of talking and remembering. 'I'm a bitch, Harris, I always have been. And I did some things in the past which I regret. I thought that Mildred might tell you all about them in this letter. So I decided that you would only read it after I was gone. Once a bitch, always a bitch.'

'You're not a bitch –'

Irma stared at her, almost amused. 'You don't know me . . . Anyway, I didn't want you to read about what I'd done – and then see the judgement in your face. I couldn't have taken your hatred. But when I'm dead, it won't matter. Just don't be too hard on me, Harris. We were a strange family, with a strange background. We were all chockful of secrets.'

'Nothing could change the way I feel about you,' Harris said softly. 'I admire you so much. I didn't value you for a long time, but now I do. I love –'

'I want to sleep now!' Irma said, cutting her off, stopping her niece from saying *I love you*. She didn't need to hear the words to know it. And being sentimental was never Irma's way.

Nodding, Harris watched her face. 'Shall I stay with you?'

'Please. Stay until the end,' Irma replied, turning to Harris and seeing her begin to cry.

Her heart shifted. The one thing she had never expected had happened. Someone finally loved Irma Simons. Someone would cry for her, miss her when she was gone. It was almost worth dying for.

But Irma wasn't going to go out on a maudlin note. 'There's just one more thing, Harris . . .'

'Yes?'

'Do something about your hair, will you? I never liked it like that.'

SEVENTY-ONE

Irma Simons died at 11.30 on 4 December 1953. Her niece was beside her. The following morning, Harris found Irma's will, and the letter from Mildred. Closing the breakfast-room door, she sat down alone and then slowly broke the seal.

Mildred's handwriting leaped off the page.

My Dearest Harris,

If you are reading this then I am no longer around. I only hope that you're an old lady! Either way, I can now talk to you about matters you need to know. Irma thinks that she knows everything – all the secrets – but there's one she *never* knew.

Well, here goes. A long time ago I fell in love with a man called William Kershaw. I know all about being obsessed – it happened to me. Yes – Mildred Simons – spinster of this parish. You never know people, Harris. You think you do, but you never know who anyone is really. I loved William Kershaw desperately, and I got pregnant by him. It was only when I told him about the baby that he admitted he was married.

Our family lived in such a strange atmosphere, Harris. Everyone hiding things, everyone living off each other's secrets. But no one found out about my lover and my pregnancy – or about the abortion.

It was a terrible time, that summer. Things were so difficult at home. The weather was hot, nights punctuated by screaming matches, all of us terrified. Never think too badly of Irma. She became hard in order to survive.

Every year either Irma or I would go away for a while, to visit an old bachelor cousin of ours in Derbyshire. I remember how eager we always were to go. Anything to escape the house – and that year it was my turn.

William had left me and I had gone for the abortion – *but I never went through with it.* Luck was on my side, for once. Our cousin hated our father and he knew what was going on. I stayed with him for four months. Long enough to have my baby without anyone knowing back home . . . I can imagine how shocking this is for you, but please don't tear this letter up now. Keep reading, Harris, keep reading.

Although I told the family differently, I had never lost touch with your father, Gideon. I loved my brother too much to turn my back on him. He was married to Kate then, and they were desperate to have a child. But it never happened.

It seemed that Fate had played into all our hands, so we set a plan in motion. When my baby was born it was never going to be adopted by strangers – it was passed over to my brother and his wife. Do you understand, Harris? *You were that child.*

No one ever knew. No one ever realised, and over the years I learned about you through letters and photographs that Gideon sent to the post office, where I would collect them from a box office number. One of those photographs was of you as a baby. And that's the one I put in my locket. The locket you should be wearing now. The one I had sealed, to prevent anyone seeing what was in it. Because *you* were the face in the locket, Harris. Your image always close, always lying against my heart.

Gideon was very kind. He would tell me where he would be with you, and I would watch you from a distance. I viewed your life in snippets, grabbing what news I could of my child, always greedy for information. That was why I was so willing to buy the salon with Irma – to get some extra money to send to Gideon. He was never very good with finances, and could never hold down a job. He had been raised to take over from Father, and when that fell through, he never found his niche.

I must admit that I didn't know until later how difficult things had become. I would never have let you suffer so much, but my brother was a proud man and never one to beg. He should have told me he was down on his luck, that the family was poor, but he didn't. You have to let people run their lives their own way. But one thing I always knew was how much he and Kate adored you. No child was ever more loved than you.

But I missed you so much. I longed for you, used to see women pushing prams in the park and ached to be like them. I couldn't hold you, or bathe you, or show my beautiful child off. All my life I was seen as a childless spinster – and I couldn't tell anyone different. My father would have killed me if he had known the truth. Times were very different then, Harris. My family would never have been supportive – and I wasn't a brave woman.

So I adjusted to the fact that I would have to watch you from a distance and I prayed that one day you would come back to me. It's sad sometimes how our prayers are answered – but the death of Gideon and Kate gave me back my child.

I can see you now walking up the path that first evening when you came to Deerheart House. A stroppy kid. A fighter in short socks. *My* kid come home to me . . . Now maybe can you understand why I was so tolerant when you did so many reckless things? When you fell in love with the wrong man – how could *I* scold you? I had done the same. I understood how you thought, because you were my child. I understood every impetuous, crazy, wilful action – because you were like me. Once. But my resistance was crushed.

Don't ever let anyone crush you, Harris. Don't ever let anyone break your spirit. As I write this you are at the salon. Working with you by my side has been the happiest time of my life. Please find a good man to love, have children and keep them close to you.

Forgive me for letting you go – and thank you, thank you so much, for coming back to me.

So now I'm signing off. For the first, the last, and the only time,

Your loving mother,
    Mildred